Praise for Baker & Goodman's
Mountains to Climb

This fourth book in the Nurseketeers series lives up to the "Finale" status we've come to expect from these authors. From the argument in the opening scene of Chapter 1, through struggles with schoolwork, athletics, engagements, graduation, and ultimately even Board exams, this book continues to entertain and is simply a joy to read. It's a trip down memory lane, returning us to the innocence of the '70s and the youthful trials and tribulations of growing up.

—Daryn Herrington

This book, the 4th in the *Nurseketeer* series, revisits the four nursing students as one of them sets out to learn to become an operating room nurse in the 70's. The story line also brings the conflict between young adults and their parents forward as both navigate separation and the independence of children.

—Carol Applegeet

Mountains to Climb is the 4th novel in Baker's & Goodman's *Nurseketeer* series about a close-knit group of nursing students. This is their senior year and the story focuses on Leslie Bleu and the challenges she faces with ambition, overcommitment, prioritization, and leadership, and how they affect her studies, her work, and her relationships with her family, friends, and fiancé.

It's an easy read, with likeable characters and lessons for readers navigating similar, and all too familiar, challenges in their careers or personal lives. And, of course, it's a must-read for fans who have followed the *Nurseketeers* through the first three novels.

—Greg Goodman

I definitely recommend this book! In addition to a good read, it may be incredibly beneficial to nursing students in helping them work through the challenges they are facing.

—**Christine Roberts**

Nurseketeer Leslie tries to juggle all aspects of a full life in her journey through her senior year of nursing school. Learn how she manages academics, sports, love, and friendships in *Mountains to Climb*.

—**Chelsie Gabel**

Mountains to Climb

JOY DON BAKER

&

TERRI GOODMAN

Published 2024
Printed in the United States of America

ISBN: 978-1-7345150-4-6 Bublish
E-ISBN: 978-1-7345150-5-3 Bublish

Library of Congress Control Number: 2024924158

Written by Joy Don Baker & Terri Goodman
Cover & Interior Design: *JETLAUNCH.NET*
About the Authors photo: *Kelly Williams Photography*
Author photo back cover: *Simao Ago*

For information:
Baker & Goodman
Dallas, TX
joydon@bakergoodman.com
www.bakergoodman.com

Table of Contents

Chapter 1

"Mom, I got the job!" Leslie exclaimed as soon as her mother answered the phone. "I'll be working in the operating room at Parkland this summer. Can you believe it… the *operating room!*"

"You can't do that," her mother demanded. "You're coming home for the summer."

Leslie's eyes widened and her smile disintegrated. "What? I just told you I got my dream job, and you want me to spend the summer in a grocery store? You've got to be kidding."

"Leslie, of course I don't want you home to work in the store. You must have known about this job for a while now and you didn't mention a thing to us. That wasn't very thoughtful. We've been planning for your last summer at home with us… a vacation and plenty of family time. You graduate next year and then you'll be gone for good. If you need to work, there are plenty of opportunities around here."

"This job is the chance of a lifetime, Mom. How can you not be happy for me?"

"Don't take that tone with me, young lady, and it's not a matter of happy. I'd be happier if we'd been part of the planning. Your family should be more than an afterthought. You don't need the money. You have a scholarship. You'll work after you graduate and you'll be sorry you didn't take vacation when you could."

"Mom, that's not fair."

"Fair? What's fair about ignoring your family?"

"It's about my future. I want to be an OR nurse and this job will open doors for me. Besides, all the *Nurseketeers* got summer jobs in Dallas. It's our last summer together, and Crestmont is letting us keep our apartment for the summer. It's too perfect to pass up. Mom, you gotta understand."

"Leslie…" Mrs. Bleu began.

"MOM!" Leslie interrupted. "This is an investment in my future… in my *career*… and it's about the money, too. I need to build my savings account. I want to have my own money to spend for Christmas and birthday presents, and I'll have expenses when I'm on my own after graduation."

"Well then, when *will* you come home?" Mrs. Bleu asked grudgingly.

"Oh, for heaven's sake. It's not like I'll never be home again, but it will have to wait. Abita Springs is too long a drive for a weekend."

"When?" her mother insisted.

"We'll see," was all Leslie could manage. She resisted the urge to slam the receiver onto the cradle as soon as her mother hung up. She replaced the phone carefully and stared at her suitemates sitting in their living room chairs, tie-dyed in shades of Crestmont University's purple and gold.

For a moment, no one spoke, then Katie said, "Les, she'll come around. "We're all lucky to have families who care about us."

Robin and Frannie nodded.

Frannie added, "I'm not going to tell my folks about my job until I go home after finals. My Mom's going to have a fit, but Daddy will convince her that it's a good opportunity. She'll have two weeks to get over being disappointed. It's going to be a cool summer. Parkland's the busiest hospital in Dallas so we'll get lots of experience, and we'll all be there together."

"My folks seem fine with my staying in Dallas," Katie said, "but it's probably because Atoka's only a two-hour drive. They know I'll get home to visit over the summer."

Robin grinned. "Now that Gram's living in Dallas, my summer job won't disappoint her at all."

"Lucky you!" Leslie groaned, then she smiled. "I can't believe I got into the OR, and with the job that Coach Mitchell got for Mike, it's going to be a perfect summer."

Robin answered the jangling phone. "*Nurseketeers* Hangout." She held out the receiver to Leslie. "It's Mike. His ears musta been burnin'."

Leslie smiled as she listened. "Sure, I would," she said, "but not there. I want barbeque." She paused, "I know Tex-Mex is your favorite, but it's mostly rice and beans and I can't afford to get fat. I don't know how you eat all that stuff and look like you do. If I didn't run every day, I'd look like the Pillsbury Doughboy… well, Doughgirl. Sure. I'll be ready," she said and hung up.

"That's ridiculous, Leslie," Robin said. "There's not an ounce of fat within a mile of your body."

"There would be if I weren't careful," Leslie insisted. "You guys can come along to dinner with us if you'd like."

"Two's company, five's a crowd," Katie said when she saw that Frannie was about to accept.

Robin added, "Count me out. I picked up a shift at the SteakHauz tonight. Maddie's not feeling well, and I need to cover the hostess station. I never turn Mr. Davis down when he asks. He's been so good to Gram and me, it'd seem ungrateful."

"True," Katie agreed. "Frannie, you and I can eat something special right here to celebrate our summer jobs. You got peds and I'm in gerontology, first choice for both of us."

Frannie brightened. "That would be great. How about an *everything* pizza? Maybe J.R. and Missy can join us; he's an honorary *Nurseketeer* after all. I did tell you that Missy got a summer job at Neiman's downtown, didn't I? Can you believe it, *Neiman Marcus*! I hope she gets a good discount. I love shopping there."

"Good to hear Missy's in Dallas for the summer, too. J.R. would miss her big time if she'd gone back to Baton Rouge," said Robin.

"Go knock on J.R.'s door while I order our feast," Katie said.

"Hang on a second, Frannie," Leslie said, picking up her purse. "I'll go with you so Mike won't have to come fetch me. It's cool that Mike and J.R. got a campus apartment for the summer just two doors down from ours."

"You look like you swallowed a lemon," Mike said. "What's got you so upset?"

"I called home to tell Mom about my OR job, and all she did was insist I come home for the summer. I thought she'd be excited for me, but *noooo*, she wants me hanging around Abita Springs just because it's my last summer before graduation."

"Must be a parent thing. My folks didn't jump for joy when I told them I was staying in Dallas for the summer. When you come from a small town and go away to college, your folks tend to hold on because they know it's not likely you'll ever be back home for more than a visit. I guess we need to cut them some slack."

"Hmmm, yeah… I s'pose," Leslie mumbled.

"So, instead of barbeque," Mike said, "let's go to Ramone's. An Italian dinner will put a smile back on your pretty face. Spaghetti and meatballs with a side of veggies or a salad would be fabulous and they're right up your alley… protein and greens."

"Next time," Leslie countered. "I'm in the mood for barbeque."

"One of these days I get to decide where we eat," Mike said. "Let's take the truck."

"You can drive," Leslie said, "but we'll take Nellie. She needs gas, so we'll stop on the way home."

Mike opened the passenger door for Leslie and put his hand out for the keys. "Wanna shoot hoops after dinner?" he asked as he climbed into the driver's seat. "You can work off the calories and the meal will be a net zero."

Leslie punched his arm.

Leslie slid into the booth opposite Mike and took a menu from the waitress. "We'll order first," she said to Mike, "then you can tell me about your job."

"Yes, Ma'am," Mike replied.

"I don't know why we bother with a menu. The buffet's the best choice. I'll get a barbeque plate and you can load up on whatever you'd like. Let's go," she said.

Mike raised an eyebrow, shrugged, and followed her to the buffet. He filled his plate with beef, pork, and ribs. He added a mound of rice and dipped two ladles of beans over it.

"Where do you put all that food?" Leslie said. "No amount of working out would save me if I ate like that."

"Your obsession with your weight never ceases to amaze me. You look great. Why can't you just accept that you're fine the way you are?"

Leslie shrugged. "You don't understand."

Mike heaved a sigh, and they carried their trays to their table.

"Tell me about the job Coach Mitchell lined up for you," Leslie said. "He's the best."

"It's at North Dallas High School and I'll be working with the basketball coaching staff."

"What will you do?" Leslie asked.

"No clue yet. Whatever the coaches need, I'll be their gopher. The team's got to be good because they just won the Division AAAA State championship."

"Wow, impressive."

"Coach Mitchell said when North Texas brings on permanent coaching staff, they look to their summer hires first. If I impress them, this could be a door opener to a job after graduation."

"Sounds like a good investment in your future," she said. "I guess it doesn't hurt to be the coach's pet."

Chapter 2

"Congratulations, Madame Soon-to-be-President," said Carol, the current president, as Leslie took her seat at the Student Nurses' Association's last board meeting of the school year. "You'll be chairing these meetings in the fall, and I know you'll do a great job for the Association."

"Thanks. You've been a great role model," Leslie said. "I hope I can fill your shoes."

"Ladies, let's get started," said Carol. "On the white board is a list of our initiatives for this year. They'll likely be repeated next year, so let's review each event for suggestions that might help next year be even more successful. Let's start with the Halloween party."

When all the items on Carol's list had been discussed, she concluded, "1972/73 has been a good year for SNA."

Leslie raised her hand. "I'd like to propose a celebration before everyone leaves. What do you think?"

"Sounds great. I love celebrating," Heidi said.

"What did you have in mind?" Carol asked.

"Something casual to spend time together and say good-bye to the graduating seniors. It could be a mixer if we want to invite friends. We can order food, or have a potluck."

"Let's keep it simple," Angela suggested. "We don't have a lot of time for planning, and the end of the semester is chaotic enough with finals and packing to go home. How about an afternoon social with a Dutch treat dinner afterwards for whoever wants to go? We can reserve a room here in the Student Union on a Friday afternoon for the social."

"I like that idea," Carol said. "Let's go with punch or lemonade and finger food."

"We can call it the *Senior Sendoff*," Leslie suggested.

"That sounds upbeat," Carol said.

"OK by me," said Angela, and the others agreed.

"So...," Leslie summarized, "I need to reserve a room in the Student Union, order lemonade and snacks, make reservations at a restaurant, and get the word out. I'll take care of it."

"Wait a minute," said Heidi. "Shouldn't we decide on a restaurant together?"

"And on the menu?" added Angela.

"Uh, right, I guess," Leslie hesitated.

"We should make as many of the decisions as we can right now," said Carol. The others nodded. "About the restaurant..."

"The *Steakhauz* is a possibility because the Davises are so supportive of campus activities," someone suggested.

"True," Carol said, "but it's a bit pricey. Let's pick something that everyone can afford. Who wants to look into our options?" She paused, then said, "Thank you," to the first girl who raised her hand.

Leslie asked. "How about snacks?"

"The Student Union kitchen does a great job on cookies," Angela offered. "We can ask for an assortment. Cookies are easy to manage while we mix and mingle."

"You've got a point," Carol said.

"We need to get the word out to the members," said Angela. "I've got a copy of the membership list."

"Leslie, do you want to take the lead on that?" Carol asked.

"Yes, happy to," Leslie said.

"How many do you think will go to dinner afterward?" Heidi asked.

"No clue," said Carol, "but I expect that every one of you at this meeting will be there, right?" She smiled when everyone's hand went up in response. "Leslie, make that a question for the call to the members. We'll need a rough count to reserve tables."

"Right on," Leslie agreed.

"That wraps it up." Carol lifted an imaginary champagne flute. "Here's to celebrating a great year for SNA."

"This should be fun," Leslie said.

Once the others left, Carol said, "Leslie, before you leave, I want to share something important with you that I learned this year."

"Tell me," Leslie said.

"I'm a *doer*, a poster child for a Type A personality, just like you. As soon as I became President last year, I started taking care of everything myself, just like you're doing. That worked until the Fall semester started. Suddenly, there weren't enough hours in the day. By the end of September, I knew I needed to step down or my grades and my relationships were going to suffer."

Leslie listened, nodding.

"When I told my roommate I couldn't continue as President, her response surprised me. She said, *I wondered how long it would take you to quit.*"

"What a nasty thing to say," Leslie said. "I thought you two were close."

"You need to hear the rest of the story, or someone will be saying the same thing to you come fall."

"What do you mean?" Leslie asked.

"Just listen," said Carol. "She told me that a leader's job is to *lead*, not just *do*. A leader motivates, organizes, delegates, and supervises others who are there to help and want to get the job done. I'm telling you this now, so *you* won't be thinking of quitting in the fall." When Leslie looked perplexed, Carol continued. "In the meeting just now, when we agreed on the plan, you listed all the steps and said you'd take care of it. Just you. All you. That's not leading, and that's what I'm talking about."

Leslie nodded slowly. "You're saying I should be assigning the tasks to others, not doing them myself."

"I'm not saying you can't participate, but you're leading a group. You're not a one-woman show. Your job is to make it possible for others to participate and do a good job."

"I'll need your help with the Senior Sendoff," Leslie announced to the *Nurseketeers* as soon as she walked through the apartment door. "We need to settle on a date and get a room, we'll have to notify all the members. I'll give each of you a list of names to call."

"Hold on!" Robin said. "We're your roommates, not your minions. Aren't there other SNA members who could be helping?"

"Well… I…," said Leslie, flustered. "Angela's going to get me the membership list. We don't have a lot of time to pull this off and Carol said I need to delegate. I'm counting on your help."

"No problem," Robin said. "But *ask* us; don't order us around."

"Sorry," Leslie said, contrite. "I'll wait until I get the list and we'll see who's available to help."

"Sounds like a plan," said Robin. Katie and Frannie nodded.

Chapter 3

"I can't wait for finals to be over," Leslie groaned. "After all this time, I'm still struggling with tests. I wish we had the option to do a project or write a paper instead of taking finals."

"Not gonna happen," Robin said. "Finals are efficient. Grading test papers is easy; reading essays or reviewing projects takes way more time."

"That's great for the profs," Leslie moaned, "but it doesn't help me at all."

"Welcome to the real world," Robin said. "The people in charge design the world with themselves in mind. With luck, someday it will be *our* turn to be in charge."

"In the meantime," Katie said, "Just remember to cover the answers when you read a test question. Answer the question in your head, *then* uncover the answers and find yours."

"And if I don't find it right away, I should mark the question and move on," Leslie added.

Katie nodded. "The important thing is to make it through the whole test and get credit for everything you know before you spend time thinking about a hard question. I'd be willing to bet that if you did that, you could skip the hard questions altogether and *still* pass the test. You never give yourself enough time to finish."

"I don't know why that's such a hard concept for you to accept," Robin insisted. "We've been reminding you for three years, but you still let yourself get hung up when you don't know an answer."

"I know what to do," Leslie grumbled. "It makes perfectly good sense and I try, but my mind short-circuits when I can't find my answer in the list of choices."

"Stop right there!" Robin demanded. "You can't let that happen. You know what to do. What I don't understand is that you have no problem being in charge of everyone else. It's time to step up and take charge of yourself."

"Can you believe it?" Leslie crowed as the *Nurseketeers* left the classroom for the last time as juniors. She brandished her Psych final with the red B prominently displayed. "I made it."

"We knew you could do it," Katie said.

"You finally listened to reason," Robin added.

"I still don't get why tests are such a big deal for you," Frannie said. "We all knew the material, so why wouldn't you pass?"

"Back off, Frannie," Robin said. "I'm not sure where you've been the last three years, but let Leslie savor her victory."

"Soon as we get to the apartment, I'll go give Mike the good news," Leslie said. "Maybe we can all celebrate together. Mike and I were talking about trying out TGI Friday's on Greenville. It's supposed to be one of the hottest places in town."

Robin grinned. "Sounds like an adventure. Maybe Tonya can join us."

"Wouldn't you lovebirds rather be alone, Robin?" asked Frannie coyly.

"Enough, Frannie." Robin barked, looking around to reassure herself there was no one else in earshot. "I'm surprised your big mouth hasn't gotten us in trouble. When are you going to develop a little sensitivity?"

"I'm sorry," Frannie whispered. "I'm going to miss her, too. It took a while, but you know that I'm okay with you two, don't you?"

"I shouldn't have snapped at you." Robin apologized and took a deep breath. "I'm grateful that you've come around. That's what friends do. We're the *Nurseketeers*, after all."

Frannie smiled.

"I'll tell Mike, and Frannie," Leslie said, "why don't you see if Missy and J.R. can join us for dinner. I'm sure they'll want to celebrate the end of the semester, too."

"Good idea Leslie. I'll give Missy a call."

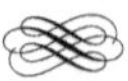

The group of eight settled into chairs at a large round table at TGI Friday's, and turned the pages of the menu. "Will you look at these desserts," Mike said. "From the photo, it looks like any one of them would feed all of us."

"I hope the meals are as tasty as the pictures," J.R. said. "This could be our new go-to eatery."

"They certainly serve a variety," Robin said. "I thought the *Steakhauz* menu was impressive, but this is amazing."

"Let's start with a cocktail," Missy said. "They look yummy."

"They have every beer I've ever heard of and then some," J.R. added.

When their dinner orders had been taken, and they'd toasted their success in completing the school year and finding summer jobs, Leslie said, "Tonya, you're the story of the evening. How does it feel to be a college graduate? And… tell us about your new job in San Francisco."

Everyone applauded, and Tonya stood and took a bow. "Wow," she said, taking her seat. "I can hardly believe it's over, but now that I'm graduating, it feels like the last four years flew by in a blur. One minute I can't wait for the future to begin and the next

I want to stay right here where I'm comfortable." She squeezed Robin's hand under the table.

"A year from now the *Nurseketeers* will be saying goodbye to one another. I can't imagine what that's going to be like," Katie said.

"It's too early to be thinking about that," said Tonya. "You have another whole year to be with one another."

"What's your new job?" asked Missy.

"With a degree in Business Administration," Katie added, "You can work just about anywhere."

"Well, this apple didn't fall far from the tree," Tonya said with a grin. "It's a restaurant. Actually, it's the Tadich Grill, the oldest restaurant in San Francisco and the third oldest in the country. I'll be their business manager with responsibility for all the restaurant's accounts."

"That's a lot of responsibility for someone right out of college. You should be proud of yourself," said Katie.

"What she isn't saying," added Robin, "is that she beat out a load of guys and she'll be the first black woman in the business office in that restaurant."

"How exciting." Leslie said. "You're starting at the top. You must have impressed them in your interview."

"It did go well," Tonya admitted. "I convinced them that I'm a quick learner and a hard worker, and they were willing to invest in me. It didn't hurt that they knew Mr. Davis from restaurant conventions. He's known my mom and me for years, and he gave me a terrific reference."

"They'll be happy with their decision," Robin said. "No doubts."

"I'm looking forward to living in San Francisco," Tonya added. "It's a unique city, one of the few in the country with a tolerance for diversity. I'm counting on the chance that a Black woman can be successful there. I know I'll be better off there than most anywhere else, especially here in the South."

"You're gonna be great," Robin said with obvious pride. "I'm gonna miss you, Girlfriend."

"What a great evening," Leslie said to the *Nurseketeers* curled up in their favorite spots in the living room. "That restaurant was amazing."

"I was surprised at how reasonable the prices were," said Robin.

"The dessert menu was the best part," Frannie said. "Mike was right about one dessert feeding our whole clan. I hardly had room for the sundae after that meal. Next time we should start with dessert."

"Tonya's excited about San Francisco," Katie said. "I hope she's right about the city being tolerant. She deserves to be successful and it's not fair that it should be hard just because she's Black."

"We need to give her a going away party," Frannie said. "If I were leaving, I'd want you to throw one for me."

"That's a great idea, Frannie" Robin said, pondering possibilities.

Frannie beamed.

"If we invite the folks who were with us at dinner tonight, we can have it at Gram's. She likes Tonya a lot and she'll want to be part of the festivities."

"Let's make it a surprise party," Frannie said. "They're the most fun. We can go in together and buy her a going-away present from the *Nurseketeers*."

"We don't have much time to plan," Robin said. "Today's Friday the 18th and she's leaving on the 25th. We don't start work for a couple of weeks and midweek would be perfect. Do you think we can make that happen?"

"Sounds great to me," Katie said.

"Me too," Leslie agreed.

"I'll call Gram in the morning and see what we need to do," offered Robin. "Just think, a year from now we'll be planning our own going-away party."

"I don't want to think about that," Frannie said. "I can't imagine what it will be like when we're not altogether. Let's just give Tonya the best sendoff ever."

Mrs. Kelly, Robin's grandmother, made sure there were no signs of a party in evidence. "She'll be here any minute," Robin said, checking the time on Gram's antique clock. "You all need to make sure you're out of sight. It won't be a surprise if Tonya sees you before we're ready."

"Maybe we shoulda picked a bigger place," Frannie said. "I hope we can all fit into your grandmother's bedroom. That's the only place you can't see from the front door."

"I've been thinking about a larger place," Mrs. Kelly said, "but for now, the bedroom will have to do." She shooed them all into the only bedroom in her garage apartment, then she and Robin settled comfortably in the living room.

Tonya knocked softly, opened the door, and said, "Yoohoo."

"Come in, come in," Mrs. Kelly said. "Make yourself comfortable," she added, pointing to the couch beside Robin. "We are truly going to miss you."

"I've been so excited about my job in San Francisco that I thought it would be easy to leave," Tonya said, "but it's harder than I expected." She squeezed Robins fingers.

Robin nodded, her eyes glistening. "I'm going to miss you more than I'd like, but we agreed that this is best," she murmured, and quickly wiped a tear from her cheek.

"It is, indeed," Mrs. Kelly said softly. She raised her voice so that the hidden crew would hear their cue. "Let's celebrate our last evening together."

The bedroom door burst open to a chorus of *bon voyage, safe travels,* and *we'll miss you, Tonya.*

Tonya's breath caught in her throat as she stood.

"I'm not the crying type," she insisted, "but this might be an exception. What a terrific surprise," she said to the group. "Thank you."

Leslie said, "You're an honorary *Nurseketeer*. We couldn't let you go without a send-off. We'll all miss you."

"I heard Mrs. Kelly say she's looking for a bigger place," Frannie said. "When you come back to visit, she might have room for you to stay."

"The Davises are keeping their eyes open for something here in the neighborhood," said Mrs. Kelly, setting the cake on the coffee table.

"I hope we'll find something before graduation," Robin added. "I plan to stay with Gram in Dallas, at least for a while, and it would be nice to have my own room."

"We got you a gift, Tonya, "Frannie blurted. "You should open it now."

Robin fetched a Neiman Marcus gift box from behind the couch. "This is from the *Nurseketeers,*" she said. "We hope you like it."

Tonya carefully removed the bow.

"Just rip into it," Fannie said.

"Jeez, Frannie, let her do it her own way." Robin said.

Tonya lifted the briefcase from the box and ran her hand across the fine leather. She traced the monogram with her fingers. "My initials," she whispered, her eyes glistening. "It's perfect. Thank you all so much."

In the kitchen replenishing drinks, Leslie asked quietly, "Robin, you're okay with Tonya's leaving for California, aren't you?"

Robin nodded slowly. "It's hard to see her go, but it's definitely the right move. After all, she represents the triple whammy of challenges… she's female, Black, and gay, all in one package… and her best chance for success is San Francisco. She's smart and talented, and it's pointless to hamstring her with the narrow-minded and unforgiving environment here in Texas."

"What about you? It's hard to have a secret like yours that you can't share."

"You'd be surprised at how many gay people there are right under our noses. Tonya taught me that being gay isn't an impossible situation. She and I are friends, and her being in San Francisco won't change that. I'm not ready for a life partner yet. For now, I'm happy to be a *Nurseketeer*. Besides, we have one more year before graduation and by then, maybe I'll know more about what I want to do with my life."

Chapter 4

"Should we try to hook up with J.R. and Missy for a movie tonight?" Leslie asked, crouching to tighten the laces on her basketball shoes. "Or we could make it an *everyone* night out and see who wants to join us."

"I was thinking more of a *Mike and Leslie* exclusive," Mike said, setting the basketball on the bench beside him and pulling her closer. With finals, we haven't had much time alone, and we'll both be working soon."

"I love the sound of *Leslie and Mike*."

"Hmmm… I could have sworn I said *Mike and Leslie*. It's a good thing I like strong women, but don't push it. How does *Mash* sound for the movies tonight?"

"Isn't that a war movie?" Leslie asked.

"Well… not exactly. Yes, it takes place during the Korean War, but no, the movie's not about the war."

"Tell me what it's about."

"Trust me. You'll like it."

"But…"

"What part of *trust me* did you miss?" Mike asked, pulling her into a hug. "Wanna grab a bite to eat before the movie?" Before Leslie could respond, Mike added, "and don't say anything after *yes*. I get to pick the restaurant for a change."

"O-K," she said slowly, unable to think of a snappy reply. "This time!"

"That was hysterical," Leslie said, as they rose from their seats in the theater. "I wasn't sure what to expect when you wouldn't tell me what the movie was about."

"My good choices are why you need to let me decide where we're going to spend our time together," he teased. "It's still early. Let's go for a drive. I was thinking of someplace quiet and private."

"Let's pick up a cold drink and snacks. Then we can drive to Bachman Lake. I like watching the planes land. It's so close to Love Field, it feels like you could reach up and touch them."

"Hmmm, quiet and private... watching planes land was just what I had in mind."

"There's plenty of time in between planes to be quiet and private," she promised.

"I know I don't start working for two weeks," Leslie said to her mother into the phone, "but there's nothing earth-shattering happening at home and I want to spend time with Mike. Last semester was a bear, and we hardly got to see each other."

"Spending time with your family should be more important," Mrs. Bleu huffed.

"If you needed me for the store or something, I'd be there," Leslie explained, "but you have four kids at home to help out."

"This is the last summer before you're gone for good. You have to come home," Mrs. Bleu insisted.

"Not now, Mom. I'm not going to disappear when I graduate. I will always be part of our family. Right now, I want to be here with Mike. We only have two weeks before we both start working. I'll make it home to visit, Mom, but not now."

"If Mike's so important, bring him home with you. You can be with us and with him at the same time."

"We'll try to work that out for later, I promise. In the meantime, please be reasonable."

"*Reasonable!*" Mrs. Bleu spat. "Reasonable is a daughter coming home when her mother wants her to."

"I'll let you know when I'll be home, Mom. I gotta go. Love you, bye." Leslie hung up before their conversation got completely out of control.

"Les," Mike began, mid-morning. "J.R. and Missy are going to Arp this coming weekend. How about I take you home to meet my parents? I checked with J.R. and they're taking Missy's Dart, not his truck, so we can all ride together."

"I'd love that," Leslie said. "When will we leave and what should I bring?"

"Bring? Like what?" Mike asked.

Leslie giggled. "Typical guy. Just do it. No planning.

"What? Planning for what?"

"I need to know what we're going to do so I'll know what to pack."

"Oh, like a bathing suit and something to wear out to dinner?"

"Yeah. Like that. How can I be prepared if I don't know what to prepare *for,*" Leslie insisted. "Do your parents dress up for dinner?"

"No, not really, but we might go out to dinner. You'll probably want to pack more than tracks shorts and a bathing suit."

"Duh!" Leslie grinned at Mike. "Ya think?"

"I can't believe this will be the first time you've met my parents. We should have done this ages ago."

"Do you think they'll like me?" Leslie asked.

"Duh! Ya think?" Mike grinned back at her.

"Dude," said Mike as the two couples spread blankets on the grass for their picnic that afternoon. "I have a proposition for you."

"What's up?" asked J.R.

"How 'bout Les and I join you for the drive home next weekend?"

"That would be so cool," Missy chimed in. "Arp's neat… for a little town, that is."

"You're on," said J.R. "Let's leave Friday morning. That will give us lots of time to hang out. We might even make it into Tyler for dinner or something."

"I wish Abita Springs were close enough for a weekend trip," said Leslie. "If my mom could spend time with Mike, I know she'd quit ragging on me."

"We should try to work something out before school starts," Mike said, rummaging in the picnic basket. "Good stuff here. Let's eat."

"How long have you and J.R. known each other?" Leslie asked Mike.

"Forever," Mike laughed. "Our parents grew up together, then so did we."

"That's small-town East Texas for you," J.R. added. "Mike's dad's the high school coach, and mine's the police chief. Lemme tell you, it was a culture shock coming to the Big D from a place you know like the back of your hand. Everybody knows everybody in Arp."

"I can relate," Leslie replied. "Abita Springs is tiny. You can get anywhere in ten minutes on a bike. If it weren't for my scholarship, I don't think I would ever have ventured this far from home."

"You guys just don't know what you missed, growing up in those little towns," Missy said. "Big cities have so much more to offer. Arp is cute, but it doesn't have a theater or any decent shopping to speak of. It doesn't even have a country club!"

Mike, J.R., and Leslie laughed. Missy shook her head in bewilderment.

"I swear parents have built-in radar," Mike said when his mother and father stepped onto the porch before J.R. had come to a full stop in front of the Hampton's house.

"Welcome home," they said, hurrying down the porch steps. "Leslie, we've been looking forward to meeting you. Hello, there, J.R. and Missy."

"Need help carrying anything?" asked Mike's father.

"We're good, Dad. Leslie, meet my mom and dad, Carla and Gene Hampton.

"Pleased to meet you," Leslie said, extending her hand to Mrs. Hampton.

"So much for formality," said Mrs. Hampton, drawing Leslie into a hug. "You can let your hair down this weekend, Sweetie. We've been looking forward to meeting you."

Leslie smiled at the warm welcome. "Thank you, especially since we gave you such short notice."

"The guest room is always ready for company," Mrs. Hampton assured her. "You and Mike feel free to spend as much time with us as you can. In the meantime, let's have lemonade out back. J.R., come in and call your folks to see if they'll join us."

J.R.'s parents joined the lively conversation on the patio at the Hamptons. J.R.'s mother squeezed her son's shoulders and planted a kiss on his cheek. "What do you have planned for the weekend?" she asked. "Can you fit in a BBQ tomorrow? Hamptons included, of course," she added.

"Dad's BBQ is the best in Texas," said J.R., "and Mom makes amazing coleslaw."

"I'll take care of dessert," said Mrs. Hampton. "Mike's bringing Leslie home definitely calls for a celebration."

"How about a movie at the drive-in afterwards," Mike asked. It doesn't get dark until nearly nine."

"I guess it won't matter much what's playing," said Mr. Hampton with a grin. Leslie blushed.

"There's enough food for an army," Leslie said as they settled into lawn chairs in the Johnson's backyard the next evening.

"You'd be surprised how much the men in our families can put away," Mrs. Johnson laughed. "Good thing, too, because Carla and I love to cook. Food's a social phenomenon in most small towns. When folks get together, it always involves a meal or if it's a community event, everyone brings a dish or two."

"It's like that in Abita Springs, too," Leslie said. "There's lots to be said about small town living. Mike says the Hamptons and Johnsons have been like family as long as he can remember."

"That we are," Mrs. Hampton said. "Susan's family and mine go back generations. Our great grandparents homesteaded this land, back when Arp was called Jarvis Junction. Susan's great grandmother was a Jarvis."

"Carla and I were best friends growing up," said Mrs. Johnson.

"More like sisters, really," added Mrs. Hampton. "My dad was the principal of the high school and Susan's dad was Arp's police chief. Are you beginning to see a pattern here?"

"This sounds like the beginning of a great story," Leslie said.

"What happened next?" Missy asked.

"Well, when Gene, Mike's dad, was a teacher just out of college, he passed through Arp on his way west looking for a good place to settle down," Mrs. Hampton began. "He stopped for gas and ran into my mother when he went inside to pay. They got to talking and she invited him home for dinner. Before the evening was over, Dad had hired him to teach and coach. Gene never got any further west than Arp."

Mrs. Johnson picked up the story. "Right about that same time, J.R.'s grandfather was lookin' to hire a deputy. A colleague suggested he check out Sam Houston in Huntsville because they have a good criminal justice program, so he went and interviewed seniors who were about to graduate. He and James, J.R.'s dad, hit it off, so he invited James to Arp and there you have it."

Mrs. Hampton continued the story. "It was love at first sight for both Susan and me. Both men married their bosses' daughters. Now, Mike's following in his father's footsteps and J.R. is breaking ground in a new profession. Ever since his little brother died, nursing is all J.R.'s ever wanted."

"Those three boys were like triplets," said Mr. Johnson. "J.R. and Mike took Davey wherever they went. As long as they had Davey to watch out for, they were good as gold, but after Davey died, there was nothing holding those two adventurers back."

"You're tellin' me," Mr. Hampton chimed in. "One summer, I was fixin' shingles on the roof. It was hotter'n blazes, so I went inside to get a drink. Couldn't have been in the house more'n five minutes. I came out to find these two hooligans hanging from tree limbs, laughin' like hyenas. Honestly, they were both dangling there, stuck, and laughing. Seems like they'd climbed my ladder and made it onto the roof. Then one of them lost his balance and took the other down with him."

"We were laughing because at first, we thought we were gonna die… and then we didn't," Mike explained. "There was nothing to grab onto to keep us from fallin' and the ground was a long way off. It didn't look like there could be a happy ending."

J.R. carried on with the tale. "Not sure how it happened, but the tree caught both of us. It was like it reached out and grabbed us. We looked at each other and we realized we weren't dead. We looked ridiculous and there was nothing we could do but laugh."

"That's when my dad came along," Mike added, "and all of a sudden it wasn't so funny. He was furious. He had to climb up and get us untangled and the whole time he was growling *what were you thinking* and *you coulda been killed* and *can't let either of you outa my sight*."

"I expected we'd be grounded for the rest of our lives," J.R. added.

Mr. Hampton broke in, "And well you should have been, considering the zillion other scrapes the two of you managed to get into. The miracle is that the two of you are still alive."

"Okay," Mike said. "Enough reminiscing or we'll be late for the movie."

"Only Disney could think up a title like *Bedknobs and Broomsticks*," said Leslie, snuggling up against Mike on the spacious back seat of Missy's Dodge Dart. "Since there are four of us in the car, we might actually get to see most of the movie."

"Speak for yourself," said J.R. as he pulled Missy close. "This gorgeous girl is way too distracting."

"The summer's gonna be fantastic with all of us staying in town," Missy said. "My job at Neiman's is cool. Leslie, y'all can use my discount when we shop together."

"Fantastic, I know nothing could make Frannie happier, and thanks J.R. for finding that notice about the summer jobs for the rest of us," Leslie said. "I'm still amazed that my roommates and I each got the spots we wanted."

"The job Coach Mitchell got me is gonna open doors big time," said Mike. "That deserves a kiss, doesn't it?" he asked, kissing Leslie before she could respond.

"Good recommendation," J.R. said, and pulled Missy into an embrace.

Chapter 5

Frannie answered the phone, then held the receiver out to Leslie. "It's your mom."

Leslie settled reluctantly into the chair by the phone. "Hi, Mom. How's everyone?" she asked as brightly as she could. "You wouldn't believe the fantastic weekend I had. Mike and I went to Arp with Missy and J.R., and I met Mike's parents, You'll really…"

"You did what?" Her mother shrieked. "If you can go to Arp, why aren't you coming home?"

"*Holy shit, why did I even tell her?*" Leslie's smile evaporated. "Mom, please don't make every conversation unpleasant. You don't have to be angry with me."

"How is it okay to spend time with Mike's family but not with your own? How can I not be upset," Mrs. Bleu huffed.

"Mom, going to Arp doesn't mean I'd rather be with Mike's family than my own. It means that Arp is two hours from Dallas, not eight. As much as I miss you, I absolutely cannot drive to Louisiana for the weekend. Please understand."

"No, you understand," Mrs. Bleu snapped. "You'll be with your friends all summer. You could have come home before your summer job starts. That would have been the right thing to do."

Leslie sighed, defeated. "I gotta go Mom. Bye." She collapsed next to the small telephone table with her head in her hands. *Mom's right I should have gone home.*

"Mike, I'm in deep shit with Mom."

"You can't do anything about it right now." Mike said. "Chill out. You'll make it home before school starts. For now, let's see if any of the gang wants to go to Six Flags this coming weekend. When we were kids, J.R. and I couldn't wait for the county fair every year. Six Flags is like the county fair on steroids. I know J.R. will want to take Missy."

"I don't think so. Six Flags is expensive just for rides and cotton candy. I'd rather go to the county fair in Arp come fall."

"You sure? It won't be that expensive. Besides, going to Six Flags would be the perfect thing to get your mind off your mom. You'd enjoy all the arcade games and I bet we'd come home with a dozen stuffed animals."

"And just where would I put a dozen stuffed animals?" Leslie laughed. "The apartment's barely big enough for four *Nurseketeers* and all of Frannie's junk. Besides, there are fun things to do that aren't outrageously expensive."

"A quiet evening alone in the park behind the cemetery wouldn't cost anything," Mike said. "That sounds practical to me."

"Hardly anything," she teased. "You have to buy me a burger first."

Mike maneuvered the car into a stand of trees while Leslie unwrapped their burgers. "We've had such a good time since finals," Leslie said, taking a bite, "and we still have a week before we start work."

"One more year 'til we graduate. Whoo-hoo," Mike said.

"I love you, Mike Hampton."

They finished eating in companionable silence. Mike leaned in to kiss her and drew her close. Warmth and contentment spread the length of her body. Their kisses deepened and Leslie's breath came faster. Their hands explored one another. When Mike gently caressed her breast, a moan of pleasure escaped her lips.

"*Much* better than Six Flags," Mike mumbled and kissed her again. "Tastier than cotton candy, too." Mike stifled Leslie's giggle with another kiss and his touch sent shivers of pleasure coursing through her.

Chapter 6

"Come on, come on," Leslie yelled, tugging at her ear lobe impatiently.

Robin came through the kitchen doorway munching a piece of toast. "Don't get your panties in a wad," she mumbled, swallowing. "Frannie's probably still primping."

"We can't be late on our first day. Go get her!" Leslie commanded.

"Yes, *Ma'am*," Robin saluted, turning, and colliding with Katie.

"Sorry." Katie said.

"Commander Leslie says we gotta get a move on," said Robin, "and Frannie's still upstairs. I'm on my way to tell her that she can walk to Parkland if she doesn't hurry."

"We'll take two cars in case someone has to stay late," Leslie announced."

"Hopefully, that won't happen too often, but it's a good plan," Katie agreed.

"I'll drive," said Robin. "Frannie can ride with me."

"You can stop messing with your ear now, Les," Katie said. "Everyone's here and we'll be on time."

"My ear…?" Leslie let go of her ear and looked at her hand.

"Whenever you're uptight, you mess with your ear." Katie said as she and Leslie climbed into Nellie.

"No, I don't," Leslie said, her brow furrowing. "Do I?"

"You don't even realize you're doing it. I used to think it was just when you were concentrating 'cuz you always do it when you study for a test, but you do it when you're on the phone with your mom, too."

"But I'm not uptight now," Leslie insisted. "I just didn't want to be late for work."

"You're uptight and you don't even realize it. You need to relax. None of us wants to be late and we have plenty of time. You gotta trust us."

"We're the *Nurseketeers*; of course, I trust you."

"That's good, because no one, not even you, has the energy to be responsible for absolutely everything and everyone."

Leslie pulled into the closest parking space she could find, and Robin pulled into a slot two cars away. As the *Nurseketeers* approached the hospital entrance, Leslie raised a fist. "Here we go, Girls! Our first day on the job."

The other *Nurseketeers* each raised a fist and chorused, "Go, *Nurseketeers!*"

"Let's look for each other in the cafeteria at lunchtime," Frannie said.

"It's doubtful we'll get our lunch breaks at the same time, but it won't hurt to look," Robin nodded.

"In any case, we'll meet here in the lobby when we get off work," Leslie said and turned down the hallways to the OR.

Robin pushed the button to summon the elevator for the rest of the *Nurseketeers*.

Leslie put on her scrub dress and left the locker room to check the familiar scheduling board.

"Good morning, Leslie. Welcome to the unit," said the OR Director.

"Thank you, Mrs. Laurent," Leslie beamed. "I'm excited to be here."

"This is Nan Holden, Leslie, another summer student. Rhonda Loving is our day charge nurse. Rhonda, you remember Leslie from Crestmont and Nan from Baylor, don't you? We'll need to focus on their orientation as they'll be starting on 3-11 in three weeks, if they're ready."

Leslie's eyes grew wide at the mention of working 3-11. She reached out to shake Ms. Loving's hand. "Nice to meet you," she said. "I'm so looking forward to working in the OR this summer. I'm positive I want to be an OR nurse when I graduate."

"We're happy to have both of you, and please, call me Rhonda." Ms. Loving's smile was warm, just the welcome that Leslie had hoped for on her first day. "I'll be making your assignments each day to be sure that you get the experience that will prepare you for 3-11. If you ever have questions, please come to me."

"I will. Thanks," Leslie said, taking her first deep breath since she'd arrived at the scheduling board. "I didn't realize I'd be going on 3-11."

"I didn't either," Nan said.

"We try to give our nursing students exposure to both day and evening shifts. You both did well in your OR rotations last semester. I expect that you'll learn quickly and enjoy the 3-11 shift. You'll have new experiences and an opportunity to be a bit more independent."

"I see." Leslie said, pleased with the compliment.

"Come along, you two. Nan, you'll be in OR#2," she said, pushing open the door and introducing Nan to the circulating nurse. Leslie you'll be in OR#4 today."

"Hi," said Troy, the scrub tech, looking up from organizing instruments on the sterile back table in OR#4. "You look familiar."

"This is Leslie. She was with us for her OR rotation last semester," Ronda said. "She'll be working here this summer.

We're getting her ready for 3-11, so I expect you to teach her everything you know."

"I'm on it, Boss," Troy said, his eyes twinkling.

When the nurse and the anesthesiologist arrived with the patient, Rhonda took Leslie to a safe spot where she could observe. "You can watch the whole room from here," she said. "The procedure won't take long. Help Troy turn the room over after the case, and you can scrub in with him on the next one." She turned to leave, then added, "Remember, you can come to me if you need anything."

Leslie nodded and dug in her pocket for the small notebook she always carried, intending to write down the circulator's name. *"What **is** her name?"* She squinted trying to remember. *"I must be losing it."*

She held on to the notebook and watched as Troy made scrubbing the case look effortless. She grinned when he called, "Betty, I need saline" and quickly scribbled the nurse's name in her notebook.

"Will I ever be as competent as those two? Betty makes circulating look easy, even though she's responsible for managing the whole room. With all they have to do, I wonder how long it took them to master their roles."

"Come on, Leslie," Troy said, when Betty and the anesthesiologist left for Recovery with the patient. "Let's get this room turned over. I'm glad you're here 'cuz we have back-to-back cases today and no time to dawdle."

"Sorry I'm late, "Leslie explained as she reached Katie in the Parkland lobby. "I got caught up watching Troy scrub a Whipple and I lost track of time."

"No problem," said Katie. "Robin and Frannie went on ahead. Let's get home and we can all share our first day at work."

"Great," Leslie said. "I spent the whole day scrubbed in with Troy. You remember him, the tech? He's going to be my preceptor until I go on 3-11. He remembered me from my rotation last semester, which, by the way, helped me big time. I was already familiar with the OR, and I remembered all the instruments for today's cases. Troy said he was impressed, even though I feel like I'll never learn enough to scrub alone, let alone circulate." She took a deep breath.

Katie laughed. "I wondered how long it would take you to run out of air. It's good that you're hooked up with a quality preceptor. You'll learn the ropes in no time."

"Leslie said she's going on 3-11 in three weeks," Katie said as she and Leslie joined their suitemates in their living room.

"What's that all about?" Robin asked.

"Rhonda, she's the charge nurse, is getting me ready for evenings. Mrs. Laurent thinks I'll be ready in three weeks, but I'm not sure what she means by *ready*. It feels like it will take all summer for me to learn enough to work on my own. There are soooo many different procedures, and all the surgeons have their special way of doing things."

"It won't take nearly as long as you think," Katie said. "You know the instruments. You just need practice time. My guess is they will continue to precept you even on evenings gradually building to intense cases."

"Lord knows you made us practice enough with you," Robin added. "Katie, I may be going on 3-11, too, so if Les and I are both working evenings, you and Frannie could take your car."

"Maybe not," said Katie. "There was talk about 3-11 on my unit, too, but I didn't pay much attention. I'll check it out tomorrow. I think I'd like evenings better than days."

"You never did enjoy the crazy atmosphere on days, especially on Med-Surg," Leslie said.

"Too true," agreed Katie. "Even geriatrics is hectic on the day shift. Besides, sleeping in sounds good."

"So," Leslie said, and all eyes turned to Frannie. "If you could do 3-11, we'd all have the same time schedule, although we might have different days off. We can sort out transportation when we get a final on who's working when."

"I was already thinking that tomorrow I'll tell my supervisor I'd like to change shifts," Frannie said. "I think they'll appreciate it because they've been complaining about how hard it is to staff 3-11. I don't want to be the only one of us left on the day shift. I'd only see you guys on weekends, and who knows how I'd get to work."

"That *would* suck," Robin agreed. "After all, how can I rag on you if I only see you when you're asleep?" She grinned at Frannie and gave her shoulder a shove.

"The summer'll be more fun if we can all spend it together," said Frannie. "After all, the *Nurseketeers* are *all for one and one for all*, right?"

"Fingers crossed," said Katie. "So, how was everyone's day?"

"I gotta admit," said Robin, "Med-Surg is more interesting than I expected, but I made two trips to the emergency room to bring patients back to our floor, and I'm thinking I might like the ER even better."

Chapter 7

"Mike, we have to make the most of our time together," Leslie said, "because I'm going to start on 3-11 in three weeks. I'll still be working Monday to Friday, but I'll be at work when you get off."

"Not ideal," Mike said, "but we'll make it work."

"At least we'll have Saturdays and Sundays together. We'll have to plan carefully to make the most of our time."

Mike laughed. "*Of course,* we will."

Leslie's brow furrowed. "What's wrong with being organized?" she huffed. "All I have to say is *plan,* and someone tells me to lighten up."

"Planning is fine," Mike assured her, "but not for everything, and not all the time. Enjoy spontaneity once in a while. We don't always need to know beforehand where we're going or what we're going to do. We might take in a movie, or we could just hang out."

"But if it's a popular movie and we don't plan to get there early, we might not get in," Leslie insisted.

"Could happen," Mike agreed, but then we'd have the whole evening free to drive to Bachman Lake or the cemetery and smooch."

Leslie laughed. "You're incorrigible."

"And you're gorgeous," Mike said, hugging her. "I'm not wild about having to wait all week to spend time with you, but I'll take whatever time I can get. Let's go to Galveston this weekend. Just us."

"A weekend in Galveston sounds like a party. Shouldn't we invite the others, too."

"*Not* the party I had in mind. We're going to see precious little of each other with you on 3-11, and I want to spend as much *just us* time with you as I can. We'll get a room at one of the beach hotels and chill."

"*Two* rooms at a beach hotel," Leslie said emphatically. "We can check out what cool things there are in Galveston to see and do, and then create an itinerary."

"A quiet weekend with my girl is what I had in mind," Mike said, and she had to smile when he added, "Let's play it by ear."

"How long is the drive?" she asked.

"It's about five hours. I'm sure I can get off early on Friday, since the students are always anxious to get their weekend started."

"Good. If you pack on Thursday, we can leave by four. Even if we stop for dinner along the way, we'll be there in plenty of time for a good night's sleep."

"Sleeping wasn't what I had in mind," Mike winked.

Later that week as they walked to the athletic complex, Mike said, "Bad news, Leslie."

"Bad news for you, for sure. I'm gonna sink the first three-pointer?" Leslie gave him a punch.

"It won't count for anything if I'm crippled," he said, massaging his arm.

"So, what's the bad news?" she asked.

"A big storm's scheduled to hit Galveston this weekend. We need to reschedule our trip."

"That's a shame, but it would be a waste to drive all that way and be stuck in a hotel room the whole weekend."

"Hmmm… au contraire, ma chère," Mike said, leering. "That sounds like a fantastic way to spend a weekend with you. Maybe we should reconsider canceling."

Leslie looked at Mike. "You're serious, aren't you?"

Mike nodded, a mischievous smile playing across his face.

"Whoa, Stud," Leslie cautioned. "I'm not sure I'm ready for what you have in mind. We can't afford to let anything get in the way of graduating. That would be a disaster."

"That won't happen, Les," Mike assured her. "I just want us to be together."

"Well, we'll have two rooms, so temptation won't get in the way of good judgment. We were both taught that sex comes with marriage, not before. I believe that, Mike, so *two* rooms."

"How about one room with two beds?" Mike suggested and continued hurriedly before Leslie could protest. "It'll be a lot cheaper, and pretty much the same thing. We'll each have a bed to sleep in. Why does it matter that we're in the same room?"

"Mike," she began. "We can't…"

"We can." Mike interrupted. "What's the big deal? We're two intelligent adults. I'll use a rubber. Those little swimmers will be stopped dead in their tracks."

"No amount of protection will make sex before marriage okay for me." She held up her hand when he started to speak. "I mean it. I love you, but I'm not willing to take even the tiniest risk of not graduating, not to mention that I can't imagine the guilt trip. All my life I've been taught that sex before marriage is wrong, and for me, it's wrong. Period. End of discussion."

Mike conceded. "If two rooms is what it takes to get you to Galveston for a weekend, I'm game. Two rooms it is." Leslie smiled. "I love you, Mike Hampton, but I don't think going to Galveston during a hurricane is a smart thing to do. Let's wait for glorious weather."

Chapter 8

"Did you see that dreamy pool of blue eyes that just walked by?" Nan asked as she and Leslie walked toward their assigned rooms.

"Which one?" asked Leslie. "Three baby docs just walked by and for all I know, all of them have blue eyes. Besides, I only have eyes for Mike, and his are brown."

"You goof," Nan said, rolling her eyes. "I meant Dr. Banks, the tall, good-looking one. He's a huggable teddy bear."

"Oh, him. He's tall, I'll give you that." Leslie chuckled. "Actually, I'm scrubbing in with your Dr. Banks on a hernia repair, but I doubt I'll have time to decide if he's a huggable teddy bear. I'll be too busy memorizing the steps in the procedure and the instruments he needs. I wish Troy were here today; he always makes it easier to learn. If I'm lucky, Esther, the OR tech who's scrubbing the case, will hold his retractors and let me run the mayo and pass the instruments."

"Good luck with that," said Nan. "I hear she's a bitch."

Harsh words startled Leslie as she entered the OR. "It's about time you got in here. I've been opening this case by myself for ten minutes already. Get me sterile saline and water for the basins. Now!" Esther spat.

"Bitch," Leslie muttered under her breath as she turned away and walked out to the fluid warmer in the center hall. "What happened to, *Good morning, Les?* Something ugly crawled outta her cereal this morning.*"* Leslie took a bottle of saline and one of sterile water from the warmer. "Here's hoping…," she tapped the two bottles together, toasting herself. "Things can't go anywhere but up from here."

"You'll run the mayo today," Esther commanded when Leslie returned. "I'll assist Banks. He's a private doc now, and the residents are all working with the attendings."

"*My wish came true.*" Leslie beamed. "Awesome."

Sharon, the RN circulator, returned from assessing the patient in the pre-op holding area. "Good morning, you two," she said. "Can one of you get scrubbed? Anesthesia is with the patient now and Banks has already spoken with him and the family. Let's get our counts done so I can go back for the patient."

"We'd be ready by now if Leslie hadn't taken so long getting in here," Esther groused.

The comment caught Leslie off guard, but she found her voice quickly. "I'll scrub right now," she said, and hurried out to the scrub sink. "*I can't believe I let her get away with that. Why didn't I tell Sharon I wasn't late?*"

Esther appeared at the sink beside her and turned on the faucet. Leslie willed the clock hands to move quickly, and she finished her ten-minute scrub in silence.

In the room, Leslie managed to don her gown and gloves without incident, grateful that Esther was still at the scrub sink. She organized the back table and counted sponges and sharps with Sharon, then Sharon left to help the anesthesiologist bring the patient into the room.

"Hand me a towel," Esther demanded. "I'm dripping all over the floor."

Leslie realized Esther had not set out a gown and gloves for herself.

"Gown me!" barked Esther. Leslie's mask hid her broad grin when Esther looked up, startled to see Leslie holding the gown ready for her.

Leslie quelled the desire to say something snarky. *"She can't complain about THAT!"* Leslie was still grinning. *"My technique was perfect."*

"Get ready to gown Dr. Banks. Make sure the gown is up high enough so the neck doesn't fall back down on his arms," Esther preached. "Then the neck would be unsterile, and you would have to start all over again."

"Wishful thinking!" Leslie knew her technique was flawless.

"Remember, right hand first unless the doc. has a preference," Esther continued her harangue. "Did you check Banks' preference card? Is he right or left handed?"

"I... I...," Leslie stammered, "I checked the preference card but I didn't notice any mention of that."

"He's right handed," Esther snapped. "You need to know that. Never mind. I'll gown and glove Banks so we won't have any more delays." The arrival of Sharon and the anesthesiologist with the patient curtailed Esther's next unpleasant remark.

Banks and Sharon helped the patient scoot onto the OR bed and Sharon cinched the safety strap across his thighs. Banks said *"Good morning"* to Esther and Leslie, then left to scrub. Ten minutes later he came into the room holding his scrubbed hands high, water dripping from his elbows. Leslie watched Esther gown and glove him while Sharon finished prepping the patient with an iodine solution.

After Banks and Esther placed surgical drapes on the patient, Leslie positioned the mayo stand over the patient's legs and pulled up the back table. Esther took her place across the OR table from Banks.

"Esther, why don't we let Leslie assist today. You run the mayo."

"Of course, Sir," Esther replied curtly, and shot Leslie a look that would have stopped a Mack truck.

Leslie didn't know whether to jump for joy or be disappointed. She had looked forward to managing the instruments on the mayo, but assisting Dr. Banks would be exciting, and she'd get a close look at the anatomy. Leslie held the retractors that exposed the operative site, watching carefully as Dr. Banks cut through the various layers of tissue.

"What do you see?" Banks asked.

Leslie was ecstatic. She identified each layer of tissue. She spotted a small bleeder and was grudgingly impressed when Esther handed Banks a hemostat without his having to ask. She accepted the scissors that Esther snapped sharply into her palm, then cut the suture after Banks occluded the vessel with a stitch.

"Nicely done, Leslie." She could hear the smile in his voice. "Let me show you something. If you hold the scissors like this, you can flip them back towards your wrist to free your thumb and two fingers to remove the hemostat without having to put the scissors down. The scissors will be right where you need them to cut the next stitch."

She fumbled the scissors as she tried to replicate the move, and Esther laughed out loud.

"Practice is everything," Banks assured her. "By the time we finish the case, you'll have nailed it."

Leslie avoided looking at Esther, whom she knew was glaring hatefully at her. "*Esther's hell bent on seeing me fail. I'll never get a chance to learn if I have to work with her.*"

Banks looked up after he placed the last suture in the incision. At 5'9", Leslie felt short standing opposite his 6'3" frame. "*Nan was right, he's as cute as he is nice.*"

"You did well," he said to Leslie, eyes twinkling. He nodded to Esther he as he pulled off his gown and gloves and stuffed them into the trash. "She's a keeper."

Leslie imagined that she heard Esther growl as she walked out, leaving Leslie alone to clean up after the case.

Leslie spotted Nan in the cafeteria and joined her.

"Sounds like you had your hands full with Banks' case this morning," Nan said, concerned. "Esther was trashing you to everyone in the locker room. She said you couldn't do anything right and Banks had to hand hold you through the whole case."

"What?" Leslie exploded. "What a bitch! How could she say that? Absolutely *nothing* went wrong in that case. I nailed it. Esther was pissed because Banks asked me to assist him and told her to run the mayo. He knows I'm a nursing student and I think he wanted to teach. He showed me how to flip the scissors so I could manage them and the hemostat at the same time. He quizzed me on the anatomy, and I slam dunked every question he asked."

"That's so cool," Nan said. "Esther is a real bitch. I've heard that she bullies new people for no good reason, and she gets away with it. I'm lucky I haven't had to work with her yet. They've had me in ortho this week and I'm told she doesn't like it. That's reason enough for me to stick with ortho."

"Do you think I should confront her?"

"That's your call, my friend. She's been around a lot longer than we have, and she does know her stuff. I'm not sure why the powers-that-be ignore her bad behavior 'cuz I can't image that they don't know about it."

"Normally I'm not one to tolerate bullying, but she threw me for a loop this morning, and I wasn't prepared to deal with it. I'll have to think about it."

"Bye Mom," Leslie said as she placed the receiver firmly in the cradle, controlling her anger as best she could. "Jeez! Mom's *got* to see what a great opportunity working in the OR is for me. I don't know how to make her understand."

"That's how moms are," Frannie reminded her. "Mine doesn't need any reason at all to wish I were home instead of in Dallas."

"My mom's just being selfish," Leslie insisted. "My family doesn't have any specific vacation plans for the summer and they don't need my help in the store. My brothers and sisters are too old to need babysitting, so there's absolutely *no* reason for me to be home, but here she is, acting like I'm committing the crime of the century… like I'm working in Dallas to spite her. She won't listen to a thing I say."

"You should promise to get home before school starts," Katie said. "Looking forward to your visit is probably just what she needs to remind herself that you're still her loving daughter who is growing up and developing priorities of her own."

Chapter 9

Leslie stood at the sink scrubbing for a breast biopsy with Dr. Banks. Esther walked by with another scrub tech and snickered loudly. She gestured toward Leslie and the other tech looked back and chuckled.

Great! Esther's ragging on me again and there's no way I can take her on now. Thank heaven she's not in this case with me. Leslie turned from the sink, holding her hands up to ensure that water would drip downwards toward her elbows, and entered the OR."

Troy looked up from the back table as Leslie entered the room. "Hey there. I'll set things up so we can count when Sharon comes back from assessing the patient. Banks will be by himself on this one. Do you want to run the mayo or assist him?"

"I'd like to run the mayo. This will be my first opportunity to do it alone, and with you, I know I'll be fine."

Troy's eyes crinkled an encouraging smile. "Then let's get on with it."

The door swished open, and Sharon surveyed the room. "Super," she said. "Looks like you guys are ready to go. Let's count."

Leslie counted sponges and sutures, missing only one suture that Troy had already loaded onto a needle driver. Troy winked and said, "Way to go, Newbie. Was that your first count?"

"Yes, and thanks for catching the needle I missed."

"You wouldn't have missed it if you'd been the one who'd loaded it. You're going to nail this case; I have faith in you."

"Thanks, I appreciate your confidence. I don't get any support from Esther when I scrub with her."

"Forget Esther. Stay focused on what Banks is doing and think about what he'll need next so you can be ready to hand it to him. You got this."

After Banks and Sharon positioned the patient on the OR bed, Banks left to scrub his hands. Leslie was ready with a towel when he came back. She gowned and gloved him, smiling at the memory of practicing with the *Nurseketeers,* a million times according to them.

Sharon finished prepping the patient, and Leslie handed Banks towels to isolate the operative site, presenting them one at a time like Troy had instructed. Troy moved to the opposite side of the table to help with the rest of the draping. Leslie worked the mayo stand into place over the patient's legs, then pulled the back table into position. A single drop of sweat rolled down the middle of her back as she picked up the scalpel and passed it to Banks for the initial incision.

"Great to have you in the room again, Leslie. Seems like you are getting in on all the best cases today," Banks said, accepting the knife from her.

Leslie's emerald eyes reflected the smile hidden behind her mask. She watched carefully as Banks dissected breast tissue to expose the lesion, then lifted the biopsy tissue with a hemostat and placed both the tissue and the instrument in the kidney basin that Leslie held for him. "Sharon, I need the frozen section results before I close."

"I'm on it," Sharon said, holding the specimen cup for Leslie to drop in the biopsy tissue. The tissue stuck to the clamp, so she shook the clamp a couple of times to dislodge it, knowing it needed to be sent to the lab quickly.

"It's okay," Sharon said. "Drop the instrument into the cup and I'll take care of it." Sharon removed the clamp and capped the specimen jar to keep the tissue moist. "This needs to get to the lab, stat," she said to the orderly whom she had summoned.

While they waited to hear from the lab, Banks wrapped his hands in a sterile towel to protect his gloves and lowered himself carefully onto the rolling stool Sharon held steady for him.

Leslie was straightening the instruments on her mayo when her eyes grew wide. *"Oh my god, if the biopsy is positive, it means the patient has cancer. Banks will want to remove the breast. I know the instruments he'd use for a radical mastectomy, but I've never actually seen one done. How did I not think of this before? The whole purpose of a breast biopsy is to see if there's cancer... and to deal with it if there is. I should have prepared. I..."* A rivulet of sweat ran down Leslie's spine.

"What's your favorite music?" Banks interrupted her self-flagellation.

"I...," Leslie stammered. "I like Simon and Garfunkel, particularly *Bridge over Troubled Waters*. It makes me a bit sad, but it's my favorite."

"It is a sad song," he agreed, "but it has a wonderful melody."

Sharon lifted the receiver as soon as the phone rang and listened expectantly. With obvious pleasure she announced, "Benign and all margins clear."

Leslie couldn't stifle her sigh of relief.

"Okay, boys and girls," Banks said heartily, "let's close and send this lucky lady home. Sharon, see if you can find some peppy Simon and Garfunkel on that music contraption, something like *Mrs. Robinson* or *the 59th Street Bridge*. Sorry, Leslie, no sad songs now. We need to celebrate our patient's good fortune."

That evening, Leslie and Mike sat holding hands across the small table in the diner. "When I'm on 3-11, we'll still have all day Saturday and Sunday together."

"Gotta be grateful for whatever time we have. Let's not fill the weekends too full. We need to leave plenty of time for smooching." He grinned mischievously Leslie shook her head. "Men and their one-track minds."

"Gotta keep the planet populated. Us guys wouldn't want to be responsible for letting the human race die out."

"Well, Mike Hampton, saving the world will just have to wait a couple of years."

"We can practice."

"We *can't* practice. I told you that isn't going to happen. I do not believe in sex before marriage."

"Spoil sport." Mike laughed and leaned across the table to kiss her.

"With me at Parkland and you a shoo-in for a coaching job in Dallas, it's likely we'll both be staying in Dallas after graduation. What do you think?" Leslie asked with her fingers crossed.

Mike smiled. "Yes, I was hoping that's what you had in mind. I thought I might have to explore coaching jobs in Louisiana in case you wanted to be closer to your family, but I'm sure that both of our careers will get a better start here."

"I want Mom to realize that it's a smarter move for me to start my career in Dallas than in Abita Springs," Leslie mused, "and that's what's got her so bent outta shape. She's torn between what she knows I want and what is best for her. I know there are great hospitals in New Orleans, but I like Dallas, and I want to be with you."

"Les, you can't lay your decision to stay here on me."

"It's not *just* you, Mike. The *Nurseketeers* all have summer jobs at Parkland and it's our last summer together as well. I don't want to work in Abita Springs, or in New Orleans. It's not right for Mom to make me choose between my friends and my family."

"I don't think she intended it that way, Les. She took for granted that you'd come home, and you sprang the news on her without giving her a chance to adjust. She's just disappointed. Talk to her. If she knows you understand how she feels, she might feel better about it."

"She's being selfish," Leslie insisted.

"No more than you are, Les. It's her last chance to have her whole family together."

Leslie interrupted, "I can reason with Daddy, but Mom isn't interested in discussing it. She just wants what she wants. I suppose it's because she's a wife and mother living an uncomplicated life in the same small town where she was born. Kids grow up and follow in their parents' footsteps. It's the only world she knows. If it weren't for my athletic scholarship, it's the only life *I'd* know."

"Not sure I buy that," Mike disagreed. "You don't fit the small-town image. You're assertive and involved. You're a *do-er.* I wouldn't be surprised if your mother didn't realize that from the beginning."

"Actually," Leslie explained. "I get most of that from Mom. Daddy's the quiet one; Mom's the doer. She manages the store, keeps up with the house, and has always been involved in our activities. She's never missed a school event for any of us. It's just that her world is so small. Looking back, I think I understand why she wasn't excited about my scholarship. She must have seen the writing on the wall way back then."

"Makes sense," said Mike. "Arp is so close to Tyler that it doesn't qualify as a small town. There are families like mine who have always lived there, but it's common for the kids to grow and go. Folks who move to Arp come to escape the frenzy of the city, so the town's population pretty much stays the same."

"You're lucky your folks don't expect you to come home."

"Daddy might harbor a secret fantasy that I'll come home and coach with him, but he knows that isn't going to happen, at least for now."

"Really?" asked Leslie. "Do you think there's a chance you'd end up in Arp?"

"A few things could make that possible. A big city might not be the best place for raising a family. What do you think?"

"I think I want kids, but haven't given it a lot of thought," Leslie said. "It's for sure I don't want any for a while. When we graduate, I'll need to concentrate on my career."

"Makes sense," Mike agreed. "First things first,"

Leslie smiled slyly as they stood to leave the diner. "Let's drive to Bachman Lake."

"I *like* that idea, but maybe we should trade the truck out for Nellie."

"Why?" Leslie asked innocently. "We can see the planes just fine from the truck."

"I…," Mike began, but Leslie's grin gave her away. He grinned back. "No problem, I have a blanket and it's a beautiful night."

They drove to the far end of the parking area, away from other vehicles. Mike pulled the truck under the trees at the edge of the lake. "This looks romantic," he said, and was interrupted by a thundering airplane flying low overhead toward the Love Field landing strip just across the lake. "Okay, not quite as idealistic as I'd like, but lovely and private… well, kinda private. It's a *Catch 22*, Les. The park is quiet, but there are more people; here we have jets, but it's just us." He reached behind his seat to grab a blanket.

"I prefer *just us*. That's romantic," Leslie said.

Mike opened her door and reached for her hand. "At your service, My Lady."

Mike spread the blanket on the grass, and they sat, arms around one another, watching the airport lights twinkle on the surface of the water.

The darkness enveloped them, and the hour grew late. "Mmmm," sighed Leslie, "We both have to be at work in the morning."

"In a minute," Mike mumbled, pulling her close for one last, long kiss before standing up.

"Ahhh, lovebirds," crooned Frannie as Leslie closed the apartment door behind her. "You two *do* make a cute couple."

"Doesn't hurt that he lets you get away with being Miss Bossy Britches," Robin added.

"What? I'm not bossy," Leslie insisted. "What makes you say that?"

"C'mon, if you had your way, you'd make all the decisions for you and Mike and for the *Nurseketeers*, too."

"Well, I'm just organized. People who can't make up their minds are frustrating, and besides, If Mike didn't like my suggestions, he'd say something."

"What would you do if he disagreed?" Robin asked.

Leslie cocked her head. "Why would he do that?"

Robin rolled her eyes.

Chapter 10

After work, Leslie changed into shorts and a t-shirt and joined the *Nurseketeers* for pizza and their daily debrief.

"I got to take care of a 10-year-old girl today," Frannie said. "I took care of two other patients, but that little kid stole my heart. She was hooked up to an IV and her grandmother stayed with her the whole day. They played cards and watched TV. I think the grandmother is addicted to *Days of Our Lives*. The kid's parents both work and they were trading off staying with her at night. When I first went in the room this morning, her dad was on his way out. He slept on a cot that the nursing staff got for him. The funny thing about it is that she's scared to death to leave her bed. She thinks bed rest means *don't leave the bed for any reason*. I could hardly get her up to go to the bathroom."

"You did get that misconception ironed out, right?" Robin asked.

"Well, I tried to, but she is one frightened little girl. I talked with her about drinking lots of water and that getting up to the bathroom was a great way to get a little exercise. She sleeps a lot, probably because she doesn't feel well, but being bored and scared may be part of it. She's gonna be okay, though," Frannie concluded. "She's getting better every day."

"I had an interesting day, too," Katie volunteered. "Since we were on the Gero floor last semester for clinicals, I'm already familiar with the routine, but the big adjustment is being responsible for more patient care than on our clinical rotation. I'm grateful that they haven't assigned me a full patient load yet. Today, I had enough on my plate with just two patients, trying to get organized for bed baths and changing sheets, transporting them to radiology and physical therapy, delivering food trays, helping transfer them back into bed after surgery, and assisting them in the bathroom. It was a struggle to keep up with it all. This summer is going to test my organizational skills, for sure. I need to take a page from your playbook, Leslie. How was your day?"

"Dr. Banks taught me something cool today," Leslie began. "Let me show you." She pulled two pairs of bandage scissors from her pocket. "I borrowed your scissors, Katie. I hope you don't mind. Imagine I'm holding a pair of scissors and I have to hand Dr. Banks a hemostat to stop a bleeder. He showed me how to manage my scissors and the hemostat at the same time. Watch." Leslie flipped the scissors she was holding out of the way and used her last two fingers to hold them firmly against her palm. "Look. I'm still holding the scissors, but I have my thumb, index, and middle fingers free to grab the hemostat. When the surgeon's tied off the bleeder, I can remove the hemostat, then flip the scissors back into place and cut the suture. TA DA! Isn't that the coolest thing you've ever seen?"

"Yep, pretty cool," said Frannie, "let me have a go at that."

Robin and Katie groaned in unison. "Shades of a zillion practice sessions from junior year," Robin sighed.

Leslie continued while Frannie messed around with the two pairs of scissors. "My day was great, until I went into the locker room to change. As soon as I opened the door, I heard my name. Esther was trashing me to a group of her tech buddies. She was telling them what an awful job I'd done all day and not a word of what she said was true."

Frannie gasped in disbelief.

"She's a bully, Leslie, plain and simple," Robin said.

"I have no idea why she has it in for me. I can't imagine how making me look bad does her any good. The worst part is that people listen to her because they don't know me."

"You can't let her get away with that behavior," Robin insisted. You gotta blast the bitch!"

Katie added, "I agree with Robin. You have to confront her, but tone it down a bit from *blast the bitch* to something more constructive."

"She's *supposed* to be teaching me," Leslie retorted, "but all she's doing is making me want to avoid her at all costs."

"That won't work, and you know it," Katie said. "It's inevitable that you'll be assigned to work with her again."

"Maybe she *is* teaching you something," Robin said. "She's giving you the opportunity to confront a bitch who has it in for you for no reason. You would never have let that happen here at school. Here, you face nonsense head on. Remember the *March Against Violence* parade our freshman year. You stood up to Stephen and that pack of bullies that day. Why is standing up for yourself at work any different?"

Leslie nodded. "You're right. We did stop those toads, but you and Katie were the ones who did the heavy lifting, as I recall. I had my hands full with other agenda items. I guess I'm gonna have to give the situation a little *cognitive effort*, as our instructors would say. So, how was your day, Robin?"

"Pretty much the same as Katie's," Robin said. "Challenging, but nothing worth sharing. Let's eat 'cuz I'm starving, and Leslie, you cannot put off confronting that hussy."

Leslie took a deep breath and began to dial. "I hope this works," she said to the *Nurseketeers* as the phone began to ring at the Bleu's grocery store in Abita Springs.

"Daddy," she said with a sigh of relief. "I was hoping you'd answer. I need some help."

"What's wrong," Mr. Bleu said, alarmed.

"Nothing's wrong," Leslie assured him, "Not really… it's just Mom. She's upset with my decision to work in Dallas this summer and every conversation with her is difficult. I can't convince her that working in the OR here this summer is a great opportunity for me. Students rarely get that chance. It's like she doesn't hear a word I say. Can you talk to her?"

"Leslie, perhaps, you should be more sensitive. She's your mother. You never mentioned the possibility of staying in Dallas for the summer, and your announcement caught her by surprise. She knows you'll probably never be home again except to visit and that's a difficult adjustment for her."

"Daddy, I'm 21 and I'm investing in my career, in my future. Why is that a problem?"

Mr. Blue chuckled. "It's not a problem for *you,* Sweetheart. You're not a mother. You're the 21-year-old off becoming the successful adult you're going to be. Your whole life is ahead of you. You have no reason to understand what your mom's going through… yet. However, there is good reason for you to be sensitive."

"Well, explain it to me… because it just doesn't make sense." Leslie pleaded.

"You're the first of her fledglings to leave the nest, and for a mom whose entire adult life has been devoted to raising a family, it's a cruel reminder that it won't be too long before her home is empty of her children. There's actually a name for it: *empty nest syndrome.*"

"You'd think after raising five kids, she'd be looking forward to time for herself."

Mr. Bleu chuckled. "Some mothers look forward to an *empty nest.* Your mother's not one of them. You need to be sensitive to how she feels. Your mother deserves that much. In the meantime, I'll see what I can do, but I expect you to do your part."

"Thanks, Daddy. I'll try to be understanding, but this summer in Dallas is important for me."

"Be sure you come home before school starts. I know that will help. When you and your mother are together, it will be easier for her to make the transition. Right now, she's focused on her disappointment that you aren't home for the summer."

"I'll make it home, Daddy. You're the best!"

"Honey, I miss you, too, you know," said Mr. Bleu. "I miss you very much."

On Monday, getting ready for the *Nurseketeers'* second week on 3-11, Leslie complained, "This isn't how I wanted the summer to go. I love the OR, but it sucks that I only get to see Mike on weekends. I can't believe how fast this weekend went by, and it'll be five days before we can spend any real time together."

"Look on the bright side," Frannie giggled, "You won't get tired of each other."

"They do say that absence makes the heart grow fonder," Katie chuckled. "Now, tell us what happens on 3-11 in the OR."

"As soon as I get there, I get assigned to relieve someone from the day shift who's still scrubbed in on a procedure. It's a challenge to step into the middle of a case, but most everyone is patient with me, and they're used to teaching."

"I knew you'd rise to the challenge," Robin said. "I told you not to worry. They wouldn't have put you on 3-11 if they didn't think you could stand on your own two feet."

"Nursing students aren't the only newbies," Leslie continued. "Every discipline has them: surgical residents, anesthesia residents, radiology interns. I'm lucky we did our clinicals at Parkland or I don't think there'd be any way I'd be in the OR."

"You've found your specialty, for sure," Katie said.

"You bet! I got to scrub in on a tough vascular case. I didn't get to do much, but the surgeon was great at explaining what he was doing. I learned a lot, and the scrub nurse complimented me on how well I knew the instruments. All that time in the practice lab paid off."

"Look on the bright side," said Katie. "You'll have the whole summer to get a head start on your career."

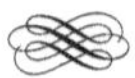

The next evening after work, Leslie hurried across the lobby toward Katie. "What a day!" she said, breathlessly. "Betty Ames, the circulator on one of my first cases this summer, is on 3-11 now. She was assigned to relieve on a tough case, and she asked me to scrub in with her. She said it would be a good learning experience, and she knew they'd need extra hands. The patient was in pretty bad shape, and they had surgeons from different specialties all working at the same time. I didn't do much besides hold retractors, but it was fascinating. Watching Betty manage a case that challenging made me feel like someday, *I'll* be able to do that."

"What happened to the guy?" asked Katie. "Was he in an accident?"

"After the case, Betty told me they call it the *Knife and Gun Club*. It means the guy was in a street fight and was shot or cut up badly. Seems that our patient wasn't the only *Knife and Gun Club* victim in the OR today, and two of them didn't make it."

"That's awful," said Katie. "Until I came to Dallas, I'd never heard of street violence. At home, there are dustups between Whites and Indians, but those skirmishes involve pushing and shoving and name calling, not knives and guns."

"I never heard of anything like that in Abita Springs, either. Big cities have better opportunities for career development, but it seems like living in a small town is a lot safer. With all the choices we'll have to make, it's a good thing we're nurses. We can work *anywhere*."

"True," said Katie. "At first, I was resentful when John decided to go back to Atoka to take over Doc's vet practice without bothering to ask me, but recently I've been considering the Indian

Health Service, and it sounds intriguing. I hope they have a presence in Stillwater so I can work there while John's in veterinary school. I know they have an office in Atoka, but I can't imagine waiting four more years to be with John."

"That would suck," said Robin.

"All we have is one more year of school, then Boards, and we'll be *nurses!* "said Katie. "Doesn't that sound exciting?"

"It would be exciting if I weren't worried about passing finals, let alone facing Boards," Leslie answered. "I can't believe that I'm still struggling after three years of college. I *know* the material. It shouldn't be that hard to answer the test questions. Maybe this year will be different."

"The *Nurseketeers* are here for you, Les," said Frannie. "Everyone learns differently, and you and I have both developed good study habits. You just have to find an approach to test-taking that works for you. The way Robin and Katie suggested has been working for me."

"I hope I can make it work for me, too," Leslie said. "I'd better go call Mom or she'll have a cow. Back in a jiff."

"Mom, it's Leslie," said Leslie as soon as her mother picked up the phone. "How are you?"

"I miss you. I'm glad you called. Tell me about work."

"The summer's going well. At first, I thought it would take me forever to learn enough to be useful, but that's happening quicker than I expected. On some cases, I can run the mayo by myself. That means I give the surgeon the instruments he needs to operate. I've had to learn what instrument he will need for each step in the procedure so I can have it ready."

"I'm glad you're enjoying the job, Sweetie. At least I'll get to see you before school starts in the Fall."

"On complicated cases, I either scrub with someone else or I assist the surgeon by holding retractors so that he can see what he's doing. I'm amazed at how much I'm learning."

"I hope you've told them that you have to quit in time to spend time with us before school starts. We haven't seen you since Easter and I expected we'd have the summer together. I can't wait to have you home after graduation."

"Hold on, Mom. I don't know where I will be after graduation. That's a whole year away. I know it's been a while since I was home but staying here in Dallas worked out for all the *Nurseketeers* to be together. We just couldn't pass up the opportunity. Having this job will make finding work after I graduate much easier. Please understand how important that is to me."

"I'm trying to be supportive, but I expected you to come home. You were going to spend this summer with the family, and it's not right that it's not happening."

"Mom, you've got to try to understand. This is important for my career."

"Remember that you have a family."

"I'll be home before the end of the summer. I miss you, too."

"Be sure that happens, Leslie. We need to spend time with you."

"I will, Mom, I promise.

Coming home from work the next evening, Frannie grabbed an envelope taped to their apartment door. "Here Les, this has your name on it."

"Wonder who left it," Leslie said

"Opening it might be the best way to find out," Robin quipped.

"What if it's personal? Shouldn't we give Leslie a chance to read it first?" Katie asked.

"It's okay," Leslie said, reading as she unfolded the paper. Ms. Reynolds wants to see me about something. She's invited me to a meeting next Tuesday at 4. It says, I don't have to call her unless I can't make it and we have to reschedule. It's got to have something to do with SNA."

"You'll have to reschedule since you're on 3-11 now." Robin said.

"Yep, I wonder what she has in mind," Leslie mused.

"Calling and asking might be a good idea," Robin said, and couldn't stifle a laugh.

The next morning after calling Ms. Reynolds, Leslie said, "We have an answer. The Nursing School is planning a clinical orientation for junior students."

"Interesting," Katie said slowly. "Last year when I was struggling with Med-Surg, I told Giffy Guts that we'd be better prepared if we had a chance to visit the hospitals before we started clinicals. Junior year was so different from our freshman and sophomore years that I thought juniors would benefit from an orientation. It would be cool if my suggestion was the motivation for the orientation."

"They obviously heard you, and it's a great idea." Leslie said, "I agree that clinicals would have been much easier for all of us last year if we'd known what to expect. Ms. Reynolds wants the senior SNA members involved because we'll make the best preceptors for the incoming juniors. She also said active participation in our professional organization is part of our career development."

"So, when are you meeting with her to get the details?" Robin asked.

"Tomorrow at 10," Leslie answered. "I'll give you all the details over lunch." A worried expression crossed Leslie's face.

"What? What's wrong?" Katie asked.

"The orientation means I won't be able to go home like I promised. I'm not looking forward to telling my mother *that*. Imagine the fit she's gonna throw when I call with this news."

"Her being upset about you not coming home is sweet in a way," Katie said. "She was counting on spending one last summer with her oldest daughter. She just wasn't prepared when you stole that from her."

"Wait," said Robin. "There's no reason you can't go home. Your job is to make the orientation happen. You don't have to be there yourself. There should be plenty of participation without you. Wait and see what Ms. Reynolds has in mind and how much support you get from the SNA members."

Chapter 11

"The nursing faculty would like the Student Nurses Association to participate in this new initiative," explained Ms. Reynolds when Leslie had settled into the chair across from her desk. "We'll have the orientation for junior students entering the nursing program the week before registration for fall semester."

"I'm glad that you were impressed with Katie's suggestion," Leslie said. "Our junior year was challenging, and it *would* have been helpful to know in advance what to expect from a senior student's perspective."

"As President of the SNA, I would like you to facilitate the senior nurses' participation as mentors for the incoming juniors. The pressure of the added clinicals could be mitigated by ensuring that each junior student could reach out to a senior SNA member for information or support. Faculty members are always available to assist students, but I imagine it would be easier to talk with someone who has experienced the same pressures."

Surprised at the professor's keen perception of the student experience, Leslie blurted, "I know the senior SNAs would love to help."

Ms. Reynolds nodded. "As for their participation in the orientation itself, they will serve as guides for the visits to the clinical facilities. Each senior participant will be assigned 2-3 incoming juniors. The tours will be personal and the juniors will have sufficient time to ask their questions."

"I reached out to a couple of seniors in SNA when I was struggling last fall. One of the OR nurses at Parkland is a Crestmont graduate, and she was helpful to me, too. Of course, my roommates were grand, and if it weren't for their support, I might not have done as well."

"I'm glad you agree with the initiative, and I appreciate your enthusiasm," Ms. Reynolds said. "Today is Tuesday. How would 10am on Friday work for our next meeting? We can explore your thoughts on how to engage the SNA members."

"Perfect." Leslie said, already thinking about how to motivate her colleagues to participate in the project. "Do we have a budget? I was thinking of sending a flyer to every senior SNA member since most have gone home for the summer."

"That can be part of our discussion on Friday," Ms. Reynolds said. "Come prepared with your plan and a budget. The SNA did well when they elected you President. You've got a good head on your shoulders."

"Thanks," Leslie said. "I appreciate that."

Leslie burst into the apartment and shared the details of her meeting with the *Nurseketeers* over lunch. "It should be fun," she said. "Just think how nice it would have been last year if we'd had mentors who'd walked in our shoes. I know I had help from a couple of seniors and without y'all, I don't know how I would have made it. Sometimes you just need someone who has been there, and friends who care."

"I hope the SNA members are as enthusiastic about precepting as you are," Robin said, skeptically. "Keep in mind there are more junior nursing students than there are SNA seniors. If any of the seniors choose not to participate, the ones who volunteer might have more than they can handle. Remember we all still have classwork and clinicals."

Leslie responded emphatically. "The students who joined SNA made a commitment to be leaders in the Crestmont nursing community. That means they have to support projects that make the school better. This project needs their support."

"You'll have to accept that people aren't always as willing as you are to participate," Katie said. "It's good to expect the best of everyone, but you shouldn't be surprised if some of our classmates have other priorities. After all, it means giving up a whole week of summer vacation."

"*You* three are in, right?" Leslie asked, a bit unsettled. "Katie, are you trying to tell me you don't want to participate? After last year, I'd've thought you'd be the first to appreciate how great it would be to have someone to talk to when things weren't going as well as expected."

Katie shook her head. "Yes, I struggled, and you guys helped me, and I'm still concerned about what is ahead for me this year. I'm just pointing out that this project might be more challenging than you think. I'm willing to explore what it will involve." She nodded toward Frannie and Robin.

"I can help with the planning," Frannie said, "but I'm going home the week before registration. The only way I got to stay in Dallas to work was to promise I'd come home before the semester starts."

"Didn't you make that same promise to your mother, Leslie?" Robin asked.

"I... uh," Leslie stuttered. "Daddy will help her understand how important this is."

Robin shook her head. "I'll help you as much as I can," she said, "but I'm with Katie. Find out what all is involved and how much of our time will be required before you ask us for a commitment. Let's also see how willing the rest of our class is to accommodate your proposal. If you get the responses you need, you can go home that week and not disappoint your mother."

"The SNA seniors had better be willing to pitch in," Leslie said. "I'm counting on them, *and* I'm counting on the *Nurseketeers* to help me plan this thing. First, we need to create a flier. Ms. Reynolds is expecting a game plan and a budget when I meet with her on Friday."

"That only gives you two days," Robin pointed out. "Keep in mind that all of us are working full time this summer. I'm also picking up extra lunch shifts at the Steakhauz, so tomorrow is my only free day this week."

"I was going shopping with Missy tomorrow morning," Frannie began, then added hastily, "but we can go another day," when a frown began to cloud Leslie's face.

"The *Nurseketeers* are in," Katie said, "but your game plan has to be flexible enough to accommodate everyone's prior commitments. You can't count on folks for more than they're able to give. If you demand too much, you might get nothing."

"What's the next step after the flyers?" Robin asked. "How do you plan to get in touch with the members who don't respond?"

"I have confidence in them" Leslie assured her friends. "They'll see how important this is and they'll be excited about participating."

"*Sure* they will," murmured Robin.

"Leslie, shouldn't you warn your mother that you might not make it home like you promised," Katie asked. "The longer you wait, the more upset she's gonna be."

Leslie took a deep breath and nodded. She reached for the phone. Her chest felt like it was being squeezed by a boa constrictor. She held the receiver, waiting for someone to answer. "*Please let it be Daddy,*" she prayed. Her shoulders sagged when her mother answered.

"Mom, I'm glad it's you," Leslie said with all the enthusiasm she could muster. "I have good news and not-so-good news."

"When are you coming home?" her mother demanded.

"Well, that's the not-so-good part," Leslie hesitated. "Let me tell you the whole story and you'll understand."

"*Not coming home* is what I'm hearing, and I'm definitely NOT understanding that. You promised to be here for a week before school starts. I've been looking forward to that, Leslie Jean."

"We'll have time together, Mom. I'll be home for the holidays, and we'll celebrate like we've always done. What I need right now is for you to understand how important this year is to me. It's my senior year, my last year in college, and I need to make the most of it."

"So, what is it that's so important you can't spend a few days with your family?"

"That's the good part, Mom. Last year we suggested that an orientation for the junior nursing students would make the transition into clinical courses easier, and the faculty thought it was a good idea. Ms. Reynolds has asked me to organize the Student Nurses Association members to help with it. I'm president this year."

"It's July. You have plenty of time to get it organized and come home."

"Not really, Mom. I can't just walk away while everyone else does the work. Besides, I can't be sure they're doing a good job if I'm not here."

"You're the president, Leslie. It's your job to organize the event and make assignments. You don't have to do everything yourself. You should trust the others to do a good job once you've given them instructions and they have accepted the responsibility. There's no reason for you not to come home."

Frustrated and guilt-ridden, Leslie said, "We'll see, Mom. I gotta run."

"You don't look like that went as well as you'd hoped," Katie said. "You could go home you know, if there are enough SNA members participating in orientation. You did make a promise after all."

"That's what Mom said, but I can't just get everyone else involved and walk out. How would that look?"

"What do you mean by *how would it look*? It would look like you did your job well. You're responsible for organizing the event. That's what leaders do. If you get enough participation, and everyone knows what's expected, there's no reason for you to stay here. You're the leader, not the only worker bee."

"But," Leslie began.

"Don't make excuses," Katie interrupted. "Just think about it. I feel sure you can figure it out on your own."

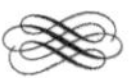

At work on Thursday, Leslie had the instruments organized and was ready for the procedure when Sharon wheeled the 17-year-old into the room for his tonsillectomy. He was built like a football player with soccer ball shoulders. "*Wow,*" Leslie thought. "*That took some major upper body work in the weight room. Bet he has a six-pack, too.*"

Sharon, the circulating nurse, held the patient's hand while the nurse anesthetist, Quig, gave him anesthesia and inserted a breathing tube into his windpipe.

"Sharon," Leslie asked, "why does the circulating nurse always stand by the patient during intubation?"

"Good question, Les. First, going under anesthesia can be frightening for the patient and the nurse's support is helpful. Clinically, taking over control of the patient's breathing is a critical step, so someone should be right there in case the anesthetist needs help. I've been asked to provide cricoid pressure so the anesthetist can insert the endotracheal tube more easily. Sometimes you'll see a resident help instead of the circulating nurse, but I like doing it because it's an opportunity to connect with the patients before they go to sleep. I feel like I make a difference."

"Is this your first time to scrub alone?" Dr. Chandler asked as he and Leslie draped the patient.

"No, Sir" she responded, "I've scrubbed procedures by myself before, but this is the first time there hasn't been someone else to assist the surgeon."

Leslie slid the mayo tray over the patient's legs and did a last-minute check of her instruments. Her hands trembled slightly as she touched each one in the order that it would be used during the procedure. Finally satisfied, she took a deep breath, laced her fingers, and placed her hands on the mayo to wait for Dr. Chandler's first request.

He plucked the retractor from the mayo and placed it in the patient's mouth.

"Hmmm… I guess he'll just get what he needs when he wants it. Good thing, too, since my hands will be full with the retractor and the suction." She relaxed into the case.

Chandler removed the tonsil on the first side and repositioned the tongue retractor to expose the other side.

"His tongue is growing. That's not right," Leslie thought, and she shook her head to clear her mind.

As soon as Chandler pulled the tonsil out of the boy's mouth, his throat filled with blood. Leslie suctioned the blood and tried to reposition the retractor so Dr. Chandler could find the bleeder, but nothing she did seemed to work. She could not find a way to keep the monster tongue out of the way. No matter how she adjusted the retractor, blood filled the throat and kept him from locating the pumping bleeder.

Time stood still.

Quig's gloved hand appeared, took the tongue retractor from Leslie, and repositioned it. Dr. Chandler spotted the bleeder and got a clamp on it.

When a gowned and gloved Esther appeared, Leslie realized that Sharon had called for help. Esther did nothing but stand there while Leslie and Dr. Chandler finished the case. Leslie's shoulders slumped and her heart pounded, imagining the gossip that evil Esther would spread throughout the OR.

When Dr. Chandler stepped back from the patient, Esther disappeared without lifting a finger to help clean the room for the next patient. Leslie, near tears, was tying up the last trash bag when Sharon returned from Recovery.

Sharon's arm encircled Leslie's shoulders. "Don't beat yourself up over this case. No one could have predicted that the young man's tongue would double in size like that. What happened would have happened to any of us. You know that, don't you? You did great."

Leslie nodded and whispered her thanks, then carried the trash bag into the hallway for the orderly to take to the dirty utility room. She squared her shoulders. *"Get a grip Bleu. FOCUS!"*

Leslie entered the crowded lounge and immediately spotted Esther holding court in one corner, probably talking about her. She heard her name and Esther's cronies giggled.

"Not again." Leslie's breath caught in her throat, and she hurried into the locker room. She collapsed onto a bench and took long, slow breaths. *"I'm not going to let that bitch derail me."*

Leslie grabbed her lab coat and her lunch and left for the cafeteria. *"I can't confront her with an audience, and I need to be anywhere but in the lounge right now."*

None of the *Nurseketeers* was in the cafeteria, so Leslie sat alone in a corner, stewing over Esther's unacceptable behavior. Her anger rose as she chomped through her lunch.

Back in the locker room, she couldn't even remember what she'd eaten. *"That bitch… I can't even enjoy a meal without thinking about her. I've got to make this right, but please don't let me run into her again today. I'm not ready."*

Chapter 12

"Wow! Nice shot!" Mike said, as Leslie's three-pointer swished through the net. "That deserves a celebration. How about Galveston next weekend?"

"Groovy. I was more disappointed than I expected when we had to cancel for bad weather last month."

"If we can both get Friday off," Mike said, "we can leave early Friday morning and start back home after lunch on Sunday. I'm pretty sure they'll give me the day. The athletic camp's going well and we're not at all short-staffed. Do you think you can arrange a day off?"

"I'll ask my supervisor tomorrow. Fingers crossed."

"I'm up for spending lots of time alone with you in the hotel," Mike grinned wolfishly.

"I was thinking more like Friday and Saturday on the beach, romantic dinners, and sightseeing. We're getting two rooms, remember?"

"Leslie, we're not teenagers." Mike insisted.

"I love being together as much as you do, but seriously," Leslie insisted, "we're getting two rooms. One room is too much temptation, and too much guilt to handle for this small-town girl."

"Guilt? What guilt? You love me, don't you."

"Of course, I do, but we've had this conversation before. I'm Baptist and I was raised to believe that you save *that* for when you're married. You're Methodist, right? You should know what I am talking about. You were raised the same as me."

Mike swallowed his frustration. "The beach should be a no-brainer… a blanket, towels, and a beach ball should do it."

"…and food, drink, sunscreen, and a good book to read…" Leslie added.

"Gee, and I was going to pack a bathing suit and a toothbrush and play the weekend by ear. If I had my way, that's all I'd need."

Leslie took a deep breath, and Mike jumped in before she could begin. "Okay, okay. I was just kidding… sort of."

"We won't have to check out before noon or one on Sunday. We'll grab lunch and be on our way home by, say, two o'clock. That will put us in Dallas in time to get a decent night's sleep. We may not get much sleep in Galveston," he concluded, grinning.

"You can get up as early as you want," she scolded, pointing a finger at him, "but don't knock on my door. It's vacation and I'll get up when I get up."

"I can think of a better way to spend our mornings than sleeping in," Mike winked.

"You are a shallow man, Mike Hampton."

"I'm a *man,* Leslie Bleu, and you are a woman, and I love you."

"I love you, too, but you'll just have to be patient."

"Not my strong suit," Mike grumbled.

"Did you pack nice clothes for dinner?" Leslie asked, as Mike pitched his duffel beside Leslie's suitcase in Nellie's trunk on Friday afternoon.

"Depends upon what qualifies as *nice,*" Mike said. "I won't be taking you to dinner in my bathing suit."

"But…"

"Lighten up, Les. We're not having dinner at the Magnolia."

"I was just…"

"Yeah, I know, but for this weekend, just relax. No planning necessary. We have hotel rooms reserved and the rest we can play by ear. I'll drive; you lean back and sleep."

"I'm too excited to sleep. Maybe I'll doze off later, but for now, we're on an adventure." Leslie sat up straight. "Mike! You're driving too close to that car. Let him pull ahead."

"Leslieeeeeee…" Mike hissed.

"Okay, okay," she said sheepishly and settled back in her seat. In no time, she dozed off.

"We're here, Sleeping Beauty." Mike said, pulling into a space in the hotel parking lot. "Let's check in and get to the beach."

Leslie stretched and rolled her shoulders. "I must've fallen asleep."

"Ya think?" Mike chuckled. "I am happy to report that we've arrived safe and sound. No close calls; no major accidents; and, I might add, no backseat, or rather passenger seat, driving."

"Well, that's a relief," Leslie said. "Perhaps you *can* function without my supervision."

Mike pulled their bags from the trunk. At the desk, Mike put his credit card on the counter. "We have reservations for two rooms for Hampton, please. I asked for them to be next to each other, with connecting doors if possible."

"One moment, Sir," The hotel clerk flipped pages in the registration book, then looked up with a troubled expression. "I have one room for Hampton with two beds."

"But that's not what I reserved," Mike insisted.

"I'm so sorry, Sir, but that is the reservation we have. We are fully booked, or I would gladly accommodate your request."

Mike looked at Leslie. "Your call. Take it or try another hotel?"

"I hate to interrupt, Sir, but unless you want to try a motel out on the highway, you won't find two vacant rooms anywhere in town. Guests are here for the convention this weekend and have taken all the rooms in the beach hotels."

Both men looked to Leslie for a decision.

She pulled on her left ear, right hand balled into a fist. Her face reddened as her jawline beat an angry rhythm, then she snarled, "We'll take the room."

"Very good, Ma'am," the clerk said, and signaled a bellhop to take their bags and usher them to their room.

Mike waved the bellhop off. "We can manage, thanks." He reached for their bags, but Leslie grabbed hers and strode to the bank of elevators.

Leslie stomped into the elevator car before the door fully opened, pushed six, and ignored Mike as he got into the car just before the door slid shut.

"Leslie," he began.

Through clenched teeth, Leslie growled, "I can't believe you thought you could get away with that!"

"What? You think I did that on purpose? You think it wasn't *their* mistake?"

She stared ahead in silence.

"I reserved two rooms." he retorted. "Trust is a two-way street, you know."

They found their room in silence. Leslie hefted her suitcase onto the luggage rack and went into the bathroom. The lock clicked like a jail house door.

"Not exactly what I expected either," Mike said, loud enough for her to hear. "If you want to go back to Dallas, that's fine, but right now I'm going to the beach." He rummaged in his bag for his swimsuit, changed, and draped a beach towel around his neck.

The sound of the hotel room door closing startled Leslie. She unlocked the bathroom door and checked the room. *"He just left; he doesn't have the right to be angry... unless the reservation was a mix-up as he claims."*

She sat on the bed, frustrated at having to manage an unmanageable situation. *"This isn't exactly what I expected either. No matter how we got here, we're still in one room."* She closed her eyes and allowed herself a small smile. *"But..., he's got to behave. I'm on the pill and I bet he brought rubbers thinking he might get some.*

But I just can't go there. Nothing would make that okay. I have to stay strong 'cuz for sure, he won't, Besides, what if Mom found out."

Leslie took her time changing into her bathing suit, lathered herself with sunscreen, then collected her beach towel and the blow-up beachball they'd brought. *"I hope I can find him."*

"So, where are we with this?" Mike asked testily when Leslie sat down gingerly beside him on her beach towel.

"I'm here, aren't I?"

"Good, that means we aren't driving back to Dallas tonight." Mike said. "Does that also mean you realize I had nothing to do with the room situation?"

"I suppose," she replied.

"I need more than *suppose*," Mike said. "You either trust me or you don't. If you're so worried about my nefarious intentions, you can sleep in the car."

"I believe you. It was an unpleasant surprise that wasn't easy to swallow. We can still have a nice weekend. Blow this up," she said, handing him the ball. "We can both use some exercise after all that time in the car."

"Whew," said Mike after three games of two-person beach volleyball. "Running on sand takes it out of you. I'm ready for a swim."

"Me, too. Beat you there," she called over her shoulder as she took off for the water.

Refreshed and dripping, they stretched out on their towels. "I love the beach," Leslie said. "Some summers my folks took us to Biloxi for a week, but that seems like years ago."

"Arp is in lake country. That's the water I'm used to, no salty skin. Gotta admit though, I'm enjoying this."

"You might be enjoying it a little too much," Leslie said. "You left without sunscreen, and you look a bit lobsterish. Does this hurt?" she asked, putting her hand on his shoulder.

"Nah, it'll be fine. We should be thinking about dinner soon."

"In a bit," Leslie said.

On the way back through the lobby, Mike said, "You go on up. I'll be there in a minute."

Leslie gave him a quizzical look. Mike grinned, shooed her toward the elevators, and walked to the concierge desk.

"What was that about?" Leslie asked when Mike came into their room.

"You'll see," he said.

Leslie gathered her outfit for dinner. "I'll shower first."

"How 'bout I join you?" Mike asked, rummaging in his duffel.

"Nope," she said, and closed the bathroom door firmly behind her.

"Les, we're a couple, right?" he said.

"Yes, but there are things that take time to get used to."

"Then now's a good time to remember that I'm the man in your life… right?"

"I'll take that under advisement," she called, and turned on the shower.

"Did you make reservations?" Leslie asked as Mike opened the hotel room door for her. "With the hotel full, we'd probably never get a table without reservations."

"Trust me," Mike said, and grinned.

"Are you going to play the *trust me* card every time you don't want to answer my question?"

"For now," Mike said, and squeezed her hand.

Leslie's eyes widened as they approached the reservations desk at the Beach Club. "Table for two under Hampton," Mike said.

"Of course, Mr. Hampton. Would you prefer the dining room or the terrace?" He smiled and added, "The terrace is quite romantic at sunset."

"The terrace, please." Mike pulled Leslie a bit closer.

"I'm surprised it's not too hot to sit outside," Leslie said as the waiter ushered them to a small table on the terrace. "How do they keep it so pleasant?"

"The fans are unobtrusive." The waiter smiled. "If you get too warm let me know," he said, and placed an ornate menu in front of each of them. "I'll give you a moment to peruse the selections."

"Peruse the selections," Mike mimicked when the waiter walked away. "Fits with the ambiance. I didn't realize how hungry I was. Let's start with an appetizer while we study the dinner menu."

"Mike, this menu doesn't have prices. That means we can't afford it."

"We started our weekend with a disappointment. Now we're making up for it. Let's order a cocktail and you study your menu while I *peruse* mine."

Leslie laughed. "This is fun. I'll have a white wine, please... and don't ask… I don't know one from another, maybe we should ask the waiter to suggest one."

"A bourbon and seven for me, please," Mike said to the waiter, "and she would like a white wine. What do you recommend with baked crab dip and lobster bisque?"

The waiter handed Mike a wine list. "We have elegant white wines here," he pointed. When Mike's eyes widened at the prices, the waiter slid his finger quickly down the list. "This chardonnay will go nicely with your selections."

"The chardonnay sounds good," Mike said, nodding his thanks.

"Keeping with elegant, are we?" Leslie smiled. "What if we don't have room for dinner?"

"Then we'll skip to dessert," Mike said, without hesitation. "We'll be *elegant and spontaneous.*"

Leslie nodded and reached for the wine the waiter placed before her.

"Cheers," said Mike, lifting his drink. "To us."

"To us," Leslie repeated, "and to an amazing evening. You've outdone yourself."

After dinner they walked on the beach back to the hotel, then settled onto a comfortable glider at the far end of the hotel patio. Mike pulled Leslie close, the glider gently rocking back and forth.

"Look at that gorgeous reflection of the moon on the water," murmured Leslie.

Mike tilted Leslie's head back and kissed her gently on the lips.

"Mmmm," she murmured, "you taste like desert."

"And you taste amazing," Mike whispered. "My whole body thinks you're amazing." He pulled her closer and their bodies melded into one another.

They snuggled close and their kisses grew longer and deeper. "Let's take this inside," Mike whispered, reaching for her hands.

Leslie remained seated, holding his hands. "Let's not let this get out of hand, Mike. We'll stay here a bit longer, then it's best we go to bed." She paused, then added, "*Separate* beds. Remember?"

Leslie woke first in the morning. She sat up and looked over at Mike in the other bed, his chest rising and falling rhythmically. *"Last night was lovely. I wanted to make love as much as he did, but he was a gentleman."* She quietly gathered her things and slipped into the bathroom to dress.

"I see you're ready for the day, Lovely Lady," Mike said as Leslie crossed the room and folded her pajamas into a drawer.

"If you drag yourself out of bed, Prince Charming, we can grab breakfast. We can come back, change, and spend the day on the beach."

"Gimme five," Mike said, sliding off the bed.

Leslie pulled the bathroom door shut behind Mike, shaking her head. "*Men!*"

When Mike came out and rummaged in his duffel for shorts and a tee, Leslie studiously gazed out the window.

"Are you always going to be this modest?" Mike teased.

"You'll have to be patient, Mike. My family has always been respectful of one another's privacy, and it takes time to accept different habits."

"You could practice," Mike quipped.

Leslie threw a pillow.

"How can it be the same temperature if Dallas is suffocating, and Galveston feels heavenly?" Leslie asked.

"It's all perception," Mike answered. "*Beach* and *hot* go well together. Sweat's not a problem. We can't plunge into the Gulf to cool off in Dallas."

"When I have a home, I think a swimming pool will be a must." Leslie mused.

"I like the sound of *a pool in the backyard*," he said.

"Nice to dream," she said. "Let's take advantage of the Gulf while we've got it." She grabbed his hand and pulled him toward the water.

"Glad you remembered the sunscreen," Mike said, as they toweled off after their swim. "I'd hate to ruin the weekend with a sunburn. Will you put some on my back?"

"You're pretty red. Are you sure this doesn't hurt?"

"Grab the ball," Mike said, shrugging off her question. "See if you can redeem yourself for yesterday," Mike said.

"You were showing off for all the broads on the beach. I didn't want to damage your image by beating the pants off you."

"Riiiight," Mike said, "but I'll be darned if I'll cut you any slack if you show off for the guys."

"It's nearly two," Leslie said when they collapsed onto their blankets, spent. "Let's grab a bite from one of the beach vendors and we can have a late dinner. It'll be romantic to watch the sun set while we eat."

"I'm game," said Mike. "A coupla hot dogs should tide me over. What's your pleasure?"

"Hmmm… maybe a taco salad."

They ate and wiled away the afternoon, sunning, swimming, talking. "Seems like forever since we've had real time together," said Mike. "Your summer schedule isn't what I expected, but we're lucky we have the same days off."

"For sure. At least, we've been able to spend weekends together. On the other hand, 3-11 has turned out to be great for me. I've learned lots, and they've given me the option of working a couple of days a week during the school year."

"Don't bite off more than you can chew, Les. Senior year is gonna be challenging, and you have more obligations than most already. You have SNA on top of classes, and working's going to cut into your study time. Be careful not to overextend yourself."

"I'll play it by ear. I hate to pass up a good opportunity."

"Not to mention that saying *no* isn't your strong suit." Mike looked around. "Must be getting late. We're about the only folks left on the beach."

"It's nearly 7. Perfect timing. We'll stop by the concierge desk and make reservations for dinner at the hotel at 8, on the patio if we're lucky."

"Sounds perfect. Let's go," Mike said rising from the beach towel and gathering their things.

Mike whistled as Leslie emerged from the bathroom in a yellow sundress with a thin silver necklace, matching earrings, and white sandals. The outfit set off the tan she had been nurturing all summer. Mike, on the other hand, was indeed lobsterish from head to toe, although he seemed not to notice when Leslie's light touch skimmed his arm on their way to dinner.

Mike held Leslie's chair, then sat beside her so both could gaze at the water.

"It's been a fantastic weekend," Mike said. Dinner came and they ate slowly, nursed their drinks, and watched the brilliant sunset on the distant horizon.

"Let's get dessert," Mike suggested. "I'm thinking something decadent like bananas foster or baked Alaska, with an after-dinner drink. We can ask the waiter to suggest something."

They were delighted by the tableside preparation of the bananas foster. "Look at that!" Leslie exclaimed, as the blue flames licked across the surface of their dessert. The waiter filled their plates as Mike sipped his brandy and Leslie enjoyed her port wine.

"The perfect ending to a perfect day," Mike said, as he touched his glass to Leslie's. "You up for a walk on the beach?"

"Let's do that before we go sightseeing in the morning, Mike."

Leslie leaned against Mike as the elevator rose to the sixth floor. "What a magical evening," Leslie said.

Mike leaned down and kissed the top of her head. She tilted her head, and their kiss was long and passionate.

They reached their room, arms around one another, and kissed again before Mike opened the door. Leslie kicked off her shoes and collapsed onto her bed. Mike leaned over to kiss her, then sat beside her. As they kissed, he stroked her hair, then her back.

"Mmmm," she murmured as she ran her fingers through his auburn hair. They held one another close. Mike pushed her gently backward until their heads came to rest on the pillow. Leslie opened her eyes and gazed into Mike's. "I love you, Mike," she whispered.

"I love you, too."

Their kisses were long, their tongues exploring one another. When Mike slid her dress off one shoulder, Leslie reached under Mike's shirt and stroked his chest. The two wriggled closer together, their bodies molding themselves to one another. Mike slipped her sundress slowly down her other shoulder. Leslie moaned and worked her arms free. Mike sat up long enough to remove his shirt.

"Mike," Leslie murmured, waves of pleasure challenging her resolve. "We have to be careful."

"We're as protected as a couple can be, Les."

"That's not what I meant."

"Do you want me to stop?" Mike asked, gently stroking her thigh.

Leslie arched her back, and soon their hands found sensitive places. She didn't push back as they came closer and closer to a union.

"I want you, Leslie," Mike whispered in her ear.

They came together in an explosion of ecstasy, then slowly settled into each other's arms.

Later, when Mike moved to go to the other bed, she pulled him close. "Stay, Mike," she murmured, and they slept wrapped in each other's arms.

Leslie woke first, Mike's arm across her torso, pinning her in place. She lay quietly, reliving their day on the beach, the sun setting on the water, the unforgettable pleasure of their lovemaking. "*He's my everything,* she thought, *I couldn't stop; I wanted him so badly, but it's wrong. We can't do that again. It's only for the marriage bed. We've barely talked about life after college. He's never actually used the m word. Oh, Lord, forgive me; what have I done?*"

Mike stirred, then raised himself on one elbow to gaze down at her. "You are so beautiful," he said.

She smiled at him. "A man who thinks I'm beautiful first thing in the morning must be the love of my life."

When Mike ran a finger gently up her middle, she shuddered, and quickly pushed his hand away.

Mike took a deep breath and smiled sheepishly. "Do you want to get breakfast and see if we can find those historical buildings you wanted to see?"

"Yes, I'd like that." She looked up at Mike. "About last night. We can't do that again."

"It was magic," Mike reminded her.

"It was, but it's part of being married. I should never have let it happen. It can't happen again."

Mike shook his head, pulled her into a hug, and planted a kiss atop her head. "Let's eat," he said.

They drove up and down the streets of Galveston and marveled at the period architecture, the stately manor homes dating back to the turn of the century.

"It's nearly two," Leslie said. "We should be starting for home. I can drive if you're tired."

"Nuh, uh," Mike answered. "You just sit here close to me, and we'll remind each other that we just spent the best weekend imaginable together."

"So, you can spend a weekend in Galveston with a man, but you can't make it home. Explain that to me," said Mrs. Bleu, aggrieved. "That's wrong on so many levels."

"Mom, Mike isn't just a *man*. We've been together two years. Besides, I'm 21, not 15. You can trust me to make good decisions."

"It's just wrong, Leslie." Mrs. Bleu insisted.

"Besides, Mom, we couldn't have come to Abita Springs in any case. Galveston's only four hours from Dallas, not eight."

"We all miss you, Leslie Jean. Your family should be more important than your friends."

"Please, Mom, this isn't a contest. Of course, my family is important, but that doesn't mean that there aren't other things that are important, too, things that can't wait."

"What can't wait while you come home for a visit?"

"Working in the OR here in Dallas is the most important thing I can do for my career. It's the only operating room where I can work as a student because they know me."

"You never even checked to see if hospitals here would accept you."

"The *Nurseketeers* all had summer jobs lined up here at Parkland before the end of the semester, Mom. This is our last summer together. Once we graduate, we may never see one another again. I want to spend time with Mike, too. My friends aren't more important than my family, Mom, but they're *here now* and they won't be after this summer."

"I miss you, Leslie."

"I know Mom, and I miss you, too. I gotta go. I'll call soon."

<h1 style="text-align:center">Chapter 13</h1>

"Excited about scrubbing this breast reduction alone?" Troy asked.

"You bet," Leslie answered. "I read up on the procedure and memorized Herringbone's preference card."

"I'll stay long enough to help you get everything set up, but I'm outta here as soon as Sharon brings the patient in. Got plans!"

Leslie took sterile saline and water from the warmer and poured the water into the basin for rinsing instruments during the procedure. When she turned to pour the warm saline into a second basin, she collided with Troy, gasping as the instruments from Harringbone's personal tray clattered to the floor.

Troy glared at the scattered instruments, then drew a deep breath and murmured, "SHIT! Every one of those instruments needs to be washed and re-sterilized. I'll never get outta here."

Leslie stood gaping, the empty saline bottle still in her hand.

Troy gritted his teeth, closed his eyes, and took a deep breath. "A little help here?" he huffed.

"I'm so sorry, Troy," Leslie murmured. She pitched the empty saline bottle into the trash and squatted to help gather the instruments. "Do you want me to take care of these or finish opening for the case?"

"Both!" he snapped, as he slung instruments into the tray, then with a slow intake of breath said, "Sorry, Les. Accidents happen. I'll get these ready and you finish opening and scrub in."

Troy's jawline pulsed as if he were grinding his teeth to dust. "We've got to hustle here, 'cuz Harringbone's been on a tear all day long. I hate it when Gilda the Hun's in charge because I'm always last on her list to be relieved, Now this, and I have a date tonight. I need to get out of this freakin' place."

"I'm sorry, Troy. I can get the instruments into the autoclave and finish the set up," Leslie said, fighting tears. "You go on. It's okay. I'll tell Harringbone it was my fault."

"Forget it," Troy said. "Gilda would skin me alive if I left before the case was set up. "You go scrub and I'll get Harringbone's instruments into the sterilizer."

As soon as Leslie was gowned and gloved, the buzzer on the sterilizer went off.

"I'll get those instruments while Sharon counts with you," Troy said, "then I'm gone."

Leslie nodded, "Have a good time, and thanks."

"Harringbone's last three cases went off like clockwork," Sharon said. "You did a good job, Leslie, and thanks for staying late."

Frannie's note was stuck on Leslie's locker door. *Katie's riding home with Robin and me. We'll see you back at the apartment.*

"Glad they didn't wait," Leslie thought. It was midnight when she pulled out of the parking lot. *"Troy always has my back. I hope my fiasco didn't ruin his date."*

She unlocked the apartment door and closed it quietly behind her, then realized all three of her roommates were sitting in the living room.

"Oh," Leslie said. "I thought you would have crashed by now."

"Nope," Katie said. "we're just hangin' out, waiting to hear what kept you so long."

"Troy had a date tonight that he'd been talking about all week. He had to stay late to help me get my first case started, and I bumped into him and knocked Herringbone's special instrument tray out of his hands. All of the instruments had to be cleaned and sterilized all over again. He went off on me, but I deserved it. I made him late for his date."

"He'll forgive you," Frannie said. "You always have good things to say when you work with him."

"The best part of the story is that the case was dynamite. After Harringbone got over his huff and into the case, everything went smooth as silk. The resident was teaching a first-year med student, so I learned about the whole procedure in detail. It was fascinating. The more I learn, the more I love the OR."

"So, tell us," Katie said. "What was the case?"

"A breast reduction. The patient's boobs were the size of watermelons. I can't imagine what it would be like carrying around all that weight."

"Can boobs get that big?" Frannie asked, staring at her own B cup chest.

"Trust me," Leslie said. "They were huge. Herringbone started by drawing all over her breast with a blue marker, and I couldn't make any sense of his chicken scratching. Then he took a small metal cup, like the ones in our prep trays, and made a circle high on each breast. Next, he took a second metal cup the size of a shot glass and made another circle on each breast over the nipple and areola."

"Why?" asked Frannie.

"The circle around the nipple and areola was to mark where he'd lift them with the tissue below to create a pedicle graft and the smaller circle was where he'd reimplant the graft when he was done. That way there should still be nerve sensation to the nipple on the reconstructed breasts. The reduction was amazing, truly a work of art. There's no doubt the patient will be much better off," Leslie said taking a deep breath.

Laughing, Robin said, "I don't know about the rest of you but, I am definitely swearing off the OR as a potential specialty for me."

"Agreed," Katie said. "I'll be staying right where I am."

"Whatever happened to Esther?" Frannie asked, changing the subject abruptly.

"Esther is still her same ole nasty self. Mostly I steer clear of her. She works days and since I went on evenings, I only run into her if I have to relieve her. I get panicky every time I see her name. I still haven't worked out how to confront her about lying about me behind my back and making me look like an idiot."

"You're going to have to confront that bitch." Robin said. "The longer you let her get away with trashing you, the worse it looks for you."

"Robin's right," Frannie agreed. "You grumble about her all the time, but you're not doing anything about it. You need a plan. You're ignoring your own advice."

"I know, I know," Leslie whined. "It's easier to avoid her, especially since I'll be part-time when school starts. I hardly ever run into her now that I'm on 3-11."

"That's only an excuse," Katie said. "You're as likely to have to relieve her as anyone else every time you show up for work."

"That's for sure," said Robin. "Get a grip, Girl. Esther isn't worth the energy you spend complaining about her, or the time we spend having to listen. Tell her off and move along. Bullies back off when they're confronted and that's exactly what she is… a bully. Find your moment and pounce. You'll see. She'll steer clear of *you,* instead of the other way around."

On the way back from lunch the next day, the *Nurseketeers* picked up the mail. Leslie thumbed through the envelopes. "Can you believe I've only gotten two responses from SNA members to the flyers we sent, and one of them said she'd be on vacation with her family the weekend of Orientation. Right now, we have five people to fill 20 positions… and that includes the three of us. Frannie, are you sure you have to go home that week?”

“I do. I promised my mother,” said Frannie, “but two responses is a start.”

“SNA members are supposed to be *responsible*. What’s wrong with these people?” Leslie frowned.

Robin interrupted Leslie’s rant. “It’s time you realized that SNA is not as high a priority for everyone as it is for you. Be realistic. Not everyone sees things the way you do.”

“Robin’s right,” Katie added. “Do you have a plan for contacting the members who haven’t responded? As I recall, you didn’t think you’d need a Plan B.”

“Don’t be snarky,” Leslie grumbled. “I can’t help it if I expect the best of people.”

“Reality check!” Robin said.

“Ignoring the invitation was easy. They’ll have a harder time refusing when we call them on the phone,” Leslie replied.

“Whoa. Who’s *we?*” Robin demanded. “Are you volunteering us without asking again?”

“Well, I thought…” Leslie began.

“You have to be more diplomatic if you want our support,” Robin said. “Remember, leaders *lead*. Only autocrats go around *telling* folks what to do. Besides, you trash your supervisor, Gilda. You call her Attila the Hun and what you’re doing is no different.”

“No, it’s not like that. We need to get the job done,” Leslie insisted.

“You’re the leader, not a dictator. This is a volunteer organization. You need to motivate people, get them to *want* to do what you ask,” Robin insisted.

Katie broke in. “Leslie, you only need fifteen more people, and whoever can’t make it will still be able to mentor junior students during the year.”

“We need a big presence during Orientation,” Leslie insisted. “We have to demonstrate the importance of SNA to the nursing program.”

"Leslie don't make this any harder than it has to be," Katie said. "Be realistic about what you can accomplish; otherwise, you're just setting yourself up for disappointment."

"They'd better come through," Leslie muttered. "Ms. Reynolds is counting on me."

"Well, this is more like it." Leslie said, reviewing her list the following week. "Two-thirds of the senior SNA members are coming back early to participate."

"Now that you have enough help," said Frannie. "I don't have to feel guilty about spending the end of the summer at home." Frannie paused, "You should go home, too, Leslie. You've done your job. You planned the whole thing, and you have enough participation. You should spend the time with your family like you promised."

"I know, but I have to be here," Leslie insisted. "I can't get everyone to come back early for the project, then not participate myself. It wouldn't look right."

"You might want to think twice about that," Robin said. "A trip home would put things right with your mother. You need to do a better job of setting priorities."

"My mother is just being silly. She needs to get used to my not being home. One week in Abita Springs isn't going to change that. She doesn't want me to grow up and that's going to happen whether she wants it to or not."

"What?" Leslie demanded, when Robin sighed and shrugged her shoulders.

"Never mind," Robin said.

"So, you're really not coming home?" Leslie's mother's voice was strident. "You promised you'd spend time with us before school starts, and now you're not coming. You haven't been home *all summer*."

"I couldn't help it, Mom," Leslie pleaded. "You have to understand. Ms. Reynolds asked me to organize the SNA members for the *Nursing Orientation*. I'm President and it's my responsibility."

"You should be delegating, making assignments. A president is in charge of making things happen, not doing everything herself."

"This is a new project. I have to stay here and make sure it goes well."

"No, Leslie. What you need to do is trust people. With a good plan and good preparation, there's no reason the others can't do an excellent job on their own. If you don't learn to delegate, you'll end up with more than you can manage."

"I can handle it."

"Obviously not." her mother murmured.

"I've had a great summer in the operating room, Mom. You'd be proud of how well I did."

"Keeping your promises would make me proud. Setting priorities that make sense would make me proud. Not going off on some rendezvous with a man would make me proud. Coming home would make be proud."

Leslie's chin dropped to her chest. "Mom, you know that Mike is not *some man*. I know it's hard for a mother to let go when her kids grow up and leave, especially the first one, but it's inevitable. We both have to get used to it. Punishing me for growing up isn't doing either of us any good. You make it hard to call home when I know you're going to be upset instead of being excited about what I'm doing with my life."

"Leslie Jean Bleu," shrilled her mother.

"I'll be home for Thanksgiving," Leslie interrupted, "and I'll call every week and let you know what's going on." Before her mother could reply, she added, "I gotta go, Mom. I'll call soon. Bye." She placed the receiver onto the cradle and slumped in the chair.

"Trouble in paradise?" Katie asked, looking up from the textbook she was studying.

"Mom's pissed that I can't come home before school starts. I told her I'll come home when I can."

"You could go home, you know. Orientation is well-covered and the SNA members can get everything done while you're visiting with your family. You've done what Ms. Reynolds expects of you."

"That's what Mom said," Leslie shook her head, "but I have to be here."

"No, Leslie. The truth is you *want* to be here. What you *have to do,*" Katie said, "is learn to delegate effectively, trust people, and keep your promises."

"That's what Mom said, too," Leslie sighed, "but I'm President. I can't just walk out on everyone, I promised that, too."

"At some point you'll figure out that prioritizing and delegating are characteristics of a good leader," Katie said. "Your plan for the Orientation is coming together. You should get the group together and see what input they have."

"I'll make the assignments first, then we can meet to determine what revisions need to be made," Leslie said.

"That will only work if the participants are okay with your plan and you're willing to listen to what they say to you."

"Why wouldn't they be okay with the plan and assignments?" Leslie asked, puzzled.

Katie sighed and shrugged her shoulders. "Because they're your colleagues, not your minions. You need to pay attention to what people tell you," Katie said. "I mean, *listen*; don't just assume you know best."

"The orientation went well, Leslie," said Ms. Reynolds as Leslie settled into the chair across from her desk on the following Monday. "The SNA members' participation was a large part of its success."

"Getting the SNA volunteers set up was harder than I expected," Leslie admitted, "but in the end, almost everyone participated."

"Valuable lessons can be learned from your experience," said Ms. Reynolds.

"Lessons?"

"Yes, lessons in leadership. Do you remember how frustrated you were that so few SNA members volunteered at first?" Ms. Reynolds asked.

"It was disappointing that the orientation wasn't important enough to them to give up any of their summer vacation," Leslie said.

"You've underestimated your colleagues, Leslie," Ms. Reynold replied. "You told me that the response to your flyers was disappointing and you needed to call each of the members personally."

"That's true," Leslie admitted.

"What made the phone call more successful than the flyer?"

"I suppose it's that I got to explain the project and answer their questions."

"Did you find that all the members asked similar questions? Was there a theme to the information they wanted?"

"They all wanted details about the project. They wanted to know what was involved, particularly the time commitment."

Ms. Reynolds nodded. "So, once they understood the program and could see its value, they were happy to volunteer. What does that tell you?"

"I get it now." Leslie said. "They needed to know what was expected before they made a commitment. I should have put that information in the flyer in the first place. That's what you meant by underestimating them. So, the lesson is that the information I share when I ask for participation makes a big difference to the responses I'll get."

"Exactly. When we met in July, if I had just given you the assignment without providing the details and sharing the benefits, how enthusiastic would you have been?"

"Not very, I suppose," Leslie said. "Also, I learned that I need a plan B. When I didn't get the response I wanted, I got frustrated and wasn't sure what to do next."

Ms. Reynolds smiled. "That's a good observation." She watched as Leslie processed the advice she'd been given. "Another thing to consider, Leslie, is the importance of delegating effectively… not just telling people what to do, but choosing the right people, soliciting their input, and preparing them to be successful in completing their assignments on their own. A leader should not be a one-woman show. By definition, a leader works with others to reach a successful conclusion. If you learn from your experiences," Ms. Reynolds assured her, "you'll make an excellent leader."

"Thank you," said Leslie.

"You're a hard worker, but that's not enough. A leader must be sensitive to the strengths, needs, and expectations of others in order to appeal to them in a meaningful way. Anyone who's asked to devote time to a project wants to know what's in it for them. They want to be sure that the benefit of participating is worth the investment of their time and energy. A leader should be able to provide that information when asking for participation."

"So, if I'm clear up front, I can expect everyone to do what they're supposed to."

"I'm afraid it's not that easy. Leading doesn't end with getting the project off to a good start. It continues with facilitating the success of the team by keeping your participants motivated, by helping them find solutions when they reach an obstacle, and by letting them know you appreciate their contributions. Although you may be responsible for doing part of the work, the project is a team effort."

"That sounds fine as long as everyone does what's expected, but what do I do when someone doesn't do their part?"

"That's a real leadership challenge," Ms. Reynolds nodded, "and there is no single answer to your question. The approach you take will depend upon the specifics of the situation. Your solution must be respectful of the individual and must keep the objective of the project in mind at the same time."

Leslie sighed.

"You look perplexed."

"It would be easier to do the work myself."

Ms. Reynolds laughed. "Doing it yourself because you can *is* the easy answer, but it's not the right one. That's not leading. As President of SNA, you will no doubt be responsible for outcomes that you won't have the resources to do alone. Sometimes the simplest of tasks takes time or a skill that you don't have. You must have confidence in the people you lead."

"I understand."

"Do you?" Ms. Reynold looked directly at Leslie. "Do you have confidence in the people you lead? I don't think so, because if you did, you would have gone home and let them get the job done."

Leslie's eyes widened. "How did you know…?"

"There's little I don't hear about, Leslie. I understand that leading effectively is no small matter, but if you learn from each experience, your skills will grow steadily. If you don't, you'll burn out."

Chapter 14

"It'll be interesting to find out what Community Nursing is all about," Leslie said as the *Nurseketeers* walked across campus to their first class of the 1973 Fall semester.

"We'll have our answer in short order," said Katie. "Walk faster or we'll have trouble finding seats together. Every senior nursing student is scheduled for this class."

"Look," Frannie said, pointing to J.R., waving to get their attention. "He's saved seats for us. Good thing, too. There's nowhere else we could sit together."

"You are a gentleman, J.R.," Robin said, as the *Nurseketeers* took seats on either side of him."

"I'm looking forward to finding out what nurses do outside of the hospital," J.R. said, nodding toward the podium where two women in white uniforms were seated.

Ms. Reynolds tapped on the microphone. "Good morning, students. Welcome back. I'm sure you're excited to begin your final year in nursing school. It will be a busy year, and graduation will be here before you know it. This morning, we have guests,

"

two Crestmont graduates who now work with the Visiting Nurses' Association."

The two young women in white stood and approached the microphone. "I'm Linda Larson," said the slender, blonde nurse, "and my colleague is Karen Long. We've been visiting nurses since we graduated three years ago."

"I always knew that community nursing would be my specialty," said Karen. "My mother has been in a wheelchair since I was seven. She was paralyzed in an auto accident. You can imagine how devastated she was, a young mother with three children. The visiting nurses were responsible for the independent and productive life she's been able to lead. Their excellent nursing care has kept her from having any of the complications associated with being wheelchair-bound, and they've always encouraged and supported her. My mother is as involved with her family as any mother with two good legs, thanks to them."

"Karen and I have been friends since grade school, and her mother is my motivation as well," said Linda. "As a community nurse, I can make a meaningful difference in my patients' lives. Each patient is unique and faces distinct challenges, and I get to counsel and motivate them through their progress, and enjoy their success over time. Every day is different."

Ms. Reynolds thanked the women for sharing their enthusiasm for community nursing and encouraged the class to ask questions.

"That's just what I'm looking forward to," said Katie as they gathered their belongings. "I want to make a difference in people's lives, and I like the idea of being able to watch it happen over time."

"That was more interesting than I expected," said Leslie, "but I can't think of any place I'd rather be than the OR. Every case is different and the relationship I develop with each patient during the assessment is unique. Instead of having a long-term relationship, I like concentrating on one patient at a time. I enjoy the intensity of the moment, and being there when they can't take care of themselves."

"I could be a community nurse," Frannie said, "if all my patients were children."

"That's certainly an option, Frannie," said Robin. "Considering community nursing would broaden your job opportunities, for sure. What appeals to me is the independence, working in a different environment for each patient, and the opportunity to think on my feet. At the same time, I kinda like the structure in the hospital. Guess I still haven't made up my mind."

"We've got two hours until lunch," Katie said, "then Research at one o'clock. Let's go to the library and review the reading assignment for Research. Then, if there's time, we can get our work for Community done. We'll be ready for Clinicals tomorrow and have the rest of the afternoon free. I vote we take advantage of our free time while we have some."

"I can hang with you for an hour after Research," said Leslie. "I have to be at the gym at three. I'm guessing Coach Thomas wants to see what her talent pool looks like this year. We have a good shot at the Basketball Championship. We came close last year."

Chapter 15

Leslie rapped the gavel to begin her first SNA meeting of the semester. "Hello everyone, we have a lot on our plate this semester. Please stand if you are a new member of SNA." The audience welcomed the new members with a round of applause.

Leslie continued, "Let me introduce your leadership team. I'm Leslie Bleu, a senior, and I work in the OR at Parkland. I'm pleased to be your president this year. I'm told that I have to practice delegating, so please help me out by volunteering when I ask."

The group responded with a collective chuckle.

"Amen to that," said Robin.

Leslie introduced the other SNA officers seated at the front table, then she announced, "In October, we have our first project. SNA joins the campus sororities in hosting a Halloween party for kiddos from two children's homes near the university."

"What can we do to help?" A freshman asked.

"For freshman, and those of you who have never participated before, let me explain. Crestmont donates party sacks full of candy and everyone in the freshman nursing seminar fills the goody bags the week before Halloween."

"So," said a voice from the audience, "Freshmen are conscript labor."

"Right." Leslie chuckled, and the group laughed with her. "It's true that during your class you don't have much choice but to participate, but you do have a choice when it comes to attending the party. It's not mandatory, but I urge you to dress up in costume and come. The children have such fun. When they arrive, we give each one a sack of candy, then before they leave, they get a second one to take home with them."

"And, you're already in costume for the Crestmont Halloween Party that evening. You won't want to miss that. It's packed full of fun," Frannie added.

"You can count me in," one senior volunteered. "I'll be there to ease the freshmen's workload."

"Me, too," another senior said, and volunteer after volunteer raised a hand.

"Thanks, everyone," Leslie smiled her appreciation. "Anyone who is free at 1pm the Saturday before Halloween is invited to join us at the party. If you've never attended, do yourself a favor and join us this year. Watching kids who have so little enjoy themselves will make you glad you chose to be a nurse."

Frannie stood up. "In my freshman year at the party, I spent time with a shy little girl who was sitting all by herself just watching the fun. By the end of the party, she was laughing and playing with the others, and I knew, for sure, that I wanted to be a pedi nurse. That decision made me appreciate school even more, knowing that it would be getting me where I want to be."

The sporadic applause turned to chuckles when someone added, "and I discovered, for sure, that I didn't want any part of pediatrics."

"Whatever you learn about yourself, your participation is invaluable," Leslie said. "Please take a moment to add your name to the signup sheet at the back of the room at the end of the meeting, so we'll have an idea of who will be attending the party next month."

There were no hands raised in response to Leslie's query, "Is there anything else we need to discuss?" She rapped the gavel on the lectern. "Meeting adjourned."

"Mom," Leslie said excitedly when her mother answered the phone. "I just chaired my first SNA meeting and it went well."

"Will you be home for Thanksgiving?"

Leslie was struck silent by her mother's abrupt dismissal.

"How can you expect me to call home when you're not interested in anything I'm doing here?" she blurted. "What I'm doing in Dallas is important to me. Why is that so hard for you to understand? How can you be upset that I turned out to be the adult you want me to be?"

"You're not an adult yet, Leslie. Right now, you're a college student and I'm your mother and I want to see you. You'll be an adult when you have a place of your own and pay your own bills."

"Mom, college is more than going to classes. The things I'm doing here will help me become successful, like working in the OR, and being the SNA president. Why can't you appreciate what I'm doing?"

"Why can't you understand that a mother misses a daughter who's soon going to be out of the house forever?"

"I *do* understand that, Mom. We'll be together for the holidays, and we'll enjoy every minute. In the meantime, please be happy for me."

Silence broken by sniffles filled the line, and the next voice Leslie heard was her father's. "Leslie, it's not easy for your mother now that her fledgling is leaving the nest. You need to be sensitive to that," he paused for emphasis.

"I'm trying, Daddy, but..."

"There's no *but*, Leslie. It's not like you to be insensitive."

"I'm sorry, Daddy, but it's hard to walk away from the responsibilities I have here."

"So, how are you doing?" he asked.

"The semester just started, so I don't know much about my classes, but my two shifts in the OR are going great. I'm learning tons."

"Working two days a week sounds like a lot for your senior year, especially with your other commitments."

"I can handle it, Daddy."

"I'll leave it to you to decide what you can manage. You should be the first to know when you're over-extending yourself."

"Thanks, Daddy. I love you. Please give Mom a hug for me. Convince her that I love her very much."

"She knows you do, Leslie."

"Can you explain to her how important it is for me to take advantage of the opportunities I have here. My classes are important, but so are my job in the OR and my other activities on campus. They're all helping me prepare for my future."

"Keep your family in mind, too, Leslie," her father said. "We were expecting you to come home before the semester began. It's not like you to break a promise."

"I'm sorry, Daddy. I just couldn't."

"You could have, but you chose not to," her father admonished. "Promises are made to be kept."

"You should write your mom a letter," Frannie said, when Leslie placed the receiver in its cradle. "Tell her exactly how you feel. You know she will read it over and over. She needs to hear that you love her."

"Thanks, Frannie. That's a great idea. Could you help me?"

"*Dear Mom,* would be a good start," Frannie said, and they both laughed.

After crumpling sheets of paper and creating a sea of white balls in the general direction of the wastebasket, Leslie said, "Listen to this and tell me what you think."

Dear Mom.

I love you and I'm sorry that you think I'm being insensitive. I can only imagine what it feels like when your first child leaves home for good. You're a wonderful Mom. You've been there for me with every success and every scrape I've ever gotten myself into. I know this isn't easy.

Before I got my scholarship, we never talked about my leaving home, but we were all excited about the opportunity for me to go to college. I never thought about the changes it would bring for you. My projects this summer gave me the chance to spread my wings.

Mom, I know it's hard, but I hope you'll understand that I can't pass up these opportunities or ignore the commitments I've made here. I love you with all my heart and I want you to be proud of me. I miss our long chats and realize the phone calls aren't the same as being together, but I'll be home for the holidays and we can spend alone time then, just you and me.

I love you so very much each moment of every day,

Leslie

"How long do you think the letter will take to get to your mom?" Mike asked.

"Maybe a week," Leslie said. "The real question is *will it do any good?* I'm sure she's not happy about being upset with me. Daddy reminded me that it's hard for a mother when her children leave home, especially the first one, but Mom's putting one big guilt trip on me. It's not like I can just get in the car and drive to Abita Springs for the weekend. I've asked Daddy to help me out. I'm sure Mom understands; she just doesn't like it. I hope the letter will make a difference."

"I think you're doing the best you can," Mike said. He slid from behind the steering wheel, scooched closer to Leslie, and put his arm around her. They settled into one another and watched the dancing reflection on the water as the moon rose over Bachman Lake.

"It's peaceful here," Leslie said, then they laughed as the roar of an incoming jet grew louder, reaching a crescendo as it passed low overhead. "Okay, not exactly peaceful, but private."

"I don't know whether to consider the planes an interruption or to thank them for creating our own private space." Mike said. "Hardly anyone comes here at night." He leaned down for a kiss.

"Mmmm," Leslie mumbled as another incoming jet approached. "That makes this our private, not-so-quiet spot."

"J.R.'s going...," Mike waited for another jet to roar over-head. "You're right about the not-so-quiet. J.R.'s going home next weekend. We can have my apartment all to ourselves. It's definitely quieter than the truck, and roomier, too," he added as he squirmed to get comfortable.

Leslie sat up. "No, Mike. That isn't going to happen. That kind of privacy is too much temptation, and I can't trust either one of us to stop when we need to."

"Les, it doesn't make sense that you..."

"It doesn't *have* to make sense," she interrupted. "I don't expect you to understand, but I do expect you respect my decision."

"It would help if I could understand it," he insisted.

"Well, you *can't!* First, you're a man and that makes a big dif-ference where sex and guilt are concerned. However, I've always believed that *sex is for marriage*, and you should understand that. We were both raised with Christian values. You're telling me that it's illogical doesn't change anything. Every time I think of our weekend in Galveston, I remember how wonderful it was to be with you and at the same time, I'm overcome with guilt. I lost my head, and I can't deal with the guilt trip, so… case closed. OK?"

"But" he began.

"The *OK* was *rhetorical*." she insisted.

Mike sighed.

"Daddy, did Mom get my letter?"

"She did. She let me read it after she'd carried it around with her for a day. It was nice of you to tell her that you understand how she might be feeling and to explain yourself. She's struggling with the decisions you're making. I'm sure that she'll accept them in time, but right now, she's hurt."

"How long will it take? I dread it every time the phone in the apartment rings."

"Be patient. Everyone adjusts slowly to changes they don't want to accept."

"I know. I know, but I've always been able to talk to Mom about everything. So much is going on, and it's frustrating that I can't share everything with her. I would have thought she'd be missing it, too."

"She is, but you broke her heart when you broke your promise to come home and you can't undo that."

"But Daddy…"

"Leslie. You made your decision and you have to own it. We'll all move forward, but it will take time."

Chapter 16

Leslie pulled into the Parkland lot for her shift on Monday, turned off the ignition, and absently pulled on her ear. *"If I hang back a little, someone else might relieve Esther. I'm not up for another confrontation. I've never done anything to that bitch, but she lies about me and not a word of what she says is anywhere close to true. At some point I'm gonna have to take her on."*

Leslie slowly got out of the car, looked skyward, and mumbled, "Please, please, please let this be a good day." She changed into scrubs, hustled to the schedule board, and groaned when she saw her assignment.

"Leslie," the shift supervisor said. "You'll relieve Esther on Dr. Chandler's procedure in room four. The patient is having gallbladder surgery."

"I like Dr. Chandler," she smiled, covering her dismay at having to interact with Esther. *"Chandler's a little old school and he can be a prima donna, but I like the little fella. Since that nightmare tonsillectomy, he seems to enjoy teaching me and asks great questions. Better hurry,"* she admonished herself. *"Esther bitches when I'm on time. I can only imagine the scene she'll make if I'm late."*

She pushed open the door to room four and stopped short when she saw that another tech was relieving Esther. She looked heavenward. *"Thank you, God."* Savoring her good luck, she left to get a new assignment.

Esther followed her out of the room and elbowed Leslie as she walked past. "Daydreaming in the hallway again, Leslie? You'd do well to show up on time," Esther chided.

"Tell me why you trash me all the time," Leslie demanded. "I've never done anything to deserve it."

"That's a laugh. Anyone who constantly makes the mistakes that you do should consider digging ditches instead of putting patients at risk."

Esther walked off, leaving Leslie open-mouthed and unable to process the absurdity of the words she'd just heard. Leslie realized, long after Esther had disappeared, that someone else would be waiting for relief. She hurried to the schedule board.

Leslie relived the encounter with Esther while she finished scrubbing an uncomplicated appendectomy. Before the room was turned over for the next patient, she had come up with a dozen responses that would have put a stop to Esther's idiocy. *"I'll be ready the next time that bitch says a word to me."*

Robin and Leslie followed Katie and Frannie to Shepard Hall on Wednesday for their Research class. "Drink too much coffee this morning?" Robin asked.

"Huh?" Leslie replied, startled out of her reverie.

"It's a quiz," Robin said. "It's not a big deal, so don't be a space cadet. You are in *nowheresville* right now. Time to come down to earth."

"It's our first quiz in Research, and I can't help freaking out. I just know that everything will fly out of my mind the minute I look at the first question. Monday night I got home from the OR too late to study. I fell asleep as soon as my head hit the pillow.

Yesterday we were in Community all day and ever since I dragged my butt out of bed this morning, nothing has gone right."

"So… you didn't get to run this morning?"

"No, I didn't run, and running clears my head." Leslie said.

"Les, listen to yourself. You're dead on your feet. You've got to quit working 'cuz you're killing yourself. You don't have enough time for the important things like school. How can you not see that?"

"I love the OR and I'm learning stuff I can't get from books or classes. I can't quit."

"None of that will be worth a flip if you don't graduate. Your plate is too full with school, basketball, SNA, Mike, and work, so something's got to give, Girlfriend."

"You work, have time for your grandmother, for the *Nurseketeers*, and you pass all your friggin' tests with flying colors."

"That's because studying is my priority and I make time for it. Gram doesn't make demands on my time. She is simply happy when I can spend time with her. I also don't have an athletic scholarship that takes up time, or SNA to deal with. I'm nowhere near as overloaded as you are."

"Everything I'm doing is important to me."

"You wouldn't be so overwhelmed if you gave more than lip service to delegating. You claim to understand, but you still do everything yourself. Work on your leadership skills, and by that I mean set priorities and delegate. That will give you the time you need."

"Yeah, but doing things myself is easier than explaining, and everything gets done right."

"That's not leadership. People learn from doing. They'll never get it right if you don't give them a chance to learn from experience."

"But they might not do things the way I want them done."

"That's your fault, not theirs. As their leader, it's your responsibility to provide the information and resources they need to do the job you expect. Then, let them *do it*. Good grief, Les, you're not the Lord Almighty! There's always more than one *right* way to get things done. It doesn't always have to be *your way*. Once you put a plan in motion, you need to trust that people will get the job done. It's not *your SNA*. It belongs to all of us."

"Yeah, but…" Leslie began.

"Yeah, but… yeah, but," Robin said. "Do you hear yourself? Instead of listening, you make excuses. I don't think you hear anything we say. Hurry, or we'll be late for class."

They slipped into their seats and Robin whispered, "just remember what you've learned about test taking. This is just a quiz."

Frannie said. "That quiz was a breeze."

Leslie pulled on her ear as they walked. "What's wrong, Leslie?" Katie asked.

"I know I didn't pass," she answered. "I got stuck on one of the questions."

"Which question stumped you?" Frannie asked.

Leslie mumbled. "I don't remember exactly. It was something like *what limits the capacity of the scientific method to answer questions about humans?*"

"I thought that was easy." Frannie said, "I picked *humans are complex.*"

"Easy for you, maybe, but I kept vacillating between *humans are complex* and the one about *shortage of theories about human behavior.*"

"I remember that one, Leslie," Katie said. "I struggled with those same two possible answers."

"When I finally picked an answer, I didn't have time to finish the quiz."

"For fu… For God's sake, Leslie, I can't believe you just said that."

"Robin, you owe the cussing jar 25 cents," Frannie said.

"I'll take care of it later," Robin spat. "Leslie, what happened to the promise you made to stick to the plan?"

"I was petrified when we started the quiz, and I couldn't make myself move on from the first question. I knew I could get the answer, and I think I got it right."

"That would be great," Robin said sarcastically, "if you hadn't left everything else blank."

"Leslie," Katie said, signaling Robin to back off, "it was almost one o'clock when you came in from work this morning and you work again tonight. This whole week's been hectic."

"Oh, no! I thought I was quiet. I'm sorry. I didn't mean to wake you."

"Waking me isn't the issue," Katie said. "The point is you're exhausted, over-extended, and you don't make the time to prepare for the courses or get a good night's sleep. That's what we mean about setting priorities. You put your fascination with OR ahead of everything and let the important things go into the dumpster."

Leslie's shoulders slumped.

"Why were you working on Sunday anyway?" Robin asked, "You work Monday and Friday. You picked those days for a reason."

"The evening supervisor had a call in. She asked if I could cover the shift. I don't like to disappoint her. So, I said yes."

"When the answer should have been an obvious *NO*. Girlfriend, you have gotta learn to say *no*." Robin said. "It won't matter if they love you to death, if you flunk out."

"I s'pose you're right," Leslie said, and glanced at her watch. "I gotta go or I'll be late for my regular shift."

In Research on Wednesday, Leslie dropped into the desk chair like a stone and began pulling furiously on her left ear. She stared at the folded quiz the instructor set in front of her.

Robin poked her. "Not looking won't change anything."

Leslie nodded miserably and slowly unfolded the test. The red 10/100 in the upper-righthand corner was no surprise, but that didn't diminish her dejection. "*Thank you, Lord, that this is just a quiz. I have to get my act together before our first test.*"

Chapter 17

Leslie left the Visiting Nurse Association office wired on coffee. She pulled to a stop in front of her patient's house and double-checked the highlighted address on the map lying on the seat beside her. She checked her watch. *"Two minutes to review my assignment and still be on time for my first solo community health appointment."* Her hands trembled, from the combination of caffeine and working in the OR till midnight. She took a deep breath, gathered her supplies, and climbed out of the car. Her new, bright blue polyester pantsuit uniform glowed neon in the sunlight.

A wolf whistle startled her. Five young men lounged, smoking, at the far end of the dilapidated porch. The one who wore a green sock cap drawled, "She been wait'n on ya."

"Never mind her," the whistler leered. "C'mon over here. You can take care of me first."

Leslie couldn't reach the front door fast enough. She knocked on the door frame and watched a fly make its way into the house through a rip in the screen-door.

"She be in the back bedroom," called Green Sock Cap. "She cain't hear ya and ain't nobody else to answer the door. Go on in."

Leslie walked through a shabby but orderly living room. "Hello," she called. "I'm from the Visiting Nurses Association." She made her way through the stifling house. All the windows were open, but the curtains hung lifeless. The house was dark compared to the bright sunlight she'd left outside.

She passed an empty, unkempt bedroom and continued making her way uncertainly through the house. The smell of bacon suggested that the next room would be the kitchen.

"In here," came a voice from the room on her left. "This thing's itchin' up a storm this mornin'."

The woman sat in a lounge chair, clad in a pink chenille robe with matching house shoes. Her legs were propped on a padded foot stool, and a cane rested against her chair. "'Spect'd ya five minutes ago," she said, her chin jutting towards the wall clock that read 9:05.

"Good morning," said Leslie, deciding not to apologize. "I'm Leslie Bleu, a student nurse with the VNA."

"Figgered. You gonna stand there all day or change this here dressin'?"

"Where can I wash my hands?" Leslie asked. "Then, I'll check your blood pressure and temperature and we'll get right to the dressing. OK?"

"OK, OK. Just get on with it, Girly."

Leslie turned on the faucet. The fixtures were old, but the bathroom was spotless. *"At least she has help, or she's managing better than I would expect with that leg ulcer."*

When Leslie returned to the bedroom, the lady pointed to the now empty footstool. "Sit," she commanded, then offered her arm for the blood pressure cuff, and opened her mouth for the thermometer.

"She's been down this path before." Leslie smiled, more comfortable. She recorded the woman's normal vital signs, then arranged her supplies, and donned her gloves. She sat on the stool, and

snapped her legs together quickly when the woman, without warning, raised her foot onto Leslie's lap.

"Your ulcer is healing nicely," Leslie said, making a mental note to record the small amount of clear serous fluid. She smiled at the lady's clean foot, sporting bright red toenail polish. "Your circulation is good, too," she reported, after palpating the foot and noting the quick return of blood flow.

"Good. That's done," said the lady, examining her newly dressed foot. She relaxed into her lounge chair. Leslie gathered the refuse from the dressing change.

"Over there."

Leslie followed the lady's finger to a trash can under a small desk. She dropped the soiled dressing in the can and then went into the bathroom to wash her hands. When she returned, the lady said nothing further and Leslie realized she'd been dismissed. "Goodbye," she said. "Have a lovely day."

Leslie pushed through the screen door and the wolf whistler stood. "I'll walk ya to your car, Gorgeous."

"Let her be," Green Sock Cap snapped.

"Lord, why me?" Leslie hurried down the steps.

"She okay?" Green Sock Cap called after her.

"She's fine," Leslie called over her shoulder.

Laughter and catcalls followed her to the car. She locked Nellie's door and made her escape.

"Let's start with Research," Leslie said, as the girls settled around a corner table in the library. "Tomorrow's our first test."

"Sure," Robin agreed. "Is there something in particular you want to review? It's been pretty basic material so far."

"Not really," Leslie answered with a look of concern. "It's just that I blew the quiz and…"

"Stop," Robin hissed. "This has gone on long enough, Leslie. No one can fix this but you. You *know* what to do, so *do it!*"

"I struggle with tests too, Robin. I could use the refresher." Frannie said.

"Leslie's issues are different from yours," Robin said. "You do fine taking tests. You just need to study more."

"Well then, where do I start?" Leslie asked.

"By listening to me, for a change," Robin snapped. "You are so worried about failing," Robin said, "that it short circuits your brain. You get stuck on the first question that takes any thought."

"So, what do I do?" Leslie asked.

"You tell me," Robin insisted. "It's not like this is the first time we've had this conversation."

"I don't look at the choices until I've read the question and decided on the right answer. Then I find my answer among the choices and move on," Leslie recited. "But, when I do that, there is usually another choice that looks as good as mine."

"That's how tests are constructed," Katie said. "One right answer; one close but not as good, and two more that you should be able to discount immediately."

"Exactly." Robin agreed.

"So how do I know which is right, my answer or the other one that looks just as good?" asked Leslie.

"You trust yourself," Robin insisted. "You've studied and you know the material. You came up with your answer based on what you've learned, so if that answer is one of the choices, *choose it and move on*. Have a little confidence in your decision."

Leslie nodded hesitantly.

"If you're unsure," Robin continued, "don't waste time thinking. Just mark the question and move on. The important thing is not to spend any time deliberating on any single question before you've gone through the entire test."

Katie added, "Anything you need to think about can wait until you've answered all the questions. That way, even if you don't have time to come back to a question, you've answered all the ones you know. Your problem is that you don't get past the first tricky question, so you don't answer enough questions to pass the test, even when all your answers are correct."

"We can't make it any clearer, Leslie," Robin insisted. "You *know* how to take a test. You're the only one who can discipline yourself to change your bad habit."

"Try this" Katie said, "Close your eyes."

"O… K…," Leslie complied and shut her eyes.

"It's tomorrow and we're sitting in Research," Katie began. "You just turned the test over to read the first question."

Leslie's heart raced and her eyes popped open. "I… I…" Her breath came in gasps. "I…

"See what I mean," Robin insisted. "You're sitting in a library with your eyes closed, *imagining* a test, and you're already in panic mode."

Leslie nodded woefully. "How do I fix this?"

"It's been going on a long time, so don't expect miracles," said Katie, "but right now is the time to start working on it."

"But what if I can't?" Leslie moaned.

"We are graduating this year, and we're doing it *together*. We're here for you, Leslie, but you have to do your part."

Leslie sat straighter and squared her shoulders.

"Here's the plan," Robin began. "Burn this into your brain. First, open the test with NO hesitation, no thinking about it. Look immediately at the first question and cover the answers. You know this stuff, so just answer the question in your head, find your answer, mark it, and move on."

"What if my answer isn't there? What if it isn't one of the choices," Leslie's heart rate and breathing quickened.

"Okay, *stop!*" Robin commanded. "You're already upset. This whole exercise is to help you get over that. You have to play by the rules. You know the answer to that question. What is it?"

Leslie took a deep, cleansing breath. "If my answer isn't there, mark the question and move on."

"How hard was that?" Robin asked, rhetorically. "Repeat after me, *MOVE ON.*"

Leslie slumped in her chair. "I can't do this," she murmured.

Katie put her arm around Leslie's shoulders. "You're the only one who *can* do it, Les. It's a choice that only you can make. As

Daddy would say, *If you think you can, or not, you're right!* It's up to you."

"C'mon, Leslie," coaxed Robin. "If Coach Thomas gave you instructions, you wouldn't hesitate. You'd get out there and *do what she said.* I'm the coach now, so listen to me."

Leslie nodded.

"Sit up straight. Take a deep breath. Get your mind in the game."

Leslie sat up, squared her shoulders, and looked at Robin with determination.

"So, what will you do?" Robin insisted.

"I'll answer each question in my head before I look at the choices. If my answer isn't on the list, I'll mark the question and move on. When I'm finished with all the questions, I'll go back to the ones I didn't answer."

"That's what *I* do," Frannie assured her.

"We all do," Katie added. "Leslie, you know the material. You'll be able to answer most of the questions and most is all you need to pass. You just have to get through all of the questions, and you're the only one who can make yourself do that."

Two days later, the *Nurseketeers* sat in their living room chairs. Leslie pulled absently on her left ear lobe.

"What planet are you on?" Katie asked.

Leslie made no response.

"LESLIE!" Robin demanded, "what's up with you?"

"Uh… sorry," Leslie said with a quick shake of her head. "I was thinking about my VNA patient visits today. The first patient required a simple injection. But the second one was strange and exciting at the same time."

"Like how?" Katie asked.

"Well," Leslie began. "I was right on time, but things went crazy right away. We've practiced catheter insertions in the lab, but this was something else."

"How so?" Robin asked.

"The patient was an 89-year-old woman with contractures. Her daughter has been caring for her with the help of an aide who comes twice a week, and a visiting nurse who comes weekly. I never realized how awful contractures can be. The poor woman was practically frozen in a fetal position."

"Wow," said Frannie, "I'll bet she had bad pressure sores."

"Surprisingly, she didn't. Her daughter repositions her frequently enough that her skin is in good shape. But that's the good news. The rest is awful. The poor woman has to be in pain because she cries out any time you move her, and there's no other way to care for her."

Frannie grimaced.

"I positioned her as best I could to change her catheter, and it's a good thing I brought two because I contaminated the first one trying to locate the meatus. I had to start over with new gloves and the second catheter. Finally, I visualized the meatus through the crook of her leg and inserted the catheter as carefully as I could. That was, for sure, not something we ever practiced."

"It's hard to picture," said Katie. "What a challenge."

"I've been praying all day that I didn't accidentally contaminate the catheter in the process. The rest of the visit went well. The daughter's been taught how to give her mom injections, and I left IM meds for her. One was an antibiotic that she'd never given before, so we reviewed the medication instructions together. I think she was grateful to have someone to talk to."

"I'm sure you're right," Katie said, "especially If she's been taking care of her mother almost single-handedly all this time. I can't image doing something like that alone."

"Her next-door neighbor comes by once in a while to sit with the mom so the daughter can run errands. There's a brother in California, but it sounds like he's pretty much disengaged from the whole situation. I felt lonely just being there."

"How long did you stay?" Robin asked.

"Close to an hour," Leslie said. "The daughter offered me tea. I wanted to escape after the catheter ordeal, but I couldn't say *no*. I stayed a bit longer than I'd anticipated because the daughter seemed so appreciative, and the tea was great. I think it was jasmine. When I left, I hugged her, then I had to hurry out before she could see how close I was to tears. About a block away, I pulled over and just cried. It's obvious that I'm not cut out for community health nursing."

Frannie sat on the arm of Leslie's chair and gave her a hug. "You know," she said, "it's not always about the nursing care we give a patient; sometimes it's simply that we care."

"That's exactly how I feel," Katie said, "and it's the kind of nursing that attracts me… where the quality time we spend with patients and their families is what they treasure most. Community nursing sounds like the right place for me. I certainly don't care much for hospital routines and time constraints."

"Well, you can have it," Leslie said with conviction. "I'm sticking with the OR where I can be focused and organized, and I like the challenge of each patient's case, except 3-11 is killing me."

"It's killing us, too." Robin said, "You're always tired and out of sorts. You order us around like we're your slaves."

"I do not!" Leslie insisted.

"Yeah, you kinda do," Katie said. "At the SNA meeting you offered up the three of us for the October children's event without bothering to ask if we had the time, or if we had other plans, or even wanted to do it."

"But…" Leslie began.

Robin interrupted. "You also told us the coach has been ragging on you. She warned you that you'll lose your scholarship if you don't get yourself into the game."

Leslie's chin dropped to her chest.

"Leslie, you need to quit working," Robin said. "If you wanna graduate, you have to drop the OR. It'll be there when you graduate, but right now it could be *keeping you* from graduating."

"Does a burger sound good?" Mike asked, as he started the truck later that evening. "We can park by the lake and eat there."

Leslie sat beside him, her eyes closed.

"Leslie, open your eyes and listen to me."

"What? What did you say?" She stammered.

"This is ridiculous," Mike said. "We have next to no time together anymore, and when we *do* get together, you can barely keep your eyes open. You need to eat, so let's get a burger."

Leslie stared at her high-top tennis shoes while Mike drove to Sonic and ordered burgers and drinks to go.

"Let's eat here in the truck and then get you home for a good night's sleep," he said, handing her a burger and of the drinks the carhop delivered.

"I want to make more time for us, but I love everything I'm doing. I don't want to give any of it up."

Mike interrupted before she could protest. "School and sports are suffering because of the OR and SNA. You've said your grades aren't what they should be, and you're dangerously close to being in serious trouble with Coach Thomas."

"I'm sorry, Mike, but Coach Thomas has got to understand."

"No, she doesn't," Mike snarled. "She doesn't owe you anything. It's her job to take Crestmont to a championship. You have an athletic scholarship and that means it's *your* job, too. You owe the team your best, and just showing up isn't good enough. Why would you expect the coach to understand when you're the one not living up to your commitment. Your scholarship is dependent upon your participation in the athletic program, not the OR."

Mike started the engine and Leslie stared wordlessly out the window of the pickup, pulling on her ear.

"You've got to drop something," Mike continued as he drove back to Crestmont, "the OR or SNA, or both if you have to. You're risking everything that's important, Leslie, and It's killing us, too."

Leslie said nothing.

"Are you even listening to me?"

"I love the OR," she insisted. "I'm learning so much, and they might not hire me after graduation if I quit."

"When you don't graduate, they for sure won't be hiring you. What then?"

"I can't give up SNA either. It would look awful if I walked out after they elected me president. Besides, I'm learning to be a leader." She turned to look at him. "I can't give them up, not the OR and not SNA."

"Listen to yourself. First you make bad decisions and ignore the consequences, then you make lame excuses for your bad decisions. The Leslie *I* know and respect focuses on her goals and does whatever it takes to make them happen. This Leslie is in self-destruct mode, and it's not doing her or our relationship any good."

Wide-eyed, Leslie exclaimed, "I thought you'd support me."

He shook his head in frustration and pulled into a space in the apartment parking lot. "I can only support you when you support yourself. I can't support your poor choices, and I'm not going to stand by quietly and watch you go down in flames."

When she didn't respond, Mike turned off the motor, got out of the truck, and strode off leaving Leslie to ponder his words as she trudged back to the apartment alone.

"Wow," said Katie when Leslie threw herself on her bed. "What's with you?"

"Mike's mad at me. He's being unreasonable."

"What happened?" Katie asked.

"He said I need to quit the OR and SNA. He should know how important they are to me. When I started to explain why I couldn't do that, he said he didn't like me anymore and walked away."

Katie looked startled, then shook her head. "I find that hard to believe. What exactly did he say?"

"He said...," Leslie frowned.

"*Exactly,* what did he say?" Katie demanded.

"He said he doesn't like *this* Leslie."

"Oh, you mean the Leslie who refuses to set priorities... the Leslie who's going to be in real trouble if she doesn't wake up soon and start making good decisions? I'm not the least bit surprised. The Leslie he knows and loves wouldn't find that at all surprising, either."

"Dammit, Katie, you sound just like Mike and Robin. Are you all in this together?"

"Do you hear how absurd you sound?" Katie shook her head in frustration. "If all the people who care about you are saying the same thing, you might consider listening. It should be obvious that everyone is trying to save you from yourself. You're putting the least important things ahead of the ones that are essential."

"But it's all important."

"Everything's important at one time or another, but graduating is what's important *right now. Graduating* should be your highest priority, meaning whatever it takes to make that happen comes first on your priority list. If you don't graduate, none of the rest will matter, not the OR, not SNA. *That's* what everyone is trying to tell you."

Leslie said nothing.

"Think about it," Katie said gently.

Robin rapped on the doorframe. "Couldn't help but overhear, Les. Sorry. We're here for you, but it's frustrating watching a friend self-destruct. Come on downstairs and let's talk."

Leslie slumped into a kitchen chair.

"You owe Mike an apology," Katie said. "You know he's right."

"Give her some space," Frannie said softly. "It isn't always easy to do the right thing."

"I'll give up my Monday shift in the OR," Leslie said grudgingly. "Fridays don't get in the way of studying."

"Give up the OR altogether," Robin said. "Having more time with Mike would be good for both of you."

Leslie shook her head and Katie said, "Monday is a start. You can give up Fridays later if it looks like the right thing to do."

"Something that would help," Robin added, "would be to practice delegating. SNA wouldn't take up so much of your time if you let the members do more of the work."

"Robin's got a point," Katie agreed. "Good leaders put their ideas on the table and motivates others to help develop strategies. You're a great idea person, and you have lots of SNA members willing to help you. Just give them the information and the time they need to get the job done their way. Focus on results, not the process."

Leslie smiled for the first time. "OK, OK, Guys, and thanks."

"Go talk to Mike," Katie said. "He needs to know that you heard him."

Mike answered the soft knock on his apartment door. He stood in the doorway, unsmiling.

"M-Mike," Leslie stammered.

Mike cocked his head, still without a smile.

"M-may I come in?"

Mike nodded, stepped aside, and followed her into the living room. He pointed to the couch, then sat in a chair.

"I should have listened to you," Leslie began.

"Ya think?," Mike deadpanned.

"I *do* listen to you." Leslie insisted.

"Not often, if you think about it," Mike countered. "Usually, you're too busy telling me what we're going to do."

When Leslie started to protest, Mike added, "But you only get away with it when I let you. I get my say when it's important to me, but I do have to insist."

"Well, what you said is important. Katie and Robin have been saying the same thing for weeks."

"So, you listen to Katie and Robin..." He shook his head.

"Actually, it was *you* who made me listen. I convinced myself that you didn't understand, but the truth is that you care about what happens to me."

"Of course, I care."

"I'm going to give up Mondays in the OR. I understand that I need the time to study."

"What about Fridays? You're exhausted and we don't have nearly enough time to spend together."

"Let's see how giving up Mondays works out. Fridays might be OK."

When Mike frowned, she added hurriedly, "That doesn't mean I'm not listening to you. Let's wait and see."

"I would think our relationship would be high on your priority list," Mike said.

"You're a fine one to bring *that* up." Leslie snapped. "I'm not the only one keeping us from spending time together. Nearly every Saturday you've volunteered to coach an event at that school. How is that different from my working in the OR?"

"I get school credit for that, Leslie, and it goes a long way toward ensuring that I'll get a good position when I graduate."

"My working in the OR does the same for me," she insisted.

"You have a point," he conceded, "although it doesn't give you school credit, and you're paying a much bigger price than I am. You're exhausted, your grades are slipping, and you're anxious all the time. How big a price *are* you willing to pay? When it's all said and done, you may regret your decision."

On Friday, Leslie changed quickly and went directly to the shift supervisor's office.

"Something wrong, Leslie?" asked Mrs. Laurent when she looked up and saw Leslie fidgeting in her office doorway.

Leslie pulled on her left ear and nodded hesitantly. "Y-yes, Ma'am."

"Come in and tell me what's wrong."

"I love working here and I don't want to disappoint you," Leslie's words tumbled over one another, "but I can't work

Mondays anymore. Can you cover the shift without me? I'll still come on Fridays…"

Lizzie Laurent held up her hand, stopping Leslie in mid-sentence. "Take a deep breath. What are you trying to tell me?"

"I need more study time," Leslie admitted.

"You're a student, Leslie, and your coursework is important. It won't do any of us any good if you don't graduate."

Leslie nearly burst into tears. "Everyone keeps telling me that, but I love the OR and I'm learning so much here."

Mrs. Laurent swiveled her chair and examined the large sheet of paper on the wall behind her. She reached for an eraser and adjusted checkmarks. "We'll be fine," she said. "I've been orienting two more nurses to this shift and they're doing well. I want you to promise me something."

"Anything!"

"Please focus on your studies. You will make a fine OR nurse."

"Suck it up, Leslie, you've got this!" Leslie said aloud as the *Nurseketeers* approached their classroom on Monday.

"That's telling yourself." Robin laughed.

The four girls settled into seats and took a collective deep breath. Robin gave Leslie an encouraging grin.

Dr. Langston distributed the Research test. Leslie hesitated, then covered the answers before reading the first question. She closed her eyes. Soon she nodded, opened her eyes, and smiled when she decided upon the answer. She circled "b" with a satisfied grin and moved on to the next question. When she uncovered the answers to the fifth question, she frowned and reread the choices. Still frowning, she shook her head and reread the question. Leslie shook her head, put a dot by question five and moved on to question six.

Leslie had only one question left when she heard, "Five minutes, Folks. You have five more minutes." She marked a response, then returned to the dotted questions and answered them as quickly as she could.

"Time's up. Put your pencils down, "announced Dr. Langston.

"I'm glad I chose an answer to those questions, even though I wasn't sure," Leslie thought. *"If I'm right I'll get credit; if not, it will be no worse than leaving them blank."*

In Research class on Wednesday, Leslie fidgeted in her seat.

"Chill," Robin said. "We'll find out in a minute. I have a good feeling about this."

"Hope you're right," Leslie whispered. "We'll see if your plan worked for me, too."

Class was nearly over before Dr. Langston distributed the graded tests. Leslie clutched the folded paper to her chest.

"Now!" Robin commanded.

Leslie tentatively unfolded the test, then her eyes widened with delight. "I did it! I passed!" she squealed.

"Of course, you did." Robin said.

Katie hugged Leslie tight. "We knew you could do it."

Chapter 18

"That's more like it," Robin said after Leslie adjourned the SNA meeting. "You did a good job of delegating this time. How does it feel?"

"Well, I'm not comfortable, but I do feel good about not having all that work on my plate."

"Why aren't you comfortable?" Katie asked.

"I know I would do a good job, but there's no guarantee that the people who volunteered will do as well, or even do the job at all."

"What makes your way better than theirs?" Robin insisted. "You're the president, but it's everybody's project. Once you've shared your expectations, have confidence that they'll do their best."

"They did seem eager to participate," Leslie conceded.

"Why does that surprise you?" Katie asked. "We all joined SNA for the same reasons you did. You can't grow professionally by sitting around watching. Of course they're eager to participate. You're not doing the members any favors by doing all the work yourself."

A frown clouded Leslie's face.

"What?" Robin asked.

"You guys were right. I could have gone home. Orientation would have been fine without me. If I had, I wouldn't feel like a shit for what I did to Mom. I don't think I've ever broken a promise before, at least not an important one."

"Too late to feel bad about that now," said Frannie.

"Mistakes can be valuable if you learn something from them," said Katie. "You owe your mom an apology. That should go a long way toward setting things right."

The *Nurseketeers* settled into their seats in Community Health and watched as the instructor placed a graded test in front of each student.

Leslie stared at the folded paper. She reached for it hesitantly, then drew her hand back.

"For heaven's sake," Robin hissed. "Open it! You said you made it through all the questions, so have a little faith in yourself." She snatched the test and unfolded it. "There!"

The *Nurseketeers* grinned as Leslie's eyes widened and she stifled a joyous yelp.

"86. I got an 86."

"Way to go, Les." Frannie said, a bit too loudly.

The professor flashed Leslie a smile before beginning her lecture.

Leslie listened carefully but couldn't stifle a grin each time she glanced down at the paper.

On the way to the library after class, Leslie said, "I feel better than I have all semester."

"You scored even higher than on the Research quiz," Robin said. "You're on a roll."

"I can't wait to tell Mike I got an 86."

Leslie and Mike collapsed onto a bench at the end of their run. "Good one," Leslie said, checking her watch.

"I was thinking," Mike said.

"About?" Leslie asked, curious.

"How will your parents feel about our relationship?"

"That's easy," Leslie said, eyes twinkling. "My parents will love you. If Mom had met you first, she'd be trying to fix us up."

"I'm not so sure about that, Les. Our relationship pretty much affirms her fear that you'll never be going back to Abita Springs, except to visit."

"She has to come to grips with that eventually," Leslie said, "and I hope it's sooner rather than later."

"But she doesn't have to like it," Mike countered, "and that might end up being a barrier to liking me at all."

"Even if that were true," Leslie insisted, "Daddy would never let her get away with it. You're everything they want for me, and *he* knows I won't be living at home after college."

"I hope you're right."

"Come home with me for the Holidays, Mike. Mom will be over the moon when I tell her I'm bringing you home for Thanksgiving and Christmas. She'll forget all about being upset that I haven't been home since Easter. You won't believe the Thanksgiving feast my mother prepares, and Christmas has always been magical."

"Whoa," said Mike. "My family goes all out for the holidays, too. I have to show up."

"But Arp is close enough for us to spend weekends with your family," Leslie insisted.

"You know that's not the same as celebrating the holidays," Mike said. "Let's spend one holiday in Abita Springs and one in Arp. Both our families need to know that we're serious about each other, and the holidays seem like the best time to share that with them. What do you think?"

Leslie's heart skipped a beat and a grin split her face. "*He said it! It's not the M word but telling our folks that we're serious is close enough.*"

"That's a great idea," she said. "Which holiday should we spend where? Both our families are counting on having us home, so we need a good reason for our decision."

"That's easy," Mike said. "Arp is closer, and Thanksgiving is only a four-day holiday. Christmas is lots longer, and the drive to Abita Springs won't seem so long if we get to stay a week or more. Besides, I'll bet my mom's Thanksgiving spread is as good as yours. We could stop in Arp on the way back to school after Christmas. That would make my folks happy."

"I've got great news, Mom," Leslie said as soon as her mother answered the phone. "I'm bringing Mike home for Christmas."

"It's about time we get to meet him. Why wait for Christmas? Bring him home for Thanksgiving."

"We need to spend one holiday with each of our families. We'll do Thanksgiving in Arp and Christmas in Abita Springs."

"You can't do that! You said you'd be home for the holidays. You're supposed to be spending the holidays with us."

"Be reasonable, Mom. Thanksgiving is only a long weekend. We'll be spending the whole winter break in Abita Springs with you."

"I guess that's something," Mrs. Bleu conceded. "But you can't renege on your promise this time. Do you realize that this will be our family's first Thanksgiving without you since you were born."

"Mom, you've always known that I wouldn't be living at home forever. Please don't make this so hard. I told you how much you mean to me in my letter."

"It was a nice letter," Mrs. Bleu said hesitantly, "and I love you, too. It's just not easy. It's been so long since we've seen you. You'll understand that when you're a mother."

"I suppose I will, but in the meantime, let's not keep fighting," Leslie pleaded. "I miss you. I miss talking to you, but it's hard to call when I know that every conversation will be an argument about why I'm not coming home. Arguing doesn't make either of us happy."

"I'd be happier if you were coming home for Thanksgiving."

"Mother, stop it." Leslie said, exasperated.

"I'm kidding," Mrs. Bleu said, then added, "well, not really. I do wish you were coming home for all the holidays, but I'm glad you chose Christmas to spend with us. Aren't Mike's parents upset that he won't be home for the holidays?"

"The Hamptons are a close family. They seem excited about everything Mike does. Maybe it's easier with boys," Leslie suggested.

"Not for me, it isn't. I'll feel the same when my boys leave home, especially if they don't come home to visit."

"Gotta go to work, Mom. Love ya."

Leslie left the locker room and spotted Esther at the end of the empty hall. She mentally pumped her fist. "*No one around. Bleu this is your chance.*" She strode purposefully towards Esther, fists clenched and fire in her eyes.

Leslie raised her hand, and Esther halted, surprised. "Esther, we need to talk, *now.*"

Esther opened her mouth to comment, but Leslie shook her head. "I said, **now**. I've had enough! You're always finding fault with me no matter how well I've done. You know I do a good job, but you trash me every chance you get. Making me look bad for no reason makes no sense, so just stop it. You're bullying me and I won't stand for that from you or anyone else."

"I don't know what you mean. I only state the facts."

"Listen to yourself," Leslie commanded. "Nothing that you say about me is factual. You take things out of context, you manipulate the intent, and what's worse, you lie whenever it suits you. Don't ever talk about me again. If you have something constructive to say, say it to my face, not behind my back."

Esther stood dumbfounded, silent for the first time since Leslie had met her.

"I… I don't know what you mean, you are making all of this up and it isn't right," Esther insisted.

"Everything I've said is true and you know it. Bullying is what you do. I've seen you bully others, like the girl who started last week. Bullies are toxic. If you can't say something nice about me or anyone else, then just don't say anything. Bully me one more time and I won't be talking to you, I'll be talking to someone who can make you listen." Leslie turned to walk away.

Esther grabbed Leslie's shoulder and spun her around. "You're lying. You'd better not be telling lies about me to anyone. Do you understand me?"

Leslie ripped Esther's hand from her arm. "Don't you ever grab me again or you'll find yourself facing assault charges. Do you understand me?" she hissed. "Don't think I'm not serious." Leslie turned, leaving Esther open-mouthed and stunned.

Leslie rounded the corner and heard Esther's footsteps hurrying in the other direction. She walked a few more steps then leaned against the wall, spent. "*I did it. The bitch had better never mess with me again.*"

Leslie let herself into the apartment, kicked off her shoes, and slumped into her chair.

"What's up," Robin asked. "Are you simply exhausted, or did you have another go-round with Esther? Give it up."

Frannie handed Leslie a bottle of Dr. Pepper. "Thought you might need this."

"Thanks," Leslie said, and raised the bottle to toast Frannie. "Where do I start?"

"Try the beginning," said Katie.

Leslie leaned forward with a twisted grin on her face and a gleam in her eye. "I did it. I have finally shut Esther up for good."

"Hip, hip, hurray!" Frannie yelled. "What did you say?"

"I don't know if it's time to celebrate yet, but there was a perfect moment to confront her. Nobody was around and I let her know in no uncertain terms that I wouldn't put up with her shit anymore. I was clear that there would be consequences. I was about to wet my pants the whole time, but I did it."

"Tell us word for word what you said and what she did," Frannie said, "and don't leave out any juicy bits."

Leslie sat up, in full story-telling mode. She relived the event as she recounted the details, experiencing elation and exhaustion a second time that day. When she finished, she slumped back in her chair and took a big swallow of Dr. Pepper.

The *Nurseketeers* all spoke at once. "Fantastic! Congratulations! You did it!"

When a loud belch erupted, all four girls burst into laughter.

"I'm glad you realize that this one encounter may not be all it takes," Katie said. "If it happens again, you need to be ready to follow through and do what you said."

"Next time I go straight to Mrs. Laurent."

"I'll bet her bullying the newbies gave you courage," Robin said. "Maybe you're a little slow on the uptake in your own defense, but you're good at taking up for others."

Robin dodged the pillow that Leslie threw. "Seriously, Les. I'm proud of you."

"Right on. Me, too," said Frannie. "Leslie's on fire! Esther had better stay out of her way!"

Leslie arrived early for her VNA appointment at the patient's home. She knew the lady would be waiting as impatiently as she had when Leslie and Shan, the Visiting Nurse, had visited the first time. "*Fingers crossed that all goes well,*" Leslie thought. "*On the last visit the nurse used the 'see one, do one, teach one model', even though she skipped the 'see one' and talked me through inserting the pessary. This time I'm on my own.*"

She reviewed the process over and over. As she climbed the porch steps, she realized she'd been reciting the steps out loud. Her cheeks flamed red. She rang the doorbell, hoping that the patient's forty-something son wouldn't notice her blush when he answered the door.

"Hello," he said. "Glad you're a bit early. I thought I would take Mom out to the park after you leave. It's such a crisp, pretty day, and she hasn't been out much lately."

"What a great idea," Leslie agreed. "I'm sure she'll enjoy it."

"Mom, your nurse is here," he said when they reached the bedroom. "I'll be in the kitchen if you need anything." He closed the door softly behind him.

"Good morning, Mrs. Foster. How are you feeling today?"

"Pretty perky, Young Lady. Today my son is taking me to the park, and I'm looking forward to it. I like this fall weather."

"Yes, Ma'am. It's a lovely day, but it's a little on the brisk side, so be sure to take a wrap when you go."

"Oh, I will. I always bundle up. These old bones get cold quick and I want to stay outside as long as I can."

"Let me wash my hands and we'll get this done so you can be on your way."

Leslie took Mrs. Foster's vital signs. "*Good,*" she thought. "*Everything is as stable as last week.*" She organized her supplies, "*take the cap off the lubricant so I can get to it easily,*" she reminded herself, "*just like Shan told me last week.*"

Leslie helped Mrs. Foster spread her legs. "Please let me know if I hurt you, Mrs. Foster."

"No problems, Sweetie. I've had a prolapsed uterus for so long, nothing phases me. You just go on and do what you gotta do."

Leslie removed the pessary that was supporting the uterus to keep it from creating more problems for the woman. She washed the pessary carefully with *Betadine* and laid it on a clean cloth. She removed her gloves, washed her hands, donned new gloves, and prepared to reinsert the pessary.

"*Lubricate, bend the pessary with the notches at top and bottom, then insert,*" Leslie chanted to herself. "*What if I can't get it to seat properly or have to take it back out? Shit, Les, get a grip. Girl, you can do this."*

Leslie helped Mrs. Foster lower her legs, tidied up from the procedure, and returned to the bathroom to wash her hands. Only then did she realize her uniform top was drenched in sweat. She was wasted, but happy; more exhausted than if she'd been shooting hoops for an hour.

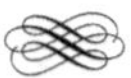

The following day, Leslie trudged behind the *Nurseketeers*, paying no attention to their excited chatter about getting their first choice of clinical rotation. *"How could I not get a single one of my choices?"*

"Good grief, Les, what's with you?" Robin asked. "Get the lead out, or we'll be late for Chapel."

Katie pushed open the Chapel doors and they grabbed seats just as Dr. Creighton began his sermon. Leslie hardly heard a word.

"I'm starved," Frannie said when the sermon finished. "Let's get back to the apartment and eat."

At their small kitchen table, Katie, Robin, and Frannie gobbled bologna sandwiches, chips, and soft drinks, while Leslie nibbled at hers dejectedly.

"Okay, Gloomy Girl," Robin said. "You're upset about something. Spill."

Leslie set her sandwich down and took a deep breath. "I made an appointment with Ms. Reynolds for right after Research class. I need her to adjust my specialty assignment. I can't go to Med-Surg. I just can't. I want the OR. Med-Surg wasn't anywhere on my list."

Six eyes widened, and Frannie blurted, "Med-Surg? You wouldn't put Med-Surg on your list. There's obviously been a mistake."

Leslie stared at her plate. "I didn't get any of my choices. The OR was first, then the ER, and I put the Recovery Room as a last choice since it would get me close to the OR. I know my grades aren't the best, but this feels like I'm being punished. I'm not a bad nurse. I'm just not good at tests."

"I don't think Ms. Reynolds is suggesting you're a bad nurse," Robin said. "She is likely trying to help you strengthen your basic nursing skills."

Leslie glared at Robin, picked up her sandwich, and bit into it savagely.

"Robin's got a point, Les," Katie said. "The assignment may be Reynolds' way of providing an opportunity for you that she thinks is important."

"I want the OR," Leslie mumbled. "I hope Ms. Reynolds will be reasonable."

"You need to be reasonable, too," Robin said. "If she chose Med-Surg because she felt it's what you need, then you need to trust her judgment."

The *Nurseketeers* left their Research class, chatting enthusiastically. Leslie lagged behind, focused on her three o'clock appointment with Ms. Reynolds.

"Research sounds like fun." Frannie said. "Just think, you can explore anything you choose with a single question."

"It does provide the option for us to explore our individual interests," Robin said. "I'll choose a research question related to family violence. How about you, Les?"

"What? Oh. Lemme think," she said without enthusiasm. "Maybe I could explore a question related to pain management for patients after a specific surgical procedure, one that doesn't rely solely on drugs."

"Interesting," Robin nodded.

"Look at those gorgeous leaves," Katie said. "Fall is such a beautiful season, particularly when the weather is as nice as it's been this year."

"Yeah," said Robin. "We could formulate a research question to explore the difference in the psychological status of ICU patients who can't see outside compared to those who can. We could hypothesize that having windows in ICU is beneficial to a patient's recovery."

Frannie nudged Leslie, "C'mon, Les. Take a look around and see what you're missing. We have a whole hour before your appointment. We could put a blanket on the grass in front of the apartment and soak up the nice fall sun."

"I guess." Leslie smiled halfheartedly. "I could read a couple of chapters before I go meet with Reynolds."

"An arrangement tailor-made for Leslie," Katie said. "She loves the outdoors *and* a plan of action."

Forty-five minutes later, Leslie hadn't turned a page in her textbook. "Gotta go," she said. "Take this back when you go, please," she said, handing Katie the book.

"Frannie had a point. I do always feel better outside." Leslie concentrated on the afternoon sun and fall colors as she made her way to Montgomery Hall, her anxiety growing with every step.

"Leslie, come in." said Ms. Reynolds, even before Leslie could knock on the door frame. She motioned toward a small three-legged table and two chairs. "What's on your mind?" she asked when they were seated.

"I want to discuss my assignment for the Specialties Clinical. It's not fair that I didn't get any of the requests I submitted: the OR, the ER, and the Recovery Room. My suitemates all got their first choices."

"I understand your concern," Ms. Reynolds nodded. "I thought that might be why you requested this meeting."

Leslie nodded.

"I had a number of reasons for putting you in Med-Surg. First, keep in mind that we do consider grades, so it's reasonable that students with the highest grades will get their first choice of assignments."

"I'm not a bad student, Ms. Reynolds. I am passing all my courses, and my grades are getting better. I should have gotten one of the three specialties I chose."

"All of your choices are specialty environments, Leslie. Med-Surg exposes you to a wide variety of patients. Med-Surg is a setting where you can hone your assessment skills and experience the broader role of a registered nurse."

"But I'm going to be an OR nurse when I graduate," Leslie insisted, "and I can practice those skills in the OR, too."

"I am sure you will make a wonderful OR nurse; however, there is good reason for not assigning students to the area where they work. First, in your case, we want your clinical specialty experience to focus on the role of the registered nurse. At Parkland you're working as a tech and the likelihood is that they will take advantage of that during your clinical rotation. That is not the intent of the clinical specialty."

"Well, what about the ER? That was on my list, too, and I don't work there. Each patient that goes into the ER is a unique person whom the nurse has to assess in order to determine a nursing diagnosis, then plan and implement the appropriate care, and evaluate the outcome. That's the same nursing process as in Med-Surg."

Ms. Reynolds sat quietly for a moment. "Leslie, you make a good point. I also know you struggle with tests, and you have one coming up in Dr. Hardwire's research course on Friday. If you can make a B or higher on that test, I will approve the ER for your Clinical Specialties rotation."

Leslie's smiled broadly. "Awesome! Thank you, Ms. Reynolds," Leslie said, nearly toppling the small table as she stood and hustled out of the office.

Friday could not come fast enough. Leslie sat, barely breathing as Dr. Hardwire passed out the graded tests. "Thank you," she whispered, accepting the folded paper.

"Breathe," Katie whispered. "I've got a good feeling about this."

Slowly Leslie unfolded the test to reveal an 82 in the upper lefthand corner above a scrawled, *Nice job, Ms. Bleu.*

Leslie's audible sigh of relief brought chuckles from the classmates around her. A red tinge climbed from her neck to her cheeks and she smiled sheepishly. "I have to go see Reynolds right after class to confirm I get the ER for clinicals," she whispered.

Chapter 19

"Best Thanksgiving ever," said Mr. Hampton, winking at his wife. "Time for some football, wouldn't you say, Mike?"

Mike glanced questioningly at Leslie seated beside him. "Go," she said. "It's a guy thing in every household in America on Thanksgiving. I'll help your mom with the dishes."

"You're on, Leslie. That's a gal thing, right?" said Mrs. Hampton. "Let's get started and you can tell me all about your family."

"Wouldn't we finish faster if I washed, Mrs. Hampton, since you know where everything goes?"

"Good idea. Mike says you're good at organizing. I think that's a gal thing, too. Dish soap is in the green jug under the sink. There are rubber gloves, too, if you'd like."

"My mother wears gloves, but the first time I tried them, a plate slipped out of my hands. It was my mother's good China, *her* mother's actually, and I never wore gloves again."

"This is *my* mother's China," said Mrs. Hampton. "It seems like your mother and I share some traditions. Tell me about your family."

"First, I want to say that Thanksgiving dinner was amazing. Mike raves about your cooking just like I do about my mom's. I'm the oldest of the five of us, and I've been helping in the kitchen as long as I can remember. I just hope some of Mom's talent has rubbed off on me."

A yell from the living room made both women smile. "I've been married to a coach long enough to have become a bit of a sports fan," said Mrs. Hampton, "but not so much that I'm motivated to scream and holler at every play. I do remember jumping up and down when my husband's team won the championship on the last play of the game one year. I guess there are times that you just can't help celebrating out loud."

"From a player's point of view, I'll tell you that when you're on the field, the screaming and hollering from the stands is motivating. It makes you feel like you're out there for a *reason*. We play even harder to keep from disappointing our classmates."

"You must come from a sports family, too. Mike says you're at Crestmont on an athletic scholarship."

"I think sports are a unifying feature in most small towns. Daddy was a jock in his day, and all of us kids are sports nuts. My folks never miss a game. I was the basketball team captain in high school, but the athletic scholarship to Crestmont was a huge surprise."

"It was obviously well-deserved. Mike says you've been team captain at Crestmont since your sophomore year. That's quite impressive."

"Thank you. Mike is Coach Andrews' favorite, you know," Leslie said. "You and Mr. Hampton must be proud of how well he's done."

"We are. Fortunately for his dad, Mike's always exceled in sports." Mrs. Hampton grinned. "Do I sound like a proud parent, or what? Tell me more about your family."

"Well," Leslie wondered where to start. "Daddy's the strong, silent type. He never raises his voice, except to cheer at games. He has this quiet smile when he's pleased or proud that makes me feel like I've gotten a bear hug."

"Girls and their daddies," Mrs. Hampton smiled. "My dad's like that, too."

"Mom's more vocal. I guess that comes from raising five kids. My folks have a grocery store so, with five kids, Mom has always had her hands full. We kids pitch in at home and at the store. Actually, we're a pretty *together* family," Leslie said, smiling at the notion. "That might be why Mom's been so upset with me for not coming home."

"Upset? What do you mean?" asked Mrs. Hampton.

"She wasn't happy about my staying in Dallas for the summer to work, and she got more upset with every phone call. It didn't make sense at first, but I guess it's hard for a mother to adjust when her first child leaves home for good. Mom and Daddy both know that once I graduate, I'll probably never be back in Abita Springs for more than a visit. Daddy seems okay with it, but not Mom. She's coming around, but only at a snail's pace."

Mrs. Hampton nodded knowingly.

"You Hamptons are a close family, yet you don't seem upset that Mike isn't planning to come home after college."

"We've always known he'd live somewhere else after college," explained Mrs. Hampton. "This town doesn't have a lot of opportunities for an inexperienced coach. Perhaps down the road," she added wistfully. "Did your folks grow up in Abita Springs?"

Leslie nodded.

"That makes a big difference. They married and stayed put. It makes sense that your mother assumed her children would do the same."

"She's glad that we're spending Christmas there. I hope that being with her for the holidays will make up for not being home all summer."

"Mike's looking forward to meeting your parents. I hope they enjoy him as much as we enjoy you."

The Thanksgiving weekend ended all too soon and by mid-week, Leslie was exhausted.

"Leslie! For god's sake," Coach Thomas shouted during practice when a pass bounced off Leslie's chest. "Get off the court. A zombie could play better basketball." Leslie's teammates cringed at the coach's unusually strident tone.

"But, Coach…" Leslie began.

"Can it!" Her raised hand silenced Leslie. "No excuses. This team needs meaningful practice, and you've been nothing but useless on the court today. Wait for me in my office."

Leslie avoided eye contact with everyone as she trudged to Coach Thomas' office and sank into a chair. Her chin dropped to her chest and she was sound asleep when Coach Thomas stormed in thirty minutes later.

"You've gotta be kidding me, Leslie!" she growled when Leslie awakened, startled. "You're dead on your feet. How do you expect the Lady Coyotes to win a basketball game when their captain is asleep on the court? They deserve better. Get your act together or you'll be warming the bench for next week's game."

Dumbfounded by the coach's harshness, Leslie stared wordlessly at her shoes.

"What gives, Leslie?" Coach Thomas demanded. "Your grades are slipping, you're dead on your feet, and you're certainly not performing like a basketball starter. Start by telling me what's going on. What's keeping you from sleeping, studying, and being the athlete, I know you are capable of being, the athlete your scholarship *requires* that you be. You must realize that if you lose your scholarship, all the rest goes away with it. So, talk to me."

"Well, I've got athletics, of course, and my classes. Also, I'm president of SNA this year, and I've been working 3-11 on Friday in the OR."

"Stop right there. You're sitting here because you're exhausted, overwhelmed, and your scholarship is in jeopardy, and you're working when you don't have to? Your priorities are all screwed up, Leslie, not to mention there are only 24 hours in a day. Your classes and your scholarship should be the first things on your schedule, not the last.”

“I know, but working in the OR almost guarantees me the job when I graduate.” Leslie hurried on when it looked like Coach Thomas was about to erupt. “I have an appointment with my supervisor on Monday. If I resign, I hope she’ll understand and be willing to hire me after graduation anyway.”

“**IF?**” Coach Thomas asked incredulously. “Resigning from working would be a start, Leslie. SNA and working are options for when you have the time and resources. My question for you is… are you serious about turning things around? Think about it. There’s a lot at stake.”

Leslie sat silent.

“Hey! Why’s Leslie on the bench? The game’s about to begin,” Katie asked.

Leslie sat on the sidelines, staring at her feet. *“This isn’t happening,”* Leslie thought, halfway between anger and tears. She carefully avoided looking up into the stands to avoid making eye contact with Mike or the *Nurseketeers* who were cheering for the Lady Coyotes with the rest of their rowdy classmates. *“I’ve started every game since second semester freshman year, and Coach Thomas cut me two minutes before the game. What’s the deal with her?”*

Leslie followed the team into the locker room at the end of the first half. *“Thomas never put me in, not once. What is she thinking? This makes no sense.”* Trapped between confusion and self-pity, she hardly heard a word of Coach Thomas’ half-time pep talk and nearly missed her name when the coach called the second half starters.

“We’re down ten,” Coach admonished. “Get out there and execute!”

“I’m playing. Finally. I hope I didn’t miss anything important about strategy. I can’t afford to screw up.”

"She's on the court." Mike gave Katie a high five. "C'mon Coyotes," he yelled. "Leslie, you've got this!"

The second half was a nail-biter and Leslie's three-pointer won the game. "You did well, Ladies," Coach Thomas said. "You pulled together and got the job done. I'm proud of you. Change and get out there to cheer the Coyote men on to victory."

"Not so fast," Leslie heard the soft voice behind her. "A word in my office."

Coach Thomas pointed, and Leslie sank into the chair. "How did it feel sitting on the bench, Leslie?"

Leslie hesitated.

"That wasn't a rhetorical question. I want an answer."

"Well..." she stammered. "I - I was hurt... and embarrassed. I wanted to hide. I've started every game since I made the starting lineup freshman year. It didn't make sense for you to bench me."

"Really? It actually made perfect sense. The bench is exactly where you're going to end up if you don't make changes. I'm still waiting to hear how you're planning to keep your scholarship and graduate. You've had long enough to think about it. I'm surprised that someone as practical as you would choose to prioritize anything above schoolwork and your athletic commitment. Lose your scholarship and all the rest goes down the drain. Not only won't you be around for track in the spring, you won't be around at all."

Leslie groaned.

"Gut it up, Girl, and get your priorities straight!"

"You first," Mike said, as he and Leslie chose up teams for a casual game of hoops on the campus' outdoor court. The *Nurseketeers* sat on a bench and cheered for both teams, until Mike's team won by one point.

"Good game, guys," said one of the players. "Hope we get a chance to do that again."

The players left the court in twos and threes. Frannie clapped Leslie on the back. "Les, that was a major slam dunk. One more like that and your team would've won."

"Close games are the best," Katie said. "You and Mike are both amazing players."

"Great game," Robin said. "Let's head back."

Mike and Leslie walked slowly, holding hands, and falling further behind the others.

"Let's get changed and get a coke at Sonic," Mike suggested. "We need to talk."

Leslie, drained from the game, would have declined but for Mike's earnest expression. "Okay," she said, hoping she'd get her second wind. "Meet you in 30."

Mike ordered Dr. Peppers and left his window down to let in cool air. "Scoot over here," he said, patting the seat beside him.

The drinks came and Leslie took a sip. She leaned into Mike, letting him wrap an arm around her and snug her in close.

"What's going on, Les?" Mike asked. "Whatever it is, tell me what's happening so I can help."

"That's just it," she said dejectedly. "No one can help. It's all on me. My grades still aren't great because I'm not studying enough. I know I have too much on my plate, but it's all too important to give any of it up."

"You're not making sense, Les. You're telling me what's wrong and at the same time telling me you won't do anything about it."

"Sometimes it seems like I can't get anything done. Well, not quite *anything.* I do okay in class, but it took so long to start doing okay on tests, that I don't have any cushion. That makes me anxious about every test all over again."

Mike listened without interrupting.

"I know you're thinking I should give something up," Leslie said. "I've gotten better at delegating, so SNA is manageable. The girls keep telling me I'm doing a good job as president."

Mike remained silent and attentive.

"It might help if I quit my Friday evening shift in the OR. Maybe I should, but I learn so much every single day that I work there, I can't give it up. It's great experience and practical, too, because working there almost guarantees me a job when I graduate."

Mike inhaled slowly. "You're *shoulding* on yourself."

Leslie giggled, "What did you say?"

"That's something my uncle used to say when I would be all over myself with what I *should* do about this or that. I knew what I needed to do but wasn't willing to take ownership of the decision. He'd say, *stop shoulding on yourself and do what you need to do.*"

Leslie contemplated the expression, then broke the silence. "I *should* give up my OR shift, but…"

"Les, there are no *buts* here. You're running out of time to decide. If you were focused on your career like you say you are, you wouldn't risk it by insisting on having more on your plate than you can manage. Think about how you felt when Coach Thomas benched you for the first half of the game. You want it all, but you're risking it all at the same time. If you wait much longer, you won't have any choices left."

"Everything I'm doing is helping me become the person I need to be."

"And at the same time, some of the things are also placing you in jeopardy of losing the opportunity to become the person you want to be. Your career hinges on your being an RN. That makes graduating your highest priority. Athletics is what's paying for school, so that's right up there with graduating. You're smart enough to know that whatever could keep those two things from happening has *got to go*. That process starts here, tonight, in this dirty ole truck, with a decision to make it happen. What do you say?"

Leslie swallowed hard, took a deep breath, and looked at Mike. "I'll do it. I'll call Mrs. Laurent tomorrow and schedule an appointment for Friday afternoon."

Mike shook his head. "Not Friday, Les. Tell her you'd like to meet with her after class. You cannot put this off for a whole week."

She pulled on her earlobe. "I don't work till next Friday."

He pulled her hand from her ear and held it in both of his. "Time is your enemy. Every day you stall, makes it easier to do nothing. Talk to her on Monday so she'll have time to cover your Friday shift. You need to share your decision with the girls tonight. They'll be pleased and they'll support you, but most important, telling them will also keep you from talking yourself out of it."

She squeezed his hand and gave him a warm, slow, grateful kiss.

On Monday afternoon, Leslie knocked softly on the OR Director's door.

"Come in," called Mrs. Laurent. "How can I help you?"

"I have to quit work," Leslie blurted, her words tumbling over one another. "I'm struggling with school and I'm too tired to live up to the demands of my athletic scholarship. I love working here but if I don't let it go...," she paused, not sure how to continue.

Mrs. Laurent nodded, then asked, "Are you wanting Friday to be your last day?"

"I wish I could stay, but I need to stop working right now. I hoped my coming in today would give you enough time to cover my Friday shift. I didn't want to put you in a bind."

"Then, thank you for letting me know this early in the week." Mrs. Laurent looked at the schedule folder opened on her desk. "We can cover you, but you realize that, if you'd stayed, you would have had the first option to fill any RN vacancies available when you graduate. Under the circumstances, I can't guarantee that I will have an opening for you."

Blinking back tears, Leslie nodded her understanding. "I know you can't guarantee my position. I've struggled with this decision because I love the OR and I learn so much every shift, but if I don't focus on my studies, I might not graduate. Thank you for being supportive of me."

"I wish you the best with the remainder of the school year," said Mrs. Laurent. "Go by the Human Resources Department. I'll call and let them know you're coming down."

Leslie reached to shake hands and Mrs. Laurent clasped Leslie's hand in both of hers. "You've done well here, Leslie, and I do wish you scholastic success."

Leslie stopped by the public restroom in route to the HR department, hoping to quell the tears that were threatening. In HR she filled out forms through a fog then fled to Nellie with tears coursing down her cheeks. She sat in the car until her tears subsided and the strength of having made the right decision made her sit straighter. She turned the key in the ignition and drove back home.

"In a way it's a relief," Leslie admitted to the *Nurseketeers* when she returned to the apartment. "Even though Mrs. Laurent said she couldn't guarantee me a job after graduation, I know it was the right thing to do."

"It was," Katie assured her. "Now the first order of business is to get some rest, prepare for finals, and end this semester on a high note."

"Amen to that," added Robin.

"Can we eat first?" asked Frannie. "It's still early."

"Of course, Nitwit," Robin grinned. "That was a figure of speech. We'll fix dinner first."

"Let's go to the library after dinner," Leslie said. "I know I can handle midterms if I put my mind to it."

Katie grinned triumphantly and Robin winked in reply.

Chapter 20

The bell jangled when Leslie and Mike entered the grocery store. "Be right with you," called Mrs. Bleu over her shoulder as she finished arranging cans of soup on a shelf.

"Do you have fresh eggs today?" Leslie called out, stifling a giggle.

Mrs. Bleu spun around, her eyes large with surprise. "You're home!" she cried, flinging her arms wide to pull Leslie into a hug. "It's been so long."

"We're here now," Leslie hugged her mother tightly.

Mr. Bleu pushed through the stockroom door. "Annette," he said, out of breath. "I should have waited for Jac to unload the truck. That boy is strong as an ox."

"Mac," Mrs. Bleu called, "Look who's here."

Mr. Bleu turned into the canned goods aisle. "Leslie! Come here, Child."

Leslie left her mother's embrace, and her father enveloped her in a bear hug. "And Mike," he said, looking up with a welcoming grin, "so glad you could join us for the holidays."

"We've been looking forward to it, Sir," Mike said, reaching to shake Mr. Bleu's hand. "Leslie couldn't wait to get here."

"Her mother's certainly been counting the days," Leslie's father said.

"It's about time you got here," Mrs. Bleu said, marshalling Leslie toward the chairs behind the cash register. "You haven't been home since Easter. That's the longest you've ever been away."

Leslie threw a *what can I do?* look over her shoulder, as she and her mother left Mike and her father standing in front of the Campbell soup display.

Mike shrugged, gave her an encouraging smile, then turned toward Mr. Bleu. "Need some help, Sir?"

A grin spread across Mr. Bleu's face. "Sure do," he replied and led Mike to the stockroom.

"Well, I'm home now, Mom. We're going to have a wonderful holiday. You're going to love Mike."

"It was cold enough this morning for a white Christmas," said Mrs. Bleu, ignoring Leslie's comment, "but it warmed up fast. It'll feel like Spring by Christmas day."

Leslie sighed.

"I don't envy the folks up north their cold weather," said Mrs. Bleu. "Give me Louisiana any time of year, even summer. I'll take too hot over too cold any day."

The bell jangled and a stout women pushed through the door. "Clarice," Mrs. Bleu called out. "Look who's here. My Leslie has finally come home."

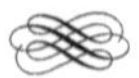

The stockroom door closed behind the men. "The Missus'll come around, Mike," Mr. Blue said. "She just needs some time with Leslie. I didn't realize it would be this hard for her to let go. She was counting on Leslie's being here for one last summer. Grab that box and have a seat. I can use a break. Coke?"

"Dr. Pepper if you have one," Mike answered.

Mr. Bleu fished a Dr. Pepper from the cooler. "So, let's get acquainted," said Mr. Bleu, pulling the tab from his can of Coke. "Tell me about yourself. Leslie says you two have a lot in common."

"We do, actually. I'm a senior and we're both at Crestmont on athletic scholarships." He paused. "I grew up in a small town, too, but I'm an only child and Leslie has a house full of brothers and sisters."

"That she does," agreed Mr. Bleu with a smile. "We have five children. You'll get to meet everyone at dinner."

"I've been looking forward to meeting Leslie's family."

"Leslie's our oldest and she and Annette have always been close. Unfortunately, with five kids to raise and a business to run, we've depended on Leslie more than the others, and she and her mom have been more like partners than parent and child. I don't think Annette realized that until Leslie left for college. She misses her friend as well as her daughter."

"That's gotta be tough," Mike agreed.

"So, tell me about your family. What does your dad do?"

"Dad's the high school football coach," Mike said. "That's what I'm hoping to do when I graduate. My coach, Coach Mitchell, got me in with the basketball coaching staff at North Dallas High School. I've been volunteering with their practice sessions. They have a dynamite program, and I hope they'll hire me when I graduate. It'd be a great place to start my career."

"Well, I certainly wish you the best," Mr. Bleu said. "That means you'll be staying in Dallas after graduation."

"For sure," Mike replied. "Leslie's hoping to work in the operating room at Parkland. She's lucky to have gotten hooked up with the OR as a student because it's difficult for a brand-new nurse to get into surgery, and the OR is what she loves."

"So, I hear," said her father. "Her mother was hoping she'd come back to Abita Springs, but I knew that wasn't going to happen. I think Annette knew it too, but she's not ready to accept it just yet. I won't be surprised if she asks Leslie about working in New Orleans."

Mike shrugged. "There's only one coaching job in Arp, and my dad's not planning to give that up any time soon, so no one's expecting me back home after college. They've always encouraged me to be independent and to think big. Arp has limited opportunities for college graduates, and the job I'd want is currently unavailable, that is until my dad retires or asks me to join him."

They chuckled. "Leslie's scholarship changed everything," said her dad. "Before that opportunity came along, we expected that Leslie'd graduate from a college nearby and get a job close to home. Crestmont has opened her eyes to the world outside of Abita Springs."

"College does that," Mike agreed, "especially if you've grown up in a small town."

"Small towns have a lot to offer," Mr. Bleu said, "but they're better for raising a family than building a career, unless you're going to inherit the family business. You go to college to prepare for the career you've been dreaming about; at least most do, I'd guess. I wish you luck with your coaching, Young Man. I'll bet your parents are proud as punch."

"They've always said that they're proud of me," Mike said, "and I plan to make sure it stays that way."

The storeroom door opened. "Leslie and I are going home to get dinner started," Mrs. Bleu announced.

"Mom," Leslie said, nudging her mother into the storeroom. "You haven't met Mike yet."

Mike stood and held out his hand. "I've been looking forward to meeting you, Mrs. Bleu."

Mrs. Bleu smiled sheepishly and took Mike's hand in both of hers. "Yes, well, of course. It's good to have you here." Bolstered by Mr. Bleu's nod, she continued, "We've been looking forward to meeting you, too."

"Annette, you and Leslie go on ahead," said Mr. Bleu. "Jaq should be here shortly. We'll close up and be right behind you. We can spend time over dinner getting to know one another."

Leslie threw her arms around her dad. "I love you, Daddy," she said. Then she hugged Mike. "Thank you," she whispered. "I love you, too."

Mike finished helping the youngest Bleu, Gabby, set the large table in the dining room. Leslie, Suzanne, and Mrs. Bleu worked together in the kitchen like a well-oiled machine. Jaq and Frank each set an armload of split logs on the hearth in front of the roaring fire. Mr. Bleu added his load of firewood and sighed, "Gotta take advantage of a fire while the cold's still with us. I 'spect it's gonna warm up soon. I kinda envy the Yankees their white Christmas."

"I honestly don't remember a single white Christmas," Mike said.

"Me either," Jaq and Frank said in unison.

"And that's just the way I like it," Mrs. Bleu stated emphatically from the kitchen doorway. "Wash up. Dinner's almost ready."

"You're in for a treat, Mike. No one serves a meal like my wife. It's a miracle that all of us aren't tubby as bears."

"You work us too hard to get fat," Jaq quipped.

"Hard work is what makes you boys strong. I don't hear you complaining about that."

"Whatever you're complaining about," Mrs. Bleu poked her head into the family room, "you can set it aside and come to dinner."

"Frank, will you say the blessing?" said Mr. Bleu when everyone was seated around the table.

They filled their plates from platters of fried chicken, potatoes, and vegetables. "I love the smell of fresh-baked bread," said Mr. Bleu. "Annette believes that the way to a man's heart is through his stomach."

Mrs. Bleu shrugged off the compliment. "You have to give the girls credit, too. This dinner is family affair. It was good to have Leslie in the kitchen again."

Mr. Bleu settled into his chair at the breakfast table the next morning and waited for his wife to take her seat before he led the blessing. The chorus of *amens* was followed quickly by forks digging into the large platter of fluffy pancakes.

"Don't be shy, Mike. My wife makes the best pancakes on the planet. Suzanne, pass the syrup, please. Annette, remember that today the boys and I are doing inventory, so we may not be finished in time for dinner."

Mike turned to Leslie and whispered, "Do we have plans for today? If I pitched in, they'd finish faster."

Leslie gave him a wide smile. "You're a good guy, Mike Hampton, and I can't think of anything that my folks would appreciate more. We'll make a family day of it. I'll help Mom in the store."

"Sir," said Mike, capturing Mr. Bleu's attention. "If I joined you guys, would the inventory go quicker? I'm a fast learner."

"Well," said a surprised Mr. Bleu, "that would be mighty fine, Mike. Thank you."

"You bet!" Jaq added.

"I third that motion," Frank added.

"The appreciation seems unanimous," Mr. Bleu grinned. "We might make it home for a family dinner after all."

"It'll be just you and me in the store today, Leslie," said her mother. "Suzanne and Gabby are helping at the church with day care. It gives the moms free time to deal with Christmas shopping and all. We'll have time to talk if the store's not busy."

"We have lots of catching up to do," Leslie agreed.

Mrs. Bleu opened the register and extracted a list. "Give this list to your father, Leslie. He'll bring us what we need to stock the shelves. We can work together and catch up at the same time. You have lots to tell me."

"I know you were disappointed that I couldn't make it home, Mom. I could have come home. I *should* have come home. I was so sure I needed to be there that I took my family for granted and let you down."

Mrs. Bleu nodded. "I'm glad to hear you say that. It was obvious to me that the rest of the group would do a fine job if you prepared them well. I'm glad that you've learned more about leadership, but keeping promises has always been important in our family, and you're right, when you didn't keep your promise, I *was* hurt."

"I know, Mom, and I'm really sorry."

Mrs. Bleu opened her arms and enfolded Leslie in a hug. "Your apology means a lot to me, Honey."

I know it's gotta be hard for you," Leslie said, "my being the first of your kids to leave home, but we both knew it was coming. As soon as I fell in love with the OR, I knew for sure that I'd be staying in Dallas."

"What's wrong with New Orleans? It has great hospitals, and it's lots closer to home."

"ORs rarely hire new graduates unless they're a known quantity, so Abita Springs and New Orleans wouldn't have been the best options."

"All I can think about is how little time is left before Suzanne will be gone, too."

Leslie hugged her mother. "I wish you could look at the situation differently. You can't stop the clock, and you're making yourself miserable. Wouldn't it be better to concentrate on being proud of the family you raised? You should be celebrating the terrific job you've done. Making yourself sad is a waste of energy." Before her mother could interrupt, she added, "I've heard you say, *pain is inevitable; suffering is optional.* Please don't suffer on purpose, Mom."

Mrs. Bleu's shoulders slumped. "You're right, Leslie," she murmured. "You can't imagine, but you'll understand one day." She looked up. "I promise to try, and I keep my promises. You need to make a promise to me, too, and keep it. Call home often and let us know what you're doing. If you keep us in your life, it might be easier to let go."

Leslie hugged her mother tightly. "I love you. I'll do my best."

"The pastor's sermon was interesting," Mike said, as the group of eight walked back to the house for lunch. "Growing up, I would have been more enthusiastic about church on Sundays if our minister had something interesting to say rather than spewing fire and brimstone for 45 minutes."

"Hmmm," Leslie looked at Mike. "We've not talked about religion much, have we?"

"Nope," Mike agreed. "I guess it's because we seem to believe the same things. There's not that much difference between Methodists and Baptists."

"They do have a lot in common," Leslie agreed. "We both believe that the Bible is the word of God and our relationship with Jesus Christ helps us lead a Christian life. That pretty much sums it up."

Leslie's parents nodded approvingly. Mrs. Bleu said, "Nice to hear that you both have good Christian values. That makes a parent proud."

Chapter 21

Leslie bounced the basketball to Mike, who flipped it back to her.

"Your mom sure made a fantastic lunch," Mike said. "Makes me dread the end of the holidays. Not sure I'll be able to face J.R.'s cooking after this."

"I'll admit that I'm enjoying every bite of home cooking, too. Our meals in the apartment are nourishing, but they fall way short of delicious."

"Every meal here is a feast. How did you eat like that and keep your figure? I'd weigh a ton."

"I sure couldn't get away with eating like that now," Leslie replied, "I have to run to keep fit and manage my weight. It wasn't a problem when I was a kid. Kids naturally burn calories. We walked or rode bikes everywhere and spent all our free time outside playing."

Mike laughed. "Those were the good old days."

"Let's go by my old high school and shoot some hoops," Leslie suggested. "It's a gorgeous day. If anyone's there, we might get a game going."

"Good idea," Mike agreed. "Lead the way."

They heard the shouts when they turned the corner and the court came into view. "We're in luck," Leslie said. "The guy who just made that shot, Damon Winters, was our star forward my senior year. You up for a challenge?"

"Les," Damon called. "Long time no see. You're just in time for a game."

"Yeah. C'mon, Les," coaxed Jeff, another of Leslie's high school friends. "You play?" he asked Mike.

"A bit," Mike said.

"Groovy. With you two we have eight. Two teams of four makes for a good game. I'm taking Les. Damon, pick your first sucker."

"I'll take the new guy," Damon said without hesitation. "I'm betting he's a ringer. You got a name?" he asked.

Mike grinned. "Name's Julius, Julius Erving, but you can call me *Mike.*"

"You wish." Leslie said, laughing. "Don't let him snow you, Jeff. Squashing them will be a piece of cake."

Damon and Jeff completed their teams with the remaining four players and the two evenly matched teams played for the next hour. "You're good," Damon said after Mike's three-pointer swished through the net.

"Thanks," Mike said. "If we had you guys at Crestmont, the championship would be a sure thing. Where do you play?"

"University of Tennessee in Knoxville," Damon said. "No scholarship, though. Les is the only one in our class who made the big leagues. She and Paul were our superstars. The two of them were King and Queen of the Fontainebleau High School Bulldogs junior *and* senior year. We were all surprised when no one offered Paul a scholarship."

"*Les and Paul, Les and Paul,*" sneered a girl on the sidelines. "Look how that turned out. Paul deserved better than you, Leslie. It should have been *Mindy and Paul.*"

"Shut up, Mindy," Damon growled. "That's a rotten thing to say."

"It's true, though," Mindy retorted. "Before Paul and Leslie, it was *Paul and Mindy,* from grade school all the way up to Sophomore year. Leslie didn't do right by him. When he didn't get a scholarship, she just threw him out like garbage."

"That's nowhere close to true," Leslie said. "Instead of being happy for me when I got my scholarship, he was so bitter he couldn't even be civil. I tried, but when he came to Dallas for my first home game, he was miserable and unpleasant all weekend. He was too selfish to enjoy anything that wasn't about him, and too lazy to do anything constructive. Then, he enlisted and left without so much as a goodbye."

"He was an unhappy camper, for sure," Damon agreed.

"Yeah, but if it hadn't been for Leslie," Mindy insisted, "Paul and I would have been together. I would never have left him for a scholarship, and he wouldn't have had to enlist. It's Leslie's fault he's dead!" Mindy squealed and ran from the group, sobbing hysterically.

Everyone watched in stunned silence as Mindy disappeared around the corner.

Damon turned to Leslie who stood speechless. "Leslie, that was a bunch of crap. You had nothing to do with what happened to Paul. It's a shame he didn't get a scholarship because he would've made some college team proud, but he never got over feeling sorry for himself. I think enlisting was an act of defiance, not a real commitment. I'm sorry he got killed, but it certainly wasn't your fault."

"Yeah," Jeff added, "he didn't have anything going for him but basketball, and when that didn't work out, he just gave up… then, dying in 'Nam… what a bummer."

Leslie shook her head. "I'm sorry, guys. I shouldn't have let Mindy get to me."

"She was way outta line," Damon insisted.

"Well… it looks like things turned out pretty well for you, Les" another girl said, winking at Mike. "He's a hunk."

"You mean this Lummox," Leslie said, giving Mike's shoulder a playful punch. "Damon, let's hand them their heads on a platter," she called, running toward the far basket, and raising her hands for the ball.

The two teams played for another hour.

"Every one of you would make a college team proud," Mike said, shaking Jeff's hand. "I hope there's time this vacation for another game."

"Do you two have plans for tonight?" Damon asked. "My girlfriend Carrie is coming in this evening. We could hook up. Les's folks keep the town posted on her activities, but we've still got lots to catch up on."

Leslie caught Mike's eye and when he smiled, Leslie said, "We'd love to hang out, Damon. Still meeting at Peppers?"

"Where else." Damon laughed. "What time can you make it?"

"What time will she get here?"

He looked at his watch and said, "Right now. I gotta scoot or she'll skin me alive."

"How's 7:30? That would give us time to help Mom with the dishes. I'm looking forward to meeting Carrie."

"About Paul," Leslie said to Mike. "You met him freshman year at our first home game. I don't have to tell you what a jerk he was being."

"Yeah, I do remember the guy. He didn't want to do anything with the rest of us."

"That's the one. I can't believe I let myself get sucked into Mindi's *crap*. She's always been a drama queen and I should have known better."

Mike put an arm around her. "I remember how disappointed you were with Paul freshman year, but I'll admit that I wasn't even a little bit sorry, considering he opened the door for me." He squeezed her shoulders. "Today was my first glimpse into your life before me, and I must admit, I'm impressed."

"I gotta make sure no one drinks too much tonight and spills any secrets."

"Hmmm. Maybe the first several rounds should be on me. Could be worth every penny."

Mike and Leslie pushed through the door to Peppers. Damon stood and called *"OVER HERE"* from a table in the back.

"Mike, Leslie, this is Carrie," he said when they reached the table.

A long-legged, lovely blonde woman with a feathered flip haircut that framed her face, rose and extended her hand. "Pleased to meet ya," she drawled in a pronounced Southern accent.

"We've been dating for two years, and this is Carrie's first visit to Abita Springs," Damon said.

"I'm from Nashville," Carrie added. "My family's much closer to school so it's easier for us to spend time with them. Nine and half hours is too long a drive for a weekend visit."

"Leslie and I have the same situation," Mike said. "This is my first time here, too, and we've been dating since our sophomore year. Abita Springs is an eight-hour drive. Arp, where I live, is only two hours from Dallas so we'll have other opportunities with them."

"It's beginning to look like we have lots in common," Carrie said. "I play basketball, too."

"Fantastic," said Leslie. "We've got to get in a game before the end of the holidays."

"Let's order," Damon interjected. "What's your pleasure?"

"White wine for me," Leslie said. "Chardonnay and pinot grigio are my favorites."

"Mine, too," Carrie chimed in. "Even more in common than we thought."

"I'll have a brew," Mike said.

"Man's drink." Damon agreed. "I'll get the first round."

"So," Leslie turned to Carrie, "what's your major?"

"Nursing," Carrie replied.

"No way! Mine, too," Leslie said, leaning closer to hear Carrie over the music and chatter. "I worked in the OR over the summer and had a couple of shifts a week first semester, but I had to give it up. I'm president of SNA this year and working was just too much. What's your passion?"

"I haven't made up my mind yet, but the ER's high on my list," Carrie said. "I enjoyed that rotation the most, and I don't like Med-Surg at all. I'm interested in sports medicine, so I'm exploring options with physicians who treat athletes exclusively. Working with them would mean specializing early, so I have to be sure sports medicine is the right career path for me. I don't have a lot of time left to decide. I graduate in the Spring and I want to have a job lined up by then."

"I agree," said Leslie. "I'm banking on Parkland's hiring me when I graduate because I've worked there before."

They accepted their wine glasses from the waitress. Carrie lifted hers and said, "I wish both of us luck. We should keep in touch."

"I'd like that," Leslie agreed, and lifted her class to toast her new friend.

"Do you two have plans for New Year's Eve?" Damon asked. "Carrie and I are going to bring in the new year in New Orleans."

"Please come," Carrie added. "That would resolve the one-or-two-hotel-rooms argument we've been having. If you come, it would definitely be two: one for the guys and one for the girls."

"Not exactly what I had in mind," Damon winked at Mike, "but the four of us in New Orleans for the New Year would be fun."

"What do you think, Les? Would your folks mind if we spent a few days in New Orleans? I've only been there once, but it was a cool trip."

"I love New Orleans," Leslie said, "and I'm sure they won't mind. Christmas is a biggie for my family, but New Years, not so much."

"Sounds like a plan," Mike said, turning to Damon.

"We'll drive," Carrie said. "My folks bought me a Ford Pinto for my 21st birthday and it rides like a dream."

"Sounds good to me," Leslie said. "Nellie manages to make it from here to there, but I wouldn't call her a dream ride."

"She does have roomy seats," Mike grinned, "… and a big trunk," he added when Leslie glared at him.

"We can drive down on Monday, bring in the New Year, and come back sometime Tuesday. I've just met Damon's parents so we should spend most of the holiday in Abita Springs."

"That works for us, too," Leslie agreed. "I need to spend time with Mom. She's having a hard time letting go."

Chapter 22

"Mom, Christmas is tomorrow. Today's the only day left for Mike and me to shop for presents. What does…?"

"I knew you'd ask," Mrs. Bleu interrupted, reaching into her apron pocket. She handed Leslie a folded piece of note paper. "Something for everyone, and nothing that costs more than five dollars. Can you two manage that?"

"Mom, you're amazing. Thanks so much." Leslie read the note. "You're not on the list."

"Of course, she's not on the list," Mike laughed. "Mothers never tell you what to buy them for Christmas."

Mrs. Bleu laughed. "What did you get your mother, Mike?"

"That's a secret," he said. "It just might be the perfect gift for you, too."

"It had better not cost more than five dollars," Mrs. Bleu insisted.

"We'll never tell." Mike took Leslie's hand. "Thanks for the list. Shall we stop by the store when we're done in case you need help today? I expect the day before Christmas in a grocery store could be busy."

"We'll be fine. You two enjoy your shopping. Just be home in time for dinner."

"The best shopping near here is in Covington," Leslie explained. "It's only a 10-minute drive. Last year, Gibson's Discount Center opened there and it's great shopping. If we can't find the stuff on Mom's list there, the Mall's close by."

"Do you think your mom would like the cannister set we got for my mother? That mushroom pattern is hot this year. If she doesn't need cannisters, there are lots of other kitchen accessories we could look at."

"I liked the cannisters. They're colorful and cheerful. How could they *not* make her smile? Hope we can find them in Covington."

"Can you believe how crowded this place is?" Leslie said, scouring the parking lot for an empty spot.

"I guess we're not the only last-minute shoppers. Do you have any ideas for presents in case they don't have everything on your mother's list?"

"Something will come to me, I'm sure. I'm not the best shopper in the world, but I know what makes my family smile."

"I'm counting on that," said Mike.

"I've always loved Christmas. Everything about it makes me happy. Christmas dinner is a feast and sometimes we have strangers at the table."

"Like me?"

"No silly, you're not a stranger."

"Mom and Daddy always seem to know when there's someone new in town who needs to be properly welcomed."

"That's one of the nice things about a small town. Everyone seems to care about everyone else."

"It took a while to get used to how distant folks seemed when I first went to Dallas," Leslie said. "Here, folks nod to one another or stop to talk when they're out and about. Freshman year, the *Nurseketeers* explored downtown, and people seemed not to notice one another; no nods; no greetings; nothing at all. I thought it was weird."

"It's easier to keep a secret in a big city, though," Mike added. "Everybody in a small town knows everybody else's business. When I was a kid, my mom knew all about my day before I got home to tell her about it. Keeps you on your toes, for sure."

"Merry Christmas," said a lady as she passed them in the aisle.

"You, too," Leslie said and grinned at Mike.

"Mike, we go light on dessert tonight," Mrs. Bleu explained at Christmas Eve dinner. "We go caroling after dinner. It's a tradition, I suppose. We walk the neighborhood singing and at about seven thirty, everyone ends up at the church for spiced cider and goodies. The pastor and his wife host the festivities, and everybody contributes something. It's a nice way to share the holiday spirit."

"I wouldn't miss it," said Mike, "but you'll be mightily disappointed if you think I have a good voice."

"No matter," laughed Mr. Bleu. "The folks with good voices sing loudest and drown out the rest of us."

"Christmas carols always sound lovely to me," said Mrs. Bleu. "It doesn't matter who's singing."

On Christmas morning, Mike found Mrs. Bleu making coffee in an empty kitchen. "Where is everyone?" he asked.

"Kids should never outgrow the excitement of Christmas morning," she said. "Our kids still have to stay in their rooms until we call them. Everyone gets to see what Santa brought at the same time."

"How cool." Mike grinned.

"It hasn't been too many years since they believed in Santa. We could never have a fire in the fireplace on Christmas Eve 'cuz it would have interfered with Santa's journey down our chimney. Now, it's just a family tradition."

"And a lovely one. Just think how much fun it will be when you have grandchildren. Another generation enjoying the warmth of the holiday."

"You're not trying to tell me something, are you?"

Horrified, Mike stammered, "No, no, of course not!"

Mrs. Bleu grinned broadly. It was obvious that Mike was having trouble regaining his composure. "I'm teasing you," she said. "You might want to go out and help Mac bring in firewood. A fire on Christmas morning is part of the pageantry, even if it is too warm for one."

Mike took a jacket from a peg by the back door. "Whoever owns this won't mind, will he?"

"Of course not," Mrs. Bleu replied, and Mike pulled the door closed behind him.

When the fire was roaring and coffee and hot chocolate were ready, Mrs. Bleu called upstairs. "Is anyone awake up there? It's Christmas morning, after all."

Five not-so-young children hurtled down the stairs. The pompom on Mr. Bleu's Santa hat bobbed as he chortled, "HO, HO, HO! Merry Christmas, one and all."

Mrs. Bleu came in carrying a large tray with cups, one pot of hot chocolate, and another of coffee. While everyone helped themselves to a beverage, Mr. Bleu began to distribute the gifts. "There's no card on this one, Gabby." He turned a book-sized package over and over in his hands. "It must be from Santa."

"Of course it is, Daddy," Gabby nodded with exaggerated emphasis as she tore at the paper. "Who else... beside Mom, that is... would know that I wanted this diary more than anything."

Everyone oohed mond aahed over gifts, and the pile of discarded gift wrap grew. "How lovely," exclaimed Mrs. Bleu when she unwrapped the ceramic cannister set embossed with brightly colored mushrooms. "It's perfect for the counter beside the stove. Such a thoughtful gift, both of you." She stood to carry the gift into the kitchen. "I'll bring a trash bag to clean up our mess, then we can have breakfast."

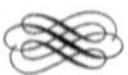

"Where did the week go?" Mrs. Bleu said when Leslie mentioned packing for New Orleans.

"We've had such fun, Mom. Mike fits in like one of the family and my friends treat him like we all grew up together. I knew the holidays would be fantastic."

"I'm glad you'll have one day left with us when you get back from New Orleans," said her mother. "It's been heavenly having you home. I'll miss you when you go back to school, Darling, but I do understand how busy you are. Just call and write as often as you can."

"I will Mom. I love you so much."

Chapter 23

"Obviously, we're not the only ones bringing in the new year in New Orleans," Damon said, threading Carrie's Pinto through the Pontchartrain Causeway traffic. "I'll be happy when we get to the hotel and get off the road for good."

"It's going to be a lovely weekend," Leslie said. "It's cool enough to appreciate that it's January, but nice enough to enjoy being outside. Yankees would consider 56 degrees hot for New Years Day, but I think it's perfect."

"Actually, it's about the same temperature in New York right now," said Damon. "Dad had the radio on before we left, and the newscaster was talking about the North having an unusually warm holiday season."

"My folks usually have friends over to watch the ball drop in Times Square on TV," Mike said. "It's only 11 o'clock our time, but if you stay up another hour, you get to bring in the New Year twice."

"Someday I'd like to celebrate the New Year in Times Square for real," Leslie said. "Don't you think that sounds romantic? It would be a once-in-a-lifetime event."

Carrie added, "That would be a cool thing for the four of us to do together."

"The Maison Dupuy is only a few blocks away," said Damon. "We were lucky to get rooms right in the French Quarter so late in the season, and affordable, too."

"The hotel just opened this year. Maybe we got guinea pig rates," Leslie said. "We'll hardly be spending any time in the rooms. Carrie and Mike need to see as much of the French Quarter as possible, so no telling when we'll get back to the hotel, and we'll be leaving tomorrow."

"We'll be too tired to do anything but sleep. What say we get one room for each couple," Damon said.

"Wrong!" said Leslie. "A room for the girls and a room for the guys. Gotta keep you two honest, don't we, Carrie?"

"For sure." Carrie said.

Leslie squealed, "There it is, the Maison Dupuy!"

Damon pulled into one of the spaces reserved for hotel guests. "Let's dump our stuff and head out. I can't wait to show Carrie around the French Quarter. It's more than 250 years old and the oldest neighborhood in New Orleans."

"You'll love it, too, Mike," said Leslie. "I want to bring in the New Year in Jackson Square. That's my favorite spot in the Quarter."

"Let's get checked in," said Carrie. "I can't wait to get started."

"Rooms 103 and 104, right across the hall from one another," said the desk clerk, and handed one key to Mike and one to Damon. He raised an eyebrow when Mike handed his key to Leslie.

"We'll knock when we're ready," Carrie said. "C'mon, Leslie, let's freshen up."

"The French Quarter is fantastic," Leslie assured her. "Good food, great music, and Jackson Square's perfect for cuddling."

The two couples strolled hand in hand through the French Quarter, wending their way among the revelers on Bourbon

Street. Damon and Leslie pointed out the famous establishments: Galatoire's, The Old Absinthe House, Marie Laveau's House of Voodoo, The Jazz Playhouse, the Cat's Meow, and Pat O'Brien's.

"It's exciting to see all these famous places I've read about in novels," said Carrie. "New Orleans is charming."

The pubs were packed, and music drifted into the street from open doorways. Every restaurant had a waiting list. "We should have thought about making dinner reservations," Damon said.

"No problem," Leslie said. "I'm glad we ate on the way down. Besides, there are food stands galore in Jackson Square. However," she said with relish, "I suggest we dine on beignets and café au lait at the Café du Monde. That will be a treat Mike and Carrie will never forget."

"We should get to the Square while there's plenty of daylight left so we can watch the artists and street performers." Damon turned to Mike and Carrie. "They call the performers *buskers*. You'll be amazed at how talented the musicians and dancers are. You can't beat expensive entertainment for free."

"I'm intrigued," Mike said as they shouldered their way down Bourbon Street and cut over on St. Peter to Jackson Square.

"What is that?" asked Carrie, pointing to an exquisite church at the edge of the square.

"That's the St. Louis Cathedral," said Damon. "It's the oldest cathedral in New Orleans."

"It's absolutely gorgeous," Leslie said, "and it's open until 4:00 so we'll be able to stick our heads in for a few minutes."

They stepped onto a path into the square. "Isn't it beautiful?" Leslie asked rhetorically, arm sweeping to take in the expanse of the park. "It's one of the best Public Spaces in the United States."

"I recognize that statue," Mike exclaimed. "It's Andrew Jackson. I knew it was in New Orleans, and I can't believe I didn't make the connection. Jackson Square... duh."

"How do you know about the statue?" Leslie asked.

"I wrote a paper on Andrew Jackson in grade school. It was my first experience with learning about something I had to look up, and I enjoyed the project. The statue of Jackson that I wrote about was in Washington, DC, but then I discovered that there was one just like it here in New Orleans. I've always wanted to see that statue in person."

"Well, Mr. Hampton, let me introduce you to Mr. Andrew Jackson, hero of the Battle of New Orleans," said Leslie as they approached the statue of Jackson astride his horse.

"Pleased to meet you, Mr. Jackson," Mike nodded formally. "I've been looking forward to this since I was nine years old."

"If we'd thought to bring a camera," said Leslie, "we could have memorialized the moment that Mike met Andy."

Mike put his arm around Leslie's shoulders. "Bringing in the New Year in your favorite spot, especially *this* spot, will be something we'll always remember."

"There's more," Leslie said excitedly. "Let's walk this way toward the music and see what's going on." The two couples made their way into a crowd surrounding an impressive juggler whose tip container was overflowing. They watched for a while, then made their way from one performer to the next, leaving a tip for each.

"This is great entertainment," said Carrie. "It's worth every nickel it's costing us."

"I thought you'd like it," Leslie said. "I think athletes have a special appreciation for talent. I'm impressed by anything that someone does particularly well, and these folks are amazingly talented."

By 5:30, it was getting dark, and Mike asked, "Did someone say something about a culinary treat that can't be found anywhere but here? Now might be a good time to check it out."

"The Café du Monde is right over there," Leslie said, pointing toward Decatur Street, "and you won't be disappointed. It's bound to be crowded, but there's lots of outdoor seating. Wait until you sink your teeth into a beignet… it's a heavenly pillow of sweet dough covered in powdered sugar, and the café au lait is the best coffee in the world."

"I can smell them already," Carrie said, as the two couples approached the famous cafe.

"Mmmm," Mike said as he gazed at a plate of beignets on a nearby table. "My mouth is watering."

"It will be worth the wait, I promise," Leslie assured them.

Two couples rose from a nearby table and beckoned to them. "Come sit," said one of the girls. "Someone was nice enough to invite us to take their table, so we're returning the favor. Happy New Year."

"Thanks," Leslie said, and the four guys shook hands.

"Have a wonderful evening," Mike said as they departed, then held out one of the wrought iron chairs for Leslie. As he took his seat, he shifted the small blue velvet box in his pocket to a more comfortable spot.

They shared two orders of the New Orleans delicacy. "You weren't kidding, Leslie," Carrie said. "I've never had anything quite so delightful. New Years Eve is a perfect time to have dessert for dinner."

"Let's get another coffee to take with us," Leslie suggested.

"Coming right up, M'Lady," said Mike. "Be right back."

They ambled back to Jackson Square.

The couples strolled through the park, enjoying the pageantry, the music, anticipating the celebration that would bring in the New Year.

Mike pulled Leslie into a hug as Carrie and Damon walked on ahead. "Come sit with me, Leslie. I want to enjoy this lovely place with you."

"I'm so glad you like it," Leslie said, "considering it's one of my favorite places on earth."

"Then it must be the perfect place for this," Mike said.

"For what?" Leslie asked, confused.

Mike led Leslie to a bench beside the path. "For this," he said, taking the velvet box from his pocket and kneeling in front of her. He opened the box. "Leslie Estelle Bleu, love of my life, the most beautiful woman I have ever met, who loves basketball as much as I do, who is passionate about everything she does, will you marry me?"

She stared at the ring, wide-eyed and speechless.

"M-Mike," she stammered.

He nodded. "If you say *yes*, I can slip this onto your finger and you will be my fiancée, the future Mrs. Hampton. I'm hoping you'll say *yes.*"

Leslie sat, eyes moist and wide, staring silently at the ring nestled in blue velvet.

Mike said, "I couldn't think of a better time or place to propose. Leslie, will you marry me?" Mike asked again.

"Mike, it's gorgeous," she sighed.

"Does that mean *yes?*"

She continued to stare at the ring.

"Leslie?" Mike prompted.

"Yes, yes, yes," she squealed. "Yes, I want to spend the rest of my life with you."

Mike breathed a sigh of relief and slid the antique diamond ring onto her finger. "Les, this is my grandmother's ring. I thought you'd like it because Gramma was an amazing woman… and so are you."

Leslie was mesmerized by the ring on her finger.

"I can get you one of your own if you'd prefer," Mike said when she didn't respond.

"No, no, Mike. It's exquisite, and even more special because it was hers." Leslie looked up and locked eyes with Mike. "I love you, Mike." She stood, pulling him up with her, and wrapped her arms around him.

They sat on the bench in Jackson Square, alone among hundreds of revelers, holding hands and watching the clouds drift across the giant yellow moon, an hour left before the New Year's celebration.

"What a perfect night for our engagement," Leslie said. "I don't want it to end. How long have you been planning this? I had no idea."

"I asked Mom about the ring at Thanksgiving. She was so excited, she almost let it slip at dinner."

"I'm glad your folks like me, and it's pretty obvious that my family adores you."

"I'd say that's a good start," Mike agreed.

"Tell me about your grandmother."

"She was an impressive woman. Her first husband died young, before they'd had any children, so she homesteaded their farm and worked it alone until she was 34 and met my grandfather. He was only 28, but no one ever noticed the age difference. She always looked young, and she had more energy than a teenager. She went through life at full tilt until cancer took her the summer before my junior year in high school. She must have been close to 90. My grandpa died the next year. I don't think he wanted to be here without her."

"Oh, my," whispered Leslie.

"She was my favorite person," Mike said. Looking into her eyes, he added, "That was before you, of course. She was wise and caring and never treated me like a little kid. She always listened to what I had to say and told me what she thought, straight up. Our deal was, if I asked for her opinion, I had to hear her out, but whatever I decided was up to me… and she never once said *I told you so.*"

"She sounds amazing," Leslie said.

"I learned so much from her, Les, and it never felt like she was teaching me. She shared her experiences and her opinions, and it was always good advice. I can't tell you how many times since she's been gone that I've wanted to talk something over with her." Mike's hazel eyes were moist in the evening light. "She would have loved you and she would definitely have encouraged me to marry you. She used to tell me that marriage is a partnership, and that communication is both the glue that holds things together and the salve that can fix whatever goes wrong. We'll have that kind of marriage. I'm sure of it."

"We will, Mike. I would have loved your grandmother. Her thoughts about communication are the same as those Ms.

Reynolds keeps sharing with me. Coming from two special people, there must be something to it. We'll make your grandma proud."

Carrie and Damon found them cuddled on the bench shortly before midnight. Carrie noticed the ring immediately. "Something you want to tell us?"

Mike stood, pulling Leslie to her feet, "Damon, Carrie," said Mike formally. "I'd like to introduce you to the future Mrs. Hampton."

Carrie hugged Leslie and Damon clapped Mike on the shoulder. "Congratulations, you two. I'll be right back." He returned shortly balancing a plastic flute of champagne for each of them. "This deserves a toast." He passed the flutes around. "To the happy couple," he announced, lifting his cup high. "May they live happily ever after."

The two couples brought in the New Year in Jackson Square with lingering kisses at the stroke of midnight. When the fireworks were over, they walked slowly back to the Maison Dupuy.

The hotel arbor was empty. The couples each commandeered a porch swing and cuddled, rocking gently back and forth.

"Would you guys mind if Carrie went upstairs with me for a little while? We don't get much alone time, and this would be the perfect..."

"No problem," Mike and Leslie interrupted at the same time.

"I don't want this night to end, Les. Let's do a bit of canoodling of our own."

"Canoodling, hmmm, only if you mean *cuddling*, nothing more," Leslie said. "Just keep thinking of the advice you know your grandmother would have given you."

Mike reached for Leslie's hand and led her in the direction that Damon and Carrie had gone. He closed the hotel room door behind them and pulled Leslie into a hug. They held each other, kissed, then sat down on one of the beds.

"Promise me that we won't ruin this perfect night, Mike," Leslie pleaded.

"I love you, Mrs. Hampton-to-Be," he said, pulling her close. "How much trouble can we get into with all our clothes on?"

Leslie laughed. "You're right. Carrie might walk through that door any minute. Hold me close, husband-to-be."

Mike kissed her passionately, and she hoped Carrie wouldn't come back too quickly.

Leslie woke slowly, sensing the rise and fall of Mike's chest beneath her cheek. The memory of their kisses and Mike's gentle touch sent shivers of pleasure through her entire body. With a contented sigh, Leslie shifted slightly, finding a cozy nook in the curve of Mike's shoulder.

"Mmmm," he murmured.

"Wake up, Sleepyhead," Leslie giggled.

"Close your eyes," Mike said softly. "I don't want this glorious night to end. I love you, Leslie."

"We'll have glorious nights for the rest of our lives," she promised, "but right now I need to freshen up." She slid off the bed and hurried to the bathroom.

A light tap at the door warned Mike of Carrie's return. He ran his fingers through his hair to tame the obvious bedhead look.

"I trust you're not angry I didn't come back," she began as soon as Mike opened the door. "Damon and I get so little time together alone that we just couldn't…"

"Not a problem," Mike said.

Leslie came into the room and Carrie threw her arms around her. "Congratulations, again. Your ring is gorgeous." She lowered her voice to a whisper. "I hope Damon's thinking along those lines."

Leslie hugged her and whispered back, "Fingers crossed."

"I'll shower," Carrie said, "and we'll get breakfast before we head for home. Maybe you can wave your hand around a bit, huh, Leslie?" Carrie said.

"Happy to oblige," Leslie said.

"Any chance we can go back to Café du Monde for breakfast," Mike asked. "I can't think of a better New Year's Day breakfast in New Orleans than café au lait and beignets. I'm hooked."

"Great idea," said Carrie. "Mike, go see if Damon's up for Café du Monde."

"Will do. Come to our room when you're ready to go," Mike said. "About fifteen minutes, you think?"

"We'll need a little more time than that. We'll knock when we're ready." Leslie said, shooing him out the door.

"Café du Monde was a great idea, Mike. I can taste those beignets already," said Damon as he slung their bags into the Pinto's trunk.

When Leslie handed Damon her bag, he said, "Nice rock, Leslie. You can tell Carrie I get the hint."

Carrie burst out laughing. "Busted. Am I that transparent?"

"You are, Sweetie, but the hint wasn't wasted," Damon said.

Café du Monde was less crowded than the night before. The two couples snagged a table and the guys went to place the order.

"Best breakfast to start the new year," Damon said, wiping powdered sugar from his lips.

"Let's order coffee and beignets to go," Carrie said. "Taking a little piece of New Orleans with us will make the trip last a bit longer."

Bellies full and café au laits in hand, the four piled back into Carrie's Pinto and Damon threaded his way out of the French Quarter toward Lake Pontchartrain Causeway.

"So, you two," Carrie began, "When's the wedding?"

"We haven't thought that far ahead," said Leslie, "but I'd marry him tomorrow if we could pull it off."

"I don't think your mom would go for that," Mike laughed. "Planning a wedding might be just the thing to get her over the empty nest blues."

"Right after graduation makes the most sense," Carrie said. "Your college friends will still be on campus, and you'll only need one apartment when you graduate. Plus, once you start working, it will be hard to find time for a wedding and a honeymoon, and it will be hard to get all your friends back to Dallas once they've moved on."

"Getting married right after graduation would be perfect," said Leslie. "Carrie's right. If we wait any longer, my suitemates will be gone… at least Katie and Frannie will be. It would be hard for them to come back for a wedding and J.R. might marry Missy and head for Baton Rouge."

"Makes sense," Mike agreed.

"Mom's going to be disappointed, but the wedding has to be in Dallas," Leslie said. "It will be too hard for everyone to get to Abita Springs."

Mike shook his head. "Just when we were making headway with her."

"Maybe planning a bridal shower for you over Spring Break would soften the blow," Carrie suggested. "She can make it a lavish as she wants and invite all of her friends and yours."

"Good idea," said Leslie.

"How come there's no big deal celebration for grooms?" Mike asked.

"Historically, a bridal shower made more sense than it does today," Carrie said. "Back when women were homemakers, they got married and followed the breadwinner. The bridal shower was like a going-away-for-good party and the presents were for the bride's trousseau and to set the couple up with necessities for their new home."

"So," Damon asked, "why don't they invite the husband-to-be to the shower?"

Carrie raised her eyebrows. "Would *you* want to watch your soon-to-be-bride opening intimate things in front of women your mother's age?"

"Point taken," said Damon, "but, Mike, what's to stop you from having a bachelor party over spring break?"

"Nah, let Leslie have her day," Mike said. "I'm sure J.R. and I will celebrate somehow, but no big deal."

Leslie burst into the dining room, her left hand outstretched. Her mother's eyes widened, and her father's face dissolved into a broad grin.

"You *knew!*" she cried, seeing her father's expression.

"Of course, I knew," he said, nodding at Mike. "A proper young man asks a father for his daughter's hand in marriage, and Mike is a fine young man. Congratulations, you two, and welcome to our family, Mike."

Mrs. Bleu remained speechless. Leslie knew that excitement was warring with the validation that her eldest was leaving for good.

"Mom?" Leslie coaxed.

The smile spread slowly across Mrs. Bleu's face. "Darling," she opened her arms. Leslie ran into the embrace, grateful that excitement had prevailed.

"Let me see." Mrs. Bleu lifted Leslie's hand and took an appreciative breath. "It's lovely, sweetheart. Intricate and antique, so much like my grandmother's."

"It belonged to Mike's grandmother. It was her wedding ring."

Mrs. Bleu looked up at Mike. "What a wonderful gesture. I can imagine how much this ring means to your family. My mother's ring means the world to me. I never saw her without it until the day she took it off and gave it to me."

"My mom and grandmother were close, too. Gramma was an astonishing woman and special to me. My parents agree that description fits Leslie as well."

"Well," Mrs. Bleu sat back in her chair. "This means I'll be planning a wedding. I'll let Pastor Bob know that you're going to be a June bride. We'll have to choose a date soon because June weddings are popular and available Saturdays disappear quickly."

Leslie gave Mike a *here we go* shrug. "Wait, Mom. Pastor Bob will preside, of course, but the wedding will be in Dallas."

"But, Leslie, this is your home. You have to be married here in Abita Springs," Leslie's mother insisted. "Your family is here, and all of your childhood friends."

"That's true, Mom, but it's our *college* friends that Mike and I share. We want them all to be at our wedding, so it has to be in Dallas right after graduation. Once we graduate, everyone will scatter."

"But, if you get married here, I can take care of everything while you concentrate on school. We'll manage to find places for all your friends to stay. No one will have to sleep in the car. It will be the wedding you've always dreamed about."

"Please, Mom, let's not turn my wedding into a family feud. It would ruin everything."

"There will be no feud, Leslie," said Mr. Bleu, "Your mother understands that you'll be married where you want to be married. The ceremony is what's important, not the location." He walked to his wife and put his arms around her shoulders. "Your mother may be disappointed with the details, but she's as happy as I am that you're marrying this fine young man."

Leslie and Mike gave Mr. Bleu a grateful smile, and Leslie hugged her mother. "Mom, you'll plan the wedding with me, and Suzanne will be my Maid of Honor. The wedding will be in Dallas, but it will be just like we imagined."

Mrs. Bleu sighed. "I suppose it will be alright."

"What about a bridal shower here in Abita Springs over Spring Break. Could you plan that for me? We can celebrate with everyone here in Abita Springs?"

"A bridal shower would be wonderful," Mrs. Bleu brightened, "and, of course, I'll help with the wedding. That's what mothers of brides do."

Mr. Bleu nodded, satisfied that his wife's ruffled feathers had settled into place.

"You'll have to tell me whom you want to invite to the shower, Leslie, so I don't miss anyone."

"You know all my high school friends. Invite them and our neighbors, our church friends, and your friends of course."

Chapter 24

Leslie dropped her suitcase in the living room and called, "Anyone home?"

"I'm here," Katie said, coming downstairs from their bedroom. "We're the only two..." She stopped in mid-sentence, then grabbed Leslie's left hand. "Oh, my goodness... *congratulations*!" she gasped and pulled Leslie into a hug. "Come, tell me all about it."

The suite door opened, and Frannie muscled her three suitcases into the living room. "Whew," she said. "It's a good thing there are porters and cab drivers to carry these things. I'd never have made it back if I had to manage this luggage on my own."

Leslie and Katie dissolved into a fit of laughter. "If Robin were here, she'd have something to say about that," Leslie said between giggles.

Frannie started to protest, then her eyes grew wide. "What's that? Did you and Mike get married? What did I miss?" she squealed, grabbing Leslie's hand to study the ring.

"Not married... not yet," Leslie assured her. "It was the most amazing proposal in history. Can you believe that Mike actually asked my father for my hand in marriage, and I had absolutely no clue. He proposed to me in Jackson Square on New Year's Eve."

"Romantic," said Katie.

"That ring is amazing!" Frannie gushed.

"It was his grandmother's wedding ring. That makes it all the more special."

"We need to celebrate," Frannie said.

"Celebrate what?" Robin said as she came through the door.

"Right on time," Katie said. "Leslie has something to show you."

Leslie dangled her left hand in front of Robin. Wide-eyed and grinning, Robin asked, "So, when's the wedding?"

"You have to get married while we're all still together, before we leave Dallas for good," Frannie insisted. "We're all going home after college and what if we couldn't get back to Abita Springs?"

"For heaven's sake, Frannie," Robin said. "Let her answer the question."

Leslie grinned. "Don't worry. You won't miss the wedding. I can't imagine my wedding without the *Nurseketeers*."

Frannie threw her arms around Leslie. "Will we be your bridesmaids?"

"Most definitely," Leslie assured her.

"Can we get back to basics?" Robin asked. "Like, what are your plans?"

"It was a hard sell, but Daddy helped to convince Mom that the wedding had to be in Dallas. We explained that our mutual friends are here at Crestmont and we want them to be at the wedding. We want to have the wedding the Saturday after graduation, before everyone leaves campus for good, if we can get the chapel."

"WOW! You're going to have your hands full this semester. Classes, clinicals, track, SNA, *and* a wedding." Katie said. "If there was ever a time to get your act together, this is it!"

"Mom will be a big help," Leslie said, "and we're the *Nurseketeers*. I can count on you guys for help, can't I?"

"Within reason," Robin chimed in. "We've all got our hands full, studying for classes and keeping up with clinicals. I don't expect there'll be much down time."

"Planning your wedding will be fun," Frannie said. "I'll help, for sure,"

"We'll all help as much as we can," said Katie.

"Just remember," Robin added. "Graduating is everyone's highest priority."

"Let's get unpacked," said Katie, "then we can catch up on everyone's holiday."

"So, Leslie, you start," Katie said. "It seems like you had the most amazing holiday of all."

"Christmas couldn't have worked out better," Leslie began. "We didn't tell the folks exactly when we'd be arriving, so we got to surprise Mom and Dad at the store. Mom was excited to see me and she all but ignored Mike when we first got there. She whisked me off to sit with her and catch up. Mike was a trooper. He wasn't put out at all. He and Daddy went into the storeroom to get some work done and get to know one another. That gave Mom a little time to get over being pissed. It was the right amount of time to get everything back on track and the whole vacation was fantastic."

"That's great news," Robin said.

"Mike was a hit with everyone. We played basketball with my high school friends. Damon and I played high school sports together, and he went on to the University of Tennessee. His girlfriend, Carrie, came to Abita Springs for the holiday. It's amazing how much she and I have in common. She's an athlete and she'll be a nurse when she graduates this year, just like us."

"I want to hear every detail of Mike's proposal," Frannie said. "Leave nothing out."

"We went to New Orleans with Damon and Carrie to bring in the New Year. Mike proposed in one of my favorite places on earth, Jackson Square. There were hundreds of people, but it seemed like we were the only two people on the planet."

"Did he get down on one knee?" Frannie asked.

"He did. He took this beautiful blue velvet box out of his pocket, then he knelt, opened the box, and asked me to marry him. He made a beautiful speech, and I couldn't say a word. I honestly didn't say *yes* until about the third time he asked."

"That's got to be a first," Katie laughed.

"Cinderella and her Prince Charming," cooed Frannie.

"Leslie's holiday trumps mine," Robin said, "but I do have good news to share. Gram and I moved into her new house. We didn't expect it to be available until Spring, but the realtors called the day after Christmas and said that the previous owners' probate had been settled earlier than expected and the house was ours if we were ready to take possession. The Davises helped with the move. The furniture Gram brought from Chicago fits perfectly and everything is out of storage. The new house feels like the home I grew up in, except the neighborhood's way better."

"You're gonna still live with us, though, aren't you?" Frannie asked, her voice a bit shaky. "I mean…"

"Of course I will, Squirt. I wouldn't abandon you at this late date." Robin put her arm around Frannie's shoulders. "You need me around to keep your head in the game."

"Will you live with your grandmother after you graduate?" Katie asked.

"Most likely, at least at first," Robin said, "and I have more news. Tonya came home for Christmas to see her mom. She loves her job; she's made friends; she likes her apartment a lot; and she said that San Francisco was absolutely the right choice."

"What great news," said Leslie. "I'm so pleased for her."

"My Christmas break was wonderful, too" said Katie, "It felt good to spend time with John. Then, Naomi and I did lots of talking about college since she's graduating this spring. She's not positive about what she wants to be, but Crestmont is her first choice on her list of colleges."

"How's John's dad?" Frannie asked.

"It's sweet of you to ask, Frannie. John's dad's recovery has been amazing. He's working the farm like the accident never happened. The Browns and the Grayfoxes are like one big family. John and his dad were with us for most of the holiday. John's going to check on the Indian Health Service in Stillwater for me. If they don't have a presence there, he'll find out what similar opportunities there might be. I'm pretty sure that's what I want to do after graduation. I can work in Stillwater while John's in vet school, and then transfer to Atoka when we move back home."

"Any idea when you two will get engaged?" Leslie asked.

"Honestly, we've not talked about it. We're so comfortable with our plans that getting engaged won't change anything. I expect John will pick a perfect time and place."

"Ever the practical one," Robin grinned. "Frannie, what about your holiday."

"I had a great time at home. The best news is that Petey will be getting out of the Army sometime this year. His tour in Viet Nam is over and he's stationed at Fort Lewis in Washington state. He says it's lovely there, but the weather is crappy. I miss him. It will be like old times when both of us are home again."

"How's your Nana doing?" Robin asked.

"She can't get around on her own anymore, but she's as sharp as ever. She's so frail that Daddy doesn't have any trouble picking her up and settling her wherever the rest of us are, so she doesn't miss out on much. She doesn't eat with us because she can't feed herself well and she can only eat a little at a time. The best part of the holiday was curling up in bed and visiting while I fed her. I'm gonna take good care of her after I graduate."

Chapter 25

"Mom, here's what I've decided so far." Leslie secured the receiver between her shoulder and her ear, ticking off items on the list in her lap. "Suzanne, of course, is my maid of honor, and my suitemates will be my bridesmaids. Jaq and Frank will be groomsmen, along with Daniel, Mike's cousin, and J. R. will be Mike's best man. Gabby's too old to be a flower girl, so how can I include her in the wedding?"

"Perhaps she can take charge of the guest book. She can make sure that everyone signs it," suggested Mrs. Bleu.

"That's a great suggestion. I hope she'll like the idea."

"I'm sure she will. The guest book is an important part of a wedding. You'll capture your memories of the day with the information in the book. All your guests will sign, and the gifts you receive will be listed to help you with thank you notes. We're all happy to do whatever we can. Mike is a delightful young man, and you two make a fine couple. I like that he's from a small town and has good Christian values. I'll make a good grandmother, don't you think?"

Leslie laughed. "The best, Mom for sure. You'll be an exceptional grandmother, but that won't be happening any time soon."

"Well, not too soon, I hope… But, not too late, either."

Before Mrs. Bleu could pursue the topic, Leslie asked, "Were you going to talk to Lenore about the flowers? It might be too difficult with the wedding in Dallas."

"Yes, I'll ask her. She's always insisted that when you marry, she would do the flowers. It wouldn't be right not to check with her."

"Of course. I wouldn't think of hurting her feelings. She's always treated me so well. The wrist corsage she made for prom was beautiful, and she only charged Paul half price. I've no idea why she's always been so nice to me."

"I would expect it's because you appreciate her work. When you were four or maybe five, you told her that the flowers she provided for Sunday service were the best part of going to church. You said they were beautiful, and they made the church smell like heaven. How could she not fall in love with that little girl?"

"I do love the flowers in church on Sunday, but I don't remember telling her that."

"It's been a few years since you were four. It's not surprising that you wouldn't remember. For you, it was a statement of fact. For Lenore it was a delightful compliment, worth remembering all these years."

"She's a lovely woman, so I'm glad I made her feel good. She deserved it."

"Ask her about Suzanne's dress," Katie whispered.

Leslie nodded. "Mom, one more thing. How shall I handle Suzanne's dress for the wedding since she can't come to Dallas for a fitting? Shall I send it to Abita Springs so she can have it altered if she needs to?"

"That's probably the best idea. It wouldn't do to find out the dress didn't fit when it's too late to do anything about it. It will be easier for her to find shoes to match, too."

"Have we missed anything?"

"You'll want to order the cake in Dallas. I'll bet that nice Mrs. Davis from the SteakHauz can recommend a good bakery."

"You think of everything. When you retire from the store, you should consider being a wedding planner."

"When I retire…," Mrs. Bleu mused, "I honestly can't imagine what that would look like. It certainly won't be happening in the foreseeable future. By the time all my children have grown up, what would there be for me to do beside work in the store?"

"After all the years you've worked and raised kids, you deserve time for yourself. You should be figuring out what cool things you might do then. I'll admit that I can't picture you sitting around eating bon bons and watching TV, but I can see you volunteering at the church, and quilting. You've always said you'd love to quilt, but you never had the time."

"Leslie, I miss you. It's been hard getting used to your growing up and leaving for good."

"It was a bit rough for both of us, but I think we're okay now, don't you?"

"I do. Once you got your scholarship, we knew that the best opportunities for you wouldn't be in Abita Springs. It just took me a little while to come around."

"Mom, I expect that we'll spend lots of telephone time keeping each other up to date. I can't imagine not having you in my life. I would miss you as much as you've missed me."

Leslie could hear the smile in her mother's voice. "Well," Mrs. Bleu said quickly, "we seem to have the wedding under control. Tell me about school. You said this would be an exciting semester."

Chapter 26

"I'm so disappointed," Mrs. Bleu said. "Pastor Benoit is booked for May and June. He's terribly sorry, but there's no way he can make it to Dallas. It never occurred to me that he wouldn't be able to marry you, Leslie. Now, what will we do?"

"I suppose I took that for granted, too," Leslie said. "But, wait. I have an idea. I'll let you know if it pans out as soon as I get in touch with Dr. Creighton."

"Who's that?" Mrs. Bleu said uncertainly.

"He's the professor who taught Old Testament our freshman year and I like him a lot. He presides at Wednesday Chapel sometimes and his talks are as interesting as Pastor Benoit's. I know he'd be happy to marry us if he's available. Keep your fingers crossed."

"It won't be the same without Pastor Benoit," Mrs. Bleu began, "but I'm sure your Dr. Creighton is a good alternative."

"You'll like him, Mom," Leslie assured her.

"I expect I will, especially if he's as good a speaker as Pastor Benoit."

"We've got the chapel and the reception hall booked, so May 25th is a firm date. It's safe to move ahead with the invitations.

Also, Mike and I have an appointment at the bakery next Monday to decide on our wedding cake. I'm going to talk him into having a groom's cake even though he thinks having two cakes is silly."

"One more thing," said Mrs. Bleu. "Lenore would love to do your floral arrangements, but flowers need to be fresh and getting them from Abita Springs to Dallas would be inconvenient and expensive. She's going to recommend a florist in Dallas, and she'll share her ideas with them so, in a way, she'll still be doing the flowers for you."

"That's nice of her. Please tell me as soon as you know who the florist will be, and I'll stop by. I know what I want my bridal bouquet to look like. I saw it in a photo in one of Frannie's bridal magazines. I'm open to suggestions for the rest."

"I'll let you know as soon as Lenore calls me."

"The *Nurseketeers* are going shopping with me for my wedding dress. That should be interesting because our tastes are so different. Frannie would have me looking like a fairy princess, and Robin would be happy with a pantsuit. Actually, I did see a gorgeous pantsuit in a *Bride* magazine Frannie brought home. She got the latest issue as soon as we started talking about the wedding. I might just be a good pants suit bride."

"A pant suit is out of the question," Mrs. Bleu insisted, "and I'd always imagined *I'd* be the one to help pick out your wedding dress."

"Mom..."

"I know. I know. But I still want to do as much for your wedding as I can. I hope you're giving me credit for... what is it you athletes say... *stepping up to the plate?*"

Leslie laughed. "That's a good one, Mom. You definitely *are* adjusting. It's much more fun to talk when we're not arguing."

"You mean it's much more fun to talk when you get your way."

"Mom..."

"I'm kidding, I'm kidding. I know you're grown up and I'm proud of you, but it's hard to be happy about one of my children leaving home for good. You'll understand some day."

Leslie let that pass. "Oh, I have something else to tell you. Robin's grandmother wants to help you with the food for the reception. She has a lovely kitchen in her new house. It's spacious, and all the appliances are new. You'll love her, Mom. She's your kind of person... kind, intelligent, and as devoted to Robin as you are to us kids."

"That says a lot about someone in my book. Tell her *thank you* and I'm looking forward to meeting her."

"What else do I need to take care of besides keeping my fingers crossed that Dr. Creighton will say *yes*."

"For the time being, I think everything's under control. You and Mike will take care of the cake; Loretta will put us in touch with a florist; I have a lovely kitchen to bake in, and a nice person to help me. Oh, and you four girls will find the perfect wedding dress. I vote for Frannie's choice. I think brides *should* look like fairy princesses."

"You could feel Valentine's Day all over the unit," Katie said after work On Valentine's Day. "It's amazing how much the flowers at the nurses' station raised everyone's spirits."

"Are you and Mike going out tonight?" Frannie asked.

"Don't think so," Leslie said. "He didn't mention anything. I didn't even realize it was Valentine's Day 'til we got to the hospital this morning and saw signs of it everywhere. With the wedding on my mind, and everything else, I'd forgotten all about it."

The *Nurseketeers* reached their two cars parked side by side in the Parkland lot. "Meet you at home," said Leslie.

"Wow, Leslie, look at this!" Frannie exclaimed when they reached their apartment door. A vase of red roses sat on the welcome mat, with a box propped against it.

Leslie plucked the card from the bouquet. Her smile grew as she read aloud, "*Leslie Jean Bleu, light of my life. Celebrate this special day with flowers and food. I love you.*" She turned the card over. "Get this, guys. *P.S. it's okay to share the candy with your bridesmaids. The flowers are for you.*"

Katie answered the phone on Saturday morning. "It's for you, Les."

"Mom?" Leslie asked.

"Nope, it's Carrie. Damon proposed on Valentine's Day.

"Fantastic! Congratulations."

"I waited two days to call 'cuz long distance phone rates are ridiculous during the week. I wish you could see my ring."

"Me too. Tell me everything."

"He brought flowers and candy when he came to pick me up, so I didn't have a clue when we left for dinner. It was a lovely meal and when it came time for dessert, the waiter said that the restaurant had prepared a special Valentine's dessert for the guests. When I thanked him and said I was too full for another bite, he got a bit flustered, like he wasn't expecting anyone to pass on a free dessert. Damon told him that he'd eat both of them."

"He hasn't changed a bit," Leslie laughed. "He could always put away more food than anyone would imagine. Mike's like that, too."

"The story gets better," Carrie continued. "The waiter came out with two desserts with silver domes. He put one in front of Damon and then said, *I'll just leave this one here until he's through, if you don't mind, Miss,* and he put the other one in front of me. Damon dug into his dessert. It looked like some fancy cheesecake. He said, *This is great. You might want to take just a bite,* and I was so curious I couldn't help myself. The waiter lifted the dome and there was my ring nestled in a silver spoon beside a cup of café au lait and three beignets. He came over and picked up the ring, and in front of a whole restaurant full of people, he got down on one knee and proposed."

"Keep going. This is priceless."

"I was speechless. I never expected that Damon would be that romantic. It was heavenly. Damon and I are following the advice I gave you and Mike. We're getting married right after graduation. We want to start out on our own, so we'll be staying in Knoxville, at least for a while. We'll get an apartment and see about jobs. Who knows what will come next."

"I'm so happy for you two. Have you set a date? We're getting married on May 25th. Wouldn't it be cool if we had the same anniversary?"

"We haven't set a date yet, but I'll let you know. There are so many details to work out."

"Congratulations, again, Carrie. Give Damon a huge hug for me. I can't wait to tell Mike."

"How are we going to do your hair for the wedding, Les?" Frannie asked.

"What do you mean, *do my hair* What's wrong with my hair?" Leslie demanded.

"I've *got* to do your hair and nails," Frannie insisted. "You can't get married looking like a track star."

"But I *am* a track star!" Leslie insisted, confused.

"Not at your wedding, you're not. You're a princess marrying a handsome prince… and you're gonna look like one," Frannie insisted.

"Hold on a minute. I am *not* wearing a gown that makes me look like the sugar plum fairy," Leslie stated firmly. "I can hardly imagine a manicure, let alone anything other than the way my hair looks every day. Besides it's cut in a shag and there's not much you can do with that. I *will not* do BIG hair. This is what I look like."

"Frannie has a point, Les," said Katie. "You don't get married every day, and it should be a special event, don't you think? Looking extra special is part of being a bride."

"Mike will be blown away when he sees the princess he's marrying," Frannie gushed.

"Your wedding will give you and Mike a lifetime of memories," Robin added. "Frannie will see to that, and I'm sure it's on your mother's agenda, too."

"You're probably right," Leslie conceded. "I'm open to suggestions, but remember, *I* make the final decisions."

"What a surprise," Robin chuckled.

"Wouldn't the gazebo on the roof of Simpson Hall be a heavenly place for your wedding, Les," Frannie asked. "It's soooo gorgeous."

"It certainly would be unique," Leslie replied. "I wonder why there hasn't been a wedding there in the four years we've been here, at least not one we've known about."

"Yours would be the first." Frannie cried. "It's gorgeous up there, particularly at night."

"It would be lovely," Katie agreed.

Leslie shook her head slowly. "Perhaps, but I don't think so. Spring weather in Dallas can be unpredictable. It could be beastly hot, or we could have thundershowers. The chapel is the practical choice. The weather might be why there haven't been any weddings up there. Thanks for the suggestion though," she added hastily, as Frannie's smile faded. "I'll let you know how cool the gazebo is after this weekend. I'm going to suggest that Mike and I check it out instead of driving all the way to Bachman Lake."

Chapter 27

The *Nurseketeers* finished their sandwiches and tidied the kitchen. Katie said, "We have tests in both Leadership and Critical Care to study for, so we should spend the afternoon in the library."

"It's Leslie's turn to get groceries for the apartment," Robin said.

"Frannie, if I give you the money," Leslie asked, "can you get the groceries for me today? "Coach Thomas called a meeting about this weekend's track meet for 3:00 and I have the SNA meeting to plan. If I study with you guys now, there won't be enough time left for a trip to the grocery store before the coach's meeting."

"Again?" Robin asked sourly. "It's not like Frannie doesn't need to study. It's as important for her to pass as it is for you. With all the other things on your plate, you've been letting your commitment to us slip. When was the last time you actually took your turn to tidy the apartment or get the groceries. We've been picking up the slack for weeks."

"I'm okay, Robin," Frannie said confidently. "I don't mind shopping for Leslie. I'll study with you guys for a bit, then go to the store."

"Not so fast," Robin snapped. "Leslie, when there's no time left to do what you've committed to do, you might want to consider making changes in your *to do list*. You won't always have one of us to keep your ass out of the fire. It's time you learned to prioritize your responsibilities."

"Tell me what's not important," Leslie demanded.

"It's not a matter of *what's* important, Leslie. It's a matter of *what's more* important than something else. That's what setting priorities is all about, deciding what's most important *for you, right now*. If you consider the consequences, your priority-setting would be a no-brainer. Graduating would be top of your list, which means that keeping your athletic scholarship is right up there with studying. Marrying Mike's obviously important, but the wedding date could be any time. The SNA would be a distant fourth in my book."

Leslie stood up, fists on her hips. "That's just mean, Robin. I would think you'd be more supportive. After all…"

"I'll shop for you today, Leslie," said Frannie. "You can take my next turn."

In research class the next morning, their graded tests were returned. Leslie's broad grin telegraphed her relief when she unfolded the research test to reveal a red 84 in the upper right corner.

"So, tell," said Katie.

"She got a B," crowed Frannie, standing to peer over Leslie's shoulder. "Same as me."

"Good job, both of you," said Robin. "We'll scrounge something up for a celebration."

"Maybe we'll make extra desserts," Frannie said.

"Sounds like a plan," said Katie. "Let's go."

"No desserts for me," Leslie said. "I have to fit into a wedding dress."

"After a second round of desserts," Katie said, "I need to go to the library. I've got stuff to look up before clinicals tomorrow."

"I'll see you this evening," said Leslie. "I've got a busy afternoon."

"Really?" asked Robin sarcastically. "Does your schedule include picking up groceries?"

Nonplused, Leslie turned to Frannie.

"Goddammit, Leslie, Frannie will *not* get the groceries!" Robin insisted. "For once you're going to do what you've committed to do. We're out of everything and it's your turn to shop. You find time for the things you *want* to do, and I, for one, think your priorities are monumentally screwed up."

"I pay for my share," Leslie insisted. "Why does it matter who picks up the groceries."

"It matters," Robin insisted, poking her finger up at Leslie's face. "I'm not talking about money; I'm talking about your commitment to us. Assuming that we'll do your share of the work around here any time it's not convenient for you is totally unacceptable. Lately, it's been *not convenient* for you to do anything at all. Frannie shopped for you last time and you promised you would pick up her next turn, but you didn't do that either. She did the vacuuming yesterday when it was your turn. You didn't even ask her; you just didn't do it."

"I didn't mind," Frannie said quietly.

"Not the point, Frannie." Robin shook her head. "The point is that Leslie hasn't lifted a finger around here in weeks. She assumes her other responsibilities are more important than her commitment to us, and I'm sick of it. We sat around this very table and agreed we would share the chores equally, and she's the only one not participating!"

"Look Guys," Leslie said, "I have been up to my ears planning for the wedding and managing the SNA meetings, even though the directors aren't doing their part. On top of that, Coach Thomas has upped the number of workouts for the team."

Katie held up both hands. "Leslie, no one is saying you are not a busy person, but I'm as frustrated as Robin. You're the one who insisted on a schedule for us to manage the apartment, and the three of us have been doing your chores for months."

"When was the last time one of us asked *you* for a favor, Leslie?" Robin demanded. "We're here for you, but it gets harder and harder to be supportive when you take our support for granted."

"It all comes down to setting priorities," Katie said. "Counting on us isn't an effective solution. We won't always be here to do what you don't have time for."

"Being SNA president and your wedding planning doesn't make either of those things as important as graduating," Robin insisted.

"That's just mean," Leslie spat.

"But it's the truth," said Katie. "You're making bad decisions, and we've run out of ways of helping you see it. Our picking up the pieces when you've promised more than you can deliver isn't helping anyone in the long run."

"I could get the groceries one last time," Frannie offered.

"Frannie! No!" Robin growled, her chair scraping loudly as she pushed back from the table.

Frannie cringed.

"No problem, Frannie," Leslie snarled. "I'll do the grocery shopping today. I'll find time this afternoon, OK?"

"YES, OK," Robin snapped. "And don't make it sound like you're doing us a favor!"

Leslie stormed out of the kitchen, grabbed her sweatshirt, and slammed the door hard enough to rattle the windows.

Leslie had run at least a mile before she realized she'd lost track of time. She jogged another block to the chapel to check the time on the steeple clock. *"Oh shit. I'm gonna be late. Coach Thomas is already on my case and she's gonna be pissed."*

Leslie ran full out and catapulted into the gym, skidding to a stop just as Coach Thomas stepped out of her office and onto the gym floor. Leslie bent over, struggling to catch her breath.

"Okay Ladies, let's get this show on the road. Ten laps to warm up, then wind sprints... and NO laggers. I want to run new relays today. You need to be at your best for the meet this weekend."

The team began their jog around the court.

"Bleu!" Coach Thomas yelled. "Get your ass in gear. You're lagging behind like an old lady."

Leslie picked up her pace but could not manage enough speed to gain the lead position that she normally held.

"There was absolutely no reason for Robin to make a federal case of Frannie's offer to help me out. Katie, too. They know how busy I am. You'd think they'd pitch in and help! I have no clue how I'll get everything done... practice, getting ready for the SNA meeting, and now grocery shopping. Oh, and on top of everything else, Mike and I have a 2:15 appointment at the bakery."

Mike was waiting as she hurried from the gym. "Ready to go?" he asked.

"Yes, please take me away from here."

"That's an odd request, Fair Maiden," Mike said, bowing deeply, "but your wish is my command."

They hurried to his pickup and climbed into the cab. "Are you okay?" Mike asked. "What's going on?"

"I'm OK... just trying to figure out how to fit grocery shopping into this day."

"Huh?"

"You heard me. I need to get groceries so my suitemates will quit busting my chops. They know how busy I am. After our appointment at the bakery, I would have had time to prepare for the SNA meeting tonight, but when Frannie offered to shop, Robin bitched me out, so we'll have to fit in grocery shopping after the bakery."

"Yeah, yeah, yeah, I get it" Mike shrugged. "Handel's Bakery, then grocery shopping. No problem. No biggie."

"My point exactly, it didn't have to be a big deal. They all knew we were going to the bakery today. They didn't have to get all snarky."

"It's okay, Les. We'll get it done."

"Not the point Mike. They were nasty... well, mostly Robin was nasty. When Frannie offered to go shopping for me, Robin quashed it just to be mean."

Mike shrugged. "It'll be okay, Les. It's not like the grocery store is out of our way. You'll come home with groceries and all will be forgiven."

"Why do I have to be forgiven? They're the ones who got all hot and bothered this morning, not me. They know I'm busy. Why can't they cut me some slack?"

"We're here," Mike said, pulling up in front of Handel's Bakery. "Let's take care of our appointment and we'll talk about this later."

Mrs. Handel welcomed them and helped Leslie choose the wedding cake and groom's cake. "Now for the groceries," Leslie groused.

Mike shook his head but said nothing as they climbed into the truck.

In the grocery store, Mike gently took over pushing the cart after Leslie nearly collided with a woman. "Easy," Mike said when Leslie tossed a jar of peanut butter into the basket. "That poor glass jar can't defend itself."

"Sorry," Leslie spat, not sounding sorry at all.

"Lighten up, Les. They're your friends, not your enemies."

"Right," Leslie muttered. "Sure."

Mike stashed the groceries in the truck. "Maybe you could..." he began.

"You need to get me home right away."

Mike drove in silence, jaw tight, staring straight ahead.

"What?" Leslie asked.

"Not now," he said, and parked the truck.

"What's wrong?" Leslie insisted.

"I said *not now*," Mike replied tersely. He lifted the bag of groceries and strode toward the apartment.

Leslie, stunned, and hurried to catch up with him.

<h1 style="text-align:center">Chapter 28</h1>

"Come on, come on, you guys, we're gonna be late," Leslie yelled up the stairs.

"Be right down," Robin called as she hustled down the steps. "Frannie's still primping, but I think she's about done."

"I don't want to miss one minute of this conference. We've been waiting months for it."

"Patience, Leslie. The first session doesn't begin for an hour, and we shouldn't run into much traffic downtown at this time of morning."

Robin answered the knock on their door.

"Thanks for letting me bum a ride," J.R. said. "One car's better than two downtown. Missy drug me to Neiman's shopping last Saturday and it took forever to find a parking space."

"I told you we needed to leave early," Leslie said.

"Chill out, Les," Robin said. "If Frannie and Katie aren't down here in five minutes, we'll take my car and you and J.R. can go on ahead."

"Deal," said Leslie, continuing her pacing in the small living room.

"I'm ready," said Katie bouncing down the stairs. "Frannie is right behind me. She can finish up in the car."

"Hotel parking is lots easier than finding a space anywhere near Nieman Marcus," said J.R. The five student nurses stopped to admire the huge banner stretched across the Dallas Hilton Hotel lobby. *Welcome Texas Nurses Association.*

"WOW!" Frannie exclaimed. "*That's* a welcome done up right."

Signage along the way led them to the banquet hall and the tables where participants were registering. They joined a line and waved to other Crestmont classmates.

Robin watched the Dean and Ms. Reynolds move along the long lines, stopping to visit with their Crestmont students. "Wonder what's up with that," Robin mused, nodding towards the faculty.

Leslie shrugged.

"What?" Frannie looked up from her conversation with a student behind them in line.

"Dean Nunley and Ms. Reynolds are on their way over here," Leslie whispered.

"Good morning, and welcome to the TNA and the Texas Student Nurses Association conference," Dean Nunley said. "Once you've registered, please join the faculty and other Crestmont students in the front of the auditorium. We're holding several rows of seats on the right, facing the podium. Following the opening session, there will be multiple breakout sessions. Attend the ones that interest you and be sure to engage with the speakers. Ask questions and interact with the other attendees to learn from them as well."

Ms. Reynolds added, "Don't miss the delegate sessions. You'll see how a large nursing organization manages discussion, debate, and voting. Seating will be limited so get there early."

"Yes, ma'am," chorused the students clustered around the *Nurseketeers.*

"I've been looking forward to this all year." Leslie said.

The *Nurseketeers* registered and pinned on their name badges. They collected a myriad of handouts and found the seats saved for the Crestmont students and faculty.

During her opening remarks, the TNA President asked the students to stand. Leslie stood proudly with her peers and marveled at the large number of students from across the state attending the meeting.

Walking to their first breakout session, Leslie asked, "Did you see that keynote speaker?"

"Duh, we were right there with you." Robin snickered.

"I mean," Leslie said, "I don't think she looked at her notes once. She spoke as if everything she had to say was in her head, and I swear there was one point where I thought she was talking to me personally."

Katie laughed. "She probably was since she was talking about being organized and not dictating to others."

"That's not what I meant." Leslie shouldered her roommate. "Take lots of notes so we can share," she added as they separated to go to different sessions.

"Didn't you hear that speaker just say *not* to dictate to others?" Katie said.

Leslie flushed.

J.R. was the first to reach the Exhibit Hall where tables were set up for lunch. "Man am I ever glad y'all showed up," he said, as the girls filled the seats on either side of him. "I thought I'd have to fight off the hordes to save these seats for you. How did your morning go?"

"Thanks for saving seats," Katie said.

Leslie began. "In one of the sessions, I sat next to an OR nurse from Presby. She's a member of AORN, the professional organization for OR nurses. She said they welcome students and if I want to attend a meeting, I can sit with her. They meet on the second Tuesday of every month."

"Leslie, how can you even *think* about fitting in one more commitment?" Katie asked. "You already have more on your plate than you can manage. If I recall, you were complaining about not getting enough running time in and the coach being all over you about losing your edge. You're forgetting your promise to set priorities and do a better job of managing your commitments. I thought you had a handle on this, but you seem to have a short memory."

Even Frannie was nodding her head in agreement.

"Think about it, Les," Robin said. "Nothing changes unless *you* change it, and it's beginning to look like you're not as interested in making that happen as you said you were."

"But" Leslie stammered.

"No *buts,* Les. Talk is cheap, especially when what you say doesn't jive with what you do. Action speaks louder than words."

Chapter 29

Leslie swiped at the bloody poop, trying not to gag as she cleaned Mr. Brimmer's butt for the fourth time in an hour. *"How can he get this crap all down his leg while he is on a bedpan?"*

The small space in the ICU was hardly a room. It was a cubical with a curtain, closed now to protect Mr. Brimmer's privacy. The confined enclosure captured and intensified the unpleasant smell of bloody human excrement.

"I'm so sorry, Leslie," Mr. Brimmer said.

"No worries, Mr. Brimmer," Leslie replied. "I don't mind at all. Taking care of you is why I'm here."

"How long before they'll come to take me to surgery?" asked Mr. Brimmer, barely above a whisper. "They *have* to find what's bleeding. I can't take much more of this."

"It will be a while longer, Mr. Brimmer. Try to get some sleep. I'll be right here with you, monitoring your vital signs."

Leslie kept an eye on the monitors beeping steadily on the shelf behind Mr. Brimmer's bed. She made sure his IV did not run dry. She had just drawn blood for another round of tests to check his hemoglobin and hematocrit and checked his vitals every 15 minutes. *"How in the world can the poor man get any rest with the noise, the constant pooping, and me trying to keep him clean one bowel movement after another? I feel like the boy with his finger in the dike."*

Ms. Rocksmith entered the cubicle with an IV bag of blood. "Will you hang this?" she asked.

When Leslie reached for the bag, she said, "First, walk me through the protocol for hanging blood."

Leslie had been looking forward to her first opportunity to hang blood. She rattled off the steps, including checking Mr. Brimmer's vital signs before and after hanging the blood. Afterward, she would check to be sure there was no rash, shortness of breath, nausea, or vomiting in response to the transfusion. She wouldn't be able to check for bleeding because Mr. Brimmer bled every time he pooped. She reached for the bag to hang the blood.

Ms. Rocksmith said, "Hold on," touching Leslie on the wrist. "Oh no," Leslie's face turned ashen. "I forgot to check the order against the information on the bag and on Mr. Brimmer's ID bracelet."

Ms. Rocksmith simply nodded, handed Leslie Mr. Brimmer's chart, and walked out of the room.

"Why on earth did I have to forget such an important step? And poor Mr. Brimmer is right here listening to how inept I am." Leslie shut her eyes briefly, took a deep breath, then hung the blood and watched the monitors. Mr. Brimmer fell asleep, and after 15 minutes, she took his vital signs, interrupting his sleep yet again. She breathed normally for the first time in what seemed like hours since Ms. Rocksmith had left. *"I hope he does okay,"* Leslie thought when the orderly wheeled Mr. Brimmer out of the cubicle a little while later. *"At least he'll get a little rest under anesthesia. Please Lord, let him be okay when he comes back up here."*

Ms. Rocksmith helped Leslie clean up the cubicle and change Mr. Brimmer's bed linen. They found a hospital-sized can of disinfectant and sprayed enough to mask the odor of excrement.

"I'm so ready for something other than this shit patrol, and the constant smell of poop and disinfectant," she thought as she walked to the desk with Ms. Rocksmith.

"Leslie, hurry over to that cubicle," Ms. Rocksmith pointed urgently. "It looks like the patient has coded."

Without having to be told twice, Leslie hustled to the cubicle, intending to keep out of the way and observe. Two nurses were with the patient, one giving compressions and the other managing his airway with an ambu bag. Gathering her courage, she stepped up and offered, "I'll take over the compressions if you'd like."

"Thank you." said the nurse with a sigh of relief. They traded places, careful to avoid an interruption in the rhythm of compressions.

"This has to be the most exciting experience I've had since starting nursing school!"

Just as Dr. Paulson arrived, Trina, the nurse whom Leslie had relieved, pulled the crash cart into the cubicle. Dr. Paulson rapidly assessed the situation and began barking orders. Trina prepared each drug he requested and placed it in his hand each time he reached out without taking his eyes off the patient.

Leslie continued compressions until a resident relieved her. The patient had not responded after twenty minutes of compressions and a boatload of IV medication. Dr. Paulson called the code. Leslie went to the break room near tears. She was devastated at the death of the patient and, at the same time, exhilarated by the experience and exhausted from delivering compressions. She sat alone wishing that one of the *Nurseketeers* were there so she could share everything that had just happened.

"I needed that," Leslie gasped as she collapsed onto the park bench where Mike was waiting. "Running is the best way to work out the kinks and clear my head, and this week has been a bear. Robin's being unreasonable and Katie and Frannie won't stand up to her. I know they're on my side, but..."

"Les," Mike interrupted, "now would be a good time for us to talk."

"About what?" she asked.

"About Monday. When someone disagrees with you, it doesn't mean they're wrong."

Leslie's jaw dropped. "What?" She stood to face him. "Are you telling me that *they're* right and *I'm* wrong? You've gotta be kidding."

"I'm telling you that it's not a matter of right or wrong. You're missing the point."

"How..."

"Just listen, for a change. It's not a game of win or lose. You're so used to thinking you're in charge that you don't listen."

"That's not true. You don't understand..."

"My point exactly. I've asked you to listen and you're arguing before you've heard anything I have to say. I love you, Leslie, but I'm your fiancé, not your lackey."

"*Lackey*. That's the kind of nasty thing Robin has been saying. What do you even mean by that?"

"A *lackey* is someone who does your bidding"

"I know what the damn word means, but why would you and Robin say something like that about *me*?"

"Think about it, Leslie. You act like you're in charge all the time. When you say something, you expect people will accept it, no questions asked."

"You're wrong, Mike. When did I ever boss you around?"

"Really?" Mike raised an eyebrow. "When have you ever asked me where I want to eat?"

"I...," Leslie stammered.

"The answer is *never*," Mike continued evenly, ignoring her. "If I tell you what I want to eat, you tell me why we're going to have something else. You don't make suggestions; you make declarations. What we eat doesn't matter to me, but I do care about the communication process."

Leslie opened her mouth, but Mike continued, "Take the groom's cake, for instance. How important is the groom's cake? Who would actually care if we had one or if we didn't? But, when

I said I didn't want one, you said we had to have one. You didn't explain or negotiate, you made a proclamation. To be honest, I could care less about the cake, and I would have been happy to agree if you'd *asked me* instead of *telling* me."

"I did ask you," Leslie insisted.

"I beg your pardon, but the conversation was short enough for me to remember it quite clearly. We chose the wedding cake, and you said we needed to choose the groom's cake. Do you remember what I said?"

Leslie paused, frowning, then said, "You said, *that one will do.*"

"That's true, but what you said right before that was, *Mike, we have to have a groom's cake. I like this one.* That was a proclamation and *your* decision, not *our* decision. I'd already told you I didn't want one. The bakery shop wasn't the place to have an argument, so I let it go."

"Why didn't you say something afterwards?"

"If you remember, I started to, but you interrupted me to tell me that we had to hurry to the grocery store and then you had to prepare for your SNA meeting. This is the first time I've seen you since then."

"Are you saying you want to make all the decisions?"

"If that's what you heard, you weren't listening. I can understand why your suitemates get upset. What I can't understand is how you can think you're always right and everyone else is always wrong."

"That's just *mean*, Mike Hampton."

"Leslie," Mike said and stood up. "Two people about to get married should be able to communicate. You and I are not communicating. I'm telling you something that's important to me and you insist that I'm wrong. End of story. No discussion. No communication. No negotiation. You're right; I'm wrong. That's not a situation I can live with."

"We DO communicate," Leslie began.

Mike shook his head. "Just think about what *communicating* means. Then, we can talk about it."

Mike stood, zipped his jacket, and walked off.

Chapter 30

"Enough already," said Robin, grabbing Leslie's arm as they hurried from their Wednesday afternoon class. "You've avoided us like the plague for days. It's time to woman up and settle this."

Katie and Frannie caught up with the pair and the *Nurseketeers* walked in silence to the apartment.

Robin began, "I should start by saying I'm sorry I yelled at you, but, truthfully, I'm not sorry at all. We're trying to help you, and you've been fighting us every step of the way."

"Yelling is not helping me," Leslie spat. "Helping me would be understanding how busy I am and not getting upset when Frannie offers to help with my chores. What's wrong with Frannie's doing the grocery shopping if she has the time and I don't? I pay my share."

"We know how busy you are, but we're busy, too," Katie said, "and Frannie's time is as valuable as yours. Her free time would be much better spent studying than running your errands. Taking advantage of Franny's good nature is abusing a friendship."

"What we've been saying all along," Robin continued, "is that you're not managing your responsibilities well, not even as well as you did when we were freshman. You led us in the March Against Violence and worked with an awesome team of leaders and volunteers. Now you're so busy that you can't get everything done without relying on others to pick up the pieces. That's being *too busy*. It's time you realized that."

"What are you talking about?" Leslie demanded. "If it weren't for me, SNA would get absolutely nothing done."

"That's where you're dead wrong," Robin insisted, and Katie nodded. "The SNA is not the work of one person. Our chapter has the talent pool to do everything that needs doing. What they don't have is leadership."

"WHAT?" cried Leslie. "I can't believe you said that!"

"You *think* you're leading," Katie said, "but that's not what you're doing. Leadership isn't telling people what to do, and it's definitely not doing the work yourself because you don't trust the members. Leaders do three things well: communicate, delegate, and negotiate to get quality outcomes. You're doing none of those."

"Barking orders doesn't count as delegating; that's dictating," Robin said.

"And thinking no one can do the job but you isn't leading," Katie added.

"You have to admit they're right," Frannie said softly, "I know it hurts, but they're right."

"You assume people know what you expect," Katie said, "and then you're disappointed or angry when they don't come through for you."

"That's not true. Last summer I contacted everyone about the orientation, and three people volunteered to participate until I called them and twisted their arms."

"That's *not* what happened and you know it," Robin insisted. "When you first contacted them about the project, did you tell them specifically what you needed from them?"

"Wasn't that obvious?"

"Perhaps it was obvious to you, but if you want others to see a situation as you see it, you have to be clear about your expectations. People aren't mind-readers, Les. You just assumed they would be as excited about the project as you were... but they weren't because they didn't know enough to be engaged. You said so yourself after you talked with Ms. Reynolds. Then, when you called them, you didn't have to twist their arms. Once you gave them the information they needed and they knew what the project was all about, they were happy to step up and volunteer."

"I would have thought if you joined SNA, you'd be excited about SNA initiatives."

"People join organizations for lots of reasons," Robin said.

"I joined just because you guys did," Frannie admitted.

"As a leader," Katie said, "you need to facilitate the success of a project. You have to help people recognize its value instead of assuming that everyone thinks and feels like you do. Bringing people together on a project is why a group needs a leader. You've been a good leader before; we want to see *that* Leslie back."

"One more thing," Robin said. "A leader is a facilitator, not a one woman show. Leaders motivate and encourage others to participate. They give direction and provide resources. Of course, oversight is important so you can make course corrections in time for the project to be successful, but oversight isn't the same as micromanaging."

Leslie protested. "I know all that."

"Actually," Robin said, "you know *about* all that. If you *knew* it, you'd be doing it and we wouldn't be having this conversation... again."

"You'd be a lot less stressed if you put your knowledge into practice," Katie added, "and I think you'd actually enjoy being SNA's president."

"I do enjoy being president," Leslie said.

"You like the *idea* of being president," Robin countered, "but you complain all the time... about the time it takes to get ready for meetings, about how frustrating it is that no one else is as motivated as you are, about how you have to do everything yourself. That doesn't sound like enjoyment to me."

"You guys just don't get it!" Leslie barked. "If you did, you'd help me get my job done."

"Leslie, you're the one who doesn't get it," Katie said firmly. "We are supporting you, caring about you, and doing things for you that you should be doing yourself. We're trying to get you to see where you're going wrong, but we can't fix it. Only you can do that."

"I don't need fixing!" Leslie insisted. "I need your support." She grabbed her jacket and left, slamming the apartment door behind her.

The sound of the ball reverberated throughout the empty gym as Leslie dribbled toward the far basket. She launched the ball.

"Dammit," she screamed as the ball bounced off the rim.

Leslie grabbed the ball and backed up.

"Ball," she said, glaring at the round, inert object in her hands, "don't let me down." She took another shot.

She groaned, grabbing the ball as it bounced off the backboard. "C'mon, you traitor. You can do better than that!"

She turned, dribbled, pivoted, and launched another shot.

Another miss.

"You, toooo, Ball?" she moaned. "Everyone's turned against me, and now I can't even score a basket. I thought I could at least count on you."

Leslie slumped to the court floor, drenched in sweat, her face a mirror of confusion and frustration. She spun the ball absently between her legs.

"Daddy always says that when things don't make sense, you're probably missing something." She lifted the ball to eye level. "So, tell me, Ball, what am I missing? My friends think I'm bossy when I'm just trying to get the job done. Why are they so unwilling to help me out? Frannie has the time to do the grocery shopping and I don't, so why isn't it okay for her to help me? It's not like I don't pay my fair share. None of this makes sense."

She shook the ball. "Are you listening to me? Nobody else does."

Leslie sat in silence, shoulders drooping, the ball between her outstretched legs. "What is it, Daddy? What is it that I'm missing?" she wailed, her pleading cry echoing off the walls of the vast empty gym.

Leslie stared at the ball, wishing it would speak up and solve the mystery. She could hear her father's counsel. *"If you're missing something, change your perspective. Look at the situation through someone else's eyes."*

"Katie and Robin are saying the same thing. Mike, too. What are they seeing that I'm not? Mike said he'd like to choose where we eat once in a while. I'll admit that I usually do make that decision, but he can always speak up if he doesn't like what I pick."

Leslie sat up straighter. "But… sometimes he does."

She shook her head. "Mike's right. When he speaks up, I don't listen. I *hear* him, but I *don't listen.*"

Leslie shook her head. "And the girls… they keep telling me I'm overextending myself. I manage to get it all done, so it *seems* like they're wrong; but, could I do it without their help?" She glared at the ball. "Probably not."

Leslie sat, breathing deeply. "I've been fighting them all along because I didn't want them to be right."

She stood and bounced the ball, listening intently to the echoing thuds. She dribbled toward the basket and sent the ball cleanly through the hoop.

"Everything I'm involved in is important to me, but they're not arguing about that. They're saying that if I don't graduate, nothing else matters. That's obvious, so why do they keep harping on it?" She took a deep breath, "Because it's true!"

She took another shot at the basket, and again the ball swished through the hoop.

"They're telling me that, above all, I have to graduate. That's what I need to care about most. I have to study, pass my tests, and keep my scholarship. It's up to me to make that happen, and I'm letting everything else get in my way."

One more toss; one more clean basket.

Leslie grabbed the ball. "You stay here." Leslie tossed the ball into a large bin of basketballs. "I hope it's not too late to tell them I get it."

Leslie took the library stairs two steps at a time. On the fourth floor she peered into each glassed-in carrel until she found her suitemates. She pushed through the door. "I've got something to tell you," she said.

"Shhhh," said Robin. "It's a *library*, for heaven's sake!"

"This is important," Leslie insisted in a loud whisper. "I think I get it, and if I'm right, I might have to apologize."

"Interesting," Robin said. "I'm not sure what you're talking about, but I like the sound of an apology."

"All this time I've been thinking that you were being mean, but it's because I didn't want to hear what you were saying. I didn't want to admit to myself that you were right, that I'm over-committed. I get it now. I promise to work on setting priorities and delegating. I hope it's not too late to say *I'm sorry*."

Smiles slowly spread across Katie's and Robin's faces. Frannie chirped, "I don't get it. I don't mind helping you."

"Of course you don't get it, Twit," said Robin, "because you're a sweetheart. It wouldn't occur to you to be mean, even for a good reason."

Robin laughed at Frannie's confused expression. "That was a compliment, Frannie. You're a twit, but a good twit."

Frannie smiled, but her expression mirrored clearly her confusion about what was going on.

"I appreciate your help, Frannie. I truly do," said Leslie, "but Robin's right about my needing to do my fair share. It's my problem to figure out when I have more to do than I can get done on my own. I have to be intentional when I make commitments. I have to learn when to say *no.*"

Robin squeezed Leslie's shoulder. "That's the first leader-like statement you've made in a long time. I know you mean it, but just saying it doesn't make it so. You have to act on it."

"I know. And I need to thank the three of you for your help and for sticking by me. I know that if you hadn't, nothing would change, and I'd be in more trouble than I am now."

Katie stood to give Leslie a hug. "We don't mind helping you, Les, but we *do* need you to ask for help, not just expect it."

"Also, please remember," Robin added, "that your way of doing something isn't the only way. Be okay with letting folks approach tasks on their own, Be okay with them as long as they get the job done. It isn't necessarily about the method; it's about the results. Sometimes it's about letting go."

"I understand that, too. I promise to try," said Leslie.

"And we promise to make sure you do." Robin smiled.

"*Please be here*, Mike," Leslie whispered as she knocked on the door to the guys' apartment. "*I need you to be here.*"

J.R. opened the door, then grinned. "Hey Mike," he called over his shoulder. "There's a tall, good-looking girl in our doorway. You should come check her out."

"Can we go for a run?" Leslie asked softly when Mike appeared, unsmiling, beside J.R.

"You *ready* for a run?" Mike asked pointedly.

Leslie nodded, certain that she knew what he meant. "I'm ready," she said softly.

Mike followed her out of the apartment building.

"Before we run," Leslie said, "I need to apologize. I'm sorry that it took me so long to catch on. Thank you for being more patient with me than I deserved. I've never had a relationship like ours before. I realize now that there has to be give and take. No one's in charge, or at least no one's in charge all the time."

"That's a step in the right direction." Mike smiled for the first time.

"In Abita Springs," Leslie continued, "I was the most adult person my age, the eldest of my siblings, and the leader among my friends. I've always been in charge. It wasn't until I came to Crestmont that I met people I haven't known my whole life."

Mike nodded, and Leslie continued. "Once I got here, I realized how big my world could be, and I wanted to be part of all of it. For instance, from my first SNA meeting, I knew I wanted to be the SNA president. Then I fell in love with the OR and I wanted to do that, too. There's so much I care about that It's hard to set limits."

"Recognizing a problem is the first step in solving it," Mike said. "Setting limits is a good place to start."

"It all feels so important to me, I hate to give any of it up."

"Giving it up might not be necessary," Mike assured her. "Honing your leadership skills would be a good start."

"Like delegating," Leslie said.

"Right… and negotiating. Delegating isn't the same as ordering people around. Everyone in SNA is volunteering their time. Delegating is telling someone what needs to be done, then providing enough information and resources to motivate them to accept the job, then enough support for them to complete it successfully. You've already seen that when you tell people what they need to know, they're willing to accept your assignments."

"Like the orientation," Leslie said. "They didn't volunteer until they knew enough to believe the project was important."

"There's even a higher priority than delegating and negotiating," Mike suggested.

"What is that?" she asked.

"Setting priorities. Only you can decide what's a *must* and what's a *would be nice*. A priority is what matters most *right now?*"

"I see your point. All of you have said *if you don't graduate, none of this will matter,* and I couldn't accept that until now. I just hope it isn't too late."

"So, now that we're on the same page, how would you prioritize your commitments?"

"Our wedding, making sure I graduate, not disappointing the girls, placing in the track meet finals next month, and SNA" she paused. "What else?"

"I'm honored that you put our wedding first on your list, but it should actually be last. If we can't pull off getting married in May, we'll get married later. It would be disappointing but not life changing. Not graduating would be life changing."

"Oh" Leslie said softly. "I get it. I do. Let me start over. Graduation has to be number one, so studying comes first. I need to stay on top of my classes. The final track meets would be next because I'm here on an athletic scholarship and I owe Crestmont my best performance. That would make Coach Thomas happy, and I need my scholarship to stay in school."

Mike nodded, smiling. "Now you're thinkin'."

"The girls would have to be next because I want our friendship to last a lifetime, which won't happen if I keep disappointing them. The SNA would be last because if I weren't president, someone else would get the job done. Once I graduate, being SNA president won't mean all that much. The experience it's already given me will help me to be active in organizations like AORN."

"You've got it, Les." Mike gave her a fist bump, "But..." he said, "recognizing what you need to do and making plans won't solve the problem. You have to stick to the plan; you have to *make it happen*."

Leslie reached up to hug him. "I'll do it, Mike. I promise."

"There's one more thing," Mike said. "Communication is a two-way process. Listening is just as important as talking, and sometimes more so. You have to learn to *listen.*"

"I'll do that, too. I promise."

"There's hope for you yet, Girl," Mike said. He pulled her close, and they never made it for the run.

The following Saturday, Katie, Robin, and Frannie piled into Katie's car, *Camel Piss.* Missy slid into Nellie's back seat behind

Leslie and J.R. climbed behind Mike who sat behind the wheel. "Open all the windows," Leslie said. "Let's enjoy the first warm, sunny day of spring all the way to Lake Texoma."

"Hope we have time to do this again later in the spring," said J.R. "A dip in the lake would be great before hotdogs and s'mores, but it'll be April before the water's warm enough."

"We'll have to settle for football and sandcastles this trip," Leslie said. "We just won't be able to wash the sand out of our pants."

"How much further, Mike?" asked Missy impatiently.

"Thirty or forty minutes according to Katie's estimate," he answered, checking his watch. "We'll be playing beach volleyball before you know it."

"I can't wait," Leslie said. "It's going to be a perfect day."

In the midst of their chatter, Mike called out, "We're *here*," and pulled into the parking space beside Katie in Eisenhower State Park on the southern shore of Lake Texoma. They piled out of the car and opened the trunk.

Katie said, "It's just a short walk to the beach. Shall we eat here on the picnic tables first, or walk straight to the beach?"

"Let's eat first," suggested Robin. "We won't have to drag all the picnic stuff so far."

"Not to mention," Leslie added, "that sandwiches taste better without sand."

J.R. handed one picnic basket from the trunk to Frannie and the second to Robin. Leslie reached for the bag of supplies and handed it to Katie. "I'll help Mike with the cooler," J.R. said as Mike manhandled a large Coleman cooler out of Katie's trunk and set it on the ground.

"Grab one handle and I'll get the other," said Mike. "We'll make quick work of this."

The *Nurseketeers* and Missy spread the red checked vinyl cloth over the nearest picnic table and set out seven plates with a napkin beside each. "PB&J sandwiches are on this plate and bologna and cheese on that one. Mike, the two sandwiches with toothpicks sticking in them are PB and honey for you."

"Aw, that's sweet," said Frannie.

When they'd finished eating and had cleaned up behind them, J.R. said, "I'll take the cooler to the beach. It's light enough for one now that half the drinks are gone. Someone get the snacks and the cookies and let's go. I'm itching for a game of beach volleyball."

They played for hours, took breaks to dip their toes into the cold lake water. When the sun went down and the warmth of the day had disappeared, the girls put on every extra piece of clothing they'd brought with them.

"Frannie, I didn't know you even owned a pair of sweats," Leslie said.

"Of course, I do," Frannie declared, as she pulled a bright pink sweatsuit from a psychedelic beach bag. "I just don't wear them on campus. Doesn't do much for showing off the bits, you know!" She wiggled her bust at the *Nurseketeers*.

Giggling, the girls joined the guys around the campfire they'd built, huddling as close to the flames as possible. "S'mores all around," Robin said, as Mike and J.R. passed around the sticks with dripping, toasted marshmallows.

"Time for stories," Missy said, "but nothing too scary. Ghosts and goblins keep me awake at night, and I need my beauty sleep."

"Honey, you are a beauty whether you sleep or not," J.R. said, snugging her in closer to him.

"Leslie, you go first. You tell great stories," Katie said.

"OK. This is the *Bleu Legend of the Cake Batter*. Once upon a time," she began, and Frannie interrupted.

"Wait a minute. I thought this was going to be a true story. *Once upon a time* is for fairy tales."

"Okay, okay," Leslie conceded, starting again. "When I was about 12, our young family was preparing for a weekend visit to my mom's sister and her family in New Orleans. Back then, we didn't travel out of town much, so we kids were all excited. Suzanne went with Daddy to the gas station to fill up the car and check the air in the tires. The gas station attendant told Daddy that the tires looked worn and he needed to get new ones.

"Daddy eyed him skeptically and studied the tires. He walked around the car and kicked each one. He scrunched up his nose, then said, *"I see your point, but they still have some life in them,"* and he and Suzanne came home to get the rest of us.

"We pulled out of the driveway on the hottest day in August. Mom had covered the seats with a quilt to keep our legs from burning and from sliding in our own sweat on the plastic.

"About midway to New Orleans, a tire went flat and we stood on the side of the highway with cars whizzing by while Daddy and Jaq worked to get the jack set under the car. Mom was pregnant with Gabrielle and her back was hurting. Francis was crying in her arms. Some things never change. He's still a crybaby.

"When Suzanne announced, *"Daddy, that gas man told you the tires were bad,"* Mom had a right healthy hissy fit, yelling at Daddy even though he was still under the car. *"You knew all along about the tires? You put our family at risk when this could have all been avoided!"*

"From under the car, Daddy mumbled, *"We didn't have the money."*

"You should have told me, Mac," Mom said. *"We could have worked something out."*

"I can visualize every word from your mom." Mike laughed.

"When Daddy emerged," Leslie continued. "Still on his knees, eye-to-eye with Suzanne, he said ever so softly through gritted teeth, *"Your mother never throws out half of the cake batter when she's baking, does she?"*

When Suzanne shook her head, he replied, *"Well, neither do I."*

"Wow, that's a great story, Les," said Katie. That could have been my dad too. He worked hard to give our family a good home and opportunities, but he still reminds us frequently to *waste not, want not.*"

"We didn't truly understand his message at the time," Leslie said. "But, as we got a little older it's come to mean a great deal to us. We've learned to *value each moment, each experience, each relationship to the fullest.* Every now and then one of us will say *"You got the cake batter out of that,"* and we all know exactly what that means. Now you do, too."

Chapter 31

On Monday morning, the girls dressed for their Management and Leadership class in their best attire, with nylons and heels.

"Man, I hate dressing up like this," complained Leslie. "What's wrong with tennis shoes, jeans, and a t-shirt? We're just practicing our interviews. We should wait for the real thing to dress up."

"I'm with you," Robin agreed.

"This is *fun*," Frannie insisted. "I love dressing up."

"I'm with Leslie on this one," said Katie. "This is my second and last pair of pantyhose. I put my thumb right through the first pair trying to get into them while I was still half asleep."

They hurried to class and took their seats. Frannie tugged at her short, short skirt.

Leslie leaned over and whispered to J.R., "Hey, Man, you clean up well. Sports jacket, wide white tie… I'm impressed."

"Thanks, but this collar is about to choke me to death. I'm a t-shirt and shorts guy."

Ms. Harris called the class to order and instructed them to count off in threes. She handed a pink sheet to one person in each group and a blue sheet to a second. "Each of you should have your resume with you. Those of you with pink sheets are employers and those with blue sheets are observers. The third person in each group is the interviewee."

Leslie was the interviewee in her group. "*This should be a piece of cake since I interviewed at Parkland last summer and got the job.*" Leslie knocked on an imaginary door.

Kathy, the employer, said, "Come in," and Joyce, the observer, recorded that Kathy did not stand to greet Leslie. Joyce put a plus in the interviewee column when Leslie extended her hand to Kathy. Kathy looked questioningly at Leslie's extended hand and finally grasped her fingers.

"*Good grief, Girl, get a grip! Daddy taught me how to shake hands properly when I was 12.*" Leslie smiled at the memory of her father instructing, "*Offer your hand and they will shake it. Interlock thumbs, and then squeeze with a firm grip, neither limp nor crushing. The woman should initiate the handshake as, out of courtesy, the man should not.*" Leslie supposed that not everyone knew the drill. The only experience they'd had so far was in their freshman year when they'd visited the university president. When he came out from behind his desk, he shook hands with each of them and offered them seats before any of them even thought to extend a hand.

Kathy began the interview. "Can you tell me a little about yourself?"

Leslie responded directly in a strong, clear voice, and after answering Kathy's final question, she stood, remembered to thank Kathy for taking time with her, and pretended to leave.

Joyce read her critique of the interview and Leslie shared her father's instructions on shaking hands. Ms. Harris was impressed and had each group practice shaking hands. Joyce pointed out that Leslie left the interview without offering to leave her resume, nor did Kathy ask for it.

Leslie slapped her forehead, "I can't believe I missed that. It took me forever to type the thing, and I didn't even use it."

"Also," Joyce continued, "you could have asked Kathy when you might hear back from her."

The small groups rotated roles giving everyone an opportunity to practice each position. When the final debriefing was complete, Ms. Harris collected everyone's resume. "You can see from this activity that the interview process is about both what the employer needs and what the candidate can offer."

The students nodded.

"My general comment about attire is that everyone has made the effort to dress for success today. However, simply because a style is popular does not make it an appropriate choice for an interview where your intent is to make an excellent first impression as a professional. You don't want your attire to be the memorable component of the interview. You want your potential employer to remember what you have to offer their patients and the facility. For instance, Frannie, while your skirt is fashionable, it is a bit too short for professional attire. J.R., your sport coat and tie are classy, but for a professional look you might want to go with dark slacks and dark shoes instead of white. You should all keep in mind that you are striving for an understated and professional appearance."

Frannie appeared perplexed. Robin grabbed her hand when she started to ask a question. "It's okay, Frannie. I'll explain after class."

"During this next month, each of you will choose a professional nursing organization meeting to attend. I have posted a list of organizations on the bulletin board with the date, time, and location of their monthly meeting. Following your meeting, you'll submit the answers to the questions on this sheet. Please take one as you leave."

The *Nurseketeers* joined the crowd at the bulletin board. "There it is," Leslie pointed with a satisfied smile. "AORN, the Association of Operating Room Nurses. That's the meeting I'll attend."

Leslie had written the second Tuesday of March at 6pm at Presbyterian Hospital in her calendar right after class and had been counting the days. She wore a light gray pant suit with knee high hose and low black heels for the Dallas AORN chapter meeting. The ensemble fit Mrs. Harris' description of professional attire and it accentuated her 5'9" height.

Robin whistled from her perch in the living room. "You're gonna wow those OR nurses tonight, Les. You get an A+ for the conservative look."

"Thanks, but I'm not trying to wow anyone. I want to make a good impression, and I want to learn all about the organization. I gassed Nelly up earlier so I wouldn't smell like a gas station. Gotta run, or I'll be late."

"Chill, Girlfriend. This is a nursing meeting, not an audience with the queen. You'll be fine."

Leslie had allowed extra time because she'd never been to Presbyterian Hospital and was concerned that she might get lost. She arrived without incident and wandered the halls of the hospital looking for the meeting. She came upon a series of 8x10 hand-lettered signs with arrows pointing the way to the AORN meeting. Leslie joined one of the lines of nurses waiting to sign in at the registration table. She looked for the nurse she'd met at the TNA meeting and was disappointed not to find her.

"You're new," said the woman when Leslie reached the head of the line. "Welcome. We're pleased you could join us tonight."

"I'm Leslie Bleu. I'm a senior at Crestmont and I'm hoping to work in the OR when I graduate."

"I'm Delores," said a woman signing in beside Leslie. "We love to have students at our meetings. Jane," she said to the woman in line behind Leslie, "would you mind introducing Leslie around? Make her feel welcome."

Jane smiled at Leslie and led her into the auditorium. "It's always nice to have students join us. Delores is our Vice President this year. One of her responsibilities is arranging a continuing education presentation for each meeting." They made their way through the large room, stopping frequently for Jane to introduce Leslie to colleagues, all of whom welcomed her with enthusiasm.

"New nurses are the lifeblood of our profession," Jane said as they slipped into two empty seats at a table at the front of the room. "The OR is a wonderful specialty and the nurses who choose it have a lot in common. Most of us are detail-oriented and love a challenge. No matter how many times you've scrubbed or circulated for a procedure, you have to stay alert because every patient is unique which makes every operation different. You never know what might happen."

"The good nurses make it look effortless," Leslie commented. "I can't wait to feel that way myself. How long does it take?"

Jane chuckled. "There's no real answer to that, Leslie. The fewer the types of procedures offered in your hospital, the quicker you can master them; however, in places like Presby or Parkland, where you said you've done your clinical rotations, it can take longer to gain confidence simply because of the variety of procedures. Don't be impatient. Enjoy every day for what it has to offer you. Eventually you'll decide what clinical specialty you like best."

"What's your specialty?" Leslie asked.

"Plastic and reconstructive surgery," Jane answered without hesitation. "I thought I'd choose heart surgery when I first started, but I'm fascinated by how the plastic surgeons can fix things that go wrong. They're like artists or sculptors, repairing defects and making new body parts with grafts and flaps. Last week Dr. Andrews made a thumb for a schoolboy who was born without one. He repositioned his index finger so he'll be able to grasp things and control them. It's amazing what a difference having a thumb makes."

The president tapped the microphone and called the meeting to order. "Good evening, everyone," she began. "We have a student with us this evening. Leslie Bleu is a senior from Crestmont. Welcome, Leslie. We hope you will join our chapter as soon as you graduate." Leslie was welcomed with a round of applause.

Delores approached the podium. "I like to introduce our speaker for this evening. Her presentation will be on the role of a nurse practitioner working as a first assistant in the OR."

Leslie was in heaven. "I can't wait to graduate," she whispered to Jane.

On Friday evening, the girls packed for Spring Break. "Can you believe that this is my last trip to Abita Springs as a single woman," Leslie said.

"Don't forget a single detail from the shower," Frannie instructed. "Knowing your mom, it's going to be the event of the year in Abita Springs,"

"She's been working hard on it," Leslie agreed. "I'm kinda surprised how much I'm looking forward to it."

"Take pictures," said Katie.

"Will do," said Leslie. "I'm off to meet Mike, but I won't be back late. If we leave by 8:30 tomorrow morning, Frannie, I'll have you at Love Field in plenty of time for your flight."

"You won't have to go far," said Robin, opening the door to admit Mike. "His ears musta been burning."

"Anyone wanna join us for dinner?" Mike asked.

"You two don't need company on your last night together for a whole week," Katie laughed.

One by one, the *Nurseketeers* returned from Spring Break, tossed their suitcases onto their beds, and gathered in the living room to share stories from their vacation.

"Unpacking can wait," Robin announced. "I want to hear all about Leslie's shower, unless someone else has something earth-shattering to share."

"Not me," Katie said. "Other than enjoying my time with John and my family, I have nothing to report."

"Me either," said Frannie, "except that spending time with Nana and Petey made it hard to leave."

"So, you're up, Mrs. Mike Hampton-to-be. Tell us all about it," Robin said.

"My mother truly outdid herself," Leslie began. "The shower was great fun. It was actually two showers in one, with me and my friends in the family room and Mom and her friends in the living room. That was a stroke of genius. My friends and I had the best time catching up, and the ladies enjoyed their peace and quiet. Everyone enjoyed Mom's fantastic spread, of course."

"Sounds like giving you the shower was just what your mom needed," said Katie.

"I agree," Leslie said. "We didn't have a cross word the whole vacation."

"Details," Robin demanded.

"Well, the sideboard in the dining room was covered with an assortment of finger food for lunch… little sandwiches, wraps, barbecued meatballs on toothpicks, and cut vegetables with four different dips. The desserts and the coffee and tea service filled the dining room table. Instead of a cake that would have been difficult to serve, Mom had cookies and pastries, fudge, and candies. My friends told her the food was too lovely to eat, but that didn't stop them."

"You promised you'd take pictures" Frannie reminded her.

"Dad took pictures of the dining room before anyone arrived. We didn't have a designated photographer for the event, but Suzanne did a great job of making sure there were plenty of photos. Mom will send me copies once she gets them developed."

"I hope they come soon," Katie said.

"Everything Mom made was a work of art and it was all beautifully displayed on her good china and silver. Lorraine brought flowers that made the whole room look like a page out of *House Beautiful.* She said she was making up for not being able to do the flowers for the wedding, and she outdid herself, for sure."

"I'm sorry we couldn't be there to celebrate with you. Did you get lots of stuff for the apartment? That's one of the best things about a shower."

"We got a whole set of pots and pans with copper-colored lids and a hand mixer and a toaster. One of Mom's friends had the coolest idea. She bought a broom with a dustpan and thumbtacked little Ziploc bags with kitchen gadgets like a potato peeler, can opener, egg slicer, spatulas, a grapefruit knife and the like all up and down the handle."

"What a great idea," Katie agreed.

"What about your china, silver and crystal?" Frannie asked. "Have you chosen a pattern? You should have gotten a good start on that at your shower."

"I always loved my Grandmother's pattern. When we were little, we had Thanksgiving and Easter and Christmas at her house and even we kids got to eat on her lovely place settings. When Grandma died, Mom promised me I could have it when I married. She'll bring it for me when she comes for the wedding."

"That sounds amazing," Frannie chimed in. "My mom's china and silver hardly ever gets used, I think people should use their pretty china, not just let it collect dust in the cabinet.

"I'll keep that in mind. I also got a four place setting of Corelle dinnerware and a stainless flatware set for every day. I don't think there's much left that Mike and I will have to buy."

"Too bad you couldn't bring the leftovers back with you," Katie teased.

"There was certainly enough food for an army. We had 28 guests in addition to Mom, Susan, Gaby, and me and even though Mom encouraged everyone to take something home, there was plenty left for the guys."

"Mike will be a lucky guy if you're half the cook your mom is," Robin said, "although, we don't get much evidence of your cooking skills."

"Yeah, I suppose that's true. We do mostly sandwiches here, and not a lot of cooking or baking," Leslie said. "Suzanne, Gaby, and I grew up in Mom's kitchen and we love to cook, especially when we're all together in the kitchen."

"I wish my mother had taught me how to cook," said Frannie. "She doesn't even let me help with the dishes. The kitchen is her domain, and I don't think it ever crossed her mind to share it with me."

"You'll be fine, Frannie," Katie assured her. "What my mother didn't teach me came right out of the *Betty Crocker Picture Cookbook* or the *Better Homes and Gardens new Cookbook*. Those two books have always been on Mom's kitchen shelf. Naomi and I love to make the recipes we discovered in them. The pictures are tempting, and the directions are clear and easy to follow. If you do that, most everything you make turns out fine."

"You're the best, Katie," Frannie said.

Leslie laughed. "I got both of those cookbooks as shower gifts, and my mom has copies, too. I think Mom orchestrated the gifts because I got just about everything Mike and I need for the apartment, and there weren't any duplicates. She's an amazing organizer. I left everything for our apartment in Nellie's trunk, but I did bring in the pretty, sexy, fun stuff to show you."

"I want to see *that* stuff right now," Frannie insisted.

Chapter 32

The following Wednesday, on the way back to the apartment after Chapel, Leslie picked up the mail and caught up with the *Nurseketeers*. She handed an embossed envelope from the School of Nursing to each of her suitemates. "Hmmm, mine must be stuck in the mailroom somewhere."

"Maybe not," said Frannie, opening her envelope. "This invitation is for induction into Sigma Theta Tau."

"Frannie!" Robin chided.

"I mean," Frannie stammered, "with all your struggles in keeping up with everything…"

Robin shook her head.

"It will probably be here tomorrow," Frannie mumbled.

Leslie worried a piece of junk mail to shreds, then squared her shoulders. "Congratulations, Ladies. It is truly an honor that you were invited into Sigma Theta Tau. You deserve it and I'm proud of you. Robin, I'll bet that paper that you wrote in the research course on agism in community nursing impressed them. Maybe you'll pursue a career in nursing research."

"Your paper *was* great, Robin," Katie said.

"I must have just squeaked by," Frannie said. "My grades weren't all that great until recently. I'm sorry, Leslie. I didn't mean to be rude."

"Not to worry," Leslie said. "I'll check with Ms. McCall tomorrow. She's the president of the Crestmont chapter of Sigma. She'll be able to tell me if there's anything I can do."

Ms. McCall's office door was wide open the next morning. She looked up from grading papers when Leslie knocked on the door frame. She turned the top paper face down and waved Leslie to a chair across from her desk.

"How may I help you this morning?"

"Since you're the president of the Crestmont chapter of Sigma Theta Tau, I have a question," Leslie said. "My suitemates all received invitations to the induction, and I was wondering if my invitation might be lost in the mail." Leslie crossed her fingers.

Ms. McCall stood, shut her office door, and sat in the chair beside Leslie. "I'm sorry, Leslie, but your grades were not high enough to qualify for induction."

Leslie fidgeted. "But I'm President of SNA and Captain of the Crestmont Women's Basketball and Track Teams."

"Those are admirable accomplishments that demonstrate leadership, but for undergraduate inductees, scholarship is the most significant qualification for Sigma Theta Tau membership. Unfortunately, your grades were short of the mark for induction at this time. Undergraduate inductees must be in the top 35 per cent of their class academically. You can become a member down the road if you demonstrate exemplary leadership in nursing."

Following a pregnant pause, Leslie stood and extended her hand. "I understand. Thank you."

Leslie wandered aimlessly about the campus, wishing she'd paid attention to her suitemates months earlier when it could have made a difference.

Mike held Leslie's hand as they walked back from the gym on Friday afternoon. "Beating you at hoops was way too easy, Les. What's up?"

"I'm sorry. All three of my suitemates are getting inducted into Sigma Theta Tau. I'm happy for them, but I can't help being disappointed that I didn't get in."

"Oh yeah, I remember J.R. mentioned that. It's like a nursing sorority."

"It's a professional organization that's focused on scholarship. You need a certain grade point average to be inducted as a student. I'll have a chance to be inducted later as a community member if I demonstrate leadership in nursing practice."

"Then it's not the end of the world, Les. Cheer up."

"It's a big deal for nursing students, and I'll be sitting in the audience watching. It's embarrassing, especially since I'm president of SNA. I promised the girls I would come, but I get this stabbing pain in my chest when I think about it. On top of that, I will be sitting in the audience with Robin's grandmother, John, and Katie's parents. Frannie's parents couldn't make it for this event."

Mike shrugged his shoulders, "Leslie, if belonging to this organization was that important, you could have made qualifying for it a priority."

"But I....,"

"It's too late for that, Les. The past is the past. Feeling sorry for yourself won't help you, move forward."

A tear trickled down Leslie's cheek.

Mike turned to her and pulled her close. "How about I go with you tonight? You won't feel alone with me by your side."

Leslie leaned into his chest and choked back a sob. "Thanks. I appreciate that. I'll try not to be a wet blanket."

Mike whispered into her ear. "You got this, Les. We all learn from our mistakes. Right now, these are your friends and you're there for them, and I'll be there for you."

Leslie dressed quickly for the Sigma induction and settled in her chair in the living room, leaving the others upstairs to primp without her. Being upbeat for their sake was draining her energy, but she'd managed not to spill any tears. *I know they appreciated the cards I gave them. I just need a minute to psych myself up for the event.*

When the doorbell rang, she took a deep breath, opened it wide, and invited Katie's parents and John to join her in the living room. "Welcome. Make yourselves comfortable. Robin's grandmother will be here shortly. The girls will be down as soon as Frannie is satisfied that their makeup is just right."

Mrs. Grayfox pulled Leslie into an enormous hug, and whispered, "I know this isn't easy for you, but you have talents that the others don't. You're an amazing athlete. You must always remember that you're special to us."

Leslie was blinking furiously to keep the tears from spilling down her cheeks. Mrs. Grayfox pointed a finger at Leslie. "None of that now. Frannie will have both of our hides if you get streaked cheeks."

Leslie laughed when Mr. Grayfox turned on the TV to catch part of a game. Mrs. Grayfox shook her head. "Men."

Mr. Grayfox was glued to the TV when the *Nurseketeers* trouped down the stairs in their finery. Mrs. Grayfox pulled him to his feet, and Katie ran into their outstretched arms. Then John wrapped her in a bear hug.

"That's got to be the rest of the gang," said Robin when the doorbell rang. She opened the door for her grandmother, Mike, Missy, and J.R.

"We should get going," said Mrs. Grayfox, "if we want to get good seats."

Mike and Leslie hung back, distancing themselves from the excited laughter. Mike squeezed Leslie's hand. "You got this, girl. Like on game day. Just like game day, right?"

"Right," she agreed bravely. "It's my own fault I didn't get into Sigma Theta Tau, and I can't let my disappointment ruin everyone else's fun. I am happy for them; really, I am. Besides, if Sigma is still important to me later on, I can get in based on leadership."

"That sounds more like the Leslie I know," Mike said.

Chapter 33

The following Wednesday morning, Leslie raced for the gym, the rhythmic beat of her running shoes keeping time with her mantra, *one... more... one... more... I... can... do... this.* When the track came into view, she increased her speed. As she entered the track, she spotted Coach Thomas in the distance. When Leslie crossed the finish line, the Coach frowned at her stopwatch. Leslie jogged in large circles around the coach, working to bring her breathing under control. "A minute and a half longer than yesterday." Coach Thomas admonished.

"I gave it everything I had, Coach," Leslie said, deflated.

"Running cross-country is not like doing wind sprints. You start too fast, then you don't have enough left for that last quarter. Tell me what you were thinking about. What was in your head while you were running?"

"I, I..." Leslie studied her shoes.

"Well?"

"I was thinking about the agenda I have to put together for tomorrow's SNA meeting."

"Lord, help me," Coach Thomas growled, pacing back and forth.

Leslie stood silent, contrite.

"Leslie," the coach said, her tone measured. "Winning the meet is what you need to be thinking about, nothing else. Hear me? Nothing else. If your head's not in this race, you don't stand a chance of winning. The Ravens' lead runner placed first last year. You came in third. At the rate you're going, you'll be following the pack, not leading it."

"I can do it, Coach. I know I can."

"I have no doubt you have it in you, but *can* is not the same as *will!* You have to want it badly enough to *do what it takes*, but so far it doesn't look to me like you want it at all."

"I...," Leslie began, but the coach held up her hand.

"Meet me here at 7am sharp."

"7am? Tomorrow?"

"You heard me! Cross-country racing requires speed, endurance, and a strategy to maximize them both. We'll see just how serious you are about winning."

Leslie nodded, and Coach Thomas turned away.

Chin on her chest, Leslie slumped to the bench and reached down to untie her running shoes. Tears trickled down her cheeks. She was startled when Mike sat down beside her.

"What's up with you and the coach? Running doesn't usually make you cry."

She collapsed against him and sobbed. Mike held her close, ignoring the dark wet tearstain spreading across his shirt.

Leslie's sobs became sniffles. "My time is off and the coach isn't happy. I have SNA tonight, so there's no chance of turning in early, and now I have to meet Coach Thomas here at 7am. I have a full day tomorrow and by the time I get to spend time with you, I'll be dead on my feet."

"Hmmm..." he pulled her close.

Leslie pushed back. "Mike, I must smell like a goat. I need to take a shower."

"I'll walk you back to the apartment. I can study while you shower... or maybe I'll help you get clean."

"Men!" Leslie punched his shoulder.

"Where are your roommates?" Mike asked, when Leslie trooped down the stairs, her hair still wet from the shower.

"Most likely at the library. Robin may be working," she answered. "I'm starving. Want a sandwich?"

"You bet," Mike said.

Leslie shut the refrigerator and announced, "No lunch meat. How about PB&J?"

"Got any honey? I'm a peanut butter and honey man, remember?"

"Check that cabinet in the corner. I saw some there the other day. Frannie keeps rearranging the cabinets, so if it isn't there, keep looking."

Mike opened the cabinet, then a second later. "Got it," he said, holding up both the peanut butter and honey jars like trophies.

Leslie smeared creamy peanut butter on two slices of bread, then added grape jelly to hers and honey to Mike's. Before placing the second piece of bread on her sandwich, she added a handful of potato chips.

"Yuck!" Mike said.

"You should try it. Adds a little salt to the sweet and makes it crunchy."

"I'll have my potato chips on the side please."

"Try it," she said, holding her sandwich for Mike to take a bite. "You'll like it."

"OK, OK," Mike replied, and took a hesitant bite of Leslie's sandwich.

"Well?" Leslie prodded.

"Not bad," he admitted. "And I can do without an *I told you so.*"

They ate, sitting side by side at the small kitchen table. "You're a good cook, Leslie Bleu. "I don't think I'll ever outgrow a good PB & honey sandwich." Mike kissed Leslie's cheek. "So, tell me what's with meeting Coach Thomas at 7am."

"Well," Leslie began, "she asked me what I was thinking while I ran, and then got all in a twit when I told her I was thinking about the agenda for tonight's SNA meeting."

"I don't think she's pissed," Mike said. "I think she's disappointed. You're the team's star athlete and she's counting on you to do your best to win the meet. Then, you tell her your mind is elsewhere."

"Why are you taking her side? It's not like I wasn't running as fast as I could."

"Stop. We agreed that you'd listen, and you're not listening, Leslie. We're not arguing and there are no sides. I'm giving you my opinion and you're arguing with me without hearing me out."

Leslie's chin dropped to her chest. "I'm sorry. Go ahead, I'm listening."

"I've never seen Coach Thomas pissed at any of you guys," Mike continued. "She gives feedback; she tells it like it is, and she doesn't pull any punches. You said your time today was slower than yesterday and your mind was on SNA, not the run. Wouldn't you expect her to be disappointed?"

"But..."

"Les, get real. You've taken on too much and you're having trouble juggling it all. That's a fact and you know it already. Your commitment to cross-country isn't an option. Your scholarship demands that it be one of your highest priorities. How can SNA be the right thing to be thinking about while you're running? You've got to concentrate on your commitment to change your behavior, or nothing will change. Pretty soon, it will be too late."

"You're right," Leslie admitted. "I can't afford to lose my scholarship. I need to focus on not getting kicked out my last semester in college. Mike, I *can* pull this off."

"We'll see about that. The race this weekend will tell. Get your head around your meeting with the coach tomorrow, and for god's sake, get some rest."

Leslie shut off the 6:15am alarm as quickly as she could. She eased out of bed and closed the bathroom door behind her. *"Good thing I laid out my stuff last night."*

She arrived at the track at 7am to find Coach Thomas waiting for her. *"I don't think that woman ever sleeps."*

"Morning," Coach Thomas said, smiling. "Let's sit and talk a bit before you stretch."

They settled on a bench and Coach Thomas said. "I see lots of potential in you."

Leslie waited for the *but*.

"But," Coach Thomas continued, "with all that you have going on, I need to know where your commitment to athletics falls on your priority list? I see how hard you're working to juggle your commitment to SNA and your classwork, but I don't see the *I want to win attitude* that you had last year. Right now, the team can't count on you; you're not there for them."

Leslie sat open-mouthed.

"Why do you look so surprised? You know as well as I do that I'm telling it like it is.

Leslie hung her head.

"Let's get down to business. Are you serious about winning?"

"Yes, Coach," Leslie nodded emphatically.

"That's not the level of enthusiasm I need from you. If you're serious about winning, I expect to hear it in your voice and see it in your actions."

"Yes, Coach," Leslie said forcefully. "I *am* serious about winning. Please believe me."

"That's more like it. So, to the business at hand. I want you to focus on this run a little differently. Endurance is a key element in cross-country."

Leslie nodded.

"Today, I want you to run only one mile right here on the track. The first quarter you'll run slower than normal, not much more than a jog. Then, at the quarter mile mark, pick up the pace to your usual speed for the middle of a run. When you pass the three-quarter marker, give me everything you've got. Run like fire is chasing you."

"I can do that."

Coach Thomas nodded. "Then let's see it."

Leslie arranged her feet on the blocks and listened for the coach's, *"ready, set, go!"* She took off, reminding herself to slow her pace for the first quarter mile.

She got a nod from the coach at the quarter mile loop and picked up her speed. At the three-quarter mile loop, the coach rotated her arm rapidly, yelling, "Pick it up! "Pick it up! Gimme all you've got!"

Leslie ran as fast as she ever had, and she knew it. She felt the fire behind her and was out-distancing it with every bit of speed she could muster.

Coach Thomas clicked the stopwatch as Leslie crossed the finish line. Exhausted and thrilled to see her coach smiling, Leslie walked in wide circles to catch her breath.

"That's the fastest mile time I've ever clocked for you," Coach Thomas said. "Well done. This pattern is exactly what it will take for you to win the cross-country meet next week: one quarter at moderate speed, faster the next two quarters, and the final quarter you run like a tornado is on your tail."

Laughing between breaths, "Got it, Coach."

"Leslie, if you can beat your own time by just seconds each time you practice, you'll be ready to take on the Ravens. The Ravens' runner who beat you last year will be the fire behind you. You pick the moment you'll run full out and pass all the rest."

"I can do that. I know I can. You can trust me, Coach."

Coach Thomas nodded. "Get out of here. You have other things on tap today, right?"

"Yes, Ma'am, I do," Leslie said, "but my head will be right where it needs to be at my next practice."

The coach grinned. "That's what I want to hear."

"Leslie, sit down, you're driving me nuts," Robin said on the day of the meet.

Leslie continued to pace the small living room, so focused that she didn't hear Robin.

"SIT DOWN!"

"What?" Leslie said, startled.

"Please sit down, Leslie. You're making us all crazy with your pacing," Katie said.

"You're acting like a Crestmont Cougar whose being pecked by a Raven," Robin said. "Settle down."

Frannie snickered, then Katie and Robin giggled at the vision of a Raven giving fits to a Cougar.

Leslie joined the laughter. "You guys are the best. I appreciate that you're always there to support me."

"We don't have anywhere else to be," Frannie said.

"FRANNIE!" Robin screeched.

"Well, we don't, do we?" insisted Frannie. "When did we ever miss one of Leslie's events?"

Katie shook her head and chuckled. "You might want to work on your turn of phrase, Frannie. You made it sound like the only reason we're supporting Leslie is that we don't have anything else to do."

"That's not what I meant," Frannie insisted.

"That's why you might want to consider *thinking* before you speak," said Robin.

"But, I…"

"It's okay, Frannie," Leslie said. "I know what you meant. Thanks for your support, Guys! I gotta go. I don't want to be late. I have to be at the gym in 30 minutes. The race is 5k and it starts in about an hour. There's one lap around the track, then through the park and back to campus, with one final lap around the track. You guys should pick a spot near the end where it will be most exciting. Wish me luck."

"Let's go with her and watch them warm up," Katie said. "We can watch the first lap around the track, then we'll cut across to where they'll be coming out of the park. When we spot Leslie, we can hustle back to the track to watch her win."

"Sounds like a plan," Robin agreed.

"Especially the *watch Leslie win* part," said Frannie.

The *Nurseketeers* sat in the bleachers watching the team get ready for the race. "Look at them," Frannie said. "They're all like Leslie. Not one of them can stand still."

"Look," Katie said, pointing. "The teams are lining up to start."

At the sound of the starting gun, the runners took off. "Leslie's in the back," Frannie said. "That's weird. She always leads the pack when she runs."

"That's probably part of the strategy she was talking about," Katie said. "I'll bet she's saving her energy for the end when everyone else is already tired."

"I hope you're right," Frannie said.

"There goes Leslie," Robin said when Leslie left the track for the trail to the park. Let's go. We don't want to miss her when she comes out of the park."

By the time the girls reached the spot where the ribboned route left the park, the first runners were nearly upon them. "There she is, there she is," Frannie yelled, jumping up and down. She's so far back. There are…" Frannie counted, "six runners ahead of her and that girl from the Ravens is in the lead."

Robin nodded. "Leslie's a harrier. She'll be concentrating on winning and won't let anything distract her."

"What's a harrier?" Frannie asked. "Leslie's a runner."

"Harriers are long-distance runners. The word comes from the 19th century when the English hunted large rabbits called hares with hounds. The hounds that chased hares were called harriers. They ran fast over natural terrain, like cross-country runners. Lots of cross-country clubs call themselves harriers, like the Chicago Harriers or the New York Harriers."

"Interesting," Katie said.

"They should call themselves runners," Frannie insisted.

"Get into the groove of the sport," Robin grinned, and hugged Frannie's shoulders.

"Come on, we need to cut through campus if we're gonna get back to the stadium before Leslie does," Katie said.

Katie, Robin, and Frannie stood by the track and listened to the disembodied voice from the loudspeaker. "Ladies and gentlemen, the first of the cross-country runners will be entering the stadium shortly. Please clear the track."

Frannie jumped up and down, hoping to catch sight of Leslie. "There she is!" Frannie squealed as Leslie came through the arches at the end of the track. "She's way behind."

"In the lead is last year's winner from Ravenwood" said the announcer.

"LES-LIE, LES-LIE, LES-LIE," Robin and Katie chanted in unison along with Mike, Missy, and J.R. who had joined them.

Leslie was moving past the runner in front of her. She passed the fourth runner and pulled up close to the third.

"Look what she's doing," Robin punched Frannie's shoulder. "Her strategy is working."

Leslie moved ahead of the third runner. "She's second," Katie squealed. "Go Leslie, go!"

Frannie's eyes widened as Leslie approached the front runner at the three-quarter mark. "She's still behind."

"She's catching up," Katie whispered.

Leslie inched ahead of the Raven runner. "She's gonna win. She's gonna win," Robin said.

The crowd picked up the chant, *LES-LIE, LES-LIE, LES-LIE,* then erupted into cheers as Leslie crossed the finish line a full stride ahead of her rival.

The girls cheered until they were hoarse.

"The cross-country race is completed," the announcer said. "The Raven's women's team takes first place, the Crestmont team is second, and the Crestmont team captain, Leslie Bleu, has won the individual award for the fastest time overall."

Chapter 34

"Apartment hunting is no fun," Leslie complained. "I didn't realize it would be this hard to find a one-bedroom, furnished apartment. Robin's grandmother's old apartment would have been perfect."

"Would have been," Mike agreed. "The rent for the one we just saw was pretty steep, considering utilities weren't included, and the two we have left to look at are all the way up by Bachman Lake."

"That's lots further north than I want to be living," Leslie said.

"So far there hasn't been a single furnished apartment available. It would be nice not to have to buy furniture right away," Mike said, "but my folks would probably let us have my bedroom furniture. Then we'd just need a table and a couple of chairs for the kitchen and something to sit on in the living room."

"Beanbag chairs couldn't be that expensive, and a couple of lamps."

"C'mon, let's get the last two out of the way. Maybe we'll be pleasantly surprised."

"I'm not holding my breath."

"Did you and Mike find a place over the weekend," Coach Thomas asked Leslie at practice. "If not, I might have a lead for you. One of my neighbors has a furnished cottage and the couple living there just said that they're leaving. The Blackwells think it will be vacant May 10th."

"That would be fantastic. Do you know how much they're asking for rent?"

"I don't, but the couple that's leaving were newlyweds when they moved in. My neighbors are Alex and Joan Blackwell. Here's their phone number. Joan's home during the day if you want to call and make an appointment for you and Mike to see it."

"Thanks, Coach. We haven't found a single apartment that wasn't either too expensive, too far away, or in major need of repairs."

"Let's hope this will work for you," Coach Thomas said. "Give Joan a call and tell her I sent you."

"Fingers crossed," Frannie said when Leslie and Mike left to see the Blackwell's cottage.

Mike maneuvered Nellie through the narrow streets of the tidy neighborhood not far from Crestmont.

"This is so convenient, Mike, and the area is lovely."

"It certainly is," Mike replied. "I hope we'll be able to afford to live here. It seems a bit pricey."

"Me, too. Joan Blackwell said that if we're interested, they won't show the cottage to anyone else."

"The next house should be the Blackwell's," Mike said, reading each house number as they drove by. "See if there's a number on the house, just to be sure." Mike slowed to a stop.

"It must be the Blackwells," said Leslie. "There's a cute little house in the back."

They climbed the porch steps and before they could knock, the door opened. A smiling young woman said, "You must be Mike and Leslie. Let me show you our little cottage. I do hope you'll like it."

Mike and Leslie followed Joan Blackwell to the end of the driveway. "I'm sure we'll love it," Leslie said. "We haven't found a single apartment that we want to live in, so we're hoping that we'll be able to afford the rent. We graduate in May and we both hope to have jobs right away," Leslie said in a rush.

"Karen Thomas recommended you highly, so I'm sure we'll be able to work something out," Joan said, opening the door to the cottage for Leslie and Mike. "There is furniture in each room, but you'll need your own towels and linens and kitchen supplies." The living room displayed a comfortable sofa and a matching chair placed at right angles around a coffee table, facing a television console against the far wall.

"It's lovely," said Leslie. "My mother gave me a shower over spring break, and we have enough of everything to get started."

"You'll have to do a bit of rearranging," Joan said, "but the sofa converts to a full-sized bed for when you have guests. Come see the kitchen. We put in new appliances before the Ashlands moved in, so they're only three years old."

The kitchen window looked out into the Blackwells backyard. "What a lovely garden you have," said Leslie. This is a wonderful view to start the day."

"It's pretty in the winter, too," said Joan. "I love to garden. Come, let me show you the bedroom, It looks out onto the backyard as well. There should be plenty of drawer and closet space for you. Also, we put a double sink in the bathroom. You'll be surprised what a difference that makes in a small space."

Mike and Leslie were both smiling, both hoping that they could afford to live in such a lovely place.

"That's about it," said Joan. "No secret rooms or hidden passageways, but you are welcome to enjoy the backyard, including the barbeque. Just coordinate your plans with us, please."

"Thanks so much for the tour, Mrs. Blackwell," said Mike. "We're anxious to find out if we can afford to live here."

Joan nodded. "First, I'm Joan. Mrs. Blackwell is my mother-in-law." She grinned. "Besides, I'm not much older than you. Let's sit in the living room and discuss the details."

In fewer than fifteen minutes, they stood and shook hands with Joan. "I'm so excited," said Leslie. "I can hardly wait to move in."

"Alex and I will be happy to help you. We're having the locks changed tomorrow, so you can stop by for your keys any time after that. I know you won't be moving in until after your wedding, but you can bring things by any time. It's easier to set up a home bit by bit than all at once."

Joan waved goodbye as they walked to the car where Mike swept Leslie into a hug and spun her around. "Amazing," he said. "It's perfect and we can afford it."

"We're off to a great start, Husband-to-Be," Leslie said, and pulled Mike's face down to meet her lips.

Chapter 35

"What's with the Cheshire Cat grin?" Leslie asked Mike. "I'm taking you out to dinner to celebrate," he said. "I got the coaching job that I was hoping for at North Dallas High School. The offer came in the mail today. J.R. handed me the envelope and I nearly tore the letter ripping it open. I misdialed the school's number three times before I got the call to go through to let them know I'd take it. This calls for a celebration."

"You bet! Do you know what you'll be doing?"

"Coaching, duh. Well, I don't know exactly, but Coach Mitchell told me a while back that North Dallas High would be the best place for investing in my future and to keep my fingers crossed for an offer. North Dallas has a great reputation in the sports community and it's only minutes from the cottage. Coach told me that three of their senior coaches will be retiring in the next few years. That means there will be promotions available sooner rather than later. This job will kickstart my coaching career if I make a good impression."

"Fantastic. You've obviously impressed them enough to offer you a job. When do you start?"

"That's the tough part. My first day is the Monday after our wedding. The coaching staff is having a retreat to plan the summer athletic program. I guess it's a good thing we weren't planning on a honeymoon right away, huh?"

"It would have been nice to have a couple of days to ourselves," said Leslie, "but we'll have our evenings together, no matter when Parkland has me starting. That is, of course, if I get the job."

"I like that you'll be working days," said Mike. "It was tough not seeing much of you when you worked 3-11 last fall."

"We'll make up for lost time when we finally get to go on our honeymoon."

"Cozumel was a great choice. It's not too far and it shouldn't cost an arm and a leg. I've been there once, just for a weekend, but I liked everything about it."

Excited, Leslie said, "Tell me more."

"The beach is gorgeous. Weather's great and the water's warm all year round."

"Sounds heavenly. I can see us soaking up the rays, margaritas in hand."

"Oh… and the scuba diving is spectacular."

"I've never been scuba diving," Leslie said. "I didn't know you knew how."

"It's other-worldly, Les. Trust me, you'll love it. We'll have to get you certified before we go. I'll ask Coach Mitchell which dive shop has the best classes."

The *Nurseketeers* sat in the Student Union, sipping their favorite sodas. "Feels good to sit a bit before I have to leave for the Steakhauz," Robin mused.

"We don't get much visit time anymore, that's for sure," Katie said.

Leslie heaved a sigh of relief. "I can't believe finals are over. Thanks to y'all, I made it. I almost choked on that last exam.

The first question threw me for a loop, but I made myself mark it and move on, just like you taught me."

"We knew you could do it," Katie said. "You just had to believe in yourself."

"You're free this afternoon, aren't you, Leslie?" Frannie asked. "Robin's gotta work, but she doesn't care much for shopping anyway. How about Katie and I take you downtown to buy some things for your trousseau?"

"No rush," Leslie said. "Mike and I can't go on a honeymoon until later in the summer."

"Good grief, Girl, it's definitely a rush," said Katie. "You need some sexy nighties, panties, and lacy bras for whenever the honeymoon happens."

"The stuff you got at your shower is a start, but considering the state of your wardrobe, we definitely need to go shopping before Katie and I leave Dallas," Frannie insisted. "The majority of your underwear drawer needs to disappear for good, and fast."

Leslie flushed scarlet. "But I…"

Katie giggled. "Come on Leslie, admit it…, Frannie' s right. You don't want Mike to see those ratty bikini briefs you wear all the time." Katie grinned at Leslie's expression of disbelief.

"Besides, your nightwear looks like something from a thrift store," Frannie insisted. "Your negligée wardrobe is in dire need of a makeover, and that's a fact."

"OK. OK. You win. Quit hounding me." Leslie said, embarrassed. "My stuff isn't *that* bad, is it?"

"It definitely is for a newlywed," Robin insisted.

Frannie and Katie nodded emphatically.

"I'm pretty sure I've got the job in Med Surg," Robin exclaimed as Leslie maneuvered Nellie into a space in Parkland's parking lot.

"From your lips to God's ears," Leslie said. "We both need to leave here with the jobs we want. I haven't talked to Mrs. Laurent since last Fall when I quit my OR job. I just pray she's still not disappointed in me. I want this job more than anything, and I don't want to think about driving all over Dallas trying to find an OR that will hire a new graduate."

"I'm sure she wasn't disappointed in you. More likely, she was proud that you were able to set priorities," Robin said. "C'mon. Think positive."

"Good luck to both of us," Leslie said, raising both hands with crossed fingers, then she turned down the hallway toward the OR.

"*Here goes.*" She took a deep breath and knocked on the Director's door.

"Leslie," Mrs. Laurent smiled. "How nice to see you."

A small sigh of relief escaped, and Leslie realized she'd been holding her breath. "It's nice to see you, too, Mrs. Laurent."

"Come in and sit down. Does this mean you'll be graduating and you're ready to come back to work?"

A smile exploded onto Leslie's face. "Yes, Ma'am. Yes it does."

"I was disappointed when you had to leave us last Fall."

"I knew you were upset with me for quitting."

"Upset? Oh, no, I wasn't upset. The Senior year in nursing school is demanding, and it's also the year when you get to explore the settings that interest you. I hoped that you wouldn't discover another clinical specialty and change your mind about the OR."

"No, Ma'am. The OR is exactly where I want to be."

"And we're happy to have you. When do you graduate?"

"Graduation is this Thursday, and I'm getting married on Saturday."

"Well, that's good news. Congratulations. How long will you be on your honeymoon?"

"That won't happen for a while. Mike has to start work the Monday after the wedding. He'll be assisting the coaching team at North Dallas High School and they're getting ready for their summer sports camp that starts the first week of June."

"Your Mike is a fortunate young man to have been hired at North Dallas High." Mrs. Laurent smiled at Leslie's look of pride. "So," she continued, "does that mean that you'll be able to start working on that Monday as well?"

"Yes, Ma'am."

"Fine, then. I'll tell Human Resources that I've offered you a position." Mrs. Laurent thumbed through the hospital directory, then wrote a number on an index card. "Call this number and make an appointment with Mr. Carter as soon as you can. He'll take care of bringing you on board. He can answer any questions you may have. Hospital orientation lasts two days. Come to my office as soon as your orientation is over, and we'll talk about your schedule." She stood and extended her hand. "Welcome back to Parkland, Leslie."

Ten minutes later, Leslie paced in the lobby, willing Robin to step out of the elevator each time one stopped.

"Hey there," called Robin from behind her. "I took the stairs."

Leslie whirled to greet her. "So, how did it go?"

"Piece of cake," Robin said. "I think I'm going to like Med-Surg better than I did in Clinicals. I interviewed with the nurse who was in charge when we were here for Clinical, and she remembered me. Maybe they are a little hard up, or maybe I made an okay impression because she didn't hesitate to offer me the position."

"Of course, you made a great impression and congrats." Leslie squeezed Robin's shoulders. "You were right about Mrs. Laurent. She wasn't angry with me for quitting. She said she was hoping I wouldn't change my mind and pick another specialty."

"Far Out! That's a nice commendation."

"Are you supposed to make an appointment with a Mr. Carter in Human Resources?" Leslie asked. "If so, we could stop by there right now and get on the schedule instead of calling back."

"Yes, I am. We can go together, then we can stop off at Keller's Drive in and get burgers and fries to celebrate."

Leslie opened the door to Parkland's HR department the following day. The woman sitting behind the reception desk looked up and asked, "How may I help you, Miss."

"I'm Leslie Bleu. I have an appointment with Mr. Carter."

The lady nodded. "Have a seat over there and I'll tell him you're here." She lifted the phone. A moment later, she said, "He'll see you now. It's the door at the end of that hall."

Leslie nodded her thanks and walked toward Mr. Carter's office. Before she could knock, a tall, slender Black man opened the door. "Come in," he said, smiling.

Leslie extended her hand like she'd practiced with her dad. Mr. Carter grasped it firmly, then pointed to a chair in front of his desk. "Thanks for coming by, Miss Bleu. I see that Mrs. Laurent has offered you a position in the OR."

"Yes, Sir," Leslie replied. "It's my dream job."

"Before I give you these documents to complete, I want to be sure you understand our policy regarding graduate nurses. Your position is conditional upon passing Boards, at which time you will become a full-time RN. You must understand that, should you *not* pass Boards, you must relinquish your position. You can continue to work as a tech until you pass Boards. When you pass, if there is an RN position available, you will be hired to work in the OR as a nurse. If there is no RN position available, your options include continuing to work as a tech until an RN position comes available or taking an open nursing position in another area."

"But I don't want to be anywhere but the OR," Leslie insisted.

Mr. Carter smiled. "Then y our first step will be to pass Boards." He handed her a stapled packet of papers. "There's a table in the next office where you can complete this application. When you're done, give the application to Nancy at the front desk. Come here to HR on your first day of work and we'll take you to the classroom for the hospital orientation."

Leslie nodded and stood. She offered her hand to Mr. Carter. "Welcome back to Parkland, Miss Bleu."

Chapter 36

"No, Mike, don't put it there," Leslie said.

Mike held up his hand. "Shhhh. Stop."

She looked at him quizzically. "What?"

"Sit." He pointed to an unpacked box. "There."

Leslie sat slowly. "What?" she asked again.

"Marriage is a partnership, right?" He paused for a response. Leslie nodded.

"We each have a say in the decisions that affect us."

She nodded again.

"So, this is going to be *our* home and *we* make the decisions about where things go."

"OK," Leslie agreed hesitantly,

"The apartment has four rooms. Choose the two you want to organize. You'll decide where everything goes in those two rooms, and I'll set up the other two." Leslie frowned, and Mike continued before she could object. "There's a kitchen, a living room, a bedroom, and a bathroom. Pretty nice bathroom, actually. Which two rooms do you want?"

"Well," she hesitated, "All of them matter."

"Of course, they do," he nodded, "but they matter to *both* of us. My sense of what's convenient and what looks good is just as important as yours, so pick your two rooms."

Leslie nodded. "I get it. So...," she hesitated, thinking. "I'll be spending more time in the kitchen than you will so, I'll take the kitchen... and the living room. I care more about the room other people will see than which side of the closet my clothes hang on."

"You got it," Mike said, and picked up a box. "This one's for the bedroom."

"You know," Leslie said. "This fits right in with what Ms. Reynolds has been teaching me. Good communication and trust. Once you've agreed on a plan, you have to accept the decisions that other people make."

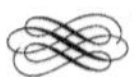

"Hello," said Leslie into the phone, "Welcome to Dallas, Mrs. Grayfox. Let me get Katie." Leslie covered the receiver and yelled. "Katie, your mom is on the phone."

Katie raced down the stairs. "Hi Mom, I thought you were coming to the apartment. Oh, OK. I hope she is feeling better. I'd hate for her to miss graduation and the party after." She looked at Leslie. "They're at the hotel, but Naomi isn't feeling well."

"Oh, no! Does that mean your mom and dad won't make it to graduation?"

"Naahh," Katie said. "They wouldn't miss it. Naomi probably got carsick. Growing up she always got the front seat. No calling dibs on shotgun when she was in the car."

Leslie chuckled.

"I'm just glad that Naomi's graduation is next week. It would suck if our parents had to choose whose graduation to attend. Besides, I wouldn't want to miss Naomi's High School graduation, either. I'm glad that John can make it to Dallas for our graduation and your wedding. I hate that we have to leave for Stillwater on Sunday so soon after your wedding reception is over. John graduates on Monday and we need to be at OSU in time for that. It's hard enough to say *goodbye* after four years of living with the *Nurseketeers* without having to do it in a rush."

Leslie teared up. "I know," she said, and hugged her roommate. "I can't imagine being here in Dallas without all the *Nurseketeers*."

Robin came in from the kitchen with a handful of potato chips in one hand and a can of pop in the other. "What's up? Are you two, okay?"

"Yeah, yeah. We're just getting soppy over the *Nurseketeers* splitting up after being together for four years."

"I'll still be here, Leslie, and we're working at the same hospital. Besides you'll be playing house with Mike."

Leslie blushed and threw a pillow at Robin. "Is Frannie still upstairs primping?"

"What do *you* think?" Robin asked. "Frannie couldn't get ready quickly if her life depended on it. I'd better go up and prod her along, or we won't make it to the stadium in time for the graduation line up."

"We need to make sure our families know we are meeting on the Chapel steps after graduation to take photos," Leslie said. "It's a lovely building and the wide steps make it easy to take group shots."

"We'll be certain that they know what we've planned, and they'll find us," Katie said. "Don't fret, Les. This will all come together."

"Door's open," Katie said in response to a knock. "C'mon in, Guys."

"See!" Frannie said, coming down the stairs. "I'm ready with time to spare." She stopped midway down the staircase. "Stand up, you Guys!" Frannie yelled. "You're going to wrinkle your gowns."

"Oh, for pity sakes," Robin said, shaking her head. "We're gonna be sitting for hours waiting for everyone to graduate. How can sitting down now wreck anything?"

Deflated, Frannie made her way the rest of the way down the steps.

"Let's go to the stadium and find our places." Leslie said. "No rush, but our families will already be sitting in the stands, and I want to find them."

The nursing students were the first group of baccalaureate graduates to march into the stadium. They stood at the head of the long line of bachelor's degree graduates waiting for the platform administrators, faculty, doctoral students, and masters' students to file into the stadium.

"I don't remember standing in line this long during rehearsal," Leslie said, rocking back and forth on her heels."

"That's 'cuz rehearsal was just with the nursing graduates. We didn't have to wait for everyone else," a nearby classmate explained.

"We're moving," someone said.

"Finally!" Leslie sighed, still rocking back and forth.

The long line of graduating bachelors moved slowly onto the field and took their seats. At 5'9", wearing 2" heels, Leslie towered over her peers. She prowled the stands with her eyes and spotted her family seated with the rest of the *Nurseketeers'* families. They made eye contact and the group in the stands stood as one, smiling and cheering for the *Nurseketeers*.

Frannie's eyes widened. "Robin," she squealed, "look. It's Petey. I had no idea my brother would be here." She waved furiously.

When everyone was seated, the President rose to introduce the keynote speaker who commenced his long-winded address.

"Will he ever finish?" Frannie whispered to Leslie ten minutes into the speech. "I want to graduate and get out of here. I haven't seen my brother in forever."

The girls met their families at the chapel. "We're not the only ones who realized the chapel steps would make for a Kodak moment," Leslie said.

"True, but there are lots of steps. We can make this work," Katie said.

"Frannie, how 'bout your family first?" Leslie directed. "Then you and Petey can have all the time you need to catch up. Welcome home from Viet Nam, Petey."

Frannie pulled Petey close to her. Mr. and Mrs. Braun arranged themselves around their offspring, and the other three *Nurseketeers* snapped photos.

Leslie said, "Now, Robin and Mrs. Kelly, you go next,"

"Yes ma'am," Robin said, giving Leslie a crisp salute.

When all of the families had taken their photos, Leslie said, "Daddy, take my camera. I want a picture of Mike and me, Katie and John, and J.R. and Missy. Then I want the *Nursekeeters*. J.R. you're an honorary *Nurseketeer, so* be sure you get in the picture."

The Bleus and the Hamptons celebrated the graduation together at the Old Warsaw restaurant. The group was seated in dark green leather chairs at a large round table. Candles in crystal cylinders flickered at each table and each dinner plate sported an intricately folded white napkin. Sparkling sterling flatware bracketed the china, a knife and two spoons on the right and two forks on the left.

"This is an elegant place," said Mrs. Bleu as the waiter unfolded the large white napkin and settled it onto her lap.

"It's my favorite restaurant in Dallas," said Mike's mother. "We celebrate our anniversary here every year."

"It's the perfect place for special occasions," Mike's father added.

"Les," Mike said, "let's split something that neither of us has ever tried."

"Like what?" Leslie asked hesitantly.

"How about escargot. That sounds exotic."

"Snails!" Leslie wrinkled her nose. "I won't be able to take a bite without remembering when I was a kid and we put salt on them and watched them melt away on the sidewalk. Ugh."

"Those were slugs, not snails." Mike said. "C'mon. Be adventurous."

"They'd better be groovy, fantastic, awesome, and the coolest thing ever, or you're in big trouble, Mister."

When the escargot arrived, Leslie said, "They're pretty with the puff pastry on top, but that might be because it keeps me from seeing them." Mike cut into the pastry and lifted the delicacy, dripping in garlic butter. She shut her eyes and took a bite. "Oh, Oh, hot hot…," she said, reaching for her water glass.

"Well?" Mike asked when she could speak.

Leslie grinned. "Other than burning off the top layer of my tongue, they're delicious."

"I hope there's something exotic on the menu at the rehearsal dinner tomorrow," said Mike. "This *try something new* could become a tradition."

Chapter 37

The rehearsal dinner was held in the large private dining room at the Steakhauz. When Maddie Davis had seated the last of the guests, Mr. Hampton stood, glass in hand.

"Welcome, everyone," he began. "My wife and I are pleased as punch to host this rehearsal dinner. Mike couldn't have chosen a lovelier woman to be his wife, and she's an athlete to boot!" The guests chuckled appreciatively. He continued, "The rehearsal went well, so we've earned our dinner." He raised his glass, "To my son and my soon-to-be daughter-in law."

While the guests applauded, Mrs. Hampton rose to stand beside her husband. "I want to add that I've always wanted a daughter, and I couldn't have asked for a better one. I'm looking forward to all of the girl stuff I get to share now."

"Leslie's *not* her daughter," Mrs. Bleu whispered angrily to Mr. Bleu. "Mrs. Hampton should know that."

"Of course she does," Mr. Bleu whispered back, "and she asked you to call her Carla, remember?"

"I'll do that when I know her better," Mrs. Bleu grumbled.

"Well, I like Gene well enough to call him Gene," Mr. Bleu stated firmly. "They're our daughter's in-laws, Annette. That's good enough reason to like them."

"Good reason to like whom?" Leslie said, startling her parents.

"I was just saying that you're *my* daughter," Mrs. Bleu pouted.

"Of course I am, Mom. What's your point?"

"Well," Mrs. Bleu hesitated, "Mrs. Hampton thinks you'll be *her* daughter once you and Mike are married, but she's *wrong!*"

"That's ridiculous, Mom. *You* will always be my mother. Tomorrow I'll have a mother *and* a mother-in-law. Why would you think that would change anything?"

"Well, Arp is so much closer to Dallas. When you have free time, you'll go there."

Before Leslie could protest, Mrs. Bleu continued. "I know why she didn't mind that Mike spent the whole Christmas vacation with us. She knew Mike was going to propose and she'd have you all to herself once you're married."

"Annette, that's enough," Mr. Bleu interjected. "Your daughter deserves more credit."

"But" Mrs. Bleu protested.

"You know better, and what's more," Mr. Bleu insisted, "you're putting a damper on Leslie's wedding weekend. You're the mother of the bride. You should be enjoying every minute of this celebration. Your grousing is not making anyone happy, least of all, you."

"Daddy's right, Mom. I know you're sad about my living away from home, but it's a waste for you to be unhappy. Of course, you'll be part of my new life. After all, you'll make the best grandma in history… and no, I'm not pregnant!" she added when her mother looked startled. "C'mon, Mom. Smile. Mike is everything you want my husband to be. Celebrate with us."

Mrs. Bleu leaned over and put her arms around her daughter. "I'm sorry, Sweetheart," she murmured. "Mike *is* wonderful, and I *am* happy."

"I can't believe we have to start this early," Leslie complained. "The wedding is at one and it's only eight o'clock!"

"Today is your wedding day, Les. It's not like any other day, so relax and enjoy all the moving parts. Every moment of today will be a memory," Katie said.

"I'm worried about my dress," Leslie fretted. "I hope it doesn't make me look too girly."

"You'll cherish the memory of looking like a fairy princess for your prince," Robin chuckled. "Your dress is absolutely stunning, and brides are supposed to look like girls… even star athletes. I've never seen a wedding with the bride in a track suit."

The *Nurseketeers* dissolved into a fit of giggles, picturing Leslie at the altar in her athletic garb.

"I guess not," Leslie said. "I'll admit that my wedding dress does make me feel special."

"As you should," Frannie concluded. "Your mother should be here any minute. She's probably as a-flutter as you are. I can imagine my mother at *my* wedding. She'll need a whole bottle of Valium to survive the day,"

"Les, your mom's been a rock star this semester," Katie said. "She took care of as much of the wedding preparation as she could to give you space to manage all the other stuff on your plate,"

"Moms are good that way," Leslie agreed.

A knock on the door was followed immediately by a smiling face peeking around it, then a second and a third, as Mrs. Kelly and Suzanne appeared behind Mrs. Bleu. "You ready for us?" asked Mrs. Bleu rhetorically.

"I think a light breakfast would be a good way to start the day," said Robin's grandmother, moving toward the kitchen. She placed a large paper bag on the table and removed its contents. "Let's see… we'll have orange juice and coffee with fresh biscuits and jam. Cereal, too, if anyone wants it. That should tide us over until the reception."

"Gram makes the most delectable biscuits," Robin said proudly. "They're light as a feather."

"Frannie, do you think you'll have enough time for hair, nails, and makeup after breakfast?" Katie asked.

"Oh, you bet. I've had lots of practice, and everything is laid out in our bathroom."

"There!" said Frannie, turning the stool so Leslie faced the mirror. "That's what a bride should look like."

Leslie stared at her reflection, both amazed and pleased at what Frannie had accomplished.

"Magnificent, Frannie," exclaimed Mrs. Bleu as she walked into the bathroom behind them. "My daughter is truly a fairy princess, just as she should be on her wedding day."

"You look lovely," said Robin. "Frannie, you could do this for a living if you ever get tired of nursing."

A smile spread across Frannie's face. "Did you really mean that, Robin?"

Robin squeezed Frannie's shoulders. "I did."

"I'll second that," said Katie. "If Leslie gets tired of nursing, she can be a model."

"Mac just arrived to take Leslie, Annette, and Suzanne to the chapel," said Mrs. Kelly. "Robin, Katie, Frannie… gather Leslie's dress and your things and ride with me."

Leslie sat alone, staring at her reflection in the bathroom mirror. "*Amazing,*" she whispered. "*Frannie truly is a magician.*"

Her father appeared behind her. He crouched beside her, their faces a portrait in the mirror. "You are beautiful," he whispered. "As lovely as your mother on the day we married."

Mr. Bleu pulled up to the chapel. Frannie was waiting beside Mike's pick-up.

"Mike can't see me before the wedding," Leslie insisted. "That's bad luck."

"The coast is clear, Leslie," Frannie assured her. "Mike and the rest of the guys are in the groom's dressing room."

"Where's that?" asked Mr. Bleu. "I need to be sure that Jaq and Frank made it here, and I want to pick up my boutonniere."

Frannie pointed the way, then ushered the women into the bride's dressing room. Mrs. Bleu stopped in front of Leslie's gown, hanging resplendent from a padded silk hanger. "Lovely," she whispered.

"Wait 'til you see Leslie in it, Mrs. Bleu. She looks amazing… absolutely stunning," Frannie gushed.

"She does," Robin echoed.

Katie answered a discreet knock on the door to their dressing room. A woman stood beside Mr. Bleu. "Katie, this is Ms. Handel from the bakery," he explained. "She has to speak with Leslie."

"Come in, please. We haven't started dressing yet."

Leslie looked up. "Ms. Handel," she said, surprised. "Is something wrong?"

"Nothing that hasn't been resolved, but I thought you should know that there was a mishap with your cake this morning." She continued hurriedly. "We didn't want you to be surprised by the substitution."

"What substitution? What mishap?" said Leslie sharply.

"The cake we have for your reception looks identical to the one you chose, and the bride and groom topper is your original."

"So… what's the problem?

"The cake is an English fruitcake instead of the traditional vanilla layers that you ordered. Of course, there will be no additional charge."

"You're kidding me!" Leslie cried. "How can that be a solution? Everyone will be disappointed. They'll hate it."

"Actually, the English fruitcake is one of our most popular choices for wedding cakes."

Before Leslie could reply, Mr. Bleu said, "Thank you Ms. Handel. I'm sure it will be fine. I'll take it from here."

When the door closed softly behind Ms. Handel, he said to Leslie, "the cake at the reception is the last thing your guests will remember about today. The bakery has behaved professionally, and who knows, the English fruit cake might taste even better than the one you ordered."

"It won't! I don't like fruit cake."

"That's enough! Put a smile back on your face. Are you going to ruin your wedding by pouting over a cake?"

Frannie, Katie, Robin, and Suzanne helped one another dress. All four bridesmaids wore the same chiffon dress with a ruffled, sleeveless bodice. The swirling skirt had an uneven hemline, shorter in the front than the back. Frannie's was a soft yellow, Robin's pastel green, Katie's lilac, and Suzanne's desert rose.

Leslie had insisted that the color of each groomsman's tuxedo shirt match the dress of the bridesmaid he ushered to the altar. Daniel, Mike's cousin, had complained bitterly. "Men don't wear *pink*," he'd contended, but Leslie had prevailed.

"Let's get you dressed, Leslie," said Mrs. Bleu, taking the dress from the hanger. "The lines of this gown are simple and yet so elegant."

Leslie stepped into the dress and slid her arms into the long, sheer sleeves.

Mrs. Bleu reached for Leslie's hand. "Such exquisite detail," she murmured. "It will take me a moment to do up these tiny, covered buttons."

The deep V of the satin bodice made Leslie seem even taller. The long flowing skirt, cinched at the waist with a sash of the same silky material, hid her feet and made it seem as if she floated on air. The four bridesmaids watched in silence, marveling at the transformation from athlete to princess. Leslie could only stare, amazed, at her reflection.

Katie opened the dressing room door when Mr. Bleu knocked.

"Annette, are y'all ready? Dr. Creighton said that as soon as the mothers of the bride and groom are seated, we'll begin the processional."

"We're dressed," Mrs. Bleu replied. "The big question is, are *you* ready, Leslie?"

"I am. All the planning and looking forward to today… and it's finally here. Actually, I can't wait."

"So, the wedding is on," quipped Mr. Bleu. He turned to his son. "Jaq, accompany your mother to her seat in the chapel. Daniel has gone to fetch Mrs. Hampton. The rest of us will be right behind you."

Mr. Bleu looked at his daughter and tears filled his eyes. "You are beautiful, My Darling," he whispered. "Absolutely stunning."

The wedding party gathered outside the chapel. Soft music entertained the guests while the mothers of the bride and groom were seated.

"Shall we?" Daniel offered Suzanne his arm and they took their places in the chapel doorway. At Dr. Creighton's nod, the couple walked slowly to the altar. The other three groomsmen followed, each ushering a bridesmaid.

"I must admit," Mr. Bleu whispered to Leslie, "the color-coordinated bridesmaids and groomsmen are impressive."

"It was Mom's idea," Leslie whispered. "I told her to quit working at the store and become a wedding planner."

Mr. Bleu caught his breath, and Leslie giggled. "But not until the rest of the kids are grown up."

"I love you, Leslie, and Mike is definitely a keeper." He leaned to kiss her check. "You look exquisite today, and I am happy for you."

Leslie had a death grip on her father's arm. "Daddy, I can't cry now," she said, blinking furiously.

He chuckled and patted her hand. "Me either."

The *Wedding March* began. Leslie took a deep breath and entered the chapel on her father's arm. The guests followed her with their eyes as she and her father made their way to the altar. Leslie couldn't help but hear their whispered comments…

gorgeous, stunning, exquisite, lovely. She smiled graciously and gave silent thanks to Frannie. She *felt* like a princess.

Leslie and her father mounted the three steps to the altar. Mr. Bleu turned toward his daughter, lifted her veil, and kissed her. He whispered, "Darling, today is the first day of the rest of your life. Cherish every moment. I love you." He presented Leslie to Mike and took a seat beside his wife who was gazing at the couple. Both mother and father were teary-eyed and proud.

Mike took Leslie's hand. "You look amazing," he whispered. "You'd win the *Miss America Pageant* hands down."

"I love you, Mike Hampton," she whispered.

"We are gathered here today," began Dr. Creighton.

"I hope the cake doesn't ruin this perfect day," Leslie said as she and Mike prepared to make their entrance into the reception hall.

"What are you talking about?" Mike asked.

"There was a *mishap,* and we have some kind of an English fruit cake instead of what we ordered. I'm afraid everyone will hate it."

"Wedding cake is a formality. People don't think twice about it because all you can taste is the icing. Don't waste time worrying. Besides, we won't cut the cake until the reception's nearly over."

They were greeted with cheers by the reception guests.

"Who's the next to marry?" Leslie asked, holding her bouquet high in the air. She turned around and threw her bouquet over her head to the excited group of young women waving their hands. Katie caught it and held it high. When she called out, "John, I think this seals the deal," everyone laughed.

Leslie and Mike made the rounds, thanking family and friends for coming. Mike agreed enthusiastically each time someone complimented him on his lovely bride.

"I've never thought dressing up was such a big deal," Leslie confided. "I must admit, it does feel special. You look pretty dapper yourself, Mr. Hampton."

"You're beautiful," Mike said tenderly, "but don't let it go to your head." He winked and she punched his shoulder.

"Ow! A princess with a punch. That's a dangerous combination."

The music started and Mike led Leslie onto the floor for the first dance.

The reception passed in a whirl of excitement, and before Leslie knew it, the music stopped. Daniel stood at the microphone, tapping a glass with a spoon to get everyone's attention. "Take your seats, Ladies and Gentlemen," he said. "It's time to roast… I mean toast the bride and groom, and there are a few folks who have something to say to the newlyweds." He handed the microphone to J.R.

"I've known Mike nearly my whole life," he began, "and do I have some juicy stories to tell."

Mike called out, "Just remember what happens to people who pinky swear and then break their promise. Just sayin'."

"Well, maybe another time," J.R. conceded. "Today a great guy married the right woman. And Leslie… you look amazing, by the way… you picked the right guy. These two are gonna make us proud." He lifted his champagne glass, and his toast, *"Here's to the newlyweds, Mr. and Mrs. Hampton"* was met with a chorus of *"Here, Hear."*

Suzanne rose, raised her glass, and said, "I guess that means I shouldn't trash my sister," she giggled. "Actually, I wasn't going to do that anyway. Leslie's the oldest of the five of us and she's always been a rock and an inspiration. She's got great taste in men, too." Suzanne raised her glass. "To my sister and my cool brother-in-law!"

Following another round of *"Here, Hear,"* Daniel said, "Mike, Leslie, please cut the cake. We're starving."

Leslie's heart missed a beat when she remembered the impending disaster.

"It'll be fine," Mike whispered as they walked toward the cake.

"They'll hate it," Leslie murmured as she reached for a cake knife.

Mike placed his hand over hers and they cut the first piece for them to share. Leslie picked up a fork, cut off a large piece, and shoved it into Mike's mouth, smearing a bit of icing on his chin.

Mike started to pick up what was left on the plate.

"Don't you dare, Mister" Leslie said.

"Mmmm," he nodded, his mouth was too full to speak. He cut a smaller piece and, a bit more gently than Leslie, fed it to his bride. He watched as her expression changed slowly from distaste, to surprise, to pleasure. "Told you so," he whispered.

Mike unlocked the door to their apartment. "Wait a minute," he said, then pushed the door open. He turned and swept Leslie into his arms and carried her ceremoniously over the threshold. "I've been imagining this moment ever since I proposed."

Leslie put her arms around his neck, and they kissed passionately. "Our first kiss in our first home," he murmured. "Mmmm, good." He put Leslie down and they kissed again.

"What a fantastic day," Leslie said. "I want to remember every single minute."

"Especially how good the cake tasted," Mike couldn't resist.

They looked at one another and burst into laughter. "It's an omen," Leslie said. "We're charmed."

"I'll drink to that," Mike said. "Wanna split a Dr. Pepper?"

Leslie nodded and Mike took a can from the refrigerator, popped the top, and handed it to Leslie. "You first, M'Lady."

Leslie took a long swallow and handed the can back to Mike. "It's going to be hard saying goodbye to everyone tomorrow. It'll be our last breakfast together. We've been together for four years, but it seems longer than that. I'll see Robin at work, and I know we'll visit Katie and John, but who knows when we'll see Frannie again after Boards in July."

"Gotta look on the bright side," said Mike. "We graduated, we're married, and tomorrow will be the first day of the rest of our lives."

"You're my Prince Charming," she said.

"And right now I'm thinking that our wedding day won't be over for another few hours. Let's continue the celebration," he said, lifting her off her feet and turning toward the bedroom.

Chapter 38

On Monday, Leslie was up at 5am to be sure she was on time for her first day of work. She was first to arrive for orientation. She took a seat in the front row and saved the seat next to her for Robin. Ms. Francine Dunn, according to her nametag, said, "I'll be set up to register everyone in a jiffy."

Robin slipped into the chair beside Leslie.

Ms. Dunn began, "It looks like we're all here. I'm Francine Dunn, Assistant Director of Human Resources. There is a folder containing all your orientation material here on the front table. Please come up, sign in, and pick up your name tag and your packet. When everyone is signed in, we'll begin."

"It is hospital policy that you wear your name tag when you are in the building, and it must be visible at all times. Today, we will tour the hospital and provide you with information about insurance, vacation, parking, and much more. We'll break for lunch, then meet back here. Tomorrow, those of you who are nurses will meet separately for specific nursing orientation"

Robin and Leslie settled their lunch trays on a corner table in the cafeteria. "Man, is this stuff boring," Robin said. "I'm glad we only have to do it once.

"Maybe the tour will be more interesting, although I'm looking forward to learning about insurance and vacation," Leslie said.

"Important, but boring. Let's hope tomorrow will be more interesting," Robin said.

On Wednesday morning, Leslie and Nan Holden, the only other OR graduate nurse new hire, met with Mrs. Laurent.

"Welcome to the OR, Ladies. I'm assuming you've met one another. Leslie, I hope your wedding went off like a charm."

Leslie blushed, surprised that Mrs. Laurent remembered.

"Congratulations," said Nan. "Great start to the summer: new hubby, new job."

"Alright now, down to business," said Mrs. Laurent. "As registered nurses, your primary role will be circulating. However, you will do your fair share of scrubbing. In each service, you'll first be oriented to the scrub role, then to the circulating role. My philosophy is that the most effective circulators have had experience at the sterile field. The needs and challenges of the scrub team are easier to anticipate if you've walked in those shoes. This is Ms. Sheila Cockerill, our OR Educator. She'll manage your orientation and be your point person."

"Thanks, Mrs. Laurent. It's nice to meet you, Leslie and Nan. Please call me Sheila."

"Good morning, Sheila," chorused the newbies.

"Here is your locker key," she said, handing one to each nurse. "Change into scrubs and meet me in the OR classroom. You know where it is."

"I'm soooo looking forward to this." Leslie said as she and Nan walked into the locker room. Esther was the first person Leslie saw. "*Shit, just what I need.*" Before she could decide what to do, others welcomed them and congratulated them on their recent graduation.

Esther walked past, mumbled *congratulations,* and left the locker room.

"Hey girl," said Betty, a nurse who'd been helpful in the Fall, "when did you get that rock?"

"Mike and I got married this past Saturday."

"Not much of a honeymoon," Betty winked. "Lemme see." She picked up Leslie's hand for a better look.

Leslie, red faced, said, "We're going to Cozumel later this summer. Mike's job started on Monday, so I figured I might as well get on the stick here."

"You don't want this rock to wind up in the laundry, so let me show you how to pin it to your bra strap through your scrub dress."

She captured the ring and Leslie's bra strap through her scrub dress with a large safety pin. "There you go. You won't be able take your scrub dress off and toss it in the laundry without undoing this."

"That's ingenious," Leslie said.

"Plenty of jewelry ended up in the laundry before someone figured it out," Betty smiled. "You're Nan, aren't you? From Baylor?"

Nan smiled. "I am."

"I'm a Baylor grad, too. Glad you're back. Welcome aboard, both of you," said Betty.

Chapter 39

Leslie pulled to a stop behind J.R.'s pickup in front of Mrs. Kelly's new house. "Come in for a bite before you leave for Austin," called Mrs. Kelly from the doorway.

Leslie hugged Katie and Frannie. "It's so good to see you. You, too, J.R. It seems like forever, but it's been less than two months."

"Feels good to be together again," Katie said. "I'm glad we decided to take Boards together."

"I'm glad to be back, too," Frannie chimed in. "It would be awful to take boards at home alone."

"You'll have a nice, three-hour drive to catch up," said Mrs. Kelly. "I've made sandwiches and snacks for the trip."

J.R. stowed their bags with Leslie's in Nelly's trunk.

"Drive carefully," Mrs. Kelly said, "and good luck to all of you.

Katie, Robin, and Frannie piled into the back seat and J.R. rode shotgun. He spread a map across his knees. "South on 75, cut across on I-30, then south on I-35, That will take us all the way to Austin," he said, "so not much use for a navigator until we get there." He folded the map and slid it into the glove compartment.

"First, tell us about you and Missy," Frannie insisted.

"Well, we're engaged, but we can't get married until fall because Missy and her mom need time to plan the wedding."

"If I know Missy, it's going to be the wedding of the century," said Frannie.

"No doubt," J.R. agreed, "but her parents are the nicest people, so I don't think I'll have much trouble adjusting to Baton Rouge. I drove down the week after graduation and proposed to Missy. Her parents helped us find an apartment and once we're married, she'll move in with me."

"What about a job? Have you found one yet?"

"I'm interested in alcoholic rehab and both Baton Rouge General and Charity Hospital have inpatient programs. I've interviewed with both of them, but I want to get a bit more settled in Baton Rouge and get boards out of the way before I accept an offer."

"So, when we get back from Austin, you'll be off to Baton Rouge for good?" asked Leslie.

"Pretty much," J.R. said. "I'm going to spend a few days with my folks and I'll be taking the last of my stuff from Arp back with me. You'll all be getting invitations to the wedding, of course."

"Speaking for all of us, congratulations, you two, and best of luck with your new job, whichever one you choose," said Robin. "I'm enjoying Med Surg more than I expected. I'm still looking forward to transferring to the ER when a spot opens up. In the ER, every day's a new day, and every now and then holy hell breaks loose and it seems like all of Dallas needs to be seen in the ER at the same time. What about you, Katie."

"First, John's loving every minute of working with one of the vets in Stillwater. John said the doc treats him like he's already in vet school and gives him lots of opportunity for hands-on practice. I was hoping to work with the Indian Health Services in Stillwater, but the nearest office is in Pawnee, so I had to adjust my plans bit. I'm working with the VNA and love being in the community. I'll be able to stick with them until John graduates. Then we'll go back to Atoka and he'll take over ol' Doc Raney's practice like we'd planned all along."

"Oh, I'm sorry," said Frannie. "I know you were looking forward to the Indian Health Service. So, what exciting adventures do you have with the VNA?"

"Well, it is the same as we did for the VNA during school. My experiences are pretty routine with dressing changes, checking in with folks post op, and making sure they're taking their meds the way they are supposed to. I haven't had to face anything like what Les did during our clinical rotation at VNA. I've had the opportunity to assist with dental care a few times and I especially like working with the older folks. Fortunately, most of my patients fit that category."

"Are we going to hear wedding bells soon?" asked Frannie.

"Not yet. We've decided to wait until John graduates," Katie said. "He'd like to make it happen sooner, but I want to get settled into the new job and see where being together takes us. It's been a long time since high school, and so much has changed since then. I want time to get used to us together as adults."

"Ever the practical one," said Leslie. "That leaves you, Frannie"

"I love peds, watching sick kids get better, especially the babies. It's amazing how quickly they can recover, but at the same time, the opposite is true. You have to keep your eyes open because they can go from doing fine to crashing just as fast. I'm getting better at spotting the warning signs. My supervisor said there's a job waiting for me when I pass boards."

"That's good news," said Leslie.

"So, looks like it's a good summer for all of us," Katie said.

"It will be better when Boards are over. Can you believe we have six exams in two days," Leslie moaned, "and we won't get our results for weeks. I'll be a basket case before this is over."

"Quit worrying and let's listen to music," Robin said.

"Good idea," Leslie agreed and turned the radio dial until she found a station playing a familiar song.

"*Leavin' on a jet plane*," Robin sang, a bit off key. "I love Peter, Paul, and Mary."

They rolled down the windows, cranked up the radio, and sang along, J.R.'s bass a nice balance for the *Nurseketeers'* higher voices.

Midway to Austin, the music was replaced with static. J.R. tried finding another station but found nothing suitable and turned off the radio.

"What kind of sandwiches did Mrs. Kelly pack for us," Frannie asked. "I'm hungry."

"Let's see," said Robin, opening the bag. "Looks like she made two for us each of us. She even labeled them. We have tuna salad, PB&J, and ham and cheese. Leslie, there are snack bags of potato chips, too. I'll doctor a PB&J for you if you'd like."

"While we eat, how about I ask questions to prepare us for the tests?" Katie said. "We can take turns answering?"

"Go for it!" Robin said.

"*Oh, Lord, no,*" thought Leslie, feeling panic creeping across her chest. "I'll listen, Guys," she said. "I can only do two things at once, stay focused on the road and enjoy this tailor-made PB&J."

"So, we'll start with Med-Surg," Katie said, "and move on to obstetrics, peds, and psych. Leslie can take over when we get to surgical nursing."

"Works for me," said Robin "Everyone, remember to answer the question before you look at the options.

"Okay. First question," announced Katie. "What's the main goal of treatment for acute glomerulonephritis?"

"I'll take that one," Robin said.

"Okay, what's the answer?" Katie asked.

"You have to maintain fluid balance because the patient can build up toxins in the kidneys that have to be filtered into the urine. Without fluids, toxins can build up and cause the body to swell up big time and make the patient tired all the time."

"Right," Katie said. "How about J.R. takes the next one, then Frannie, and we can keep rotating."

J.R. said, "Sounds like a plan."

"Here's your first question. A patient who received spinal anesthesia four hours ago during surgery is transferred to the surgical unit and, after one and a half hours, he reports severe incisional pain. The patient's blood pressure is 170/90, pulse is 108, temperature 99, and respirations 30. The patient's skin is pale, and the surgical dressing is dry and intact. What should you do?”

“The patient needs pain medication,” J.R. said, “All those vitals are normal for the situation, so that was an easy one.”

“*Whew,*” thought Leslie. *“I got those two right.”* She crossed her fingers and wrapped her hands more tightly around the steering wheel.

When they reached Austin, J.R. navigated from I-35 to the hotel. Leslie sighed with relief as she pulled up under the awning at the Holiday Inn. “We’re here,” she announced, “and none too soon. My shirt is stuck to my back.”

They clambered out of the hot car and hurried inside to enjoy the air conditioning.

“This Holiday Inn goes straight up, more like a hotel. All the ones I’ve seen are spread out like motels should be,” Frannie said.

“We’re downtown in a big city,” Robin explained. There’s not enough room to spread out. Nowhere to go but up,”

“Hmmm,” Frannie mused.

They got their room keys, the four girls in one room and J.R. by himself.

“Les, I’ll take your luggage up to your room while you park the car,” J.R. offered.

“Thanks. I’ll be up in a jiffy.”

“Let’s have dinner here in the hotel,” Robin suggested. “It’ll be easier than trying to find a restaurant in a city we don’t know.”

“Good idea,” Katie agreed, “and, I’m up for *early to bed* and a good night’s sleep.”

They turned in before 10. Long after the other *Nursketeers* had fallen asleep, Leslie turned the pages of the practice manual, reading through sample questions and answers.

The next morning, the *Nurseketeers* and J.R., with graduates from all the nursing programs across Texas, gathered outside the Austin Convention Center. The anxiety level was palpable.

"I'm not the only one who's nervous," Leslie thought. *"I wish I'd slept better. At least my tossing and turning didn't wake the others."*

Leslie slumped on a low brick wall, trying in vain to tune out the chatter about what the tests would be like and how anxious everyone was. Frannie babbled nervously, and Robin cursed about anything and everything. Katie, always stoic, said nothing, but she couldn't hide the anxiety in her eyes.

Finally, the huge double doors opened, and the graduate nurses were beckoned inside. In return for the admission card Leslie handed to a proctor, she received a slip of paper with a row and seat number. None of the *Nurseketeers* were seated near one another. It didn't matter because they were reminded repeatedly that there would be *absolutely no talking.*

"This looks like a prison mess hall... without the food," Leslie thought, examining the sea of six-foot tables, each with two widely spaced chairs. The tense atmosphere was not helping her efforts to remain calm and collected.

From a raised platform at the front of the room, a woman gave instructions about the test booklets that would be distributed, and where to turn them in when they finished the exam. "Raise your hand if you need to go to the restroom, and a proctor will escort you. Personal belongings must be placed on the floor and left untouched until you exit the room when you're through with the exam. If you need a tissue, raise your hand and a proctor will provide one." The litany continued. "If you need to put on or take off a jacket or sweater, please raise your hand, and a proctor will come to your table and monitor the process. If you need a new pencil raise your hand."

"I really am in jail," Leslie moaned.

The first exam was finally under way. *"Surely I can pass this one,"* Leslie reassured herself. *"We've spent loads of time on Med-Surg floors."*

She picked up her pencil and read the first question, then the answers, and froze, her commitment to cover the answers abandoned. *Is it A or B? They're both reasonable responses.* Her heart was pounding and she realized she'd been holding her breath. After what seemed like an eternity, she marshaled her resolve, put a dot by the question, and moved on. Leslie had to remind herself more than once not to linger when a second response made her doubt her first choice. When she reached the last question, she was surprised at the amount of time she had left to review the ones she'd marked. When she stood up to leave. There were five minutes left on the clock. *I wasn't the last to finish. That's got to be a good omen.*

When the group met outside after the last test of the day, Leslie said, "I'll get the car," hoping the walk would settle her nerves.

"Let's get Mexican for dinner," suggested J.R. "I saw a restaurant right by the hotel. We can walk. The exercise will do us good."

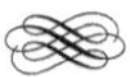

"I slept pretty well," Leslie said the next morning at breakfast. "Knowing what to expect helped a lot. Today should be easier now that we've survived Day One."

In fact, the crowd at the convention center was mellow compared to the day before. Leslie chatted comfortably and avoided any discussion about the tests.

The tests crawled by, hour by hour. When the group finally united outside the convention center, Robin said, "Let's get started for Dallas. I want outta here."

"Me, too," Katie agreed. "We can stop for a last dinner together on the way home. I saw several good restaurants right on the highway in Waco."

"Let's see if we can find a steakhouse," Robin suggested.

"Sounds like a plan," J.R. agreed. "I'm up for ribeye and a baked potato."

"I want out of Austin in the worst way," said Leslie, "but dinner sounds great and it's a good opportunity to talk together one last time."

"I miss you all," Frannie said. "I love my job and it's great to spend time with my brother now that he's home from the Army for good, but I don't have friends in Philly like all of you. Most of my high school girlfriends are married, and nobody works. I can't believe I used to think the things we did were fun. I'm just not interested in any of that anymore. The people I work with are the best. My best friend at work and I are thinking of getting an apartment near the hospital. The commute from home every morning is a killer, and living with her would be so much fun. I need to tell Petey first. He'll help me deal with the tantrum Mom's gonna throw when I tell her my plans. The only bad thing is how much I will miss Nana and and only being able to care for her when I visit."

"You've come a long way from the clueless brat I roomed with four years ago," said Robin.

"Thanks loads," Frannie said sarcastically.

"The four of us have been more like sisters than friends, when you think of it," said Katie. "We've been through a lot together."

"You know what would be fun?" said Leslie. "A chain letter. For instance, I could write to Katie, then Katie would add her news and send it to Robin or Frannie. When I get it back with everyone's news, I'll start a new one."

"I'd love that," said Katie. "It would probably take a couple of months for the letter to make the whole circle."

"That's cool, Les. You're always full of good ideas," added Robin.

"You know, I'm not much of a letter writer," J.R. said, "but I'll bet Missy would love to get in on the chain letter too. She and could keep you updated on our wedding plans."

"Awesome!" Frannie said.

Robin spotted a steakhouse between Temple and Waco for the *Nurseketeers'* farewell dinner.

J.R. said, "Ya know, goodbyes are tough. Let's order dessert and say our goodbyes here. By the time we drop everyone off at Mrs. Kelly's, it will be late enough to call it a night."

"That's probably best," Robin said. "This is how I want to remember us, sitting around and shooting the shit."

"And," added Leslie, "laughing instead of working my way through a box of Kleenex."

Chapter 40

Leslie had heard murmured conversations in the cafeteria about Board results. Mike was singing in the shower when she got home, exhausted after her 3-11 shift. *"Maybe I'll join him."* She avoided glancing at the kitchen table where the serpent with fangs of death was potentially hiding in each of the unopened envelopes sitting there. She poured a glass of orange juice and took a deep breath. *"Open the mail, Leslie Jean. Being a coward won't change anything."*

She picked up the stack of mail and flipped slowly through the envelopes, tossing the junk mail back onto the table. Mike had opened all the envelopes except for the official-looking one at the bottom of the stack. The embossed *Texas Board of Nurse Examiners* was clearly visible in the upper left-hand corner.

She held the envelope, hands trembling, unable to summon the courage to open it. *"I'll wait for Mike to get out of the shower and we can read it together. ...No, maybe I'll let him read it and tell me what it says. ...No, maybe..."* She ripped it open like she was pulling a dressing off a wound. *Failed to pass* was the first thing she saw, and she couldn't read another word.

Mike strode into the room, a towel tucked around his waist, his incredible abs on display. "I thought I heard you come in. How was work?" His words, muffled by the towel he was using to dry his hair. When Leslie said nothing, he stopped and draped the towel around his neck. Her expression told him everything. He dropped to one knee in front of her, his towel gapping, which at any other time would have led to bedroom gymnastics... but not tonight.

Leslie sat silently, tears streaming down her face. Wordlessly, she extended the letter. He read it in its entirety, then sat and gathered her to him. In Mike's embrace, Leslie's tears flowed unabated, and her sobs were unrelenting. Mike held her close until her sobs gave way to hiccups.

"This changes everything, Mike. My career, my life, our future, everything. If I can't be a nurse, then what?" Her hiccups reverted to sobs.

"Honey," Mike said, still holding her close, "Did you read the whole letter? It doesn't say you can't be a nurse. It tells what you have to do next. Obviously, lots of people miss something the first time, or they wouldn't have a process in place to move forward. Let's read what it says." He gently wiped the tears from her cheeks.

Leslie took a long, cleansing breath, and curled closer to Mike. She read the letter he held for her. "I failed the surgical test, of all things. I work in surgery. You would think I would know that stuff best of all, but... I guess if there is anything good about this letter it is that I only have to take that one test over, not the whole damn thing."

"See, Sweetheart, you can still achieve your dream."

"Maybe... but right now it feels like my entire world has collapsed. What if I'm the only *Nurseketeer* who didn't pass? How can I face them?"

"Leslie," Mike chuckled, and shook his head. "Your friends would never quit on you any more than I would, especially over one lousy test."

"One lousy test! It's not just any test, Mike. It's my Boards, my license... my career!"

"OK, OK, Les. Of course it is, but you're going to take care of that."

"I know" she said sobbing again and rubbing her temples.

"Come on, Les. I love you. That alone should give you the courage to manage this."

"I love you too," she said, hugging him close. "Who else would put up with me when I turn into an emotional wreck. I can't be an RN until I take the test again. I'm going to be a surgical tech for at least six more months. It doesn't pay as much, Mike. We were counting on the bigger paycheck."

"None of that matters. I love you, Les. *That's* what matters. Come on." Mike pulled Leslie to her feet. "You're exhausted. Let's go to bed and I'll make you feel better. MUCH better."

After Mike left for work the next morning, Leslie lay in bed, mired in self-pity. "*How am I going to tell my parents I'm a failure after all the money they spent, even with my scholarship? I'll have to pay them back. And the Nurseketeers… I'm probably the only one who didn't pass.*" Her eyes widened. "*What am I saying? How could I wish one of them had failed. I'm a terrible person.*" Leslie dissolved into tears. "*Oh lord, …Esther… that wicked witch is going to have a field day with this.*"

Finally, out of tears and emotionally exhausted, Leslie lay in bed staring at the ceiling. "*C'mon, Girl. Nothing you say or do is going to change the facts. Mike's right. I have to deal with this. It won't be the end of the world, as long as I pass next time.*"

Leslie got out of bed and strode into the bathroom, resolute. She washed her face, brushed her teeth, and stared at herself in the mirror. "*You look like hell, Girl. That won't do. If you're going to deal with this, you have to look the part.*" She practiced a variety of expressions of resolve and determination in the mirror, then burst out laughing. "*Mike believes in me; I know he does. He's my rock. I can do this for us.*"

Leslie dressed, made the bed, and ate a late breakfast. *"I'm meeting Robin in the cafeteria this evening. By that time, I'll have talked to Mrs. Laurent, and I'll have done whatever I have to do."* She looked heavenward. *"Please let me sound like I have everything under control. This is the perfect time to fake it until I make it."*

Resolved to move forward with confidence, she left for work, concentrating on maintaining a positive attitude, and found herself parking Nellie without remembering anything about the ride to work.

"Will you please tell the folks in Room 9 that I'll be right there," Leslie asked the charge nurse. "I have to stop by Mrs. Laurent's office."

The nurse nodded and Leslie knocked on Mrs. Laurent's door.

Come in," Mrs. Laurent said, "and close the door behind you," she added when she saw the concerned look on Leslie's face.

"I have to retake my surgical nursing exam," Leslie blurted before she'd even taken a seat. "Can you believe the one test I didn't pass is the one I thought I knew the best?"

"I'm proud of you," Mrs. Laurent said, surprising Leslie into silence.

"What?" asked Leslie.

"I am proud of your positive attitude, Leslie. Instead of *I failed*, you started with what you're planning to do about it. I knew I made a good decision when I hired you. You're going to be a good nurse. Mark my words."

"Thank you so much, Mrs. Laurent," Leslie said, fighting back tears.

"You are hardly the first to have to retake Boards, my dear. Except for a period of inconvenience, this should make no difference at all. Try to avoid talking or thinking about it and concentrate on studying for the retest. Can you do that?"

"I'll do my best," Mrs. Laurent. "I won't let you down."

"Now hustle along. I'm sure they're waiting for you to scrub your first case. We'll take care of the details tomorrow. In the meantime, keep up that good attitude."

Leslie left with a weak smile and another *thank you*.

Leslie's first case was a breast biopsy, a procedure she'd done repeatedly. She scrubbed effortlessly and found herself watching the circulating nurse, disappointed that it would be six months before she could assume the challenges of that new role. She hadn't realized how much she'd been looking forward to it. *"Well,"* she thought," that's even more incentive to study and pass the retest." She smiled at her next revelation. *"If the important people in my life like Mike and Mrs. Laurent believe in me, I certainly should believe in myself."*

Robin was all smiles when Leslie met her in the cafeteria. "I got my letter from the Board. I passed." she said as soon as they'd settled at a table.

"Congratulations, Robin Hart, RN." Leslie said without hesitation.

"Some of us are going to meet up to celebrate."

When Leslie said nothing, Robin asked, "Have you heard anything?"

Leslie surprised herself. "I won't be celebrating quite yet. You're not gonna believe this, but the one test I didn't pass was surgical nursing, and it's the one I expected would be my best."

Robin's face fell. "Oh, Leslie, I'm so sorry. I didn't mean to brag."

"You have every right to brag. I was a basket case when I read the letter, but I'm okay now."

"The good thing is that it was only the one, and that's stuff you know. You passed all the others, so you have a handle on the process."

"I'm going to keep it to myself as much as I can."

"I understand."

"Mike was a rock and Mrs. Laurent was supportive when I told her this morning."

"Of course they were," said Robin. "Having to retake one test is hardly the end of the world. I'll be happy to help you study for the retake if you want."

"I'm not sure how I'm going to tackle studying yet, but I'll let you know."

"Leslie, I'm glad you told me, and for now it will be our secret. Just let me know if there's anything I can do."

Leslie gave Robin a hug. "The *Nurseketeers* are a force to be reckoned with, that's for sure," she said.

Leslie had two more procedures to scrub before the end of her shift. She was pulling the table with the instruments and supplies for her next case into the room when Sharon returned from assessing their patient.

"Hey Leslie, looks like it is you and me for the next case."

As much as Leslie liked Sharon, she just wanted the day to be over. "Looking forward to it," Leslie said with feigned enthusiasm.

Sharon gave her a quizzical look but said nothing while she helped Leslie open the sterile supplies. The procedure went well, and when Sharon returned from giving her report to the recovery room nurse, she said, "My 1,000cc bladder is about to rupture."

"Mine too." Leslie said with a smile, that didn't reach her eyes.

The two were alone in the locker room. "Les, what's up with you?" Sharon asked. "You're not your usual bouncy self?"

"I know, I'm sorry." Leslie said, holding back her tears.

"So, give," Sharon encouraged. "What is it?"

Leslie melted onto a bench. "I..., I didn't pass all my Boards. I have to retake one. That means I'm a tech for another six months."

Sharon sat on the bench beside Leslie and pulled her into a hug. They sat silent for a long moment, then Sharon looked directly into Leslie's eyes. "I didn't pass boards the first time either. I had to retake the whole battery because I failed two of the tests. Trust me, this is not the end of the woodld. You will get past this."

Leslie was stunned. "Thanks," she said quietly.

"It turned out to be a good thing for me," Sharon said. "I was surprised that I didn't pass. It was a wakeup call. Failing made me realize how much nursing means to me, and now I work at being the best nurse I know how to be because what we do is important. We're here for our patients. It's why we became nurses in the first place."

Leslie held her breath, her eyes laser-fixed on Sharon, pleading for her to continue.

"So, yes, there will be boatloads of tears, but you will take back your life, one step at a time. You will study better than you ever studied in school, and you will relax when you take the test. You'll look at the question, pick the best answer, and move on. Understand me?"

"Yes." Leslie said, with just a glimmer of a smile.

Two days later, Leslie was getting ready for work when the phone rang. *"Leslie?"* asked a female voice.

"Yes, this is she."

"This is Ms. Gifford, one of your Med Surg professors from Claremont."

"Uhm, yes, Ma'am?" was all Leslie could manage.

"We have been advised of the State Board results for the Claremont graduates and I want to make you an offer. I would like to help you prepare for your retest," Ms. Gifford said. "I can meet with you weekly if you're interested."

Leslie was speechless.

"Leslie?"

"Yes, Ma'am. Yes. Absolutely! When can we start?"

"Next week. I know that you're working 3-11, so I propose that we meet in my office from one to two on Tuesdays. That should give you enough time to get to work."

"Thank you, Ma'am. That would be perfect."

"I expect you to come prepared so that we can use our time wisely. Read the chapters on surgical nursing in your Med-Surg textbook. Do you still have that text?"

"I do. I've kept all my books."

"Good. Read those chapters before next Tuesday, and we'll begin our review. We'll discuss the material, and you'll take sample tests. We'll also work on test taking skills."

"This is marvelous, Ms. Gifford. I don't know how to thank you."

"Crestmont has offered this assistance for the past several years. Passing your test and becoming the capable nurse I know you will be is all the thanks we need. I'll see you on Tuesday."

That evening in the cafeteria, Leslie was adding potato chips to her PB&J when she saw Robin come through the line. She waved, and Robin joined her. "You'll never believe what happened this morning. Giffy Guts called me." Leslie tapped her chest. "Me! She offered to work with me once a week until I retake boards."

"Our Giffy Guts?" Robin asked. "WOW! That's great!"

"Yeah, awesome, but a little scary. I hope she won't be disappointed in me."

"In you? I doubt that. When do you start?"

"We're meeting in her office every Tuesday from one to two, starting next week."

"She knows her stuff, Les. I know we struggled with her now and then, but she's good with surgical nursing."

"You're right. She is," Leslie said around a mouthful of sandwich. She choked and grabbed her milk carton.

Robin couldn't help laughing. "You do know that sandwich is meant to be chewed, not swallowed whole."

Chapter 41

Leslie and Olivia, a newly hired registered nurse from Colorado worked seamlessly together, preparing for a breast biopsy with Dr. Banks, their third case of the day.

"You're good, Olivia," said Leslie with admiration. "I hope someday I'll be good enough to come to a brand-new place and practice like I've been there forever."

"Thanks," replied Olivia. "That's a lovely compliment. Everyone has been gracious and helpful. I've worked in three hospitals and they're all different, but circulating is circulating wherever you go. Once you've learned enough names not to feel like a complete stranger and you know where everything is kept and what they use to document, you can concentrate on doing what you know needs to be done. Doctors and patients everywhere expect you to pay attention and do your job well."

"Have you circulated for Dr. Banks yet?" Leslie asked.

"Not yet, but I've heard he's delightful."

"That he is. I hope the biopsy will be benign. He's invested in his patients. When we send off the biopsy, he tells us about them and their families, and it really gets to him when the diagnosis is cancer."

"That's impressive. More doctors should be like that," Olivia nodded. "Go scrub and I'll finish opening. I'll tie you up and we can count before I go to meet the patient."

The procedure went smoothly and the biopsy was sent to pathology. Olivia smiled and glanced at Leslie when Dr. Banks said, "She's a single mother and she's doing a wonderful job of raising her daughter. I do hope it's benign because cancer would complicate things terribly for her."

The door opened and Esther backed into the room, forearms raised and eyes scowling. Leslie could imagine the frown behind the mask.

"Gown me," Esther growled, "and you'd better get back from lunch on time. I have other people to relieve, you know."

Leslie bit back the *of course you do!* and said, "Have you transferred to 3-11, Esther?"

"Not on your life. I'm doing Mrs. Laurent a favor."

"I'll be back," Leslie said to Olivia who looked confused by Esther's demeanor.

The disappointing biopsy results had just come back from pathology when Leslie returned from lunch. She sent Esther on to her next relief and organized the instruments Olivia had just opened for the mastectomy.

Lunch relief arrived for Olivia as Dr. Banks placed fresh towels around the surgical site. "Let's do this, Leslie. What a shame." He began to dissect breast tissue. "On a brighter note, Olivia is a fine addition to our staff, don't you think? She's quite competent."

"I agree. I hope I'll be as good as she is in that role."

"Without a doubt you will be, Leslie. You are a competent young woman."

As the case wound to a close, the evening charge nurse came in and asked Olivia if she might be able to stay and finish a procedure that would not be done for another hour or so.

"Of course," Olivia said. "I'd be happy to help."

"Olivia, when you and Dr. Banks take our patient to Recovery, you go on and I'll finish up here. I've enjoyed working with you today."

"I agree, Ladies. It's been a pleasure," added Dr. Banks.

Leslie finished cleaning up the room, dropped the instruments off for Sterile Processing, and pushed open the lounge door in time to hear Esther say, "She's useless, that new nurse from Cincinnati. Olive, I think her name is."

"Chicago," someone said. "She's from Chicago."

"Wherever!" huffed Esther. "She's a scatterbrain. You don't want her circulating for you, that's for sure. She couldn't do a thing right in Banks mastectomy today."

"Colorado," growled Leslie as she approached Esther. "Her name is *Olivia* and she's from *Colorado.* Esther, you are lying through your teeth, and I can't figure out why you do it. Dr. Banks was impressed and complimentary of Olivia. She's an exceptional circulator, organized and quick. I have no idea why you lie, or why anyone would believe the ridiculous things you say," she said, staring at each of Esther's acolytes in turn. "Mrs. Laurent will be getting a full report, and I'll be talking with Dr. Banks as well."

Esther began to protest. "Of course you'd defend her," she huffed. "You nurses stick together."

"That's enough!" Leslie's voice was low and menacing. "Be *very* careful what you say from now on." She left the lounge, hoping to catch Dr. Banks. She'd leave a detailed account of the confrontation for Mrs. Laurent before she left for home, with a request to meet with her tomorrow before her shift began.

Leslie felt surprisingly calm. *"Doing the right thing isn't as hard as I expected,"* she thought. *"I couldn't let that witch ruin things for Olivia."*

The next day, Leslie stopped by Mrs. Laurent's office before her shift began.

"Come in," said Mrs. Laurent, looking up from her desk. "I've been expecting you. Go change and I'll have Esther join us."

In the locker room, Leslie tied her scrub dress and secured her ring through her bra strap with the large safety pin Betty had given her on her first day of work. She took a deep breath. *"I should have dealt with Esther a long time ago."*

Esther was seated in Mrs. Laurent's office when Leslie returned. "Close the door, Leslie." Mrs. Laurent said, "and take a seat." Leslie sat in the only vacant chair and a glimmer of a smile flicked across Mrs. Laurent's lips when Leslie moved the chair a bit further from Esther. "Esther," Mrs. Laurent began. "I believe that Leslie mentioned her intention to report your conversation in the lounge at the end of yesterday's shift. Tell me about that conversation?"

"I don't remember," replied Esther, her expression sullen.

"I understand you were criticizing the practice of one of our nurses, Olivia. I believe you described her as *useless.*"

"That's a lie." Esther rose from her chair, hands on hips.

"It's not a lie," Leslie insisted. "That's exactly what you said. She's been trashing me just like that ever since I started here as a student last summer."

"Esther, please sit," said Mrs. Laurent. "The report of your conversation has been corroborated by others who heard it. Dr. Banks has also assured me that Olivia is a skilled circulating nurse. He complimented Leslie and Olivia on their efficiency and teamwork."

Esther stared at her shoes.

"Leslie, is there anything you wish to add to this conversation?"

"I wish I hadn't waited so long to confront her. I suppose it's easier for me to speak up when someone else is being bullied than when it's happening to me."

"Esther, do you have anything further to say to Leslie before I let Leslie return to work?"

Esther remained sullen and silent.

"Esther, this is not our first conversation about bullying," Leslie heard Mrs. Laurent say, as she pulled the office door closed behind her.

Chapter 42

"Thanks for coming to Austin with me, Mike," Leslie said, as they pulled into the same Holiday Inn where she had stayed six months before.

"Truth is, Leslie, I want to be here with you. You've poured your heart and soul into preparing for this, and you deserve a celebration. You've only got the one test to take, so why not make this weekend a getaway for the two of us? We've paid for the hotel room."

"I love you, Mike Hampton."

Leslie completed her exam and walked out of the building fifteen minutes before the deadline. *I can't believe how good I feel right now. I could almost hear Giffy's words as I read the questions.*

She was sitting on the stone wall when Mike arrived to fetch her. "It was good, but I'm afraid to say that out loud. I don't want to jinx it."

Mike's expression changed quickly from concern to elation. "I knew you'd be fine, and you can't jinx anything when you have me in your corner. You worked so hard to prepare, so of course, you'll pass."

"Working with Ms. Gifford gave me the confidence I needed, Mike," Leslie said. "I'd like to get her something to let her know how much I appreciated her help and her support.

"She'll get every bit of thanks she needs when she sees your test results," Mike assured her, "but a thank you note would be nice, maybe some flowers. She deserves your appreciation."

Chapter 43

"So, how are you going to spend your day off?" Mike asked as he and Leslie ate breakfast.

"I thought I'd run some errands and get the laundry done because I'll be working on Saturday."

"That sounds like a plan," Mike said. "I'll be home about four."

"Have a good one. Anything special you want for dinner?"

"I'm just looking forward to eating dinner with you. I'll take treats like that any time I can get them."

"I'll think of something special."

Mike kissed her and closed the door behind him.

Errands run and laundry done, Leslie set out to run. When she rounded the corner at the end of three miles, the mailman had reached the other end of her block. She jogged to a stop in front of the mailbox that sported a *Hampton* decal and pulled out the contents. She walked up the path, flipping through the mail. "Oh," her breath caught when she read *Texas Board of Nurse Examiners* on the last envelope.

"This one gets opened right here and now," she said out loud, ripping open the flap. She squeezed her eyes shut, held her breath, and gingerly pulled out the letter.

She whooped with delight when she read the first word, *Congratulations.* "*Yes, yes, yes!*" She pumped her fist and jumped up and down, hugging the letter to her chest.

The Blackwell's kitchen door opened and Joan emerged, laughing. "Wanna share what we're celebrating?" she asked.

Embarrassed, Leslie stammered, "I… I just got my exam results. I passed."

Joan let out a whoop of her own and grabbed Leslie's shoulders. "Fantastic, Leslie. You did it!"

"I'm an RN," Leslie whispered. Then she shouted, "I'm an RN!"

"Congratulations, Nurse Hampton." Joan said and hugged her again.

Leslie hurried into the apartment and read the letter from beginning to end, twice. She savored every word. "*I'm an RN,*" she breathed. "*Mike Hampton, you and I are going to celebrate tonight! We're not waiting for our honeymoon!*"

She checked her watch. "*Mike will be home in an hour.*" She got dinner started, then showered, put on makeup, attached her white nylons to a lacy garter belt, and slipped on one of Mike's white dress shirts. "*Women's lib be damned,*" she hissed, and unbuttoned two more buttons. She pinned on her nurse's cap with the black velvet stripe and smiled at her reflection in the mirror.

She was standing in the bedroom doorway, letter in hand, when Mike came in.

"Leslie, I'm home. Mmmm, dinner smells heavenly."

She waved the letter to get his attention. "Dinner can wait. I passed boards and I'm ready to celebrate."

A gigantic grin split Mike's face as he took in the sight before his eyes. "Congratulations, Leslie Hampton, RN!" He swept her off her feet, flooded her face with kisses, and carried her into their bedroom.

Acknowledgments

Writing about the *Nurseketeers'* world is an adventure. We've engaged with a host of individuals who help us provide detail and depth to our stories. We are grateful to our reading team: Carol Applegeet, Chelsie Gable, Greg Goodman, Daryn Herrington, and Christine Roberts. They provided perspective and helped us refine our final manuscript of *Mountains to Climb.*

We are appreciative of the talented folks who help put the finishing touches on the book's cover and interior design (*jetlaunch.net*), printing (*Vervante*), and distribution (Bublish). A heartfelt thank you to our families and friends who encouraged us to stay focused on authoring the *Nurseketeers* series and to advance our mission of *sharing enjoyment, writing, and learning through meaningful stories about diverse nursing characters.*

Authors' Note

We hope that you enjoyed *MOUNTAINS TO CLIMB* the fourth in the *Nurseketeers* series. Reader ratings are instrumental to the success of a novel. We value your comments and always appreciate your taking the time to leave us a review.

Don't miss other books in the series:

The Wake-up Call - Frannie's book
Against the World - Robin's book
Silent Struggle - Katie's book

Visit our website at: https://www.bakergoodman.com and join our mailing list for notification of new releases and our blogs. *Friend us* on Facebook at Baker & Goodman Authors. https://www.facebook.com/jt.bakergoodman and follow our Author page at https://www.facebook.com/bakergoodmanbooks/ or email us at joydon@bakergoodman.com.

About the Authors

Joy Don Baker and Terri Goodman were nursing students in the '70s, like the principal characters in their four novels. None of the *Nursekeeters'* exploits are based on the authors' personal experiences, however they remained true to the reality of that era. Baker & Goodman's mission is to give readers a glimpse of the nursing profession in the 1970s through diverse characters and meaningful stories.

Both Baker and Goodman are well-established leaders in perioperative nursing and published authors in nursing professional literature. Dr. Baker teaches at the University of Texas at Arlington and served as the editor-in-chief of the *AORN Journal*. Dr. Goodman is an approved provider of continuing education credit and the owner of Terri Goodman & Associates.

Baker and Goodman have also published the award-winning book *A, B, & Cs of Author Partnering*, the definitive how-to guide that leads readers through the process of creating a writing partnership, establishing a productive work environment, and producing a work of fiction, non-fiction, or a journal article.